Neither Angels Nor Demons

By the Same Author:

The Wind in the East
The Rich Pass By

NEITHER ANGELS NOR DEMONS

PAMELA POPE

C

CENTURY

LONDON SYDNEY AUCKLAND JOHANNESBURG

First published in Great Britain in 1992 by
Random Century Group
20 Vauxhall Bridge Road, London SW1V 2SA

Century Hutchinson South Africa (Pty) Ltd
PO Box 337, Bergvlei 2012, South Africa

Random Century Australia Pty Ltd
20 Alfred Street, Milsons Point, Sydney, NSW 2061
Australia

Random Century New Zealand Ltd
PO Box 40-086, Glenfield, Auckland 10
New Zealand

The Catalogue data record for
this book is available from the
British Library

ISBN 0 7126 38548

Typeset by Pure Tech Corporation, Pondicherry, India

Printed in Great Britain by

Mackays of Chatham PLC, Chatham, Kent

For my mother, with love,
and in memory of my dear father.

'For I am convinced that neither death nor life, neither angels nor demons, neither the present nor the future, nor any power, neither height nor depth, nor anything else in all creation, will be able to separate us from the love of God that is in Christ Jesus our Lord.'

Romans VIII. 38 and 39
(NIV)

Author's Note

Although this story is fictitious, the historical background and the lives of two of the characters are based on fact.

MARY ANN GIRLING was born to William and Emma Clouting at Little Glemham, Suffolk, on 27 April, 1827. She was one of a family of eleven. At the age of twenty she married a seaman, George Girling, and bore him ten children, only two of whom survived.

In 1864 she claimed to have received a revelation that she was the incarnation of the Deity in female form, and it is well authenticated that at that time she also received physical manifestations – stigmata similar to those on the body of St Francis of Assisi, and resembling the marks of Christ's Passion and death. She then began the preaching which was to take her from Suffolk to London and Hampshire, leading a life very like the one in this book. She was a remarkable woman who brought joy to many people for seventeen years, and she was much loved and respected.

It was from the custom of dancing and gyrating at religious meetings that the name of Shakers was given to Mother Girling's followers, though she disliked the name and always referred to her flock as The Children of God. In the past they have been known as the Walworth Shakers, and later the New Forest Shakers. No definite link has been established between these people and the Shakers in America, a sect of Believers founded a century earlier by Ann Lee. But there are many similarities.

Mother Girling died on 18 September, 1886. She is buried in the churchyard at Hordle, Hampshire, in an unmarked grave close by a row of macrocarpa trees which were planted for each Shaker who died. Hers was said to be the twelfth, and nearest to the church.

ANDREW PETERSON was born at Wakefield in 1813. He qualified as a barrister at Cambridge and went to India, where he became leader of the Calcutta Bar. When he retired he returned to England a rich man.

In India he had been very interested in the extensive use of concrete as a building material, and he put his knowledge into practice when he bought property in Hordle and settled there with his wife, Charlotte. There were many people out of work locally, and after experimenting with building work in concrete on his estate, he decided in 1879 to build a tower, thus providing much employment. Through Mrs Girling he had also become interested in mesmerism and he claimed the plans for the tower were given to him by Sir Christopher Wren, through a medium. It was completed in about 1885.

Andrew Peterson died at the age of ninety-three in 1906, and after cremation his ashes were placed in an urn on the right-hand stone table in the crypt of his tower. In 1957 they were moved to Sway Parish Church.

The tower still stands, resistant even to hurricanes, and renovations have made it possible to open part of it as a unique hotel.

Acknowledgements

I should like to thank the many people who have helped me in different ways with the writing of this book. In particular I gratefully acknowledge the help of Arthur Lloyd and Geoffrey Gale, who provided me with so many facts about the Shakers.

Pamela Pope

Peterson's Tower, Sway

PART ONE
Suffolk
1869–70

Chapter One

It began as a simple prank, sister teasing brother. No harm was intended. It should have ended in laughter that bright July day in 1869 and then been forgotten, but the far-reaching effects of the trick Hannah Jerram played so innocently on her brother Luke was to change the course of the family's future. Nothing would ever be the same again.

The most significant outcome was that it brought into their lives the woman called Mary Ann Girling. They might still have come under her influence at some other time, of course, but it's doubtful whether her impact upon them would have been as great in different circumstances.

Luckily Hannah had no gift for seeing into the future.

It wasn't easy for Hannah to remove the ladder. It had two long spikes which anchored it to the thatched roof and she had to dislodge them while Luke was singing noisily, his back towards her as he trimmed the long straw. When it was done she was betrayed by her laughter.

'Caught you!' she cried. 'Reckon you'll be up there till someone takes pity on you, Luke Jerram, and it won't be me.'

'You varmint! Put that ladder back this minute.' He was stranded on top of the barn, his feet planted on one of the rafters because the ladder wasn't long enough to reach the ridge he was thatching. When he saw what she had done he brandished an eaves knife he had made himself from an old scythe. 'Put it back, I say!'

But she had no intention of doing that. 'It was my turn to get even, remember?'

His straight hair was falling across his forehead, bleached by the sun to a paler gold than the reed yealms he was attaching to the wooden rafters with tarred twine. In contrast, the moustache which covered his upper lip was dark enough to have been fashioned with the twine itself.

'Hannah! You just wait till I catch you.'

His sister was down below in the field, her face alight with tomfoolery and her golden-brown eyes triumphant. 'Don't pull all the Jupiter's Beard out of the thatch or we'll have devils indoors.'

'There's always a devil indoors as long as you're there. Put that ladder back, I say.'

Hannah only laughed as she ran off, her faded cotton skirt lifted above her ankles and honey-coloured hair escaping from the stiffened brim of her sunbonnet. He could yell all he liked but she wouldn't give in. At nearly sixteen she didn't have a care in the world and today she was enjoying herself enormously. A warm July sun high above scudding clouds sent shadows hurrying across the flat Suffolk fields, chasing her like Luke would do when he eventually got down, and they overtook her relentlessly.

The rusty iron gate sounded like an ailing goose when it swung open. Hannah stood on the bottom bar and draped her arms over the top as she let it carry her across a quagmire at the field entrance. The cattle had churned the ground to mud. At four of an afternoon the congestion of cows vying to be first through the gate to the milking shed was as ill-mannered as village women at a bazaar. The cows were already ambling towards the gate, hiding her from Luke's view, and she hoped to reach the outbuildings before he found a way down and set off in pursuit.

She pushed the gate shut and brushed flakes of red iron from her apron before starting off along the stony path to the hen-house. Her smile was so wide her cheeks ached with it and she swung the egg basket back and forth, beheading stalks of yellow flea-bane and scattering hemlock seeds. Every year the hemlock seemed to grow higher. It almost hid the wall which skirted the lane leading into Seggenham village, growing five feet tall where it was sheltered from the cold east wind. On the opposite side of the path there was a still, green pond haunted by dragonflies and water beetles, the surface too clouded to reflect the farmhouse behind it.

Kean's Farm belonged to Squire Kean of Seggenham Manor and the Jerrams had been renting it for well over twenty years, ever since the marriage of Hannah's parents. It was neither large nor prosperous, an area of some seventy acres suitable for dairying and small crops which showed very little profit. Since it had passed into Luke's hands there was continual dissent with the Land Agent over

4

late payment of the rent and argument over the marshy ground which needed new drainage. In Pa's time it would have been different, as he always gave the Squire his vote, but Luke held radical views and spoke out for Mr Gladstone since he had become Prime Minister last December, so relations between owner and tenant had become strained of late.

The house with its thick chalk walls faced with flint was warm and enduring, and far enough away from the village to be a landmark against the wide skyline. Seggenham was equi-distant between Woodbridge and the sea, and Ipswich was a day's journey which was seldom undertaken unless business there was necessary. There was almost a primeval feel to the silent land where in the distant past conquering Vikings from across the North Sea had taken local women and bred tall, strong men with fair hair and blue eyes to farm it. The Jerrams, it could be said, showed all the traits of their spirited Norse ancestors.

Hannah seldom left the village. When Pa was alive he had sometimes taken her in the waggon to Woodbridge, and occasionally she had been to Ipswich, but now that Luke was head of the family there were no such treats. If Luke needed a companion on a journey he was not likely to choose either of his sisters, and anyway Ma couldn't spare her now that she was old enough to do a fair share of the work.

As she approached the hen-house, fifty or more sparrows flew out through the open door and holes in the brickwork, the flurry of their wings creating a wind. She covered her head with her hands and bent down to avoid them. Inside, the smell of birdlime stung her nose and she had to get accustomed to the dimness before putting her hand in the nest-boxes. She leaned against the crumbling wall, panting a little from running.

Luke would pay her back. He always did. He never allowed a prank to pass without thinking of something equally outrageous to do in return. On the last occasion he had bided his time after she had put duck-eggs under one of his broody turkeys. She'd thought he had forgotten, but a week later she had found a ferret's skull in the bottom of the glass jar of blackcurrant wine she'd been making. It had glowed through the blood-red liquid, magnified and evil-looking, and it had been his turn to laugh when she had all but fainted with fright.

A hen fluttered through the trapdoor on the far side of the wooden shed and made soft crawing noises as it looked around with beady eyes. Another came in, and another. Someone was outside. Luke must have sprouted wings to get here so soon. The fourth hen entered with ruffled feathers and a loud *squark* as if it had been frightened. A shadow darkened the doorway, shutting out what little light there had been.

'What was all the hurry then?' A deep masculine voice asked the question.

Hannah flattened herself to the bricks, her hands against her mouth to prevent a shriek of alarm. She'd been watching the chickens instead of the door, thinking she was safe, but Ben Rutherford had seen her. She hardly dared to breathe, hoping he would go away.

Ben was like a second brother, though he was no relation. He had come to Kean's Farm as a boy of ten to work in the fields, an orphan from the Union House at the other end of the village. At first he had been paid a wage, but Ma had taken to giving him meals with the family and Pa had found it cheaper to feed him than pay him, so after a while he'd moved in. Ben had stayed on, becoming ox-strong and intelligent as he grew to manhood alongside Luke. No one knew who his parents had been but they had given him brains to keep the farm out of debt in the last three years since Pa's death. If Luke had been on his own they would have been in a sorry financial state by now, so the orphan from the Union House was as necessary to Kean's Farm as sun and rain.

Luke and Ben were now wild young men of twenty-two and no example for Hannah to follow, as her mother and older sister Emily were always telling her, but Hannah was wilful. Until lately she had followed them, fought with them and worked beside them while Emily churned the milk and helped Ma in the house. But since this spring Ben had changed. He had broken up the closeness, become sharp, and she was no longer at ease when he was around.

'You've been up to something,' he said, ducking his head to come inside. His blue shirt had no buttons and the sleeves were rolled up past his elbows, exposing a mass of black hair on his arms. 'Tell me what you've done or I'll drop you outside in the muck heap.'

He made out he was going to pick her up but she dodged sideways, laughing again. The hen-house was not high enough for him to stand straight and the rafters pressing on the back of his neck

6

made it look as if he was supporting the roof. But he caught her all the same. 'Now, miss, what have you been up to?'

She squealed and capitulated. 'Don't! I'll tell you. Luke's mending the thatch on the barn and I've taken the ladder away.'

'He'll pay you back good and proper, and it'll serve you right.'

'Now I suppose you're going to spoil it by getting him down.'

He still held her by the arm. 'Maybe I should take you with me.'

His dark head was on a level with hers and light from a gap in the bricks made his eyes shine like jewels. He had the most beautiful eyes she had ever seen. She struggled to get away, ducking and squirming but both his arms now held her. A besom broom fell from the wall and the crown of her bonnet caught in the nails where it had been hanging and was dragged off her head. He bundled the thick mass of her hair in one hand and lifted it clear of her neck, then quite unexpectedly brought his mouth against the hollow at the base of her throat between ear and shoulder, tormenting her until she screamed for mercy. The exquisite yet unbearable sensation almost drove her mad.

'Don't!' she cried. 'Please, don't.'

'You've been asking for it.' He was breathing fast.

She curled closer to him, her chin lowered and shoulders hunched to force him to give up. She butted his chest with the top of her head and the smell of sweat on him was as pungent as the birdlime. Strange, exciting feelings coursed through her body. He had never touched her like this before and she shivered deliciously.

'Stop it! I didn't ask for nothing.'

They tussled and laughed but she couldn't match his strength or lithe agility. And her laughter was tinged with hysteria. This was no brotherly struggle, no innocent game such as she had played with both Ben and Luke countless times before. For the first time she was becoming frightened of a situation she had created, feeling as if it was somehow getting out of hand. Her struggles made her feet slip on the damp, lime-covered straw carpeting the earthen floor and she landed on her back in the dirt. For a moment there was no sound except for the agitated clucking of the hens. The urge to laugh had died away.

He stood over her for several seconds, a dark expression clouding his face. They stared at one another as if they were strangers, and he wiped his hand over his mouth.

7

'Get up,' he said. 'You'll get in a dreadful mess down there.'

She got to her feet slowly, brushing her skirt which was now coated in chicken manure.

'It's all your fault. Ma'll be terribly mad at me.'

'My fault, is it? You've been asking for a toss in the hay for months.'

She was shaken. 'I haven't! How can you say such a thing?'

'Leading me on. Always teasing.'

'No more than I tease Luke.'

'It ain't the same, and you know it.' Ben flicked a finger under her chin. 'You're not innocent and you know damn well what you're about when you flash your eyes and play games. Best look sharp if you don't want to lose your virginity.'

'I can take care of my virginity, so don't think I can't.'

'*I* think you're ripe to lose it.'

'Leave me alone,' Hannah cried. 'I don't like you any more.' Her legs were trembling and there was a vast ache in the middle region of her body which she attributed to anger. It wasn't like him to say such things. She didn't know what had come over him.

'Grow up, Hannah,' he said, even more sharply. He turned and went out through the low door, making the hinges squeak in protest as he thrust a balled fist against the powdering weather-bleached wood.

She ran after him. The encounter had left her feeling frustrated and bewildered, and she wished she hadn't been so childish.

'Don't be angry with me.' There was a suspicion of fear in her voice as she caught up with him.

'I'm not angry.'

'You are. You're getting old and dull like Emily, and you're no fun any more.' She darted ahead on the narrow path, snapping the hemlock stalks. When she had barred his way she faced him indignantly. 'And don't think I want you the way you're making out. You're the last person I'd make me bed with, so if you want a girl go and find yourself one who's likely to be more obliging.'

Maybe she *was* getting ready for love, but she'd not have Ben Rutherford chasing after her like she was a bitch in season. His unpredictable moods lately were spoiling everything and she hated always having to be on the defensive.

Anxious to dispel the seriousness that had descended on them she mischievously snatched at the red handkerchief round his neck and drew it off.

'Let's be friends again,' she said. She was relieved to see his tense expression ease a little. He caught the end of the handkerchief and hung on to it until a tug-o'-war developed.

When the square of red, sweat-stained cotton was again in his possession he wiped the perspiration from her face with it and they were so close she could have reached up and kissed him. She wondered what he would have done. The impulse to put it to the test was so strong her lips tingled and she pressed them together. Their eyes met. His were unwavering, holding her gaze firmly from the moment he had captured it and she saw the varying shades in the irises that made them shine so wonderfully grey. His mouth curved into a penitent smile.

'I'm sorry,' he said. 'I never meant to say the things I did.'

'Reckon I didn't neither.'

They stood there, close enough to touch, and she felt as if her body was melting. But they didn't touch. An awkwardness developed, tying their tongues so that there seemed nothing either could say. It was almost a relief when sounds of a commotion suddenly carried across the field. Her sister Emily was screaming like a banshee.

'My God, what's happened?' Ben made off towards the gate.

Hannah's legs trembled and her heart raced as she looked towards the barn and saw to her horror that her brother was no longer on the roof. She chased after Ben, fear providing the speed to catch up with his giant strides. The cattle had now congregated at the field entrance in an immovable mass, flicking at flies and impatient to be milked, and when the iron gate swung open they herded forward, nose to rump and hides chafing. Ben swore at them and pushed his way through, but Hannah was left standing in the mud until they had passed, water oozing through the soles of her worn boots. When she was at last able to get through Ben had covered half the distance between gate and barn, and Emily was flying towards him over the coarse grass. Serious, sedate eighteen-year-old Emily who never approved of unseemly behaviour and hadn't run since the day she had pinned her plaited hair neatly across the top of her head to signify she had left childhood behind.

'It's Luke,' Emily was shouting, her voice so shrill it must have been heard in the village. 'Luke's fallen off the barn roof. He's dead. I just know he's dead.'

Ben Rutherford was glad of the need for action. Emily's screams didn't alarm him too much since she was inclined to panic easily, and he welcomed the excuse to run. It helped to work off his disgust with himself.

He didn't know what had come over him in the hen-house. He'd said things to Hannah that he'd had no business saying. In spite of her farm upbringing she was as innocent as the doves on the chapel roof and her teasing was naught but childish fun. She knew right enough what he'd been after, but he was honest enough to admit she didn't really encourage male attentions and the hired hands always got short shrift if they were too saucy.

Emily was flying across the grass but he couldn't yet hear what she was saying. She bore a resemblance to Hannah in height and colouring, but it ended there and Ben had never been in any danger of looking upon her as other than an adoptive sister. She always wore two aprons, keeping the under one clean for serving dinner, and Will Baxter who'd been courting her for months reckoned she must wear two pairs of drawers as well since he'd got nowhere with her. She was strong-minded like her Pa had been, but youthful exuberance such as Hannah's had passed her by.

It was since Christmas he'd taken to noticing Hannah too much and it made him restless and moody. He liked the neat little waist she had, the way her hips swayed when she walked, and sometimes the pout of her full lips was so provocative it didn't seem fair. She had slender arms and long fingers which had strength to wield hoe or pitchfork as industriously as any man, yet when she was set to mending of an evening the candlelight caressed those busy hands and made them so feminine it were a right shame not to be able to hold them. As for her hair, the need to crush it in his fist had overcome him today and he'd gathered it up before good sense could warn him not to. The feel of it, silky and heavy, had driven him on to greater daring and the aromatic smell of her skin when he'd put his mouth against her neck had been sweeter than a summer meadow.

How wicked to feel as he did. If Matt Jerram had been alive he would have taken a whip to him for the way he'd just treated his

10

favourite child. There were enough willing wenches around, yet every waking minute Ben seemed to be fighting a battle with himself to put aside thoughts of Hannah which had no business troubling him. He'd been in the same house with her since she was eight years old and she'd been kin to him same as the others. Lusting after kin was more than wicked. It was sinful. Ma Jerram had taken the precaution of telling him right from the start that in becoming one of the family he accepted moral responsibilities, as if she had known he might one day take a fancy to one of her daughters.

He pushed impatiently through the cows, and then he heard what Emily was shouting in her panic. His blood ran cold.

'Luke's dead!' Emily shrieked. 'He's fallen off the barn roof and he's just lying there.' Her face was red and tears were streaming down her cheeks. She flung herself into his arms.

'Maybe it ain't that bad,' he said. But he thought his heart would stop. The Jerrams were the only family he'd ever known and he loved them as if he'd been born to them. He'd taken a good many beatings from Pa Jerram but he'd had a great respect for him and it'd taken a while to get over his death. Now Luke.

'Just come quick. I found him when I went over with his tea. He looks awful,' she sobbed.

Ben wasted no time. He thrust Emily aside and left her to provide answers for Hannah who was now catching up; Hannah who had taken the ladder away. He raced towards the barn, his throat dry and temples throbbing. It was a tall building with tarred walls and it had been used for stabling horses at one time so there was a hayloft above. A long drop from the roof to the ground. A devil of a long drop.

Luke was lying by a bed of stinging nettles, his moustache contrasting starkly with the whiteness of his face. His right leg was doubled under.

Ben bent over him. 'You speak to me, d'you hear! Luke, can you hear me?'

Praise be, Luke opened his eyes, and they reflected the pain he was in so acutely it was like looking into a dark abyss.

'Leg's . . . broken,' he muttered, hoarsely.

'Hold on,' said Ben. 'We've got to get you back to the house.'

He was so relieved to find Luke still breathing he could have pulled him up and hugged him, but he could see it was going to need great care to move him at all without causing terrible pain. There might be more than his leg broken. The unthinkable was that he might have broken his back.

'Straw was wet. I . . . slipped,' Luke gasped.

Hannah was crying hysterically. She had stopped a few feet away and had gathered the corners of her apron up to cover her face, but on hearing her brother's voice the edge of the apron inched downwards again. Tear-filled eyes peered over it.

'Luke, I'm sorry,' she wept. 'I didn't mean this to happen, honest I didn't.' She rushed forward and would have fallen on Luke with relief if Ben hadn't stopped her.

'Don't touch him. You don't want to do more damage than you've done already. Find an old door or something that we can carry him on.' Both sisters were now staring anxiously. 'Emily, go and help her.'

When the girls had gone he knelt to see how best to cope with the emergency. He was worried sick how Ma Jerram was going to take it. Luke's mother was a capable woman, but when it came to a crisis she was apt to rely too heavily on her religion, as if faith alone would solve everything. Likely the first person she would send for would be the Minister instead of the doctor.

Luke's forehead was creased with the pain. 'Get me up. Maybe I can walk.'

Ben snorted. 'Ain't no chance of that for a week or two. I'm going to make a couple of splints.'

Hedgerows stretched behind the barn. He took the eaves knife which was lying a few feet away to cut the stoutest and straightest branches he could find, tearing his hands on thorns as he thrust them into the dense growth. There was a kind of relief in ignoring the viciousness of the thorns. It added fuel to the fire that had been burning in him since the scene with Hannah, who had caused this to happen to her brother.

Luke was moaning when Ben got back but he hadn't lost consciousness again.

'D'you think you can move, bor? Can you sit up, d'you reckon?'

This was the test. If he couldn't then Ben would be leaving him where he was until the doctor came. But Luke made a brave effort and managed to raise himself up on his elbows, so he hadn't damaged his back. Hannah and Emily had found an old hurdle and they struggled with it between them.

'We'll cover it with our aprons,' said Emily.

Ben inspected the rotting timber, testing its strength, and when he was satisfied it would hold a man's weight he let them go ahead with padding it as best they could. Then he turned back to Luke.

'Right, now I'm going to straighten your leg,' he said, with a calmness he was far from feeling.

'Hell, man . . . have a heart!'

'I've got to do it.' Ben felt sick himself at the thought but there was no alternative. 'Emily, come here and keep his other leg straight.'

He sounded so sure of himself – he mustn't let any of them know how scared he was of doing the wrong thing. A little of Ma Jerram's faith wouldn't have come amiss at that moment.

'I'm right sorry I've got to hurt you, bor,' he said. 'Grab hold of something and grit yer teeth.'

'Grab hold of me, Luke,' cried Hannah. 'I don't care if you bruise me black and blue.'

'You ain't going to salve yer conscience that easy,' Ben said to her. 'Reckon *you'd* better run like the devil and get Dr Parkin.'

She didn't argue. She rushed off with her hair flying loose and skirt lifted high. But she had a distance to go and Ben didn't wait. He carefully extricated the bent limb and turned it. Luke screamed and blacked out again, which was a mercy because when the leg was straightened the broken bone was sticking through his shin.

Chapter Two

Seggenham was a straggling village. At either perimeter the cottages and farms thinned out like the fraying ends of a rope, while several houses, the general store, a saddle-makers and an inn gathered tightly round the church like a knot in the middle. To the north lay the manor house, a jewel hidden from the road by a border of elms which also sheltered it from winds blowing off the sea. To the south and east were water-meadows and marshes. Land to the north was rich, ideal for crops and good for grazing, but bogs encroached on the opposite boundaries and the ground was permanently wet in places, even in summer. Kean's Farm lay southwards.

That afternoon, Lilianne Jerram had been to visit an old lady who was bedridden, a kindness she undertook once a week, and she was walking home along the main winding road from one end of the village to the other. She was a fine-looking woman, two years short of forty but youthful enough to be taken for ten years younger in spite of the hard life she led.

'You're a good woman and you've raised a good family, Mrs Jerram,' the old lady had said only half an hour since.

Yes, Lilianne supposed she was lucky. Her brood was large enough to be useful and not too large to be expensive. She had always managed to dress her two girls tidily in garments made over from her own, and she'd kept the boys' clothes clean and decently patched. It hadn't been easy since Matt, her husband, had died. In the last three years since he was taken she'd noticed grey hairs appearing but as her colouring was on the fair side they didn't show up overmuch. Not that it would have worried her if they did. She believed that too much interest in one's looks after marriage was unhealthy. Peace of mind was far more important. She'd not been unhappy with Matt. True he'd wandered after other women from time to time, but what man didn't, and though she'd never admitted it, even to her husband, the intimate side of marriage had given her a fair amount of pleasure. She missed him still, but she was happy with her children. It didn't occur to her that tranquility was a better aid to beauty than any potion ever invented.

Thinking of Matt always made her sad, even after all this time. Maybe it was the terrible way he had been taken from her. She would never forget the day he had been carried home on a makeshift stretcher by two hired men, bleeding from wounds inflicted by the bull he had always said was as gentle as a lamb. He hadn't died straight away from the goring. He had lingered for a week while the poison from it crept up through his body and no one could save him, not even the doctor with his blood-letting. She'd spent hours in chapel and at the cemetery afterwards, weeping when she was needed at home, but it hadn't brought him back. It had brought hardship instead. Luke worked well enough, but when left with sole responsibility he didn't have his father's dedication and though she hated to admit it the farm would have gone to ruin if it hadn't been for Ben Rutherford.

She tried to like Ben. Matt had treated him like a son but Lilianne had never got over the feeling that he was an intruder. Likely it was jealousy. The cottage she had been visiting was at the Union House end of Seggenham where orphaned children gazed through the railings in silent appeal. She never passed by without wondering what Ben would be doing now if Matt hadn't been so generous, and she was never moved to offer a home to another orphan.

The walk from the farm to the cottage was about two miles each way, a tiring trek on a warm day with a basket full of provisions. It wasn't so bad coming back. She always stopped at the store, partly to rest on the splay-legged stool Mr Chambers provided for his customers' use, and partly to refill the basket with family requirements. Then, of course, there was usually someone with whom to gossip.

'Good-day to you, Mrs Jerram,' said Mr Chambers, as Lilianne went in the shop to the accompaniment of a jangling doorbell. 'Mrs Wigg here and meself was just talking about a strange woman who's about the village. Likely you'll have seen her.'

'No,' said Lilianne, her curiosity immediately aroused. 'I ain't seen any strangers this past month or more.'

'She's different shall we say, Mr Chambers,' said Mrs Wigg, who was married to the parson. She purposely didn't address Lilianne who was staunchly Methodist and therefore, in her eyes, lower on

15

the parish social scale. Her black straw hat, flat and primly pinned in place, was like a grim inverted image of her mouth with its thin upper lip. Her basket had a lid to conceal her purchases.

'Who's the woman staying with?' Lilianne asked. She was unruffled by the snub. Petty snobbery only made her smile.

'Don't rightly know. Seems she travels about preaching.'

'Preaching! Well, I call that a strange thing for a woman to do and no mistake.' Mr Chambers dropped some tallow candles in Mrs Wigg's bag. 'Are you sure I can't interest you in this new paraffin lamp, ma'am? You'll be amazed at the extra light it gives.'

'No, my dear man, I couldn't abide the smell.' She paid for the things she had bought, carefully counting out coins. Then: 'My husband says he'll move the woman on if she causes unrest among his flock. Unless, of course, she only mixes with chapel people, in which case it won't be Reverend Wigg's responsibility. Now, he has a parochial meeting and he asked me to be punctual with his tea.'

Mr Chambers eased his bulk through the little gate separating him from his customers and opened the door for her with a flourish which clanged the bell again. He stood on the step chatting to Mrs Wigg a few minutes more, but turned to smile at Mrs Jerram apologetically.

Lilianne sat down on the stool. It was warm in the shop and flies buzzed among the flour sacks and got stuck on a cask of treacle. Her neck was hot and she lifted up the looped hair under the curtain of her sunbonnet to wipe away sweat, glad of a few minutes quiet to absorb the mixture of fragrances in the store which she found soothing. Linen and wool, cheese and bacon, soap and candlewax. She looked around at the assortment of stock spilling out of drawers and tubs, and she marvelled that Mr Chambers always knew exactly where to find even the most obscure item. She would have liked to own a shop.

'Now what can I get for you, Mrs Jerram?'

'Sugar, if you please,' she said.

'White sugar or yellow crystals will it be? Or I've powder sugar new in stock.'

'White. I've enough strawberries to make another batch of jam.'

The storekeeper leaned over the counter. 'Can I perhaps sell *you* a paraffin lamp? Queen Victoria herself couldn't ask for better.'

'If I could afford one of those I'd leave the curtains open for all the village to see.' She watched the sugar being weighed, light catching the grains to set them sparkling as they slipped from scoop to bag. 'This strange woman, Mr Chambers, what would she be preaching about do you suppose, and where does she come from?'

'Heard tell she's from Little Glemham but other than that I don't know. Perhaps she's a gypsy.'

Lilianne was intrigued. Any stranger in the village was bound to be remarked upon, but this one seemed to be more unusual than most.

'Well, I don't reckon so. A gypsy would be thieving, not preaching,' she said. She filled her basket, adding to the list of things on tick which was pinned to a board behind the counter. 'I hope I'll be able to pay you next month. I'm right sorry to keep you waiting for the money.'

A short time later she was walking slowly home enjoying the peace of the afternoon. The chapel came into view. It was a newish oblong building of whitewashed bricks which sat uneasily on a corner of waste ground which Squire Kean's father had graciously granted to the Methodists thirty years earlier, and it was close enough to Kean's Farm for the hymn-singing to be heard every Sabbath. The green-painted door stood open.

Lilianne paused, surprised that someone was inside since it was the Minister's day for visiting. She was about to go and investigate when a woman came out of the chapel, surely the one who had set tongues wagging. She stared at Lilianne with strange, piercing eyes which sent shivers down the spine, and though her dark dress was neat she had an air of nonconformity. She smiled. Lilianne smiled back. The woman's charisma was so strong she would have crossed the lane in front of a galloping horse if she had called her. The air seemed ominously charged.

Across the fields the cows which Emily and Hannah were due to start milking could be heard lowing unhappily as if a dog was rounding them. And anxious voices came from Dr Parkin's house opposite. When two people emerged from the house she saw Hannah dragging the elderly physician by the arm and begging him to make haste.

'Hannah!' Lilianne dropped her basket by the doctor's gate, the woman forgotten. Dear God, what calamity had brought this about?

The girl came running to her mother, face wet with tears, untidy as a scarecrow and upset like she'd been after her father's accident.

'It's Luke, Ma. He's by the barn and we daren't move him. His leg's broke.'

The doctor was impatient. 'If you want me to hurry make yourself useful, girl. Carry my medical bag. I've just had a large tea and it's all I can do to get meself along.'

'How did he do it?' Lilianne cried.

'He fell off the roof.'

'Oh, my God.'

The woman who was said to go about preaching, came over to Lilianne's side.

'How wise to call on the Lord for help,' she said. Her voice was strong, the words coloured by a Suffolk accent every bit as broad as that heard locally. 'I'll come with you. You may need an extra pair of hands.'

Hannah had never been so frightened. Every bit of the blame was hers and she felt as if she had stepped over a great chasm to leave childhood behind. Never again would she play a dangerous trick like that.

The stairs were far too narrow and steep for Luke to be taken up them. Ben was carrying one end of the hurdle and the girls struggled together with the other, but they had to put it on the yellow brick floor in the kitchen. Everyone gathered round. There was Ma with tears on her cheeks, giving instructions with as much clarity as a clucking hen. Emily was more sensible. She was already bringing a blanket to cover her brother who was thrashing about in pain, oblivion having been short-lived.

The woman whom nobody knew was standing quietly in the background. She gazed at the scene with a penetrating look, her features too sharp and prominent to be attractive and her skin too bronzed for decency, as if she had spent time outdoors without the protection of a bonnet. She wore a black merino dress and a dull purple shawl which was held across her thin chest by a brooch with turquoise stones. Her black straw hat wouldn't have disgraced Mrs Wigg. She looked to be much the same age as Ma and much the same height, which was tallish, but her hair was darker than Ma's and hung down her back in long curls. No one took the trouble to ask why she was intruding since there were far more urgent things needing attention.

18

Dr Parkin had his bag open again and Hannah felt sick at the sight of the stark fear in Luke's eyes.

'Don't let him use the saw on me. *Please* don't let him use the saw on me,' he cried, terrified as the physician took out his tools. 'I'll be a useless cripple for the rest of my life if my leg's taken off.'

'It'd be better, bor,' said Dr Parkin. 'Ain't no way we're going to save it.'

The old man was known to relish an amputation. Once he'd actually performed one in a meadow to free a boy trapped in a thresher. Hannah clasped her hands together in anguish. There had to be another way to help Luke.

'You ain't taking his leg off,' said Ben. He stood, his own legs astride, determination evident in the way his muscles tensed. 'Come spring he's going to be walking again if I have anything to do with it. I didn't cut my hands to ribbons making splints for nothing.'

'If you think you know best why did you send for me?' asked Dr Parkin, peeved at the lack of respect for his trade. His pessimism was malevolent. 'Gangrene'll set in, I warn you, then it'll have to come off to save his life.'

'We'll risk it.' Ben looked down at Luke. 'Ain't that right, bor?'

'Aye, we'll risk it,' said Luke.

Dr Parkin put the tools back in his bag. 'On your own heads be it. I wash my hands of you.' He left ungraciously, words of disapproval rumbling inaudibly in his throat.

Ma went down on her knees beside the hurdle and sobbed against her son's chest while Hannah and Emily cleared the long whitewood kitchen table and wiped it down with a dwile. When that was done Luke was carefully lifted on to it.

'If you'll permit me, I'll put a kettle on the fire,' said the woman, speaking for the first time since coming in the house. There was an air of authority about her. 'You'll need hot water for bathing the wound, and likely a pot of tea would help us all.'

It should have been Ma being practical.

'I'll get some water,' said Hannah, and she escaped outside to the well, afraid she might be sick.

She let the rope out too quickly and the bucket dropped down the well with a loud splash. The effort to draw it up full in half the usual time made perspiration collect on her forehead and her heart seemed to be bursting. A terrible cry from indoors rent the air a few minutes later, and then everything was quiet. Hannah untied the bucket and set it down, leaning exhausted against the wall.

'Pull yerself together, girl.' The woman had followed her out and her voice was stern. 'Would you know where there's some comfrey?'

'Who *are* you?' Hannah asked, uneasily. 'You don't belong round here. Where have you come from and what are you doing?'

'My name's Mary Ann Girling and I do whatever God wills me.'

Hannah moved a step back. 'You're touched.'

'I asked if you knew where there was some comfrey,' said Mrs Girling. 'It's urgent I get some.'

The light in her bluish-grey eyes had a mesmeric effect and Hannah's skin tingled with a curious foreboding. Refusal to cooperate was out of the question.

'There's some by the pond I reckon. I'll see.'

'Bring the root.'

Hannah hurried round to the front of the house hoping the woman wouldn't follow, and she picked her way through tall grasses edging the stagnant water a few feet from it. Mud squelched up with every step and soaked the hem of her skirt which had only just started drying out.

What if Luke should die, like Pa? It didn't bear thinking about. She had loved her father with a passion that had surpassed anything she felt for her mother and his death had left a great yawning gap in her life. That love had, to some extent, been transferred to her brother and she wouldn't let anything bad be said about him, although she had to admit he didn't have Pa's strength of character, nor the same will to work. She suspected he gambled away family money when he went into town on market days. Once, soon after Pa's death, there had been a terrible scandal when cock-fighting had taken place in the barn. It had brought the Land Agent round with threats of eviction if it ever happened again, and Ma had blamed Ben Rutherford for allowing it to happen. But Hannah knew it had been all Luke's doing. Very often at night she leaned out of the bedroom widow to eavesdrop on Luke and Ben when they came home late. Emily tried to shame her out of doing it, but she overheard a lot of things while she was hidden by the virginia creeper, and she had witnessed Ben's attempts to persuade her brother not to be such a fool just before the cock-fight troubles.

But for all his weaknesses Luke was very amiable, and it was easy to believe him when he said that the deterioration in the farm was only temporary. He was going to make money – to breed horses and sell them for large profits. Oh, he had plenty of ideas, and he'd done some schooling. The Jerram children, including Ben, had all attended the village school long enough to learn to read and write. Pa had insisted on his family getting an education.

Hannah looked for the pink, bell-shaped flowers, found plenty without much trouble and tugged at the winged stems until the roots of the plant came free. Ma had grumbled for years about the way it spread. She broke off the flower heads and filled her apron with the roots, but was reluctant to go back. It wasn't just nervousness at facing Luke again – there was something about this Mrs Girling that disturbed Hannah greatly. She felt an uncomfortable premonition about the woman.

What a terrible day it had become. Frightening. Apart from the anguish over Luke's accident there was her guilt at the way she had behaved with Ben in the hen-house. The wonderful sensations in her body when he had kissed her neck were repeated just thinking about it and she had to suppress them. There were plenty of young men in the village angling after her but none of them could arouse mysterious longings in her the way Ben Rutherford had done this afternoon, and it was wrong when he was part of the family. She didn't think she could ever look him in the eyes again.

Emily was bathing Luke's head with a wet cloth when she went indoors, and it was quiet enough to hear a fly buzzing round a flitch of ham hanging from the beam nearest the range. Luke's eyes were closed and she didn't know whether he was aware of Ben placing stout splints either side of his broken limb. The bone no longer protruded but there was a nasty wound where it had pierced the skin and her brother's leg was the colour of a black storm sky.

Mrs Girling took the wild flowers from Hannah without a word. She broke off the stems and washed the roots.

'Find me a knife,' she said. 'And I'll need the pestle.' She set to work cutting and bruising the comfrey roots and when she was satisfied the juice was running she went to the table. Ma and Emily moved aside to give her room and she made Ben stop what he was doing. 'Wait. Put this on before you bind it.'

'Will it do any good?'

21

'Comfrey heals wounds. The good Lord didn't put plants on this earth just to make it look pretty. They all have a purpose.'

Hannah watched Mrs Girling place the concoction on the wound which Emily had cleaned. She worked swiftly, staunching any blood with strips of cotton folded into thick wadding. No one questioned her capabilities.

'There,' she said, when the job was done. 'You'll have to put a fresh lot on when this dries, but you can bind the splints tight now. Likely it'll be a good many months before he can walk again, but have faith and he won't have to lose his leg.'

'Reckon we all have a lot to thank you for,' Ma said.

'It's the Lord ye have to thank. It'd be fitting for us all to get down on our knees and you can join me in a prayer.'

The woman sank down on the yellow brick floor and clasped her hands together. Ma and Emily had no hesitation in following suit, but Hannah held back. There was something uncanny about Mrs Girling, a strong aura which frightened her because she couldn't account for it. Goose pimples stood out on Hannah's arms and she felt cold to the core, as if icy fingers were clutching her. The hand which dragged her down was Ma's, forcing her to be obedient.

'Oh, Lord, bring Thy healing on this, our brother, we pray. We thank You that he still lives. Mend his bones and cool his body if he takes a fever. Keep him strong in heart and mind.'

The praying went on for several minutes and the woman opened her eyes, trance-like, as the exhortations increased in fervour. She raised her hands in the air and swayed. The final amen had a ringing sound, as if there should have been a bell or an organ accompaniment, and then she went limp.

Into the silence which followed Ben poured words of normality.

'Hannah, come and hold the other end of these splints steady.' He hadn't bent his knee and he scowled as he took charge again. It was plain to see he didn't hold with a stranger issuing orders.

But her gaze was riveted on the woman who got to her feet as if her behaviour was nothing remarkable and went to hold a piece of clean, wet wadding in place on Luke's leg. The most extraordinary feeling paralysed Hannah. She was trembling.

'What's the matter with you, girl?' Ma demanded. Her voice seemed to come from miles away.

'Nothing,' Hannah said.

22

She made herself go to the table. Luke was muttering incoherently and Emily was trying to soothe him with encouraging words. Ben had started to knot some rope to one of the thick, straight branches he had cut from the hedgerow, and Ma was holding Luke's foot which was now straight but terribly swollen.

Had none of them noticed?

Mrs Girling had the most curious white marks on her hands, as if nails had once been driven through them.

Chapter Three

For over a week it was doubtful if Luke would live. He developed a fever and tossed on his bed until the pain that movement caused to his leg made him scream. Someone had to sit with him day and night.

An apology to Dr Parkin brought the physician once more to the house and Lilianne watched Luke's blood being drawn off with a brass instrument which transferred it in frightening quantity to a glass basin, but the fever persisted and he grew thinner and paler. Sometimes he was unconscious and it was too quiet. It was almost a relief when his leg had to be held steady again to keep the bone in place, and then he could be heard outside in the yard.

She'd given up her own bed so that he could be comfortable. For hours she would sit beside her son, bathing his face and praying for the fever to leave him. Praying this wasn't a repetition of the terrible days she had spent watching her husband's life ebbing away. But Luke was only half the age that Matt had been. He was young and strong and would fight to come through this with all the stubborn tenacity she so often condemned when it went contrary to her own wishes. He was a fighter anyway. Among the local youths he was known for the quickness of his fists and tendency to use them at the least provocation.

There was plenty of time for thinking while she sat listening to Luke's incoherent ramblings. She thought of all the children she had lost, the five infant sons birthed and buried the same day they were born, and she prayed that having been granted the privilege of raising this wayward son she wouldn't lose him now.

One thing was certain – she couldn't have done without Ben right now. He would lift Luke while they washed him to cool the fevered body, shave his bony chin as best he could and see that the splints held firm. He was coping with most of the outside work alone and he'd taken on boys from the Union House to work in the potato field since they only needed paying a shilling a week. And on market day he loaded eggs and vegetables in the cart and drove it himself to save her. No one could have asked for greater loyalty.

Lilianne gave a lot of thought as to why she resented Ben Rutherford and decided she'd been jealous of Matt's overt affection for him as a boy. It had almost seemed as if he was blaming her for losing five of his true sons. Luke, their one precious boy, her treasure, her joy, should have had his sole attention, but the only one of his three surviving children for whom he'd shown real love had been Hannah. For some reason Hannah had enslaved her father. It hadn't been fair to Emily, who was by far the more amenable of their two daughters. Emily was always willing, always thoughtful and dutiful, and Lilianne felt closer to her than to anyone.

'You need rest, Ma,' Emily said that evening when the first week was up. Shadows were creeping over the broad window-sill and smudging the pattern on the faded, flower-strewn wallpaper. 'I've made some soup for you. Make sure you eat it all then get some sleep. I'll see to things here.'

'You're a good girl.' Tiredness and reminiscing increased the ache in Lilianne's heart and she sought refuge in the arms Emily extended.

Soon she went down the narrow stairs with plodding feet, holding on to the flimsy pole which served as a handrail. It was dark in the kitchen and Hannah was lighting the candles.

'I'll sit up with Luke tonight,' Hannah said. She was so repentant and so dreadfully distressed it was impossible to think of any punishment greater than the weight upon her conscience. She had never been so subdued.

'It ain't like you to be so willing,' Lilianne said. 'I remember when your father was ill you was off to the fields quicker than a hare rather than take a turn at his bedside.'

'I was three years younger then.'

'Maybe so. But you ain't changed that much, surely.'

'Reckon I've had a warning to mend my ways.'

She was pale and she wasn't eating. Not that anyone fancied food, but Lilianne continued to cook on pot-days and saw to it they ate enough on the others since there was work to be done whether Luke was ill or not. The cows still needed milking, the chickens feeding, the butter making, and the potatoes were ready for picking up in the pightle. Hannah toiled from sun-up till sunset. Since the accident she had done everything she could to make up for the trouble she had caused, but she was not one to spend time in a sick-room.

Lilianne pulled the curtains and settled in the deep armchair covered with turkey twill which had been Matt's favourite. Likely Matt would have given his mischievous favourite child a beating at the start, but after that he would have tried to help her.

'You're blaming yerself too much, child,' her mother said. 'You'll be ill too if you carry on moping the way you're doing.'

'It were wicked what I did. I'll never forgive myself if Luke dies.' Tears filled Hannah's golden-brown eyes, drenching them like rain on autumn leaves. She had such a sunny nature and rarely cried, though she'd been known to weep when a favourite cow was sent to market.

The sight of her tears now upset Lilianne. 'Things are only wicked if we *mean* to hurt someone. You didn't want to hurt Luke, and he could have climbed down easy enough if he'd been more careful. It were his own fault he slipped.'

'Oh, Ma . . .'

'There, there,' said Lilianne, drawing her close. 'Dry your eyes and share my soup. You'll need some if you're sitting up all night.'

For a few minutes Hannah snuggled against her breast, but the words didn't seem to have reassured her. She was trembling.

'Ma, I'm so afraid the woman'll come back and take him after all.'

Lilianne gaped in astonishment. 'What're you talking about, you silly mawther?' She took the girl by the shoulders and set her away.

'The preacher woman. She as much as said she'd been sent from God and I reckon she'd come to take Luke, else why would she have appeared right then? She scared me, Ma.'

'Mercy on us!' Now she'd heard everything. 'What on earth put such rubbish in your head? The woman helped us, didn't she? The comfrey's taken the swelling down. And she prayed for Luke. She told us we'd need to have faith so maybe we should pray some more.'

'But where's she gone? She came from nowhere and then she disappeared just as fast.'

'She's a travelling woman. A gypsy most likely.'

'She had marks on her hands as if she'd been crucified,' said Hannah.

26

If Lilianne had belonged to the Popish order she would have crossed herself. A cold fear touched her heart. She'd hardly given the woman a thought since she had refused the offer of a bed for the night and gone walking off down the lane, but something about her had certainly frightened Hannah out of her wits. She looked at her own hands. They were ingrained with garden dirt and stained from fruit-picking and potato-peeling. The nails were worn down and ugly. She turned them over and studied the backs.

'See,' she said, holding them out. 'There's marks on my hands too. Brown marks what come with age. We all get them and I reckon Mrs Girling ain't no different. So stop your worrying, girl, and let's see you smile again. Luke won't want to see such a gloomy face when he starts to get well.'

Hannah was dubious, but the tightness eased a little in her face. 'Maybe you're right,' she said.

'I know I am. And I doubt we'll ever see the woman again so put her out of your mind.'

The talk did some good after all. Colour gradually returned to Hannah's cheeks and when she was at Luke's side she began chivvying him the way she always did when they were together, until he smiled in the midst of his fever. But she had transferred some of her uneasiness to Lilianne who began to wish, for no real reason, that Mary Ann Girling had never crossed her path that fateful day.

The tide turned on the ninth day.

Emily was curled up asleep on a rag mat beside the bed when the first fingers of daylight stole over her. Sunshine soon warmed the room and early-morning sounds filtered through the stillness of a lavender dawn. A cock crowed in the yard and a blackbird trilled a few notes. The fire in the kitchen range was being stoked and the well handle creaked as it was turned, but all was peaceful upstairs.

It had been a long night and Emily had grown stiff and tired on the rush-seated chair, so when her brother was no longer restless she had crept down to the floor. The sounds outside failed to disturb her, but when there was a slight noise from the bed she was immediately aware. She awoke guiltily, ashamed of having fallen asleep when she was supposed to be watching for any change in Luke's condition, and on opening her eyes she was astonished to see him propped on one elbow looking down at her.

27

'Do you reckon Ma's brewing tea?' he asked.

'Oh!' gasped Emily, jumping up.

'What's the matter – is it too much to ask?'

'No. Oh, no. It's just wonderful.' Emily's eyes shone with relief as she started at the thin, pale face. 'It's so wonderful to see you better.'

She gathered up her skirt and sped down the stairs, calling her mother with such excitement it caused consternation.

'What is it? What's happened?'

'Luke wants a cup of tea.'

Ma clapped her hands together and gave a cry of joy. 'Praise the Lord!'

Hannah, hearing the excitement, rushed in from the yard and the three women joined hands and danced round the kitchen table before Ma hurried upstairs to see the miracle for herself.

'I must tell Ben,' said Emily.

Her sister tried to stop her. 'I will. I'll find him.'

'I said *I'd* go. You stay here and help Ma.' Emily was insistent. Mostly she found it simpler to let Hannah have her own way, but lately she had been driven to express her feelings. It angered her that no one had taken Hannah to task for what she had done and a deep resentment had been building up over the last few days. If you were tall and pretty, playful as a puppy and beguiling with it, you could get away with anything, it seemed.

She had seen how Ben looked at Hannah, his eyes following every movement of her slim figure if he thought no one was watching, and Emily suffered pangs of jealousy. Will Baxter had been courting her in a very proper fashion for months and she'd taken pleasure in the thought that one day she would be his wife. Then she'd seen the hunger in Ben's eyes when he looked at Hannah and suddenly Will's polite attentions had become tiresome. She was envious of her sister's ability to attract the man who was chased by every girl in the village.

In all honesty she couldn't accuse Hannah of being provocative. She was too childish for that. Life, to her, was a game and she played it with an openness which made her both lovable and irritating. Luke adored her. Pa had made no secret of the fact that she was his favourite child, and even Ma forgave her too often, though she would be apologetic about it, as if it was against her better judgement. Envy was an ugly thing, yet lately Emily's feelings for Hannah were

28

perpetually tinged with it. She would have given much to change places with her, if only to know what it was like to attract Ben Rutherford.

She set off for the cowshed, her hair falling either side of her face from the centre parting like mouse-brown curtains because there'd been no time to brush and plait it. Her high, smooth forehead accentuated the clarity of her eyes which were the colour of the wine Ma made from barley, and when she smiled the movement of her lips showed the delicate fashioning of her cheekbones. Given a different way of life and a bit of trouble taken with her looks, Emily would have been recognised as a beautiful girl, delicately made and far more refined than her sister.

Ben was forking wet straw from the stalls and the pile he'd tossed through the open door on to the midden was already steaming in the warmth of the sun. Muscles rippled in his powerful arms as he worked. For a moment she watched without his knowledge, the way she'd sometimes seen him staring at Hannah, and a now familiar heat extended upwards from her legs to her face, bringing colour to her pale cheeks. Ma would have a fit if she knew how she felt. Come to that, so would Ben.

She remembered her news and was ashamed of delaying even a second.

'Ben, the fever's gone. Luke's better – ain't that marvellous!' She hurried to him, stepping through a rivulet of yellowish water running down the gutter between the stalls.

A smile spread across his face, lighting up his eyes, then he gave a shout of joy. 'Hey, that's what I been waiting to hear. I knew he'd come through.'

He threw down the fork and hugged her impulsively. She was shaken by the unexpected physical contact and trembled, clinging to him with great daring until he must surely know the effect he had on her. But he put her aside without a sign and strode off into the yard, heading for the house.

'Does Hannah know?' he called over his shoulder.

Emily sighed. 'Yes, she knows.' Always Hannah.

She stared up at the rafters to stop tears of disappointment. To take her mind off him she focused her attention on a peg that had been driven in one of the beams. Hanging from it was a hag-stone, a flint with a hole in it to ward off the Night Mare, the hag which

29

warned of death and made horses sweat. Over this past dreadful week she had looked at it several times, fearful that it might fall to the ground the way it had done just before Pa died. Ma said it was wrong to be superstitious, and with all her chapel-going Emily ought to have scoffed at it too, but the flint had been there for longer than anyone knew and she was thankful for anything which had helped to keep her brother alive.

Hannah was full of fears about the strange woman who had come. For a while she had almost made Emily believe that she had something to do with the hag-stone, but no one had come riding in the night for Luke. The flint was still hanging there and he was going to get better.

Once the fever had left him Luke recovered well. His appetite was enormous. Ma was having to cook on more than the three pot-days a week to satisfy him, and the supply of pigeons in the dovecote on the front wall of the house was dwindling. She dropped extra dollops of dough into the hake which hung over the fire bubbling with vegetable stew so that there would be more helpings of spoon-puddings, and the rabbit hutches had never been so empty. But no matter how much he ate it didn't help his left leg to mend any quicker. The weeks passed and he was still unable to bear any weight on the broken limb.

'You'll be walking right as rain by Christmas,' Ben kept saying to him.

By November he had been four months with the splints on it and there was no sign of any strength returning. He fretted and fumed, hobbling over to the window and back again countless times a day to exercise it, his face drawn with pain. It was terrible to be so helpless. He watched Ben doing more than his fair share of the work outside and was aware there were jobs not done because there wasn't time. No one had finished repairing the barn roof so water had come through, and he knew Ma didn't get to market with the produce as often as she used to so money was short.

During the long hours spent alone the frustration building up in him began to poison his thoughts. He no longer felt disposed to forgive Hannah for what she had done. The prank she had played took on new proportions, becoming a cruel, wicked deed which had gone far beyond the rules of all their previous childish games.

30

For a while, after the fever had left him, friends in the village had come visiting. He'd enjoyed the importance and been able to laugh and joke with them, but now the visits were less frequent and he seldom saw anyone. Most of all he envied Ben his success with the village girls, especially now he was not around himself to give him competition, and he longed for an evening at the pub with the prospect of a willing maid at the end of it. His leg was not the only part of him in need of exercise.

Christmas came. One of the turkeys was killed for dinner, and a surfeit of barley wine helped to dull the mind to hardships. Ben brought in the yule log on his shoulder on Christmas Eve. It was coaxed to burn gently on the parlour fire and left to smoulder through the night and all the next day or, it was said, there would be bad luck. By late the following afternoon only ashes were left and the fire was almost out.

'Right,' said Luke. He began unknotting the rope round his splints while Ben was still out in the yard. The girls had just come in from the milking that had to be done even on the holiest days of the year. 'There ain't never been a Christmas Day when the fire didn't last and there ain't going to be one now.'

'What d'you think you're doing, son?' cried Ma.

'One o' these I'll keep as a stick. The other can burn. I ain't being burdened with splints any longer.'

Emily flew to him, grabbing his busy hands. 'You can't, Luke. If yer leg ain't set properly you'll be making fresh trouble for yerself.'

'It's had long enough to mend.'

'Let Ben look at it first,' said Hannah.

'I make my own decisions, miss.' He pushed his younger sister away when she would have come to Emily's assistance. 'You caused me enough trouble and I won't have you meddling. Never again, d'you hear.'

Hannah's face crumpled at his harshness. He'd never spoken to her like it before and she looked stricken, but he wasn't sorry.

'I wish it had happened to me,' she wept. 'I do, Luke.'

'Well it didn't.' In spite of Emily he began to wrestle with the ropes binding the stout wooden splints which had kept his leg rigid for months. 'There's a party of mummers at the Bull's Head tonight and I mean to go.'

'No,' said Ma. 'Don't be a fool.'

31

She, too, tried to stop him but he was too strong to be thwarted and managed to untie the final knot, letting the splints fall to the ground. When they crowded round he raised his voice even louder in exasperation.

'Will you all get out of my way!'

The three women stepped back. While they watched he stood up, holding on to the table beside him, and he put his left foot cautiously to the ground. It felt as if a thousand red-hot needles were thrusting upwards from the sole. He clenched his teeth. Very slowly he increased the weight he was putting on the damaged limb and to his relief it didn't give way, but he found himself leaning sideways. It was impossible to straighten up while he was standing on both feet and to his horror he discovered that he now had one leg shorter than the other.

They stared at him, Ma, Emily and Hannah. Their mouths dropped open but they said nothing.

He straightened up and his left foot was about two inches from the ground.

'Help me,' he croaked. 'What am I going to do?'

Ma was there to support him. He leaned against her, feeling the softness of her breast through the cotton dress which was too thin for winter weather, and he wished he could cry like he'd done as a small boy with a grazed knee.

'It's all right, son. It ain't nothing.' She tried to comfort him, smoothing his hair back from his forehead and murmuring softly.

'Nothing! Nothing? I'll be a cripple for the rest of my life and you say it ain't nothing.'

The holly boughs decked round the room to bring a bit of Christmas cheer seemed to mock him, and he couldn't look at the mistletoe. It had been making him anticipate kissing Sally Radford, though she'd never needed any encouragement. Since leaving his sickbed the memory of the tantalizing mounds exposed at the top of her bodice when she served ale at the Bull's Head had been an incentive to get walking again as quick as possible. He'd been set on winning her. Now she would never look at him.

'You could have died,' Emily reminded him.

'It would've been better if I had.'

Hannah sobbed. 'Don't say that, Luke. That's cruel.'

He sank back in the chair, his Pa's chair that Ma had given over to him since he'd come downstairs, and when his little sister came near he lashed out with a backward sweep of his arm, causing a blow to the stomach which winded her. She cried out in pain.

'Cruel, am I? I'll never let you forget what you've done to me.'

'Ain't I been punished enough, seeing you so ill all these months? I never meant to hurt you and you know it. It was only a game, same as the other times.'

'That were no game. You had it in for me after the ferret's skull scared you. Well, you played the devil once too often and you'll suffer for it.' He knew he was being irrational but the shock of his discovery had brought on a temporary madness. Emily tried to pacify him while Ma transferred the protection of her arms to her younger daughter. He pointed a finger at Hannah. 'If I'm to be a cripple then *her* life ain't going to be no bed of roses either. She'll be made to pay.'

From that day on the change in Luke was enough to break his mother's heart. If Hannah spoke to him he either ignored her or became abusive. It was as if the old Luke had departed and someone completely different had come to take his place.

It was all to do with the woman, Mrs Girling, with her pierced hands and eyes like a hawk. She'd spoken of the Lord, but it wouldn't have surprised Hannah if she was in league with the devil. She had no doubt at all that her brother's soul had been taken that day, and what remained of Luke Jerram was an empty shell. He had no thought for anybody, even Ma, and he wouldn't accept help. When he was strong enough to work again he went about the farm in dour silence, never permitting comment about his lob-sided gait, never shirking a task or making his disability an excuse, but doing everything he had done before and more. He attacked the heavy manual work with a savagery which made him sweat and would take no rest even when it was plain to see he was driving himself too hard.

'Can't you do something, Ben?' Ma would ask. But Ben received the sharp end of Luke's tongue the same as everyone else.

'It's two inches off my leg I've lost, not my health and strength, so don't go telling me what I can or can't do.'

For a while he spent all his evenings at the village pub and he seemed to be happier. He was coming to terms with his disability.

33

Hannah watched the smile returning more often to his lips and was relieved when at last he spoke civilly to her, but the improvement was short-lived. One night he came home roaring drunk and he never went to the Bull's Head again. As soon as the work was done he would saddle his horse and ride off in the direction of Ipswich, telling no one where he was going. Some nights he didn't return until well past midnight. Hannah was always awake, listening for the sound of the horse clopping through the yard when all else was quiet and she knew there were times when he was too drunk to do more than doss down on the straw in the stable beside his hard-ridden animal. Emily was usually awake as well. In the bed they shared they held each other in mute understanding, worrying together about the strange new life their brother was leading, both knowing the futility of interference.

One moonlit night at the end of February, Hannah saw Ben waiting for Luke in the shadows of the stable wall and she crept downstairs to hear what would be said. She tiptoed through the outhouse, cold striking up through her feet from the stone floor, and she hid by the almost empty sacks of vegetables which had to last until there was a new crop to pick.

'Sal Radford keeps asking for you,' she heard Ben say. 'What's the matter with you, bor?'

'Asking for me, is she? Well, maybe it's her guilty conscience.' There was bitterness in Luke's voice which made his sister fear what was to come. 'Made a fool of myself. I asked her to marry me and she laughed in my face. Said she didn't want to be tied to a cripple when there were plenty of better men after her.'

The words were like a dagger to Hannah's heart. It seemed she'd ruined his life in more ways than one since her wickedness had wrecked his chance of marrying the girl he wanted. She could have killed Sal Radford for being so insensitive, but it was only to be expected of a girl like that.

It didn't seem possible that anything else bad could result from that calamitous game she had played, and she thought she had reached the depths of despair, but worse was yet to come.

'I ain't going down to the Bull's Head no more, d'you hear?' Luke went on. 'I ain't going to be laughed at. And I don't want no one's pity, neither.' He got down from his horse and flung the reins to Ben while he limped over to open the stable door. He had started to wear rings in his ears and the gold glinted as he stepped into the moonlight. 'I'm telling you, bor, there's more to life than Seggenham and Sal Radford. You should come with me to Ipswich. P'raps my accident wasn't all bad since it showed me there's easier ways to make a living than bending yer back over a hoe or a plough forever.'

'Easier but not so honest I reckon,' said Ben. 'Tell me more.'

'I've made new friends and they respect me. They've asked for me help and if I give it I needn't be scratching around here for a copper or two. I can make sure Ma won't ever have to worry where the next meal's coming from. Are you with me?'

Luke led the horse into the stable, followed by Ben, and Hannah lost the sound of their voices. What she had heard already was enough to make her feel as if icy water was running through her veins. The discovery that Luke was mixing with bad company now played havoc with her already over-burdened conscience.

'What did you hear?' Emily wanted to know when she got back to bed.

'Seems Sal Radford treated Luke right badly and our brother finds there's more to do in Ipswich,' said Hannah, and wouldn't be drawn further. She didn't want Ma or Emily worried, so the less said the better.

She stayed awake for most of that night. Fear for Luke made her feel sick and she blamed Sal Radford for sending him towards the promise of an easier living. If she had been kinder and caring he would never have gone to Ipswich. She didn't want to know the kind of people he'd met or what they were involving him in, nor would she dare to ask him questions while he was in his present mood. She was just frightened at the change in him, and angry with Ben for doing nothing to discourage it. It made her angry to think he'd shown no surprise that Luke might be heading along a dangerous path, but had sounded instead as if he was interested in treading it with him.

Since the incident in the hen-house Hannah had been careful. She was never alone with Ben and didn't seek his company. Although she knew that what had happened between them that afternoon had no real bearing on Luke's accident, she nevertheless fostered a feeling of guilt which grew as the weeks passed. The two events were linked in her mind – she couldn't separate them. But it didn't stop a strange feeling akin to shock striking her body whenever she

35

looked in Ben's direction and met his grey eyes burning steadily into hers. A few seconds only the contact would last, sending her heartbeats into chaos, then he would turn away quickly.

It was a relief to take refuge in anger, and she allowed the emotion to grow. It was healthier than letting a few feverish glances confuse her. So she was still full of resentment when she saw him making for the low pasture two days later, likely to see how long it would be before it was safe to let the cows out on it.

February had brought heavy rain which made the marshes flood and the cattle had nowhere to graze while the field was under water. It happened almost every year. Marshmen had been along the river banks cutting reeds since the beginning of December, except when there was a hoar frost, but now they had left with their bundles of best thatching reeds and all the farmers along the swollen river waited for the water to subside and leave the marshes a luscious green.

Hannah followed Ben. It was the opportunity she needed to speak to him on his own. There was no fear of losing sight of the giant figure etched against the vast expanse of Suffolk sky and he became part of the great solitude which seeped into her soul whenever she was alone in this part of their land. The flat landscape seemed to have no beginning and no end. Gradually her wrath cooled and she stopped to watch his progress. He was as strong as the wind which blew across the marshes where no hill or house or tree hindered it, and her heart hammered painfully. Ben Rutherford belonged in this beautiful, empty land. He was a part of it in a way that her brother Luke had never been, and a lump came in her throat.

She called him. 'Ben! Wait for me.'

He turned, and though she wasn't near enough to see she knew there was a scowl creasing his forehead.

'What're you doing out here, girl?' She was stepping over the tussocks of grass dotted like hundreds of small islands over the boggy ground. 'It ain't safe.'

A fierce wind was blowing and she held her hair to keep it from lashing across her face. She kept on purposefully until she was almost level with him, the hem of her skirt now heavy with mud. 'I want to know what Luke's up to and I know you won't tell me when he's around.'

'I ain't Luke's keeper.'

36

'But you know who it is he goes to meet in Ipswich.'

'And if I do?'

'I want you to stop him getting in trouble. I heard the pair of you talking when he came home one night.'

'Snooping, were you? Shame on you. Ain't no good ever comes of that.'

She clenched her fingers into her palms, determined to get at the truth. 'I'm frightened for him, Ben. And I'm mad at you for doing nothing to put a stop to whatever tricks he's up to. I want to know why he goes to Ipswich and comes back so late.'

'Then ain't it Luke you should be talking to, not me?'

'You know he won't hardly speak to me since the accident.'

For a few seconds he met her gaze and she thought he was about to trust her, but a flock of lapwings appeared overhead, wheeling and crying their mournful peewit lament as they dipped and tumbled in search of dry pasture on which to run. He lifted his head to watch, then swung away and started off westwards, thrusting a long stick scored with burn marks into the ground to register the depth of the water. His final words were flung into the wind.

'Mind your own business, Hannah, and leave Luke to mind his. He has to rebuild his life and it ain't easy. Now get off back to work.'

'Don't you speak to me like that. Don't you go telling *me* what to do.' She shouted after him, but couldn't follow any further. The tussocks were getting wider spaced and she was hampered by her skirts. 'You could stop Luke making a fool of himself if you wanted to, but you're worse than he is. It's a devil you are. I'll never forgive you if Luke gets hurt any more.'

She stood ankle-deep in mud yelling but he ignored her and she was forced to retrace her steps, shaking with cold and anger. Rain slanted down suddenly from the grey, neverending sky and struck her face with a needle-sharp ferocity which almost blinded her. She stumbled on until she reached the barn and hurried inside for shelter. Before Christmas Ben had covered the hole in the roof with reed mats and sacking to keep out the worst of the weather until the job could be done properly, but it had been too late to salvage all the hay. The best of it he'd transferred to the waggon shed, leaving the barn unused.

Hannah sank down on a heap of straw, her eyes blurred by rain and tears. She could hardly get her breath and for several minutes lay back panting, more worried than when she had set out. There *was* something bad going on. And it was Ben she blamed. Luke always listened to Ben and would surely see sense if he tried to talk him out of whatever stupid business he was contemplating.

It smelt damp in the barn but though the rain was heavy it didn't seem to be coming through the leaky roof where she was lying. She rolled over on to her stomach and looked about, wondering when Ben had managed to make the barn watertight again and why he hadn't said anything. It was then she heard a movement only a few feet away, and she clasped her hands to her chest in alarm. She wasn't alone. She edged backwards, still on her stomach, hoping to reach the door and dash outside without being seen, but before she had wriggled an inch there came a quiet whinnying sound and when she dared to raise her eyes she saw a horse watching her from the other side of the straw bale with equal curiosity.

'Oh, what a fright you gave me,' she said, with relief. The horse shook its head and snorted but didn't move towards her. It couldn't. It was too tightly tethered to an ancient iron ring in the far wall. Hannah got up slowly and went over to it. 'What's the matter, owd girl? And what're you doing here?'

Now that her eyes were accustomed to the poor light she could see its eyes shining and knew it wasn't one of their animals. This one was far too well-bred to be a farm horse, and the only place she'd seen such a one was at Squire Kean's. Her heart began to beat like a hammer against her ribs as suspicion gnawed at her. The barn was far enough away from the house and outbuildings for things to go on that nobody knew about.

She was murmuring soothing words to the horse when a hand clamped over her mouth and she found herself caught in a grip of steel. Her body went rigid with fear and she tried to scream but it was impossible even to draw breath.

'If you tell a living soul you've seen that horse I swear I'll see you in hell.'

She bit the hand which gagged her, fear giving way to fresh anger as she recognised Luke's voice, and he loosened his grip so that she could spin free.

'You fool!' she breathed. 'You stupid, wicked fool. What good do you think horse-thieving's going to do you? You could get deported for it.'

'I ain't reckoning on getting caught.'

'That's one of Squire Kean's mares. You just let it go this minute. Ma would die of shame if she knew.'

'Ma ain't going to know. And if you open yer mouth about it yer life won't be worth living.'

She snatched at the rope and frantically tried to untie it from the iron ring, but Luke was too strong for her. His grip almost broke her wrist. They fought until Hannah begged for mercy and he dragged her away from the snorting animal before it, too, became frenzied.

'I don't know you any more, Luke,' Hannah cried. 'You've changed so much and I'm real scared for you. Why are you doing this?'

'You mean you care what happens to me? After what you did!'

'I love you, you know I do. We all love you.' She was weeping with anguish, and shivering with the cold.

He dropped his hands and she could see by the rise and fall of his prominent Adam's apple that he was trying to control his temper. His shoulders were hunched and he was trembling. So it was partly bravado. Perhaps he was far more frightened than she had been.

'I'm going away, Hannah,' he said, in a gentler tone. 'I want to go to America but I can't get a passage without money.'

'But this ain't the way to get it!'

'I couldn't earn enough money farming if I stayed here the rest of me life. I had to take a chance.'

He clasped her arms and she could feel his unsteadiness. When he looked into her eyes there was an unspoken plea for her to be understanding.

'This is the last one, I promise. I'm taking it to Ipswich tonight, and when I get the money I'll be leaving.' The door was just far enough ajar for a shaft of winter light to penetrate and it touched on his moleskin jacket and the round beaver hat he always wore in cold weather. 'So you see, me life is in your hands, and if you betray me I reckon as how you'll never live peaceful again. Now get out of here and forget you ever came in.'

'No, Luke!'

'Get out, I said.'

He pushed her out into the rain and she ran along the field path to the gate where once last summer she had swung so joyously.

The next morning a small bag containing coins and a five pound note was left on the kitchen table with a note for Ma in Luke's ill-formed writing to say that he wouldn't be back until he could make her proud to call him her son.

Chapter Four

The woman came again to Seggenham before Lilianne's tears had hardly dried. Luke left on the Friday, and early on Sunday evening Mrs Girling was preaching at the roadside to a group of curious onlookers, having been refused permission to use the chapel.

'Which of you wants to die? Not one of you, I'll wager. Yet it's written that whoever wants to save his life will lose it.' She was speaking in strident tones, her voice carrying beyond the circle of open-mouthed villagers who had never seen a woman like her before. Lilianne Jerram heard every word clearly long before she reached the edge of the group. 'There is only one way, brothers and sisters. Only one way out of sin into everlasting light. Jesus said: "I am the way, the truth and the light; no man cometh to the Father but by me." Those be the greatest words ever written, and I'm telling you *I* know. Read your Bibles and you'll know it too.'

The gaunt woman appealed to them in simple but emotive words, her piercing eyes settling first on one and then another in her audience with soul-seeking directness. No one turned from her to go into the chapel. She gesticulated wildly, lifting her arms wide, and the white plume in her battered bonnet inscribed an arc across the leaden sky with every movement of her head. Lilianne was captivated.

'The Lord called me,' Mrs Girling said, climbing on to a grassy bank so that she could be seen. 'He told me to spread the Word and that's what I'm doing. But it ain't no use you standing there gawping at me. If you can hear me, and I don't just mean with your ears, then you'll want to do something about it, so let's sing, brothers and sisters. Let's sing with hearts and souls and voices. Let's all be filled with the Holy Spirit right here, right now.'

The crowd grew, and when an old man with a squeezebox started to play *How Sweet the Name of Jesus Sounds*, there came a murmur of voices in unison which gradually swelled until the cold, wintry afternoon was ringing with joyful song. Mrs Girling closed her eyes

41

and began to sway to the rhythm. Everyone swayed with her. More hymns followed, interspersed with further admonishing, and the fervour increased. The road became blocked with people who left their cottages to witness the extraordinary gathering, and the Minister stood alone on the chapel steps, unable to start a meeting without a congregation.

Lilianne couldn't take her eyes off the woman. The angular, swaying body and the plain face were transfigured, ablaze with an inner radiance which changed her completely, and for the moment at least Lilianne's troubles were cast aside in a great desire to become part of this spiritual revival. She felt uplifted. She moved involuntarily as she sensed an ecstasy which could only be expressed in a stretching of the limbs and gyrations of the body and she lifted her head high, seeking conversion for herself in the rain-laden heavens.

After a while the singing died down and everyone was still. No one moved so much as a muscle and even a blackbird cut short its late call.

'Listen,' breathed Mrs Girling. And in the silence every soul was tuned to hear only sounds of the spirit. 'Listen while I tell you that I've had the Divine Call. Oh, my brothers and sisters, it was as if my body couldn't contain the happiness I felt. I was bursting with it, my heart gushing like a new-dug well and I felt as if I was being carried into God's presence with all the force of windmill sails in a gale. Oh, the glory of it. And God told me it was time for the Messiah to come again. Yes, the Second Coming ain't something way off. It ain't a promise what no one thinks they'll live to see. It's a fact. There was a great light and I couldn't tell where I was or what day or year it was, and the light was so bright I couldn't look. I couldn't look I tell you, because it was God Himself and no mortal ain't ever set eyes on the Lord. But I heard His voice. "Mary Ann," He said, "I sent my beloved Son to earth that all men should be forgiven their sins through the spilling of His precious blood, and I made a promise there would be a Second Coming." He talked words too wonderful to tell you, but you must know this. It was *me* He chose to go on with the work of Jesus. Me, a woman. "This time it shall be a woman, Mary Ann," He said to me, and I promised to obey Him for better, for worse. Then there was pain in my hands and feet and in my side like a branding iron was going deep through my flesh.'

There was a rumbling through the crowd, the first sign of dissent, and a man beside Lilianne voiced his disbelief.

'Garn, you don't know what you're mardling about, woman.'

'Are you sure a farmer hadn't set light to a bush!'

Another said: 'Reckon you'd taken a drop too much.'

A laugh went up and the spell was broken. Mary Ann Girling no longer held them captive. The comments became more ribald, but Lilianne was lost in admiration and awe, and she hated the ridicule now coming from all sides. She wanted to go and stand beside Mrs Girling and protect her from the scorn, beg these idiots who knew no better to see that she was telling the truth. But abuse only made the woman's smile happier if that was possible.

'You can shout all you like,' cried Mrs Girling. 'I ain't afraid of anyone 'cept Him who chose me, and it brings me joy to suffer for His sake, that it do.'

'You're mad,' someone called out.

'It's written the Kingdom of Heaven's like a grain of mustard seed. If I could plant that seed in just one of you here today I'd feel God ain't called me for nothing.'

''Twere nowt but a dream you had,' another scoffed.

'A dream, was it?' The woman raised her arms and held her hands aloft so that all could see the backs of them. Her voice was pitched so that it could be heard above even the loudest dissenter. 'Were these marks made in a dream? If it's more proof you need then I'll show you my feet and my side.'

She paused to let the words be understood, and the marks on her hands which had frightened Hannah gleamed in the twilight, white and sunken as if nails had pierced the translucent skin. The last scornful remark rippled away.

'Hallelujah!' cried Lilianne. And a chorus of voices echoed her.

'I tell you,' said Mrs Girling, 'none of us knows what the Lord has in store for us, but if we give our lives to Him we've nothing to fear.'

Several more hymns followed the revelation, during which the same strange swaying took place and Lilianne became carried away. She danced with her eyes closed, her whole body shaking in response to a strange compulsion which made her hunch her shoulders with exquisite joy and spread her fingers to the limit. Everything was forgotten except the eyes of Mrs Girling when they had rested on her momentarily. When the music stopped she fell to the ground breathless and those who had not joined in stepped over her to move away now the show was over. There would be talk about Lilianne Jerram tomorrow.

It was growing dark. The Minister closed the chapel door and went home, and Mrs Girling sat on the grassy bank which had been her pulpit, her face pale and plain again.

'You saved my son's life,' Lilianne said to her, when only the two of them were left. 'If it hadn't been for you I reckon he would've died of the fever after his leg was broke.'

'I remember. I prayed for him plenty.'

'I thank you for that. But now I've lost him and I don't know what to do. He borrowed money off a friend in Ipswich and left me a note to say he's gone to America. It ain't like him and I'm real afraid.'

'Sit down by me,' the woman invited, patting the ground. The grass was damp but it didn't matter. She turned her mesmeric gaze upon Lilianne and studied her for several seconds. Then: 'You love Christ Jesus, I could tell by the way you looked when you sang. So trust Him. There ain't nothing happens without His knowledge, and likely it's meant for the best. Your son'll do fine for himself in America. Much better than he could do round here, so be thankful instead of selfish.'

Lilianne pondered the words and knew they made sense. Since Friday she had been sunk in depression, unbearable to live with and no use to anyone. Emily had tried her best to give comfort and Hannah had worked doubly hard to keep things going, but her misery at Luke's sudden departure had weighed so heavy she hadn't been able to lift a finger herself. It was true she had been selfish. The girls had been upset too, especially Hannah, but she'd not spared them a thought. She'd hidden herself away upstairs to nurse her broken heart and pray for Luke to change his mind and come back. But that was wrong. She loved him more than her other two children put together, and that being so she should be rejoicing that he had found the means to better himself. After all, in the note he'd said he would come home as soon as he'd made enough money.

'*I aim to make my fortune, Ma,*' he'd written in an almost illegible scrawl. '*Don't worry about me. When I come back you won't have to work no more.*'

It wasn't as though she was never going to see him again. Her heart felt lighter already.

'Reckon you're right,' she said. 'But that don't solve how we're going to keep running the farm. Ben can't do everything with only the girls to help and I can't afford to pay no one.'

'Trust in the Lord, sister,' said Mrs Girling, as though she were a teacher repeating a lesson. 'None of us is expected to carry a heavier burden than we can manage. You'll get help.'

Suddenly the future no longer looked so black. Lilianne's heart went out to her companion and she felt a strong affinity with her, as though bound by an unseen cord.

'You're a good woman,' she said, touching one of her hands. 'I can't thank you enough.'

'It's God you should be thanking.'

'Him too,' said Lilianne.

She walked back to the farm in a daze, her mind full of Mary Ann Girling, and so strong was her influence she almost expected to find a stranger at the gate offering to work for nothing. Instead there was Hannah and Emily, drawn to investigate the louder than usual singing which had carried on the evening air.

When Luke left home he was riding the stolen mare, and there was enough money in the bag tied to his belt for him to have some over after he had paid his passage to America. He was rich. Having accumulated the wealth so easily he ought to have been happy, but he wasn't. There was something inside him which seemed to be eating at his guts and he was never free from pain.

If Hannah hadn't found the mare he might have chanced one more job before quitting, but his accomplices in Ipswich were becoming too daring and the risk of being caught was greater. So he had kept the proceeds from the last illegal sale instead of sharing it out, and together with what he had saved from similar jobs he was going to start a new life. Of course, if Shem Whitfield, Rob Douglas or Roger Perry caught up with him before he boarded ship they would tear him to pieces for his treachery, but he reckoned he could get clean away before their suspicions were aroused. Shem was the most dangerous. He was the one who hadn't wanted Luke to make the last sale alone, and when he didn't turn up with the money as arranged Shem was going to cause trouble. By then though he would be beyond their reach.

It was a rough night with low cloud touching the swaying treetops.

He left the farm and turned into the wind. It stung his face, and the ache in his belly gnawed at him more than ever. He looked back at the darkened building where he had spent his life, fixing the familiar outline in his mind so that it would always be there, and he had never felt so lonely or so bitter. Hatred of his sister was like bile in his mouth. Frustration with his crippled leg built up until he almost screamed aloud.

He couldn't travel alone. He would die. He needed someone to share the burden of his anger and fear, someone who knew him and would be a link with home in the unknown future.

For a brief moment his thoughts flew to Sal Radford and the cosy marriage he had planned. It seemed like years since he had been one of the village youths with nothing to do except work and drink and lark about. He'd forgotten what it was like to be carefree. Pain had changed him. And then there had been Sal's rejection which had hurt so much it might have been a branding iron marking him as useless, no good to anyone. The gall of it had sent him in search of the most demanding work he could find to prove he was not finished as a man, and it was then he had met up with Shem Whitfield, a fellow about his own age who had challenged him to steal horses. Shem had never talked about his background, but it had been plain that he, too, was disillusioned with life and sought the excitement of crime to compensate. The danger had fired Luke with new energy for a while, but the bitterness remained.

He'd thought Sal loved him. Certainly he'd been able to rouse her to feverish heights before the accident and she'd told him he was a better lover than any man she'd known, which made her cruelty worse when it came. He cursed her frequently, but he still wanted her. Picturing her voluptuousness was torment, an agony which fuelled his temper and made him impossible to live with. He'd always known she was wanton, but when she had promised to marry him he'd boasted wildly, putting it down to jealousy when others who'd coveted her warned him Sal was fickle. She liked a good time.

The money at his belt was heavy. He buttoned his coat tighter and turned round so that the wind was behind him, sending him in the direction of the Bull's Head before he had time to consider what he was about to do. He dismounted from the mare and tethered it to a fence before he reached the yard, not wanting to clatter across the cobbles and risk waking the wrong people. There was a cart beneath

Sal's window. Oh, he knew which was hers right enough. Awkwardly he climbed into the cart and hoisted himself up on to a wall which was within reach of the pane. He tapped it and called her name softly, the way he'd done many times in the past.

'Sal o' my heart.' He waited, then repeated the call.

She appeared at the window, and when she saw him she sneered, 'Clear off, Luke Jerram. Ain't I made it plain I never want you in my bed again?'

'I've got money, Sal, lots of it. If you fancy coming with me to America I'll wait five minutes in the shelter of the copse. I've got a fast horse.'

He climbed down again with surprising agility, daring to put weight on his bad leg to get out of the cart. The pain didn't seem quite as bad. Then he led the mare into the shadow of a clump of trees, out of sight of the inn windows, and settled to give Sal the promised time. He knew she could be bought and he despised her for her lack of principles, yet it didn't deter him. When she came she was carrying a canvas bag full of her belongings, and her pert mouth was lifted in a smile.

'Always knew you'd amount to something, Luke,' she said. 'Guess you knew I didn't mean the things I said.'

He was standing straight, one foot on a tree stump so that he was level, and it might have been the old Luke. He snatched her into his arms and claimed that lying mouth with dominating force. Sal Radford appeared to like it. She pressed herself against him, and checked that the money bag was genuine. A few minutes later he lifted her up on to the horse and swung into the saddle behind her, one hand on the reins, the other round her warm waist. The road ahead was dark and long, but he had company for as long as he had money to pay for it.

Hannah knew something good had happened to Ma as soon as she saw her. There was a light in her eyes and a smile on her lips which hadn't been there when she went out, yet if she'd only been to chapel it wasn't likely the Minister had wrought such a transformation. He was a dour man, as solemn as the black clothes he wore and she always thought his wide, flat hat looked weighted down by the troubles he saw heaped upon his head as a result of taking on the sins of his flock.

She didn't have to wait long to find out what had taken place. Ma could hardly contain her excitement and she drew both her daughters into her arms before they reached the house.

'Emily, Hannah, I've seen the woman – Mrs Girling. She was preaching outside the chapel because the Minister refused to let her in, and the words she spoke had us all dancing for joy. Oh, it was wonderful. I wish you'd been there.' She took a deep breath and held the air in her lungs rapturously before breathing out again. 'And, Hannah, I saw the marks on her hands. She showed us them, and they ain't made by age. She's truly an extraordinary woman.'

A chill swept through Hannah and she was filled with a most peculiar dread, like the time when a travelling man had knocked on the door to tell them the end of the world was nigh. It hadn't happened, of course. Now mere mention of Mrs Girling set her heart beating so hard she could hear the pounding in her ears. The woman frightened her beyond all reason.

'You ought to have come away, Ma,' she said, her voice trembling.

'Why? She made me feel safe . . . uplifted. Yes, I reckon I could face anything if she was there to turn to.'

'If she's so marvellous, why wouldn't the Minister let 'er preach in the chapel?' asked Emily.

Ma pondered over this. 'Perhaps he's jealous. He couldn't move a congregation like that no matter how hard he tried.'

'How does *she* do it, then?' Hannah's tone was derisory.

'By her faith. D'you know, God spoke to her. She told us.'

Ma went through everything Mrs Girling had said and the light in her eyes grew brighter with the telling in spite of sceptical interruptions from her daughters.

Later, when her mother was upstairs out of earshot, Emily questioned Hannah. 'What do *you* think? Seems like the woman's bewitched our ma.'

'Bewitched is right,' said Hannah. 'I don't like Mrs Girling. She scares me.'

'Let's hope she doesn't come this way again then,' said Emily.

The fear in Hannah persisted, becoming a gnawing ache. It was silly, of course. If the woman's influence could make Ma so happy she wanted to dance, then surely there could be nothing wrong in it. Maybe things were about to take a turn for the better. Maybe Luke would come back.

The next day two constables arrived at the farm.

It was clear by their uniforms that the policemen had ridden over from Ipswich. They were no country joskins. Hannah was coming out of the hen-house and she saw one of them lean over to open the main gate without dismounting. Her heart began to pound uncomfortably as they rode in.

'D'you mind if I take a look round, miss?' the first asked, after a salute that was almost military.

'What for?' asked Hannah.

'There's been horse-thieving in this area. We're just making some inquiries.'

'We dun't know nothing.'

'I hope not, miss. So you won't mind us looking inside your stables.'

Ben had heard voices and he appeared from the cowshed, his hands covered in blood after helping with the premature birth of a calf. He wore a sacking smock over his shirt and a red and white handkerchief round his neck.

'What's going on?' he wanted to know.

'The constables are looking for a horse-thief,' said Hannah, running over to him. Her eyes were wide as she tried to warn him to be careful.

'We ain't lost no horses,' Ben said.

'No, sir. It's Squire Kean who's lost them. The last one was a valuable mare. We'd just like to have a look round if we may.'

'The stable's right ahead of you.'

One constable dismounted and tethered his own animal to a post. The other remained seated, straight-backed in the saddle while he surveyed the land around like a hound sniffing its quarry. Ben strolled over to the well and washed his hands in the iron trough full of water.

'Ben, what're we going to do?' Hannah breathed, when they were out of earshot.

He took off the smock and wiped his hands on it. 'Act natural,' he said. 'We ain't got nothing to hide.'

He followed the man inside the stables and they were lost to view. She stood in the middle of the yard, nervously watching the one who was still astride his horse, and for the first time since Friday she was glad that Luke had left. He would have lost his temper.

Ben was right, there was nothing on the farm for the constables to find. Luke had taken the mare to Ipswich to sell and he'd had the money in his pocket when he left, so there was no evidence. All the same, Hannah found it hard to act natural. She clenched her hands under her apron and wished the men would hurry up and go, this one in particular.

'Who else lives here?' The question was flung at her as if she were a hired hand. She hated him. He looked down at her from the height of the horse's back, authority giving a mean twist to his lips and a coldness to his eyes that made her shiver.

'Only Ma and my sister Emily. There ain't no one else.' Her mouth felt so dry she could hardly swallow. His voice was loud and she hoped Ma wouldn't hear. If she came out she'd tell him Luke had set off for America and then he'd want to know how he'd come by the money.

'And yer father?'

'He's been dead three years and more.'

'No other men about the place?'

'No, sir.'

He got down off the horse. 'All right, you can go.'

She escaped to the hen-house before he changed his mind and started asking questions she daren't answer. Ben would know what to say. The hens squawked and fluttered as they flew out of her way, shedding feathers which she brushed aside before going to one of the holes in the brickwork. When she peered through she saw the policeman crouching down to study something on the muddy path. She had no idea what he had found but he was so intent it made her even more nervous. After a moment he went along further, still examining the ground, and a smile of satisfaction curved his cruel mouth. Then he stood up and looked towards the old barn.

'Girl!' he called.

Hannah darted back into the dimness, tempted to stay hidden. Her legs were shaking and she dreaded speaking to the man again, but it would look suspicious if she refused. When he repeated the summons she quickly put some eggs in the basket and went to the doorway.

'The barn over there, is it yours?' he asked, pointing across the field with his riding crop.

'Yes, sir,' said Hannah.

He put his foot in the stirrup and swung back into the saddle, then headed the horse towards the barn without another word. His eyes raked the ground as he rode very slowly through the soft mud.

She watched him fearfully, wishing she had wings to fly on ahead and make sure that Luke had left no evidence. It'd only need the wretched man to find a pile of fresh horse dung and he'd be calling them guilty. There was no sign of Ben and the other constable so she had to wait alone in the cold March air, unable to do anything except shift from one foot to the other with anxiety.

The cold made her face hurt. It stole through her thin blouse and she drew her shawl round her more tightly, clasping her body until her arm muscles ached and there was a pain in her chest. When she could bear it no more she ran to the stables in search of Ben, her look of innocence lost in the speed with which she covered the ground. She found him talking to the first constable, his tone indignant.

'We rent this farm from Squire Kean,' Ben was saying. 'The Jerrams have had it nigh on twenty-five years. Ain't that so, Hannah?' He verified it with her as soon as she appeared. 'There ain't no one here who would want to steal horses from the Squire. He's a decent bloke who's always treated us right.'

'Glad to hear you say it.' The man was almost apologetic as he led the way outside again, his leather boots squeaking with every step.

'I hope you find the culprit,' Ben said. 'Our own nags ain't worth much but we'll have to watch 'em if there's a thief about.'

He was able to speak so easily, discussing the crime with the constable as if surprised such wickedness could happen in the village, and the man had actually remounted and faced his horse in the direction of the main gate preparatory to leaving when his companion came galloping back across the field, sending up clods of mud in his wake.

'Arrest that man!' he shouted, pointing at Ben while he was still some distance away. His voice carried like a bull bellowing.

Hannah's heart pounded with renewed fear as the horse came near and was reined so abruptly it reared and snorted. Ma came running out of the house with Emily behind her and the pleasant constable's manner changed immediately. He leaned over and made a grab at Ben's arm, though it was quite unnecessary. Ben shrugged him off as easily as flicking a mosquito.

51

'Are you mad? Don't try blaming me for something I ain't done.'

'What on earth's the matter?' Ma cried, and a frightened cat streaked away across the farmyard like a grey shadow. She had a wooden spoon in her hand and she brandished it like a weapon. Then seeing it was the police she went deathly pale. 'It ain't bad news about Luke, is it?'

'Who's Luke, ma'am?'

'My son. He's left home.'

'Hush, Ma,' warned Hannah.

The constable who had investigated the barn came into their midst. 'You,' he said, prodding Ben with the riding crop. 'We're taking you back with us to Ipswich to answer some questions. Saddle your horse.'

It was Emily who protested first and loudest. 'No!' she shrieked. She had buttermilk down her apron and grease in her hair. 'You can't take Ben away from us. You can't.'

'What's he supposed to have done, anyway?' asked Ma.

'Horse-stealing,' said the accuser. 'It's a serious crime that merits a serious sentence. Reckon those black locks'll be grey by the time he gets back here. If he ever does.'

Emily began to sob hysterically and Ma put an arm round her, but Hannah forced herself to stay calm. She went to Ben's side and clasped his arm with both hands, pressing herself against him to let him know that they shared this ordeal.

'I ain't guilty and I ain't going with you,' Ben said.

'Let him go. He ain't never stolen anything in his life,' said Hannah.

'Then explain why there are hoofprints on your land made by Squire Kean's mare no more than a few days since. The mare had a shoe missing. Prints in the mud are the ones we've been following, and there's been a horse up in that barn recently. Its tracks have been well-covered, but not well enough. There's no doubt the animal was here.'

Protests were useless. In vain Ben declared his innocence. For several minutes there was argument and questions and abuse until Hannah could stand it no more. In desperation she shouted out the truth.

'It's me brother Luke you want. He's the one! Not Ben.'

And at that Ma nearly threw a fit. 'That ain't true neither. Hannah, how can you say such a wicked thing!'

But the two constables exchanged glances of satisfaction. She'd given them the confession they needed as easy as shelling peas and she realised the enormity of her mistake as soon as the words had left her mouth.

'Thank you, miss. That's all we wanted to know,' said the hawk-eyed man who missed nothing. His tone rang with sarcasm. Everyone else was silent. 'However, it takes more than one to commit a crime like this and I'm sure your friend here is just as guilty.'

Her fingers dug deep into Ben's arm until she tore his shirt. The warmth of his body, added to the fearfulness of the situation, brought heat to her own. There was a smell of the earth and the horses about him, familiar and poignant in the tense atmosphere, yet exciting in a most alarming way. The danger heightened her awareness of everything. She heard the word 'Assizes' and they were saying he would be kept in custody until a case was brought against him. Now they were going to lose him too. Likely he was guilty just as they said but indirectly it was all her fault and now she had added betrayal to her list of sins.

'Ben, I'm sorry,' she wailed. 'I only said it to help *you*.'

Since last summer the word sorry seemed to have been continually on her lips. Nothing she did was right.

He pressed her hand tight against his side. 'Don't worry, I can take care of myself,' he said.

The men had difficulty dragging her away from him, and when she kicked and struggled to be free Ben let fly with his fists. He felled one of them at a stroke. The affray which followed had Ma and Emily cowering back against the wall with their hands to their mouths, but Hannah would have joined in if there'd been the slightest chance of getting rid of these trespassers in the name of the law. For several minutes the three men rolled in the mud and Ben's advantage lay in his great strength. He'd taken them by surprise. But with two against one he was never likely to come out the victor and his resistance only made them more sure of his guilt. When he was finally beaten it took both policemen to rope his wrists and he strained against their hold like a captive lion.

Hannah was sent to get his horse. Huge gulping sobs shook her body as they made him get up on it without help, and she wasn't allowed near. She had to stand at a distance and watch his humiliation. Across

53

that divide he looked at her but the expression in those beautiful grey eyes was unfathomable. She had failed him and who knew what he was feeling.

She cried because he didn't have a coat. The cold wind filled his shirt so that it billowed out from his back like a sail and his hat was trampled in the mud. But the constables who had arrived in their smart uniforms were leaving the worse for battle as well, and the departing trio was a sorry sight.

'If there's any justice I'll be back in time to plough the top meadow,' Ben said. 'If there ain't then God help us all.' His back was unbowed, but he bent a little to speak to Ma as he passed. 'You've been good to me, Ma Jerram, and I thank you for that.'

'Bastard!' shouted Ma. 'It's all your fault my Luke went away. He was too ashamed to stay and let you corrupt 'im any more.'

The pigs needed feeding, the cows were clamouring to be milked, and the number of jobs to be done before dusk were too numerous to count, but Ben Rutherford would not be there to do any of them. He rode out through the main gate beside one of the constables, their horses tethered together so that there could be no escape. The other brought up the rear.

'Ben!' cried Hannah, starting to run after him. But it was useless and she returned to her mother's side.

For Luke's sins Ben had been taken away, and he left behind him three broken women, huddled together like grey ghosts.

Word of what had happened at Kean's Farm spread round Seggenham before the next day's sun had chance to rise. The arrival of two constables in the village was remarkable enough, but the sight of Ben Rutherford accompanying them on their journey back to Ipswich, bound like a prisoner, provided a feast of gossip and conjecture. Neighbours came calling that same evening, ostensibly to see if there was anything they could do to help, but it didn't need half an eye to see it was curiosity that had brought them.

Lilianne Jerram, holding court in the kitchen, didn't have a good word to say for Ben Rutherford. Her tears had dried and she resorted to resentment, declaring she had never trusted him, not since the day her husband had given him shelter. She blamed him for every misfortune that had befallen them.

'He were a bad influence on Luke right from the start,' she said.

'Before he came there was never any trouble.'

'I can't remember a time before he came,' said Emily. Her eyes and nose were red from weeping and she wished they would all go away.

Will Baxter was one of the people who had come visiting. He was a shepherd, a large but quiet young man with a round face marred by scars from youthful spots. Through the summer months he went sheep-shearing, travelling from farm to farm, and the shirt he wore had sleeves set low, same as a smock, so that there was plenty of room to move his arms when he was working.

'Come for a walk, Em,' he said. 'The air'll do you good.'

He helped her to put her shawl round and out they went. Like as not he would ask her again to marry him. He did it regularly but Emily always turned him down, and Hannah knew why. She'd seen the hungry eyes her sister surreptitiously turned on Ben, and Will Baxter would never match up to him no matter how hard he tried. But she would never catch Ben. It was a right merry-go-round.

Hannah felt drained of every emotion, empty inside like a husk of wheat with the heart taken out, and she sat in the darkest corner of the kitchen. There was an eerie feel to everything. A desolate silence, as if man and beast waited with held breath for Ben's return. He hardly ever stayed indoors long after his evening meal, finding work to do until it was dark and then disappearing in the direction of the village to indulge in whatever recreation pleased him. There were only two bedrooms in the house so he and Luke had shared a loft above the stable for sleeping, which meant he could return at any hour without observation. Yet his absence tonight was so marked it seemed as if he was gone forever.

She stoked the fire where turf was burning and brought a flame to it, but there wasn't enough heat to melt the ice round her heart. Ma had been busily blacking his name all evening when she should have been grateful that Ben Rutherford cared enough to protect the family who had given him a home all these years. It was wicked and cruel.

Maybe he was truly innocent. Yet he must have known what was going on, and even if he hadn't been an accomplice he'd certainly turned a blind eye. She remembered his interest that night when she'd seen them in the light of the horn lantern and heard Luke ask if he'd be with him. What answer had he given? Perhaps the thought of easy money might have tempted him to carry on the illicit trading Luke had started.

It was all her fault. Luke's fall, his deformity, his changed personality, Sal Radford's cruelty, the horse-stealing, and now Ben's arrest. Every one of those terrible things were attributable to the jape she had played so thoughtlessly. Her guilt made her feel ill.

A draught down the chimney made smoke billow into the room, and the smoke jack turned the empty spit in noisy reminder that from now on meat to hang from it would be increasingly scarce. Ma put a kettle on the trivet and swung it over the fire.

'Idle fingers make for mischief,' she said, pointing to Hannah's clasped hands. 'I haven't forgotten your treachery, you wicked mawther. I've forgiven you many things but I'll not let you get away with trying to spoil your brother's good name.'

'Leave it be, Ma.' Hannah picked up her sewing basket. There were men's socks to darn, but no men to wear them.

'Luke's gone off to make a decent life for himself and when he comes back to this village I want him to be able to keep his head high. He ain't ever been a horse-thief.'

'Where do you think he got enough money to leave home? Open your eyes, Ma.'

'He never brought a stolen horse here.'

'He did. I saw it.'

Her mother slumped down on the seggen mat in front of the range.

'Well right or wrong I'm glad it's Ben and not my son who'll come up before the magistrates. You can bet your sweet life it were his idea in the first place. Seems to me you've more thought for that Rutherford scoundrel than's good for you. His good looks have turned your head.'

Hannah slipped down to the mat and buried her face in her mother's lap, but she didn't get any comfort. Lilianne's hands remained folded together and she didn't even bend towards her daughter.

The next day brought two more visitors, neither of them pleasant. The first was Mr Chambers, the storekeeper. When he arrived Hannah was loading cabbages into the old farm cart that had once been painted red but now showed only a faded pink through the dirt.

'Is your Ma in?' he asked. The weather was more spring-like and the walk out from the village had made him sweat.

'I'll fetch her,' said Hannah.

He pushed her aside. 'I'll go in and find her.'

She had the feeling her mother might need moral support so she followed him, but kept just outside the door. Ma had her hands in the flour bin. She took them out and dusted them off in her apron.

'What can I do for you, Mr Chambers? This is an unexpected call.'

'I've brought me bill, ma'am, and I'd be pleased if you can settle it right away.' He took a paper from his pocket and waved it in front of her. 'Your debts have been mounting up these past weeks and from what I've been hearing this morning you've got troubles that're going to make matters worse, so I thought I'd best look to my own interests. Three pounds fifteen shillings and tenpence I make it you owe me.'

Ma's voice rose in alarm. 'As much as that?'

'I take it you don't have the means to pay.' Hannah could see them through the crack in the door. Mr Chambers puffed out his barrel chest and took off his hat. Perspiration trickled down into his white moustache and he flicked it with the back of his hand. 'Well, Mrs Jerram, there's another way you can settle. You're a very handsome woman . . .'

'If you're about to make an improper suggestion I think you'd better leave straight away,' said Ma, indignantly.

There was a broom beside the range and she picked it up with alacrity. Her cheeks had turned pink and her eyes flashed. The storekeeper took a step backwards, his hands outstretched to keep her at bay.

'How could you think such a thing, dear lady! I was about to offer you marriage. You've always told me you had a fancy for running a shop, and you could give up the hard life you lead here.'

Hannah leaned back against the wall and pressed her fingers to her lips to suppress laughter. The thought of Ma married to Mr Chambers was so funny her sense of humour was restored for the first time in weeks.

A polite but firm refusal followed. 'I'm honoured, Mr Chambers, but I ain't the marrying sort these days. And you're wrong about me not having the money to pay.' She went to the mantelpiece and took down a tin box that Pa had kept his tobacco in, and from it she took a piece of folded paper. When she spread it on the table Hannah saw it was a white five-pound note. 'I ain't penniless, so I'd be obliged if you can take what I owe and give me the change, then that'll be the end of it.'

It was the money Luke had left for her.

The second visitor was Squire Kean. He came riding high on a chestnut stallion just before noon, the reins in one hand, the other hand thrust into the pocket of his grey buckskin trousers which fitted his thighs too snugly. His jacket was the colour of mulberries, his waistcoat finer than any Hannah had seen. From his new bowler hat to his highly polished boots he was gentry. It wasn't often he was seen around the village, his business being mostly conducted in London, so his arrival in the farmyard took both Hannah and Emily by surprise.

'You are the Jerram girls, I presume,' he said.

'Yes, sir,' they answered together, both bobbing a curtsey.

A spaniel capering round the horse's legs started to bark and two mongrels came out of the stable, spoiling for a fight. The horse reared but the Squire had him under control within seconds.

'Get your mother for me.'

Ma didn't need a summons. She emerged from the cowshed with a pail of milk, still looking flushed after the success of her en-counter with Mr Chambers. It had given her the confidence to face Squire Kean proudly.

'If it's the back rent yer after, sir, I've got it handy,' she said, speaking first so as not to be put at a disadvantage.

'I'm not a rent collector,' said the Squire. 'Nor do I want paying with money got from the sale of something which belonged to me.'

'Sir!'

'I've come to give you notice.' The man had a long nose and he looked down it imperiously. 'This land belongs to me and I'll not have it going to ruin. Nor will I let it out to thieves and vagabonds. I owe a favour to an honest man and I've promised him the farm. By rights I should also let him have your cattle in payment for what you owe, but your husband was a good man and for his sake I'll overlook it. I'll give you a week to sell your stock and be gone.'

Shock registered in the faces of the three women staring up at him. None of them had expected anything as terrible as this to happen after yesterday.

It was Hannah who found her tongue first. 'You can't do this, sir. You can't turn us out. This is our home. Where will we go?'

'I can do exactly as I please with my property, miss, and where you will go is not my problem.'

'Please, Squire Kean, give us a little time,' pleaded Ma.

Emily said nothing. She stared with tear-filled eyes at the man on the horse, her pale face almost ethereal, and he put the tip of his riding crop under her chin to tilt her head so that he could see her better.

'You, girl, can have employment at the Manor. There's a place in the kitchen for you, starting the day after tomorrow.' The crop had made a mark on Emily's pale skin. 'Your mother and sister would do well to go to a hiring fair. There's sure to be one soon with the spring coming on. Remember, within a week of this hour I want you off my land. Good-day to you all.'

The spirited horse hardly needed a touch to spur it. The Squire took off at a gallop, leaving the three Jerram women too stunned to take in the hopelessness of their plight. They would no longer have a home. And not long ago they had been a family, but one by one the members of it were being scattered like seeds blown from a dandelion clock.

Hannah took her mother's arm. 'Whether you like it or not, Ma, it's going to be just you and me left,' she said.

Chapter Five

There was so much to do and a week was no time at all to do it in. Lilianne spent one whole night in tears and prayers, and after that she knew not a second must be wasted. The home she had known for nearly twenty-five years had to be packed up, the livestock sold, and she had to find somewhere for herself and Hannah to live. It meant she was busy every hour of the day, not allowing herself any rest, but she didn't get tired and she was not unhappy. In fact she was strangely excited, though she took care that neither of her daughters saw it.

Emily in particular had thought the shock would be too much for her mother. 'I ain't leaving you, Ma,' she declared. 'I ain't going to work up at the Manor and leave you and Hannah with no home. I'm staying with you.'

But Lilianne was adamant. 'You'll go into service, sweet mawther, and be grateful. My mind'll be easier knowing one of us has somewhere to go.'

Every time she trudged through the yard with swill for the pigs she felt relieved that she wouldn't be doing it for much longer. She didn't feel quite the same when she milked the cows because over the years she had found it a mite relaxing to sit on a stool and pull the udders gently to a soothing rhythm. That was when she'd had time to think. It was when she did most of her thinking now, away from the tortured gaze of her girls.

Anticipation. Yes, that was the most uplifting of her feelings. At the age of thirty-nine she would have to make a new start, and instead of being afraid she welcomed the challenge. Squire Kean certainly wouldn't change his mind and let them stay so there was no point spending the last few days in her home moping. The worst thing about having to leave was the memories of Matt stored within the flint-faced walls, but those would be the lightest of burdens to carry with her. And now that Luke had left there was nothing to keep her here. She worried that he might return one day, expecting to find things the same, but in her heart she admitted that he was not likely to show his face in Seggenham again for a very long time.

The morning dawned fair when Emily had to leave to take up her position at the Manor, but though there were tears enough to wash down the kitchen floor they didn't alter anything.

'Be glad,' Lilianne said. 'Jobs in service are hard to come by and you've been offered one without even asking. Just mind what you say "yes" to, if the Squire makes any suggestions. You're a pretty girl and 'e must have taken a fancy to you since he chose you to go and live up there. Don't stand no nonsense and you'll be all right. No one has to give more of their body to their employer than willing hands and feet to do the work they're paid for. Remember that.'

'I don't want to go,' sobbed Emily.

'There's one way you can get out of it,' said Hannah. 'You could wed Will Baxter.' But that suggestion brought forth an even greater howl of objection.

'I don't want to wed Will Baxter. I don't love 'im.'

Emily's few possessions were packed into a carpet bag with a pattern of roses all over it, a present Matt had brought for Lilianne once when he had been called away to attend a family funeral at Lowestoft. He'd also brought her a pretty blue and white china jug which she cherished and intended to keep at all costs.

'Enjoy yourself,' she said to her eldest daughter. 'And don't spend all your wages.'

'But Ma, what're *you* going to do? I can't bear to think of you going to a hiring fair.'

'Don't worry. Hiring fairs ain't for the likes of us. I intend to find work of a different kind. Reckon I've had enough of farming.'

'But you won't go away and leave me here on my own.'

'No, girl. I promise I won't do that.' She put a small bag of coins into Emily's hand. 'That's the rent we owe and a few pence for yourself. Now be on your way, and when you give Squire Kean the money tell him it's from the sale of me cows, even though it ain't yet. I won't have 'im thinking I came by it dishonestly.'

It was terrible to see Emily walking forlornly through the farm gate with the carpet bag almost scraping the ground, her fair head covered by her shawl. She didn't have the courage that Hannah had and it wasn't going to be easy for her to fend for herself, but she wasn't a child and likely it would do her good.

One thing Lilianne knew with absolute certainty. If she hadn't met Mrs Girling and joined in her unorthodox form of worship she would never have been able to face her present situation so philosophically. Something had happened to her at that prayer meeting. Dancing was an activity quite foreign to her, yet she had swayed and moved to the hymns as if the Spirit controlled her, and long after returning home she had heard the woman's words repeating in her head. She had been conscious of a mysterious force and already it was affecting her life. 'Who knows what the Lord has in store for us,' the woman had said. She had declared emphatically that there was nothing to fear if your life was given to Him, and Lilianne kept thinking of that all day long. God had something different in mind for her. He didn't want her to go on toiling in all weathers with nothing to show for it but hardship. He had other plans, and all she had to do was wait and see, for He would show her what they were in due course.

By the fourth day of the seven allowed her Lilianne managed to find a buyer for her cows. The pigs and hens went the following day, and Lilianne's only consolation was being able to count the money accumulating in Matt's tobacco tin. She had never seen so much cash. It was all she and Hannah would have to live on until they could find work, but likely there was enough to rent a cottage so she was determined not to spend a penny more of it than she could help.

She didn't want to get rid of the furniture. She didn't have much that was any good anyway, but during the week several visitors came with the intention of trying to get things for nothing. There were friends, of course, to whom she willingly gave pots and pans and the like, but her marriage bed, the blanket chest, the bacon settle and all the big items of furniture were a different matter. She didn't want to part with them, and when Abraham Moore from the next farm down offered to let her store what she wanted in his barn she accepted gratefully. It was arranged that the man and his son would help her and Hannah to load the waggon the day they moved out and a dry corner would be found for it. The Minister begged her to let a penniless family have any bits she didn't want, and mindful of her new faith in the Lord she hoped it would please Him when she freely gave the last of her possessions.

All of this Hannah watched with an ever-lengthening face. After the hens had gone she continued to haunt the hen-house, sitting for hours at the entrance with her hands on her knees and a piece of straw between her teeth. Lilianne's heart ached for her, but since it was partly her own fault the whole unhappy business had come about she didn't waste her time with sympathy. The girl would have to get used to changes, same as her mother.

When all the money was together there was almost too much for the tobacco tin. The lid kept bobbing up and she had to tie it with a piece of ribbon. She was afraid to leave it around in case gypsies were about, and afraid to lose it if she carried it with her so she hid it in the bottom of her straw work-box.

'It'll be safe there,' she said to Hannah, showing her what she'd done.

On the morning of the sixth day she washed outside at the well, dowsing her face with the ice-cold water until her skin tingled and looked as fresh as a young girl's. Then she brushed her hair neatly and set a black bonnet on it, put on a clean apron and shawl and set off for the village just after noon. Her steps were sure and she held her head high in case anyone she met felt inclined to think she'd been bowed by the trouble that had befallen her.

Doorways stood open as the day was mild for March, and she could see through to cottage gardens beyond where old men tilled vegetable patches and women hung out washing. She glanced in at the grocery store as she passed at a slightly quicker pace and saw Mr Chambers busy with a customer, his white head bent over the scales where he was meticulously weighing sugar. A smile curved her lips at the memory of his extraordinary proposal and she was glad neither of the girls had heard it. She would have been mightily embarrassed.

Her destination was the Bull's Head, as she'd heard a small piece of gossip yesterday which had made her think it might be worth her while to have a word with the landlord, Timothy Berger. Arriving there she stood for a few moments outside, never having entered the establishment before. A clamour of voices jangled inside even though it was the middle of the day when she had thought it would be empty, and the sound of male laughter was daunting. But a malty smell seemed to surround the building like a smoke ring and had a certain friendliness about it which encouraged her to enter. The wooden floor had sawdust scattered over it and a log fire sent out a welcome blaze. High-backed settles against the walls on either side were both occupied and tankards stood on tables made from a barrel cut in half. A few other men who were too old to work in the fields stood around, all familiar, and they made way for her in surprise.

'Ain't never seen you 'ere afore, Mrs Jerram, that I ain't,' one old codger remarked.

'There's a first time for everything,' said Lilianne. 'Is Mr Berger about?'

'Aye. Out back with the blacksmith from Nunscorn. He'll be in straight way if yer wait.'

'I'll go and find him,' she said. It suited her better. She didn't want to discuss her business in front of locals with big ears.

She went down a paved passageway to the yard, her heart beating unevenly. She'd never realised there were so many outbuildings behind the pub and she looked around in surprise at the storehouses and stables which surrounded a cobbled courtyard, not knowing where the landlord might be. Through one window she saw barrels stacked high, and through another there were sacks and sieves and implements of every kind. Then she located voices coming from an open door across the far corner and she approached diffidently.

Timothy Berger was a man of fortyish with a publican's paunch and small black eyes like currants in a fat suet pudding. He was giving instructions to another man who was measuring the iron door hinges which age had worn so thin the nails would no longer keep in.

'Can't risk having the spirit store broken into,' Mr Berger was saying. 'Reckon it's time the door was seen to.' He turned at the sound of Lilianne's footsteps and peered out. Surprise wrinkled his brow. 'Mrs Jerram? And what can I be doing for you?'

'Might I have a word with you, Mr Berger?' she asked. 'It's about you having lost Sal Radford from the bar. I wondered if maybe you could do with someone else to serve.'

'You know of someone, then?'

'Myself, Mr Berger. I'm a good worker and if you'd let me and Hannah have the empty cottage next door I'd cook and clean for you and do any jobs you need doing.'

He scratched his balding head and looked at her keenly, like a farmer at a cattle sale. She didn't like it but she stood straight and suffered the scrutiny.

64

'Reckon it's someone young we're after. A pretty mawther's what my customers like to see,' he said. His scathing tone made her feel a fool for asking. 'I'm afraid you ain't suitable. And I don't need anyone to do the skivvying and cooking. My wife does it.'

The snub was intentional but Lilianne kept her dignity. She'd never liked the man. His attitude merely confirmed the poor opinion she'd always had of him and she had to bite her tongue to stop herself letting him know it.

'Would your decision be anything to do with the fact Squire Kean's seen fit to make me homeless, though I ain't done nothing to deserve it?' she asked, appearing humble. 'If so I beg you to think more kindly. I've been in this village all my married life and there ain't never been a stain on my character.'

'I know that,' Timothy Berger said. 'What I don't know is how you've got the cheek to come to me when your son's gone off with my best barmaid. I thought Sal Radford would've had more sense than to go off with a horse-thief.'

'What!' cried Lilianne. This was different. 'What're you talking about?'

'Dangled money before her eyes he did, and off she went.'

'Oh. Oh, my dear Lord.' She clung to the doorpost, feeling quite faint. She was so surprised she didn't even think to correct his description of Luke. 'I didn't know that was where she'd gone.'

The landlord unbent a little. He put his hands on the rolls of fat beneath which his hips were to be found, but his expression held a hint of cunning.

'If Hannah wants work I reckon I could use her,' he said.

Lilianne took an angry breath. She was no fool. Hannah wouldn't be safe five minutes under his roof. 'No. I thank you all the same. There's only her and me left and we've got to find somewhere to live, so we'll have to look elsewhere. Good-day to you, Mr Berger.'

She gathered up her skirt with stiff fingers and prepared to leave. It was then that the man who had been measuring the hinges stepped out into the light.

'Pray don't go yet, Mrs Jerram,' he said. He had a deep voice which rumbled warmly round the enclosed yard. 'We may be able to help each other.'

She had a good look at him. He was tall, with strong shoulders and biceps. His tanned face was furrowed with lines caused by constant squinting against bright light and his eyes were deep-set. He had a beard which was a tweedy mix of black and grey, and his dark, over-long hair glinted with silver in the March sunshine. She felt a quiver of agitation as his eyes rested on her.

'And how might that be, sir?'

He folded the wooden rule he'd been using and put it in his pocket. 'I'm Jonathan Whitfield and I've got an invalid wife. She ain't been well since the stillbirth of our second child and I need someone to look after her. And there's Clemmy who's just on two. I can't afford to pay a wage, but I've a big enough cottage to take in two more and I'll provide your food. If you think it might tide you over for a while I reckon it would be a satisfactory arrangement for us both.'

'Praise be,' murmured Lilianne. 'I'm sure it sounds like I was sent here today, Mr Whitfield.'

'You'll do it, then?'

'Yes, I will,' she said, without any hesitation.

66

Chapter Six

Hannah felt as if the whole world was collapsing round her. And she couldn't understand her mother at all. Ma had accepted the situation so well after she'd got over the shock. Instead of going to pieces it was as if she thought of it as an adventure. She hadn't shed a tear when Emily left, nor when the horses and cows went either, yet to Hannah parting with the animals was nearly as traumatic as losing the family bit by bit.

The farm was like an empty shell. If a plague had struck it there couldn't have been a greater feeling of desolation. Hannah moped from place to place wishing it was all a nightmare and she could wake up and find everything was back the way it used to be.

There was no word of Ben or Luke. It was more than a week since her brother's departure and she hoped he was safely at some port awaiting passage to the other side of the ocean, but Ben was behind bars and whether he deserved it or not it made her ache to think how desperate he must be for his freedom.

'I ought to go to Ipswich to see him, Ma,' she said, halfway through the week. 'We owe it to 'im to find out what's happening.'

But Ma rejected the suggestion firmly. 'You'll stay right here. We don't owe Ben Rutherford a thing after what 'e did.'

No use to argue. Mentioning Ben was like putting a taper to a fuse. It seemed to be the only subject that could shake her mother's calm acceptance of the situation so Hannah wisely refrained from saying any more. Her worries were locked away in her heart and she had never felt so lonely.

Now, on top of everything, Ma had agreed today that they should leave the village and go to Nunscorn to look after a family neither of them knew. Not a word had she breathed about where she was going when she set out, but the outcome of her visit had brought a sparkle to her eyes.

'It were meant, Hannah,' she said. 'Mr Whitfield was plainly as pleased as me with the arrangement and I know you'll like him. He's right worried about his wife and the little 'un. Seems he lost his first wife in childbirth, and now this one's so weak she can't get out of bed since her second one was born dead. I felt so sorry for him.'

'He wants us in his house when he doesn't know a thing about us?'

'The Lord's looking after us, like Mrs Girling said He would,' Ma declared.

'That woman's turned yer head, Ma, and no mistake.' Hannah couldn't hide her doubts.

They talked about it for hours before going up to bed. It seemed Ma was right taken with this Jonathan Whitfield whom she said looked to be about her own age, and tomorrow, as soon as the furniture was stored, they were to walk the ten miles from Seggenham to Nunscorn so as to start working for him straight away. Hannah had put up plenty of argument, but she had finally accepted that they were lucky to be finding a new home so easily, even though it might only be for a short while.

Alone in her bed at last she shed tears. The blacksmith might well be as agreeable as her mother had said, but Hannah had a funny feeling about him – a suspicion that things had been decided in too much of a hurry. Maybe it was because Ma had taken to him so quickly. It wasn't like her to form opinions about people on first acquaintance, but then she was doing a lot of things lately that she'd never done before, like singing about the house and going off on her own without saying where she was going.

Hannah deliberately turned her mind to more familiar things, else she knew she would never sleep. That afternoon she'd walked for miles by the river, straining her eyes to make out every landmark between herself and the horizon as if she were never going to see them again. She remembered the reeds over on the marshes that were beginning to turn green as they did regularly at this season, and the splashes of gold that had brightened the quagmired land where marsh marigolds were already lifting their heads to the sun. The tarred brick walls of Heytop Mill had been silhouetted against the sky, its sails turning lazily in the breeze. She loved the little drainage mill with its boat-shaped cap and twirling fantail and she'd always looked for it the way she would look for a friend. Picturing its continual activity had a soothing effect on her and at last she slipped into an uneasy slumber.

She was awakened some time later by the sound of something hitting her window. For a moment she lay still, thinking it had only been in her dreams, but after a minute there was no mistaking that a pebble struck one of the leaded panes. She peered down to the yard, at first seeing nothing in the darkness, but there was a reasonable moon which was only temporarily hidden by scudding clouds and a break in them revealed a tall masculine figure standing below in the silvery light. She drew in her breath with sudden excitement. It was Ben.

'Hannah, come quickly. I daren't stay long,' he called to her in a hoarse whisper.

She didn't answer for fear Ma would hear. With no time to put on her clothes, she wrapped her shawl round her, covering the top of her flannel nightgown to give a semblance of decency, carried her boots to put on when she reached the yard, then tiptoed with infinite care down the narrow stairs, hoping that none would squeak. Ben was in the backhouse warming his hands at a small fire which still burned, and the glow from it illuminated his face. She had never been so pleased to see anyone in her life.

'Oh lordy, I'm real glad to see you,' she breathed. 'How did you get away?'

He turned to her, holding out his arms, and without thinking she ran to them. He crushed her against him wordlessly for a few moments. Then: 'I gave them the slip when I was being taken to the Assizes. I made for home because I need your help, but it's the first place they'll come looking for me.'

'We can't talk here. If Ma heard us there'd be real trouble.' She broke free of his embrace. The feel of him so close was as dangerous as a flame to a dry rick.

'The cowshed then.'

They left the house, crossed the yard quickly and reached the byre with scarce a sound. They had to feel their way in the dark to find the ladder leading to the loft since it wasn't safe to light the horn lantern. He held the ancient ladder steady for her to climb and when she reached the top where it was dry she sat down on the hay. There was a strong smell of mildew, and an owl she had disturbed flew out through a gap under the eaves. Moments later Ben joined her.

'Now tell me what you want,' she said.

The spontaneous warmth of their welcoming hug had worn off

and she was nervous. She pulled her nightgown tightly across her legs trapping the overlapping material beneath her thighs in case he was tempted to let his hands wander more intimately. But this was not the same Ben Rutherford who had waylaid her last summer in the hen-house, full of lustful intentions. He was solemn and anxious.

'I need a horse.'

'Why didn't you steal one?' She couldn't help the barb.

'I ain't a horse-thief. You know I ain't.'

'I don't know for sure.' Old resentments came rushing to the surface and she almost forgot to keep her voice low. 'Reckon you were as guilty as Luke. Don't tell me you weren't.'

'That's not what you made out to the constables.'

'I didn't want them to take you away, but that didn't mean I believed you was innocent. You knew that horse was in the barn the day I followed you across the marsh. I saw it, so I'm certain sure you did.'

'Maybe I did. I was so bloody angry with Luke I didn't trust meself near him. I had to walk off my temper.'

Hannah remembered his abruptness when she'd tried to question him about Luke, and the way he'd gone off on his own across the boggy ground, his expression as dark as the rain clouds. 'All right,' she said, grudgingly. 'So you weren't in on the stealing. But it's no good you coming here for a horse. There ain't one.'

'Where are they?'

'Sold. What you and Luke did cost us our home. Squire Kean's turned us out. Emily's gone to work at the Manor, and Ma and me leave tomorrow. Ma's found us a place to live at Nunscorn, keeping house for a blacksmith with a sickly wife.'

Her eyes were getting accustomed to the dark and she could see clearly enough to be aware of Ben's shock. He moved his head from side to side as if to deny it and a groan escaped him.

'That ain't fair. That ain't fair at all. Ma Jerram's a good woman and Squire Kean had no right evicting her.' He leaned closer. 'Is she real upset?'

'Ma's turned different,' she said, wishing she knew how to explain. She told him about Mrs Girling and the way the prayer meeting had affected her mother. 'It's like she's been enjoying herself since then. I'd never've believed it. Reckon it frightens me.

And I ain't too sure about the blacksmith either. I get a queer feeling in me stomach, like he's going to be bad luck.'

'It ain't like you to be afraid.'

'No. Maybe it's just I'm more upset than Ma at leaving the farm, though it's been hard since you and Luke left.' She twisted round on to her knees. Only a foot or so separated them and his warmth was a magnetism that made her sway even nearer. 'I've been worrying about you. Tell me how it's been.'

'What I've been through ain't fit for your ears to hear,' he said. 'Enough to say I ain't never going back to that jail in Ipswich. Never. Reckon I'd rather hang meself first. Nobody's going to keep me locked up for the rest of me life.'

He was alert to every sound for fear of discovery. Ma wouldn't have had any sympathy, but the pain and bitterness in his voice finally convinced Hannah he'd been telling the truth all along. It touched her heart and guilt plagued her once again.

'What can I do to put things right? What can I do, Ben?' She had to make up to him for her lack of faith, whatever the cost, and he mustn't get caught a second time.

'Nothing, seemingly. Except forget I ever came back.'

Suddenly she remembered the tobacco tin in Ma's work-basket. 'There's money you can have.'

'Luke gave that to Ma.'

'No. This is from the things Ma sold. Reckon it's as much yours as ours since you're part of the family.'

'I can't take it.'

'You *must* take it,' she urged. 'You need it more'n we do.'

'But it's all you'll have to live on.'

'Jonathan Whitfield's providing a home for us in exchange for the work we do. Seems fair enough.' She hesitated, reluctant to ask the next question. 'Where will *you* go?'

'Since I'm branded a thief same as Luke I might as well join him and make for America. We'll both get a new start there.'

It was what she'd half-expected and a wave of dread swept through her. America was just a name she kept hearing and she knew nothing about it except that it was a million miles away. It crouched across the sea like some greedy giant with its mouth open ready to gobble up Luke, and now Ben, and she hated the very sound of it. With Luke there'd been no chance to talk him out of

71

his plans, but she had to stop Ben from going. Until now she hadn't thought how she would feel if he never came back at all. It would be like living in a world where the sun never shone.

'Not there. Not to America. I might never see you again.'

'It's the only place I'll rest easy.'

'I don't want you to go,' she cried. 'I won't have a brother no more, and I couldn't bear that.'

'I ain't your brother. It's a while since I had any brotherly feelings for you.'

Tears filled her eyes. 'You hate me for what's happened.'

There was a noise in the eaves. The barn owl returned with a mouse in its beak and flew overhead in search of a place to devour its feast undisturbed. She was sitting back on her heels, but Ben took her hands and raised her up so that they were facing each other.

'I didn't come back here just for a horse,' he said, urgently. 'I came because I couldn't go anywhere without seeing you first.' He smoothed her untidy hair away from her forehead. 'I love you, Hannah. I really do. Reckon I've loved you always. I shouldn't be saying it but I can't leave without you knowing so you don't think all bad of me.'

The surprising, softly-spoken confession stirred her so deeply she couldn't find words to acknowledge it. Love? It wasn't what she had expected from Ben. He wasn't the sort to commit himself to such an emotion, yet here he was declaring it in tones she couldn't doubt for a minute were sincere. Her heart was now beating more powerfully than the owl's wings and she felt shy with him for the first time ever. She responded to the pressure of his hands and drowned in the compelling gaze of his grey eyes.

'Reckon I love you too,' she said.

Funny, she'd never realised it till now, yet she was so instantly sure of it she had no hesitation in telling him. The truth dazzled her.

His mouth met hers slowly and she quivered like an aspen in a breeze. This was Ben whom she'd known since childhood, wrestled with, fought and worked with, but had never thought of loving until now. She had seen his mouth when he was angry, watched his lips when he spoke and admired the curve of them when he laughed, but the only time she had known the feel of them touching her skin had been when he'd kissed the most sensitive part of her neck, just once. Since then she had guiltily imagined how it would be to have him kiss her properly. Exciting, passionate, demanding. It was all these things, and more.

He cupped his hands behind her head and tenderly kissed her eyes before claiming her mouth again with more urgency. The pulse at her temples raced. He was a man of the soil, strong and forthright, but she was equally strong and as eager as he to express this new-found emotion. She put her arms round his neck, pressed her body close to his to prove her willingness, and all gentle pretences vanished.

He pushed the shawl and nightgown from her shoulders and kissed her breasts. She tipped back her head and arched her back as exquisite sensations rippled along her spine. And she could hardly draw breath for excitement when his hands moved down to her hips so that he could mould her to him intimately.

'I don't want to hurt you,' he groaned.

'I love you so much,' she gasped, unafraid.

She suffered the minimum of pain when he took her virginity. Up and up with tender movements. Rising. Soaring. The rafters over-head seemed to disappear and she floated on a different plain where nothing was real except the ecstatic throbbing in her body. No one had told her that love was as wonderful as this. She clung to him, bruising his back with fiercely gripping fingers as his passion was spent. Still locked, he rocked over on to his back and took her weight, cradling her in his arms a moment until both had ease from the overwhelming spasms that had shaken them. Then she slipped into the nest of hay beside him, so happy she wanted to shout aloud.

How magnificent he was. How beautiful his body. What rapture to know he'd possessed her. She touched him with a trembling joy, letting her fingers play over his chest and stomach until he kissed her once more.

'Why didn't you tell me before that you loved me?'

'Would you've wanted to hear?'

'If you'd told me seriously instead of making out I was a trollop asking for trouble.'

'I was afraid.'

'Of me?' She was incredulous.

'Afraid you'd laugh, maybe. Last year you never took anything serious.'

'No. Reckon I didn't.' She leaned up on one elbow and her nipple brushed so lightly against his chest it set up a renewed feverishness. A laugh bubbled up. 'But look at the time we've wasted.'

He teased her some, and they laughed together with muted glee. The light was slowly increasing.

'I must leave,' he said.

'No!'

'I must.' But he kissed every part of her, and then took her again with a passion that was neither gentle nor tender. In anguish they climaxed, clinging together so desperately she finally cried out. Still gasping for breath they lay side by side, gazing at each other with eyes unable to drink their fill.

'Take me with you, Ben,' she begged.

'I can't.'

'We'll be married and go to America together. I'll be a good wife to you. I'll help you, I promise.'

He started pulling on his clothes. 'I'm wanted. It ain't no life for a woman being tied to someone the police are after. No, Hannah. We'll be married when I can provide for you proper.'

'But who knows how long that'll take. That ain't what I want. I want *you*.' She was shedding tears again. 'How can I live without you now?'

'You'll manage fine.'

'You don't want me,' she sobbed. 'You didn't mean it when you said you loved me.'

He tucked his shirt in his trousers, then bent down to her, gripping her shoulders. 'I thought you'd grown up,' he said. 'That's a child-ish argument and it won't work. If I didn't love you I wouldn't care what happened to you, would I? Of course I love you. But I care too much to drag you around in the shadows. I'm real glad you're going with your Ma to this blacksmith. I'll know you're safe.'

She sulked. 'Maybe I won't wait.'

'You will. We belong together. I'll get word to you. I'm making for a place called California where men dig up gold. Two years at most I'll be, then you can join me. You're my woman now and I'll work my fingers to the bone to make a home for you.'

'I'd rather come with you.'

'No, Hannah.'

There was no persuading him so she returned stealthily to the house and delved to the bottom of Ma's work-basket for the tobacco tin. She took out most of the money, tied it in a neckscarf and went back to Ben who was waiting on the darkest side of the cowshed.

'Hurry now,' she said, pushing the bundle into his hands. 'The sooner you're gone the sooner you'll be back.'

She couldn't bear the parting. It felt as if her soul was being uprooted and the pain spread through every vein and every pore of her. One final embrace was all that time allowed.

'I'll pay back the money soon as I can,' he promised.

He didn't leave by the main gate, but set off across the field and past the barn, not once looking back. The sky was tinged with pink but it was not yet light enough to see what direction he took. She stared after him with uncheckable tears scalding her eyes. Ben! She wanted to call him back even now.

He ought to have taken her along. How cruel of him to have awakened her to love and then leave her with only a memory of it. Her tears dried and itched on her cheeks so that she had to rub them hard. Likely he hadn't meant a word of what he'd said and had only used the moment to get what he had always wanted. It wasn't being childish to doubt him. She was old enough to share his life, for good or bad, and she would have put up with any hardships so that they could be together. But he hadn't wanted that.

'You don't really love me,' she cried aloud. It was easier to be cross with him, the only way she could cope with this new heartbreak. She stamped her foot. Then tore her gaze from the distance where he could no longer be seen and covered her eyes. 'But *I* love you.'

She crept indoors and upstairs to hide beneath the blanket on her bed. Ma would soon be stirring. There was scarcely an hour left in which to indulge her secret grief.

Chapter Seven

The day was warm and the road was long. Hannah trudged beside her mother along the lanes from Seggenham to Nunscorn. It was more inland and they followed the River Deben which they knew flowed through the village, each mile seeming further than the last. It wasn't that the distance was exceptional. She was used to walking and wouldn't have thought anything of it if she'd had a happy companion. Ma was far from happy.

'I don't know what I've done to deserve you, Hannah,' she said, after an angry silence that had lasted nearly half an hour. Her heavy tread demonstrated the strength of her anger. 'I'd rather have given the money to gypsies than fill Ben Rutherford's pockets with it. Such wickedness! Such stupidity. I swear I'll never understand you.' All this was nothing compared with her outrage first thing this morning when she had discovered the money was missing.

'Ben needed to have the same start as Luke,' Hannah said. 'Without money he'd have no chance.'

'If I'd seen 'im last night he'd be on his way back to jail by now. That's where he should be.'

'Then that's where Luke should be, an' all. Ben ain't never going back there, not if I can help it. I'd rather be in prison meself.'

'Hah!' Ma's voice rang with contempt.

'Reckon I love him, Ma.'

'Love! I thought you had sense, girl. You've got straw for a brain if you go giving yer heart to the likes of him. Where did you say he was going? America? Well, that's the last we'll ever hear of 'im, mark my words.'

'He's going to find Luke.'

'So he says. Well, I hope he doesn't. Luke don't need him, and neither do you.'

Lilianne sat down on a milestone and took off her boots. Her feet were red and swollen from the effort she'd put into walking and there were still about three miles to go. They'd been taking it in turns to push the handcart containing their few possessions but it looked to Hannah as though her mother could do with riding on it instead. She put an arm round her shoulders.

'Don't let's fight,' she said. 'We've only got each other. And it won't look good if we arrive at Mr Whitfield's in bad humour. We've got work to go to so we don't need the money that much.'

'All we'll get is our keep,' said Ma, rejecting the overture. 'That money was our independence. While we had it we were doing the man a favour. Now we'll be beholden to 'im and that's not the way I wanted it. We shan't be free to leave if we don't like it.'

The first twinge of guilt tugged at Hannah's conscience. She hadn't thought of Ma when she'd given the money to Ben, yet it was all she had left after years of hard work. Hannah had denied her the only chance to improve herself. She felt miserable.

'I didn't think, Ma.'

'That's your trouble, you never do.'

They sat down and unpacked the bread and onions they'd brought for the journey and she hoped that food might sweeten Ma's temper. There was cider to wash it down. If one didn't work maybe the other would.

It was early afternoon when Nunscorn Church could be glimpsed between a cluster of trees springing clear of the hedgerows. It stood gaunt and square on the skyline at the edge of a field where a ploughman was driving two horses and guiding the share. Ben should have been doing the same, ready for the potato planting. The even furrows converged in the distance, pointing to the ruins of a priory which had once housed the nuns who had laid claim to the corn in earlier times, before the Black Death had wiped them out. Half a mile further on the lane curved to the left, and a hedger-and-ditcher had already been busy with a scythe cutting back the tangle of black-thorn so that summer growth wouldn't hinder waggons or carriages.

Hannah brushed against catkins as she pulled the cart towards the hedge to let a pony and trap pass, and pollen fell on her honey-coloured hair like gold dust. The man driving the vehicle wore clerical black and he doffed his hat, stopping when he saw that she and Ma were strangers.

'Are you coming for the funeral?' he asked.

'No,' said Ma. 'We're come to look after the blacksmith's wife and little 'un. Can you tell us where we'll find 'im?'

At once the man got out of the trap, his expression full of concern. 'My dear ladies, you'll not have heard. How fortunate I came this way in time to tell you the sorrowful news before you arrived at Jonathan Whitfield's cottage.' He cleared his throat. 'I'm sorry to have to say Susan Whitfield died yesterday, while her husband was away from home. He came back to find the Lord had taken his wife only an hour after he had left to do business in Seggenham. So sad . . . so *very* sad.'

Hannah and Lilianne looked at each other in dismay. Here was yet another blow, one which left them lost for words, and the shock dissolved Ma's temper.

'Poor man,' she murmured. Tears welled up, but whether in sympathy for a man she scarcely knew or for their own plight it was impossible to tell.

'I'm sorry to be the bearer of bad news,' said the clergyman.

'Perhaps we should go back home, Ma,' said Hannah.

Lilianne stood in the middle of the lane looking lost and forlorn. 'And where might that be? We ain't got a home any more, nor any money either. Seems we'll end up in the workhouse.'

Compassion flowed from the stranger. His face resembled a walnut shell, brown and lined, yet kindness made light of his imperfections. He put a hand on Ma's arm.

'You're distressed, quite understandably. I was on my way to visit one of my flock, but I think your need of me is greater. It might be a help if I come with you.'

'We don't want to be a nuisance . . . '

'Perhaps, ma'am, you'd like to ride.' It took a moment to turn pony and trap in the narrow lane and while he was doing so Ma protested that she was well able to walk, but she finally allowed him to help her into the seat. 'I'm the Reverend William Mitchell, Rector of this parish for the last twenty years. You two are mother and daughter, I can see quite plainly.'

'Me name's Lilianne Jerram, and this is my daughter Hannah,' said Ma.

'I'm pleased you've come. It's been concerning me greatly that the Whitfields had no family to call on in their need. Would you be any relation?'

'None,' said Hannah, who felt as if events were overtaking her and she no longer knew what was happening. They set off again in the direction of Nunscorn with William Mitchell leading the pony and Hannah pushing the handcart in silence while Ma told him how she had come to make the acquaintance of Jonathan Whitfield.

The Rector was a talkative man. He was pleased to tell them in return about the blacksmith's family.

'Jonathan's only been living in the village again since he married Susan. She was a sweet child, left in the care of an elderly aunt from the time she was born. So sad . . . so *very* sad.' He paused to sigh. 'When the aunt died Susan had no one. But at the same time as she was left, Abel Whitfield upped and died as well and bequeathed the smithy to Jonathan, his only son, who came back to run it. He was a lot older than Susan, of course, and a widower with a son, but they took to each other straight away. It was the happiest of marriages until their second child was stillborn.' He shook his head. 'Now she's gone too. So very sad.'

The village was as uninspiring as the one they had just left, but whereas Seggenham straggled out along a two-mile length Nunscorn gathered closely about its green. Geese strutted down to the pond which February-fill-dyke had caused to spread way beyond its normal edges, and as the water level sank in the sun it left weeds and mud for their greedy beaks to investigate. Old men mardled idly against a warm fence. The scent of wallflowers drifted from cottage gardens. And viewed from within the close-knit circle, the church had a more friendly look.

'I hope you are a church-goer, Mrs Jerram?'

'Chapel,' said Lilianne. 'Primitive Methodist.'

He flinched slightly. 'Ah, yes. Well, the Lord chooses many ways to spread the Word.'

'Would you be knowing a Mrs Girling?' Ma asked. 'She preaches.'

Now there was a distinct stiffening of his features, and Hannah wanted to curl up with embarrassment at her mother's indiscretion.

'The woman is a pogramite if ever I heard one,' said the Reverend Mitchell, looking down his nose. 'She came and held forth in our church hall a month since and it grieves me to say she had quite a following. I trust she hasn't turned *your* heads with her ranting.'

'No, she hasn't,' said Hannah, quickly. 'We don't want anything to do with her.'

'I'm glad to hear it. To my mind all that "shaking" is a heathen way to worship.'

79

He continued with his opinion but Hannah's attention was distracted. There was no one else around to notice a small child toddling across the green towards the geese and it started to chase them, quite unafraid when the birds set up a cackling. One spread its wings and stretched its neck in anger. It was bigger than the little girl and started to move towards her menacingly. The others followed.

'Where's that child's mother?' cried Hannah. 'It could be killed.'

She dropped the handles of the cart and went running over the rough grass just as a young woman appeared at a cottage door and screamed, 'Clemmy! Clemmy, come back 'ere. Stop!'

The old mardlers took notice. William Mitchell left Ma to get down from the trap on her own and a man came rushing from a shed in the shadow of a chestnut tree, but Hannah reached the child first. She snatched it into her arms and ran a safe distance from the angry geese before easing up. Her heart was racing.

'Thank God you saw her,' cried the man from the shadows. The little girl gurgled and held her arms out to him immediately. As he seemed to own her Hannah relinquished the child. 'If anything had happened to her . . . '

'Her mother should be more careful,' said Hannah, her eyes flashing as she stared at the young woman who reached the group in a tearful state and could hardly speak coherently.

'I'm sorry. I only left 'er a minute and she was gone.'

'Sheer carelessness,' said the Reverend Mitchell.

The man spoke gratefully to Hannah. 'Clemmy has just lost her mother,' he said. His voice was deep and he had an impressive face, craggy and glowering and black-browed. His black hair and beard were threaded with grey and to the youthful Hannah he was a mite intimidating. 'I shall always be in your debt for what you did.'

She realised who he was just as Ma joined them.

'Mr Whitfield,' said Ma. 'To think we've come at a time like this. I'm more sorry than I can say that you've suffered such a sad loss. Perhaps you'll not be wanting us after all.'

The little girl wriggled and squealed to be free, kicking her feet against her father's stomach. He tried to calm her but she was as slippery as an eel and so full of life it was easy to see how she had given the slip to the neighbour who'd been doing a good turn.

'Mrs Jerram, I'm right glad you've come. Of course we're wanting you.'

Jonathan Whitfield looked from Hannah to Lilianne with relief, then thrust Clemmy into Ma's arms.

Emily hated it at the Manor. All her life she had been free to breathe in the bracing Suffolk air, but here she was confined to a hot kitchen with scarcely a moment to look outside the door. She felt as if she was suffocating, and she wanted nothing so much as to leave. She missed her home and longed for her mother. Her hands were ingrained with soot and dirt from coal she had to handle in order to keep the fires going, and no amount of scrubbing would remove it. Milking cows, cooking and cleaning on the farm had never made her hands sore and ugly like they were now and she could have cried just looking at them.

Her day started at five when she had to be down in the kitchen to clean and light the coal-fired range. If it wasn't blackleaded by five-thirty she earned a scolding from Mrs Cotton, the cook. It took Emily so long to sift the cinders ready for banking up the fire later she found herself having to allow an extra ten minutes each morning if she wanted to avoid Mrs Cotton's wrath. The fire irons had to be polished with emery paper and the hearth whitened. The flues had to be cleaned out once a week, and the first time she did it so much soot came down on her she thought she would be blinded for life. Lighting a fire at home had never been a quarter the bother.

'You're a sight too pernickerty, miss, always looking at your hands,' the cook grumbled. 'What Squire wanted to hire you for beats me. Didn't you do any work on that farm of yours?'

'Yes, Mrs Cotton.'

'I suppose the animals were scrubbed before you touched 'em.' The fat woman laughed unkindly. 'What did you condescend to do?'

'I looked after the cows and made butter and cheese, and I helped Ma with the baking. I'm a good cook.'

'Hmmph, I'll be the judge of that when the times comes.'

Emily was instantly humble, her wide eyes so full of innocent sweetness it would have taken a heart of iron to resist her. 'I'm very sorry, ma'am, I didn't mean to sound forward. I was learning from Ma, but I'd reckon myself very privileged if *you* was to show me how to do things.'

Mrs Cotton held her gaze for a moment, and then she preened slightly. 'Well, all right. Maybe you can start helping me this evening so I can see how well you cope with large numbers. Squire's shooting party makes a lot of work.'

'Oh, thank you, ma'am,' said Emily. She picked up the coal scuttle she'd been taking upstairs to the drawing room, and her lips curved into a sly smile which belied the innocence of her eyes.

She had a very tiny attic room all to herself. For the first time in her life she didn't have to share a bed, and once the door was closed she could lie quietly in the dark and indulge in private thoughts without the interruption of Hannah's chatter. Though too often she was so tired she fell into exhausted sleep the minute her head touched the hard pillow.

She was desperately anxious about Ma and Hannah. There was no news of them and she didn't know where they were going once they left the farm. But more worrying still was the fate of Ben Rutherford. Emily would never forget his courage as he rode out of the yard between the constables with his wrists tied. They wouldn't break his spirit in prison, that was for sure, but thinking of him behind bars was a mental torture which made her head ache and her frustration mount. The few pence Ma had given her were carefully hidden and each night she felt for it in the drawer to kindle a spark of hope. As soon as she was paid she would add to it, and when there was enough she would go to Ipswich to try and see him. Somehow she had to let Ben Rutherford know she would love him till her dying day, and stop him looking and lusting in the wrong direction.

Emily had been at the Manor for two weeks when a wheelwright called to deliver a note from her mother saying that she and Hannah were settling in a village called Nunscorn about ten miles away, where they had found work. The news cheered her as nothing else could have done, until she overheard something quite startling. She was in the pantry one morning washing down the marble shelves ready for a new batch of preserves to be stored. The door was ajar. The bailiff, a dour bachelor called Joseph Nelson, who was courting the widowed Mrs Cotton, had stopped by the kitchen to see her.

'Can't get any sense out of Squire this morning,' he was saying. 'He was hoping Rutherford would be back behind bars by now.'

'Young Rutherford's too clever for him. I don't hold with horse-stealing, but you've got to admire him for skipping jail. I reckon as how he's across the sea by now if he's any sense.'

Emily dropped the scrubbing brush on the marble, and there was silence in the kitchen. When Mrs Cotton and her visiter started talking again it was of mundane things.

She pressed her fingers to her face and her body tensed with excitement. Ben was free. She didn't have to worry about him being held prisoner any longer. The relief brought tears to her eyes and she had to hastily dash them away so that she could carry on scrubbing as if nothing of the conversation had reached her. It was the most wonderful news.

Her relief and joy were heightened by the fact that Hannah was out of his reach.

Jonathan was a man of moods. Susan had often complained that he was so changeable she had to watch him walk up the path to know whether he would be angry or laugh at the mess she had made of the dinner. Well, now she would never look out of the window again, and Jonathan's heart was broken.

It didn't stop him enjoying the meal that Lilianne cooked though, since he hadn't eaten properly in days. The woman had lost no time making herself useful and he could see that she was capable and hard-working. She respected his mourning and didn't prattle. Neither did the daughter. Both settled in within the hour and the cottage lost some of its chill.

Susan was lying in her coffin in the front parlour and he kept going in there to talk to her, but the pale face and closed lids distressed him unbearably. She had been such a sweet creature, a girl meant for loving if only he could have taught her to overcome her aversion to the physical side of marriage, and he yearned for life to return to that slender body. Only two nights ago he had vowed to love her always.

'Promise me, Jon, you'll be faithful to me forever,' she had said, the feeble pressure of her fingers within his strong hands like the fluttering of a butterfly. It hadn't been a selfish request. She had meant that she wanted him to keep her memory evergreen, but he had sworn that he would never take another woman.

After dinner he showed the Jerrams the room under the eaves where they would sleep, helped them to carry up their possessions, and then forgot about them. The funeral was to be tomorrow and he wanted to spend all the time he could with Susan, so he closed the parlour door and sat with her for the last time.

It was unbelievable that a month ago she had appeared to be in the best of health, heavy with child and happily looking forward to its imminent arrival. It was overdue. She'd been nothing like this size with Clemmy, and they joked about the son they would have who would be helping his father in the smithy as soon as he left the cradle.

'He'll be like you, Jon. And I'll not know which of you to love the most,' she teased. Then she frowned and voiced the first hint of worry. 'He's lazy, though. It's two days since I felt him kick. Mebbe if we go for a walk it might stir him.'

It was Sunday afternoon and they set out with Clemmy for a short stroll, but it was the day that a strange woman came to the village and started preaching in the church hall. Reverend Mitchell objected and tried to throw her out, but so many people gathered to join in the hymn-singing he was outnumbered. Within half an hour the overflow was spilling into the lane and both doors had to be propped open.

'You'll be hurt,' Jonathan said, anxiously shielding Susan with his own body when they joined the crowd. 'This is no place for you.'

But she was so excited by the event she wouldn't come away. 'No, wait. I want to hear what she says.'

The tall thin woman was standing on a dais, neatly dressed in black with a lace collar at her neck and a feather in her hat. He could see her face clearly. Such animation. The fire in her eyes fair sparked and she waved her arms in prophetic fashion as she leaned towards her congregation.

'Brothers and sisters, I'm telling you the Holy Spirit could be in every one of you, if you'd just repent of your sins and let God take care of everything,' she cried. 'The Lord Jesus wants you for Himself. You, and you!' A bony finger pointed at one after another in the crowd. 'There must be no half-measures. I beg you, give up everything and follow Him and you'll know the greatest joy in heaven or earth.'

'That's all very well,' Jonathan said to his wife, 'but what would we live on?'

'I don't reckon she means money,' said Susan. 'It's our souls she's after.'

The incitement in the woman's voice carried clearly and a few hecklers who tried to cause trouble were soon cried down.

'Remember Ananias?' she asked, raising her voice. 'Peter'd been preaching about sharing and the people were all of one mind. They sold everything and shared all they had, but Ananias and his wife only gave part of their profits and kept the rest for themselves. It were Satan filled their hearts, and Peter knew it and told them. Reckoned Ananias'd lied to God he did, and Ananias dropped dead. So did his wife.' She paused, and the upturned faces were receptive to every word. 'Let that be a lesson to you. God wants us to give everything for Him, then He'll look after us so we never want for anything.'

'Don't make sense,' said one sceptic.

'It wouldn't do me no good if I sold everything,' said another. 'Where would I live?'

A chorus of argument threatened to turn the crowd into a rabble but the woman had a way with her which no one could ignore and she restored order by just uttering three words loudly.

'God ... is ... love,' she declared. An uneasy quiet followed. 'Don't you see, if you all loved each other like He loves you then you'd want to share all your possessions. None of us needs more than enough clothes to keep us warm, a bed to sleep on and enough food to keep our bodies healthy. And we don't need to be coupling neither.'

'Sounds dull to me,' someone scoffed. 'What d'you know about it, anyhow?'

'I was called. Yes, me, plain Mary Ann Girling.' She smiled for the first time, showing projecting teeth, but as she began to tell of her visions her plain face was alight with a beauty all its own. Everyone listened. 'Christ came to me while I was praying one day and said, "Daughter, I forgive all thy sins. A new age is coming and I've called thee to be my Messenger." I was changed from that day, but I kept what I'd heard and seen to myself. I couldn't believe it. He'd called *me* what couldn't hardly read nor write. Twice more I was told I had to declare the immediate Second Coming of the Lord, and when Christ spoke to me that last time He told me to leave my husband and children and go out declaring the message. I was afraid, I tell you. Wouldn't you be? Then I fell ill and couldn't speak. I couldn't speak, my friends, till I made up me mind I had to obey. The minute I did that my voice came back and I set out to spread the Word.'

'Leaving your family?' a girl asked, incredulously.

'Leaving everyone and everything. I tell you, we've all got to be ready for the return of our Saviour, and that means giving up all our sinful ways and living together as brothers and sisters. Brothers and sisters, I'm saying. If you follow me, I'll teach you the most important thing in life is to praise the Lord and trust in Him.'

She talked at length and not one person in her audience got up to leave. A seat was found for Susan, and Clemmy went to sleep in Jonathan's arms.

'Believe in Him,' said the woman. 'The Lord will provide. He works in mysterious ways and He'll never leave you without hope. Now who'll come and join me?'

There was a shuffling of feet but no one moved forward. She waited, then started singing a hymn, her voice rising to the rafters in exaltation, and one by one the congregation joined in. The woman closed her hypnotic eyes and swayed, trance-like, in time to the music, danced and shook until those near her did the same, and gradually the compulsion to dance took hold of everyone both inside and outside the hall. Jonathan put Clemmy on his shoulders so that she could watch and Susan rocked gently to and fro with her arms clasped across her swollen middle as if cradling the child who, though he hadn't known it, was already dead inside her. There was a peculiar hush when the music stopped, as if everyone breathed the same breath.

Mary Ann Girling opened her eyes and gazed towards heaven, at the same time spreading her arms wide. 'Praise the Lord! There's some amongst you are willing to give up sin, I can tell.' She turned to the man who had been playing a squeezebox, a rough labourer in a broadcloth coat and corduroy trousers. 'Harry here has given up everything for the Lord. Think on it. Soon there'll be others and we'll band together to live as God wants us to live . . . without sin. Brothers and sisters, let's all live pure, celibate lives, then I reckon there'll be no such thing as death for us.'

The controversy she caused set the crowd shouting and such noisy disorder ensued Jonathan insisted on taking Susan away, much to her annoyance. Mrs Girling had captivated her. She'd hung on every word the woman uttered and on the way home she was still singing hymns.

That night Susan delicately broached the subject of celibacy to Jonathan.

'Maybe she's right, Jon. We shouldn't . . . be doing the things that . . . well . . .' She was sitting up in bed in her nightgown, the material stretched tight across her stomach which no longer twitched with the kicking of infant feet. She laced her hands across the tender mound. 'Well . . . the thing that gets me like this.'

Jonathan was angry. He wished they hadn't gone out that afternoon. It was several weeks now since he had touched her and the enforced restraint was telling on him. He was looking forward to the child's arrival as much for his own well-being as for hers, and he was counting the days until they could resume a physical relationship. Now here she was boldly suggesting there should be no more of it.

'The woman's mad,' he said. 'We was sent on this earth to procreate, else there'd be no one. How can she talk such nonsense.'

'We'll have produced two children. Ain't that enough? From now on we should be living for the Lord, like she said.'

'We'll do no such thing. It wouldn't be natural. You'll be a wife to me, just like you've been since we married, and I'll hear no more ridiculous talk.' He tried to get her to lie down but she firmly refused.

'When the baby's born reckon I'll sleep in another bed.'

'You'll continue to share mine or I'll take a whip to you,' he declared, with a passion born of frustration.

He didn't mean it for a minute, but Susan began to cry and at once he was repentant. He'd never spoken to her in such a manner before and was so ashamed he tried to take her in his arms and beg her forgiveness. She shook him off, weeping as if her heart would break, and Clemmy woke up to demand attention.

'You're a beast,' wept Susan. 'I never thought you could be so cruel.'

In vain he apologised. 'Dear mawther, I'm sorry. You know I'd never hurt you. I love you too much.' He tried to stroke her hair but she brushed his hand away. 'It's because I love you I want to prove it to you the only way I know how.'

'If you really love me you'll respect my wishes. I don't want any of that ever again.'

It was the first serious row they'd had and it upset them both. The next morning he operated the forge bellows so hard the fire almost scorched him, and steam rose thick from the water trough in front of the hearth. When he wielded his favourite hammer, the one he'd made from cart springs, the force of the blows ruined the work he'd already done on repairing a plough. He didn't know how he was going to make his wife see reason. Finally he decided that her unacceptable ideas were all due to her condition and hoped he would be able to make her see sense as soon as she'd been confined.

Two days later Susan went into labour, but though her muscles contracted strongly the child resisted all efforts to make it enter the world and for hour after hour she screamed in agony.

'Reckon it's dead,' said the midwife. 'It's too big a baby for a little thing like her to carry.'

Jonathan knew a bit about such things. Eighteen years ago his first wife, Maria, had died giving birth to their son Shem, and he was weighed down with the terrible fear that the same thing was going to happen to Susan. He kept watch by the stairs, listening to the dreadful sound of her suffering, but there was nothing he could do to relieve it. After a day and a night the doctor had to be called and his skilled hands saved Susan's life when he manually removed the dead boy-child from her body while mercifully she was unconscious. It was a trauma Jonathan never wanted to inflict on her again.

She never left her bed after that. Each day he hoped she would regain some strength, and sometimes it seemed she was a little better, but she didn't eat enough to feed a sparrow and he could see her fading before his eyes. His own health suffered too. By day he worked from first light till candles were lit, while kind neighbours saw after Clemmy. All night he sat with her, afraid to sleep in case she slipped away in the dark hours.

The day before yesterday had seemed to be the turning point. For the first time there was a faint colour in her cheeks and she asked for a pillow so that she could sit up. He was overjoyed.

'I'm much better, Jon,' she said. 'Reckon I'll soon be up and looking after you and Clemmy like I should.'

'Plenty of time for that. Just get well and I'll be the happiest man alive.' Neither of them had mentioned the son they'd lost. Susan had been too ill to know that he'd been christened John after himself, then buried in a pathetically small coffin. He took her frail hand. 'I've bin thinking. You were right to agree with what the woman said. I'll not force myself on you ever again. From now on we'll live as brother and sister.'

Her eyes were awash with weak tears. She said, 'I'll have to make up to you for the son we've just lost.'

'We've got Clemmy. And there's Shem. I know we don't see him much, but he's my son and I'll not expect you to provide another.'

He said it to soothe her until she was well again, though the subject of Shem caused more tension between them than anything. When the boy had stayed with them briefly soon after their marriage Susan hadn't taken to him at all and it had pleased her greatly when he had left. Shem Whitfield was an arrogant youth, even his father admitted it. Nevertheless, he was Jonathan's firstborn and would eventually inherit the business and property.

'Reckon I was being selfish though,' said Susan. 'Like you said, it isn't natural for husband and wife not to . . .'

'Let's not think about it.' He held a cup of beef broth to her lips. The Rector's wife had brought it for her, and it was encouraging that she sipped a little and didn't seem quite so tired. 'Reckon I could ride over to Seggenham tomorrow and see about the job Tim Berger wants done. It won't take long and Mrs Mitchell said she'll keep an eye on you.'

'I'll be fine. You're a good man, Jon, and I thank you for being so understanding.' Her eyes sought his. 'Promise you'll always be faithful to me, though.'

He kissed her, and lightly gave the answer she needed. 'I'll never take a woman again. There, is that what you want me to say?'

The words filled her with fresh strength and she sat forward, her expression alight with a kind of exaltation. If he hadn't known her better he might have called it triumph.

'Swear it on the Bible,' she insisted. When he hesitated she was persistent. 'For your own good, Jon. We must love each other the way the Lord loves us, not with our bodies.'

He got the Bible and she made him take the vow with his hand upon it. At that moment he genuinely intended to keep it, for she was a sweet, caring wife who had suffered great trauma, and when he left the room she was lying back against the pillows looking more like her old self again.

Returning from Seggenham yesterday afternoon he'd felt as if the tide had turned, and he'd recalled Mrs Girling's assurances that the Lord would provide. Having renounced sin he had immediately had the good fortune to find someone to help in the house until Susan was strong enough to take over again, proof indeed that what the woman had said was right. Then he'd turned the corner by the green from where he could see his blacksmith's shed, and Mrs Mitchell had been running towards him with the news that Susan had haemorrhaged so badly the life had flowed out of her.

He dreaded the coffin having to be nailed down. She looked so pretty lying there at peace and he feasted his eyes on her like a man doomed. First Maria, and now Susan.

After a while he returned to the kitchen where Mrs Jerram and her daughter were still busy, and Clemmy played on the floor near them, perfectly contented. He studied them surreptitiously. The mother was a fine-looking woman with an open, honest face. She was quite tall, as was the daughter who had shown great initiative in rescuing Clemmy from the geese. Susan's death had shaken his faith, but he was prepared to keep an open mind when he considered that he still needed a housekeeper, someone responsible with whom he could safely leave Clemmy. He had no doubt at all that he could rely on Lilianne Jerram, even though Tim Berger had called her son a horse-thief.

'Would you like to see my wife?' he asked.

The two women followed him into the parlour on tiptoe, as if afraid they might disturb Susan, and their ruddy faces paled a little in sympathy as they gazed down at the waxen figure in the plain elm coffin.

Hannah and Lilianne didn't attend the funeral. Ma felt their presence at the graveside would hardly be appropriate, so they stayed behind to look after Clemmy and to prepare a meal for the mourners who would be returning to the house.

At two o'clock, as the church bell tolled for the service to start, Ma opened the parlour window wide.

'The poor soul's spirit needs to be set free,' she said.

Hannah was relieved the coffin had gone. Last night she'd looked down on the face of Jonathan Whitfield's wife and a faint lingering smile on the delicately shaped mouth had sent a shiver down her spine. If the eyes had been open there'd have been a message in them for sure. It was silly to be so fanciful but she had an uncanny feeling that the dead woman didn't intend to go away and that if all the windows in the cottage were opened her spirit would still stay exactly where it was.

The baby, Clemmy, was a handful. She had no fear of anything and had to be watched all the time. Hannah, who was not used to small children, found more patience was needed than she possessed and she was glad Ma was there to cope. Animals were less trouble by far, but when she held the little squirming body in her arms there was something about its warmth and scent that touched her maternal instinct. A child, if it were her own, would likely be a lovesome thing.

She was not sure about the little girl's father. Jonathan was a handsome man, as Ma had said, but they'd come at a bad time and it wasn't fair to judge him. He seemed friendly enough. And there was the strength of an oak tree about him which would give confidence to any woman he chose to protect.

Very early in the morning the farmer's wife who lived half a mile down the lane brought round some pork and chitterlings, and she showed Hannah where the apples were stored. Lilianne put layers of pork and apple in a deep dish until it was full and cooked a pie big enough for half the village, then she made bread, and while it was rising she picked rhubarb from the garden to stew with elderflowers. A backhouse had been built at the rear of the cottage with a brick chimney and oven on the outside. Inside there was a large fireplace with an open hearth and a hob on either side of it where Hannah was tempted to sit and enjoy the warmth, but washing and cleaning had to be done, and there was Clemmy to keep out of trouble.

The sun was shining. It didn't seem right somehow. Hannah always pictured funerals being held on rainy days, but this one took place amidst primroses and cowslips and celandines, all yellow bright. None of the mourners were family, since the Whitfields had no one, so faces were not so long as they might have been. They filed into the cottage in respectful silence it was true, but once they were settled in the parlour with plates of Ma's cooking and glasses of homemade wine their tongues were loosened. Only Jonathan had no appetite.

Hannah watched the proceedings from the backhouse door once the serving was done. A beam of sunlight touched on her, turning her honeyed hair to gold and her cheeks to apple blossom. Her shoulders were relaxed, her mouth gently smiling, and her tawny-coloured eyes were dreamily seeing beyond her present surroundings to remembered moments with Ben. For several minutes she remained thus, leaning against the door jamb, until she became aware of being watched. When she turned she saw that a young man had entered by the back gate and was observing her through the open window with undisguised admiration.

'We've not met before, more's the pity,' he said. 'Are you a friend of Susan's, and why haven't I seen you till now?'

He had light brown hair bushing out beneath his hat, intense brown eyes set deep and a sensual smile which suggested he had a high opinion of himself. His looks seemed a mite familiar, though she was sure their paths had never crossed. His impertinent manner was irritating.

'If you've been to the funeral why didn't you come in the front door like all the others?' she asked. 'There's food in the parlour.'

He continued to lean on the sill. 'I've come late. But then I've only come for me father's sake. If it was just to say farewell to me charming little step-mother I wouldn't have come at all.' He left the window and entered the backhouse, but didn't take off the soft felt hat of sludge-green which was tilted at a rakish angle. 'Shem Whitfield's the name. And what might yours be?'

There was some likeness to Jonathan which explained why she'd thought she knew him. It sounded as if he'd not cared a great deal for Susan.

'I'm Hannah Jerram,' she said, out of politeness since he was the blacksmith's son. She didn't particularly want to get better acquainted. 'I'm living here for a bit.'

'Under me father's roof?' He raised his eyebrows and his lips twisted cynically. 'He wasted no time finding 'imself another young girl to fill the gap, did he. I must ask him how he does it. Crafty old devil.'

The insinuation was not lost on Hannah and she was furious. He was a brash, impudent upstart, and apart from the slur he implied to her own character she didn't like the disrespectful way he referred to his father. Ma had taken Clemmy out for a walk while the meal was going on. She decided not to enlighten him about her situation, but to be obtuse and make a fool of him later.

'You're misjudging your father, and at a time like this it's disgraceful.'

'Since when has he cared about me?'

'I don't know. We've only just met.' Luckily she was saved the necessity of keeping up the conversation. The woman who had allowed Clemmy to go running after geese came out with a stack of dirty plates. When she saw the newcomer she gave a cry of surprise and thrust the dishes at Hannah.

'Shem, you've come back at last.' She plucked his sleeve as if to test that he was real, then shouted over her shoulder. 'Jon, your son's here. He must've got your message after all.'

A chorus of approving voices rang from the parlour and Jonathan came quickly, his step much lighter than it had been all day. The two men greeted each other with slight restraint, but it was plain to see the older one was pleased.

'I prayed you'd come, Shem,' he said. 'I needed you. It's been a terrible time.'

'You ain't had to face it alone, though,' said his son.

'No. I've got good neighbours. Come and meet them.'

The young fellow had an air about him, a charisma which would appeal to women of all ages. Maybe if he hadn't started off by jumping to wrong conclusions Hannah might have been more impressed. She filled a bowl with hot water from a kettle and started washing the plates.

Presently he returned to the backhouse and leaned against the door jamb which she had used earlier for the same purpose. For a moment he said nothing, but watched her intently with an artful smile.

'Well?' she asked, without turning round. 'Was there something you wanted?'

'There's something you're going to give me ... but not right now.' His voice was as smooth as silk and there was no mistaking his meaning.

Her hands were red from the heat of the water. She was tempted to make an equally red mark across his face with one of them, but she kept her dignity.

'You're wrong,' she said. 'I ain't the kind that gives favours.'

'Expect payment, do you? Well, maybe you're worth it. I'll wait and see.'

'You can go to hell, Shem Whitfield. Now, either get out of me way or give a hand with the dishes.'

The thought of work frightened him off. He strolled back into the parlour, and to hear him being so sociable it was hard to believe the cruel streak that lay beneath the surface.

Soon Jonathan shook friends and neighbours by the hand and thanked them for coming to the funeral. When the last one had gone he returned to the backhouse with his son just as Ma came in with Clemmy. The little girl ran to her father.

'You ain't seen your sister since she was born, son,' Jonathan said. He picked the child up and hugged her. 'Time you came home. We need you.'

'Seems you do right well without me,' said Shem.

'I've been fortunate. Mrs Jerram here took pity on us and she's agreed to look after Clemmy and the house. This is her daughter Hannah.'

'How d'you do,' said Ma.

The brash young man showed no sign of discomfort. The allegations he'd made might never have been voiced as he turned on the charm.

'I'm glad you're here, ma'am. It's relief to my mind knowing Pa ain't having to cope alone.'

'I'll see he doesn't go hungry,' Ma promised.

'How long can you stay, bor?' asked Jonathan. 'Until tomorrow?'

He gave a rueful smile. 'Things ain't going quite so well for me as they were. Reckon I might stay home for a bit and learn to be a blacksmith, if that's all right with you.'

It was as if a cloud lifted from Jonathan's face. His eyes shone suddenly, and he nodded with satisfaction. 'Nothing could please me more, though it's a pity it had to be Susan's death that brought you back.' He put an arm round the boy. 'Welcome home, my son.'

'Thank you, Pa.'

Shem Whitfield shrugged off the sign of parental affection with a flick of his shoulder. He gave Hannah an insolent smile.

Chapter Eight

Luck was with Ben Rutherford when he left Seggenham. He didn't chance walking along the turnpike in daylight but kept to the fields for the first hour, heading south until he felt he'd gone far enough to risk stopping at a store for food. The money in his pocket meant he could afford a decent breakfast, but he was loath to spend more than a copper since he would be needing it all for more important things. Neither did he want to draw attention to himself by appearing to be too wealthy. He tied some bread and cheese in the scarf from his neck and walked on, crossed the river at Woodbridge and kept well clear of the Ipswich road. When he had put about fifteen miles between himself and Seggenham he came to a deserted barn, and being early afternoon he decided to sleep at least until darkness fell.

He slept deeply from exhaustion, it being more than thirty-six hours since he had escaped from his captors, and when he finally stirred the shadows were already lengthening. A noise disturbed him and through half-closed eyes he saw that he was no longer alone. He remained motionless until he saw that he was sharing his resting place with a pedlar who had flung down his canvas-covered pack and himself with it, as if another step would have been the end of him. The man was old. White hair stuck out in wisps beneath the brim of his hat and a beard spread over the front of his jacket like a white cover as he lay back with his eyes closed.

Ben thought it prudent to move before he was discovered, but the man had acute hearing.

'Where be you going?' he asked, without lifting his lids. The voice was firm and it halted Ben before he reached the door.

'Time I was on the road again.'

'What's the hurry? Thought you was going to be a bit of company.'

'I'm meeting up with my brother. We're going to America.'

'From here? At this time of night?' There was a snort and the old man sat up. 'Tall story that one, bor.'

'It's true.'

'And where do you reckon to go from? Ain't no ships heading for America from this side of the country. Lest it's from London.'

'That's right. I'm heading for London.'

'Are you on the run from the law?'

Ben sighed. The pedlar, a regular cheapjack, was wiser than he appeared and it was no use thinking he could fool him. 'Reckon I am. But it ain't for nothing too serious. Leastways, I ain't never hurt anyone. Me brother stole a horse but I was the one who got caught while he made off.'

'Don't have to tell me about it, bor. I ain't too partial to the law neither.' He took a bottle from his pack and swigged the contents. 'For me chest,' he said. 'Tell you what, I've got a horse and cart outside and I'm heading for London myself. If you don't mind it taking the best part of a week we can travel together. That way you'll not be thought suspicious. Then I can take you to my son in Billingsgate. Likely he'll know a ship you can board. Have you got any money?'

'Thought I'd work my passage,' said Ben. No sense in letting on that he wasn't penniless.

'That's sensible. Get to America first, then look for your brother. Reckon it'll be easier.' After a short rest he went to feed the horse and returned with cold lamb pie which he shared generously, though he was quick to point out that further meals would have to be earned. 'You'll have to work, mind, if you come with me.'

'I ain't afraid of hard work,' said Ben.

The cheapjack's name was Amos Hanberry and he began relating the story of his life, which saved Ben having to talk about his own. He droned on the way lonely people do when they have an unexpected audience and only an occasional yes or no was needed in reply. Ben could think of Hannah. He loved her, no doubt of it, but he ought not to have taken her. His physical need had overruled all else and he had given no thought to possible consequences. Pray God he hadn't made her pregnant with his child, not while he couldn't support her. Every step he'd taken away from her today had seemed like a mile, and the idea of going to America became far less inviting. Now Amos's scorn put large doubts in his mind and he wondered if maybe it might be better to find work in London instead, until the hunt for him had died down.

In the morning the skinny nag was hitched to the cart and they set off at a pace which tried Ben's patience. He could have covered more ground on foot. They stopped at the first village of any size, a place called Stratford St Mary, and Amos spread out his wares at the roadside. Ben put up a painted backcloth of an Eastern scene depicting a snakecharmer and a dancing girl, against which he had to stack bright coloured vases, crockery and tinware.

'Come and buy!' yelled Ben, his young voice carrying with a confidence that made women emerge from their cottages like mice from holes. In no time quite a crowd gathered. 'Who can resist this?' he asked, holding up a slender vase of pink pottery. 'Meant for roses, though I declare there ain't a rose as can match one of you lovely ladies.'

He sold three of them. Cups and saucers went to a large farmer's wife, two tin saucepans to a waif of a woman who didn't look strong enough to carry them, and basins to a sour-faced spinster after Ben had charmed her. It was easy and he enjoyed himself immensely. At the next hamlet the performance was repeated, and by evening Amos's glum countenance had been replaced by a wide smile.

'Ain't never done so well, bor,' he said. They sat down to ham and pickled eggs, a crusty loaf and a jug of ale before stopping for the night at the next barn on his route. 'I'd made up me mind I was too old to peddle any more and I was going to me son's, but now we've met up I reckon I've changed me mind. I ain't enjoyed meself so much in years as I've done today. What d'you say to a partnership?'

'I'm used to working on the land,' said Ben. 'This ain't for me, though I thank you for the offer.'

Amos wouldn't let up. He tried all ways to change Ben's mind but failed. However his companion was no longer so impatient. The next day they skirted Colchester and crossed the River Colne, travelling vaguely in the direction of London, and whenever they stopped Ben was quite a showman, attracting more people at every village. Amos joined in with enthusiasm until he seemed to shed ten years. The Eastern backcloth became a stage set and Ben flirted with the life-sized painting of the dancing girl as if she were real, while Amos pretended a snake was about to appear from the snake-charmer's basket. Laughter rang out across village greens. The tomfoolery sold wares. After each performance the women would buy anything just to catch Ben Rutherford's smile and attract his grey-eyed gaze.

'We're making money, bor. Real money,' Amos said, at the close of another day. He tried a little more persuasion. 'Reckon we could get rich. And I'm danged if I don't like you better than I like Titus, my son. You'll make a success of whatever you do.'

But Ben was adamant. 'I'm sorry, my friend. I'm enjoying myself hugely. Can't say otherwise. But I've got to move on.'

'Maybe you're wise.' The old man said it grudgingly. 'You're too clever to be a cheapjack all your life.'

They reached the outskirts of London five days later, having travelled a circuitous route to sell off all that was left of the stock. The roads became busier, the horse less willing, and Ben wanted to strike out on his own, but he felt duty-bound to see Amos Hanberry safe at his son's house in Billingsgate.

'Titus were a joskin once,' Amos told him. 'Went to sea after the harvest when there was no work on the land, but one morning he went to London on the fish train and there he stayed. Said the city was more to his liking. He's a fish merchant and was doing right well the last I heard.'

'And when was that?'

'A good few years ago. We ain't needed to keep in touch.'

The change from country ways to city ones stimulated Ben. He'd thought London would be like Ipswich only bigger, but it was like no other place he had ever been and his excitement mounted. There was smoke and dirt, strange and often unpleasant smells the nearer they got to the river, and so many people he felt dizzy until he got used to it.

He was certain of only one thing. Looking for Luke would be the biggest waste of time. He'd never find him here.

That evening they reached the Thames downriver from the city proper and were told they could be in Billingsgate within a couple of hours. It was almost dark, starting to rain, and Amos was tired.

'Reckon I'd rather we put up somewhere for the night,' he said. 'T'ain't as though we ain't got the money.'

Ben was surprised. 'We're nearly there. Wouldn't you rather press on and get to your son's?'

'Tomorrow, bor. Tomorrow'll do. A day won't make no difference.'

Amos had become quieter, as if he had things on his mind. It wasn't in Ben's nature to be inquisitive so he didn't ask too much, but it was plain the old man was putting off meeting his only kin for as long as he could. The kindest thing was to play along, so at the next hostelry they stabled the horse and went inside.

They were served ale by a wench in the most revealing bodice Ben had ever seen. She edged between the tables to the accompaniment of ribald remarks and fingers pinched her where she was plumpest. It was tempting to order more ale just to see the movement of her breasts when she bent forward to serve it and they consumed more than they had intended.

'Where've you been all me life, ducks?' she asked Ben, drawing his head against the tantalizing mounds. 'If you was to ask me I daresay I'd be kind to you any night of the week.'

'Reckon I couldn't afford you,' he said, but turned his head to make the most of his opportunity. She squealed and darted off with a laugh.

'I could afford 'er,' boasted Amos, loudly. He was soon back in high spirits and drew the girl down to speak in her ear. 'Me and Ben made money on the way 'ere. Lots of it.' He wouldn't be silenced, though Ben tried.

They were given a garret overlooking the yard, so narrow there was only just space for two mattresses on the floor. Barns they'd slept in all week for free had been palaces to this. Nevertheless Amos was snoring within minutes, but Ben was afraid to close his eyes. He felt trapped, and hated it. He stared down into the dark yard, planning a means of escape if it was needed. There was going to be trouble before the night was out, he would have almost betted his own carefully hidden money on it.

Sure enough no more than an hour had passed when the door opened a fraction and a thin, wiry figure crept in, making straight for the old cheapjack who had gone to sleep clasping his money bag. He carried a knife. Ben waited, motionless, until the intruder bent over to snatch the bag, then jumped on him. The two fought in the dark, but the wily wretch was as nimble as a monkey and in the confined space Ben's size was a disadvantage. It was Amos who picked up the knife when it was dropped in the tussle and he thrust it in the youth's arm, but the wound didn't prevent him from disappearing down the garret stairs with the money in his possession.

'Quick, Amos! The window!'

'We won't catch the bastard.'

'Of course we won't, but he's dripping blood. We don't want no one following the trail up here and arresting us.'

Ben grabbed the old man and made him climb out of the tiny aperture. Pushing him when he protested since there was no time to lose. It was even more difficult to squeeze his own large body through, but necessity made it possible, and seconds later they were clambering over a roof and down a drainpipe.

'The cart!' gasped Amos.

'We'll have to leave it. We can't get the horse.'

'But I can't walk. I'm too old.'

'You'll have to. You're still alive so be thankful.'

Ben made him hurry. They weren't the only ones around, but in the dark hours the streets were peopled with tramps and footpads and he had no wish to be set upon again. The art of self-preservation was something he'd learnt quickly in the city and his wits were rapidly becoming keener.

They came to Billingsgate very early in the morning, before it was properly light. Ships galore congested the river, some emerging through the gloom with sails set, others flat and ungainly and coal-blackened. Brigantines, schooners, lighters and a few steamships heaved on the grey-brown water. The voices of watermen carried on the clear air. It was here that Ben had his first glimpse of the Tower of London, and though it was still so early he saw the market carts from Kent that had started their daily trundle across the dark, deep river.

Billingsgate had nothing to recommend it. The tide was low and two narrow gangways descended to the foreshore, along which white-coated figures in four lines hurried to and fro unloading fish from small boats that had crept upriver overnight with the catch from fishing smacks. Ben and Amos watched them fill their baskets, four large cod to one, six small ones to another, and even smaller sizes packed in dozens. The porters carried them up to the fish-market entrance where they stood in a line like runners waiting for the start of a race. And indeed that was what it was, for the instant the clock on the campanile struck five, each man rushed at top speed to whichever salesman he was consigned, the rules being that none should have an unfair start.

Every street round the fish market was now jammed with carts and vans. Ben helped his companion along and they entered the market with its fine arcades of brick and stone to look for his son. The ground was slippery with fish scales, porters with baskets on their heads pushed and swore as they kept up an incessant run between boats and buyers, and fish heaped on stalls gasped in their last agony. Soles, plaice, turbot. Each salesman sat with his back to another with a wooden board between them so that they were enclosed in a recess to protect them from pick-pockets. The sales were by Dutch auction, prices coming down until a bargain was closed. Ben was fascinated. He watched buyers shifting rapidly from one salesman to another demanding prices, and he was amazed at the speed with which transactions were concluded. In Seggenham it took all day to haggle over the price of a cow.

'I ain't never going to find Titus in this mob,' said Amos.

They asked several stall-holders but no one knew a Titus Hanberry and everyone was too busy to care.

'Are you sure this is where he'd be?'

'Sure as I can be after fifteen years.'

'Fifteen years!' cried Ben. 'You didn't tell me it was that long. He might be dead for all you know.'

'Reckon it were a mistake coming. I had a feeling last night. Now we've no money and no place to go.' The old man's voice quivered and his expression was dejected. 'You won't leave me though, will you, bor?'

Amos found a spare basket upturned in a corner and sat on it. It was gone six o'clock now and the initial rush was over, but people of a different class were coming into the market. Hawkers, house servants and merchants appeared and Ben hoped Titus Hanberry was one of the latter, but there was no one Amos recognised.

A large vessel was coming slowly down the main channel, heading towards the sea. Ben stared after it wistfully, then looked at the cheapjack who had befriended him. He fingered the roll of money at his waist.

'No, Amos, I won't leave you,' he promised. 'I'll see after you.'

America would have to wait.

Chapter Nine

'Let me help you with that, Mrs Jerram,' said Shem Whitfield, taking the basket of wet washing she'd brought out from the back-house to hang on the line.

Lilianne was used to carrying heavy loads. She was *not* used to anyone offering to help her with them and the novelty brought a flush of pleasure to her cheeks.

'That's real kind of you, Shem.'

'Glad to do it,' he said. He put the basket on a stone near the line so that she wouldn't have to bend so far, fetched the prop from across the garden, and went on his way.

He was the nicest young man she had ever met. He charmed her with his thoughtfulness and she was pleased he had decided to stay after the funeral. It wasn't entirely for his father's sake, of course. It was plain he had his eye on Hannah and intended to remain until she smiled on him favourably, though that was likely to be a long time since her daughter did nothing to encourage him. Hannah was still hankering after Ben Rutherford, but time would soon dampen her ardour. Then the girl would see that good fortune awaited her in the form of a young admirer who was so much more suitable.

'Shem Whitfield pesters me, Ma,' Hannah complained, when they had been there a week. 'I wish he'd leave me alone.'

'He's a very well-mannered boy,' said Lilianne. 'It's time you spoke nicely to him instead of dodging out of his way.'

'You may be impressed by him, I'm not,' she said. 'He's as sly as they come under all that charm. Open yer eyes, Ma.'

'Open yours, girl,' Lilianne retorted. 'Shem likes you a lot and maybe he'll soon be wanting a wife. You could do far worse.'

In spite of Hannah being difficult, Lilianne was enjoying herself. She liked keeping house again for a man her own age. She liked Jonathan Whitfield. He had a fierce look about him but he was not unlike Matt in many ways. He was appreciative of the way she ran his home and looked after his child, and she made allowances when

102

he fell into a moody silence every now and again. She understood. He was mourning his wife and had every right to shut out the strangers in his life until he had come to terms with his grief.

She missed Emily very much. A week after the funeral she had met a wheelwright in the village with work to do for Squire Kean, and had asked him to take a message to Emily to let her know where they were. On his return the next day he came to the cottage to see Lilianne.

'Your daughter sends her love, ma'am,' the wheelwright told her. 'She said to tell you she's settled in, but you're not to forget her.'

Lilianne sighed. 'How could I forget the sweet child? She's never caused me a minute's trouble in her life.'

'Not like me,' said Hannah, when the man had gone.

'No, not like you.'

'Then maybe I should get out of your way, Ma.'

'That's exactly what you will be doing,' her mother said. She'd been putting off telling her and she looked at the ground. 'There ain't enough work for both of us here and Mr Whitfield can't provide for you as well as me, so I asked him to look for a job for you. He's spoken to a farmer across at Five Elms and you're to start there on Monday as a dairymaid.'

Hannah showed her astonishment. 'Without you even having talked to me about it!' She was angry. 'That ain't fair, Ma. I ain't a child and I don't like arrangements being made for me without any asking. Reckon if it were Emily here with you instead of me you wouldn't have been so quick to push her out.'

Lilianne didn't answer. She couldn't when it was the truth. She had been guilty of wishing that Squire Kean had chosen Hannah to go and work in his kitchen instead of Emily. In all fairness the arrangement would probably have suited Hannah better too.

That same evening when they were all at table Hannah aired her displeasure publicly the minute Grace was said.

'So you've found me work at Five Elms, Mr Whitfield. I'd have been grateful if you'd consulted me first.'

'I'd left it to yer mother,' said Jonathan. 'I happened to know Elijah Springly needed a girl in the dairy and I thought you'd be glad to earn money.'

'You've no right arranging my life,' said Hannah.

Lilianne was ashamed of her. 'You just apologise for being so rude, my girl. And be grateful to Mr Whitfield. It ain't your place to speak your mind like that.'

Shem leaned back in his chair and laughed. 'All families are alike. Reckon it's the same with the Jerrams as it's bin between you and me, Pa.'

'Mebbe so,' Jonathan said.

It was a relief when Monday came and Hannah set off to start her job. A satisfied smile played on Lilianne's lips as she watched the girl walk proudly down the lane towards the hamlet of Five Elms. She was now the sole occupant of the blacksmith's cottage until evening, except for the child, and she felt as if she had found a new, permanent home. She was intent on making herself indispensable to Jonathan Whitfield.

As the days passed a work pattern was established. Lilianne got up before five each morning to see Hannah off, and to get the fire going in the backhouse so that she could cook the men a good breakfast. Jonathan allowed her to get whatever food they needed in the general store and each Friday he paid the bill. She frowned at the state of the cupboards. At Kean's Farm the shelves might not have been so well-stocked, but they had been spotlessly clean. It seemed Susan Whitfield had cared more about her parlour which was cluttered with useless knick-knacks, and her garden with little box borders and roses coming into bud, than cleanliness. Lilianne soon set to work with a scrubbing brush in the pantry, and kept the parlour door closed so that she wouldn't have to be reminded all the time of Jonathan's wife.

At first he didn't stay indoors after the evening meal. He would kiss his child goodnight and then go out, and Lilianne worried that he didn't feel at home with her around. She was pleased when he began to linger a while longer. She liked seeing him at rest of an evening in the wooden rocking chair, and the smell of tobacco when he smoked his clay pipe was better than perfume.

'You're good with Clemmy,' he said, on one such evening.

The fire was drawing well and Lilianne was sitting at the table with some mending to get the best light from the lamp. A warm glow sent shadows dancing round the walls and there was a companionable atmosphere like she'd known with Matt.

'I've become right fond of her.' The child had been badly missing her mother, but now she turned naturally to Lilianne for the affection she needed. She clung to her and would hardly let her out of her sight. 'It's a while since I looked after a little one and I'm enjoying it.'

'And I'm grateful. Reckon it was meant we should meet that day, Mrs Jerram. The preacher woman was right. If you repent the Lord looks after you.'

'The preacher woman?' Lilianne looked up eagerly from her sewing. 'Do you mean Mrs Girling?'

'Heard tell that's her name.'

'You've listened to her, then? Oh, glory, I'm so glad. Ain't she wonderful?'

'My wife thought so,' said Jonathan. He drew on his pipe and stared into the fire. 'Susan was right taken with Mrs Girling, same as you. Mebbe if she'd lived she would've been converted.'

'And you, Mr Whitfield? What did you think of the woman?'

'What I think ain't neither here nor there.'

To her disappointment he stood up and left. She'd already discovered that he wouldn't talk about anything which might lead to a probing into his past. All conversation was at surface level and he seemed to put a barrier between them.

If he could have known her thoughts when they sat together in the firelight he would have been very surprised and likely he would have taken fright, or thrown her out. She wanted to smooth away the furrows on his forehead which deepened when he shut his eyes, as if the pictures behind his closed lids were too painful to watch, and she would have eased the tension in his thick neck where cords tightened. Sometimes he rounded his shoulders, maybe to relieve an ache in them which she could have eased away with sympathetic fingers. Matt had always liked her to loosen the taut muscles at the back of his neck after a long day in the fields.

What a way to be thinking at her age. Lilianne felt as if she were a young girl again, full of eager anticipation and waiting to see if the object of her sexual fantasies was likely to respond in reality. It was disgraceful, especially when he had only just buried his wife. Yet she couldn't help it. From the moment of setting eyes on the blacksmith she had been attracted to him. She guarded the secret carefully for fear of making a fool of herself.

The forge was in the centre of the village, edging on the road which wound past the green and the pond. A bit further on the road divided. One fork had a pitted milestone at the corner and it was just possible to read that it was ninety-two miles to London in that direction; the other led to Debenham via Five Elms. At the turn of the century a row of cottages had been built along the north side of the Debenham road to house nine families and they were now so overcrowded children spilt out on the front cobblestones at all hours. The least savoury of the two inns in Nunscorn, the Plough and Plover, was situated right opposite and it never wanted for trade. And with the coming of the cottages there had been need for a general store, so that had opened close by.

Clemmy loved to be taken to the shop. Sometimes the shopkeeper would give her a sweet from one of the bulbous jars, or a prune from a saucer on the shelf, saying it would be good for her 'innards'. The child had a mop of reddish-gold curls and elfin features resembling the prettiness of Susan Whitfield. She was sturdy and impish, bright for her age. Lilianne had hoped that through Clemmy she would quickly get to know people in the village, but though folk spoke to the little girl and let her play with their dogs or cats, few were friendly towards herself. She found the people of Nunscorn exceptionally withdrawn.

It was when she was walking up past the nine cottages one sunny afternoon that she discovered the reason. A group of women had collected round the pump at the end of the terrace where a low wall made a seat for two of them, and their youngest children played about their feet. All eyes turned to Lilianne, who was wearing a dress of flowered cotton which contrasted sharply with their plain homespun skirts.

'How d'yer do,' she said, hoping they would invite her to stop. She had missed mardling with friends since leaving the farm.

Her greeting met with stony silence. Not one of the group answered her and their stares seemed to bore into her back. She went on her way with Clemmy dragging and whining that she wanted to play with the other children, but no notice was taken. Then she heard the unkindest of comments.

'Picked up with her before his wife were dead, 'e did. It's a disgrace.'

'Came from Seggenham way. Made 'erself right at home in poor Susan's place. The brazen hussy.'

'Who do she think she is? The Queen o' Sheba?'

There came the sound of coarse laughter. Lilianne walked on, but her stomach seemed to turn over, her throat became dry and her cheeks red. It hadn't occurred to her that she was resented here, or that her presence in Jonathan's house would be misconstrued. Her enlightenment was made worse by the fact that she was already guilty of hoping one day she might take 'poor Susan's' place. The truth sounded terrible coming from village gossips and she had to walk another quarter of a mile before she felt calm enough to face them on the way back.

They hadn't moved. Pride came to Lilianne's rescue and she walked slowly with Clemmy balanced on one hip and her head held high. She wasn't going to be talked about as if she were some husband-stealer.

'Ain't you got nothing better to do than take a person's name in vain?' she asked, when she was level with the women.

They stared at her.

'Decent people live in this village,' said one.

'If you're meaning I ain't decent let me tell you I've never done a thing to be ashamed of. What right have you to judge me when you don't even know me?'

One of the women sitting on the wall got up and drew her child to her side. 'Reckon living with a man who ain't yer husband, and right after he's just buried his wife, is downright immoral. Susan Whitfield must be turning in her grave.'

'Then she'll be wasting her time. I'm a housekeeper, nothing more,' said Lilianne, and she stalked away before temper got the better of her.

When they got back, Clemmy wanted to see her father and Lilianne took her to the door of the forge so that she could look inside. Jonathan was stripped to the waist in the shimmering heat and as he wielded his hammer the muscles rippled in his powerful arms. The sight of his strength filled Lilianne with the sort of excitement she had never expected to experience again, and even spiteful tongues couldn't curb it.

Springly's Farm covered several hundred acres and was far bigger than anything Hannah had been used to. Elijah Springly owned it himself and he was not short of a penny or two, of that she was certain. He was thin and miserly, his meanness renowned, but he kept the best stock in the district and commanded the best prices at market. His wife led a lady's life.

'Don't know who'll have his money when he's gone,' said Martha Croppit, the girl with whom Hannah shared the work in the dairy. 'There's no children for 'im to leave it to, not that I know of, so what's the sense of hoarding it. What a waste.'

'Mebbe his wife spends it,' Hannah suggested. 'Her dresses ain't ones she's made herself.' She was standing at the great stone dairy sink making butter, and she had a lot to think about as she worked with the wooden pats to remove buttermilk from the golden mound piled high in a cooper-made vessel. There was too much on her mind to care about the Springlys and their money.

It was three weeks since Ben had left for America and not a day went by without her wondering about him. While she worked she tried to picture the road he had taken, the boat he must be on, and the land he would come to at the end of his journey, but it was very difficult when she knew so little about the world beyond her own environment. At school there had been a screen by the door to keep out draughts and it had been pasted with scrap pictures of foreign places. For a while Hannah had dreamed of travelling when she was grown up, but that was before she had seen the sea on a rough winter's day. It was the first time she'd walked across the marshes towards the coast with Pa and she never forgot how grey and fearsome the endless expanse of water had looked. It had made her feel ill just watching fishing boats pitch and roll, and when they'd tipped into deep troughs she had been afraid they would never reappear. After that she'd had no further inclination to travel abroad.

It was dreadful to think of Ben cooped up on some sailing ship with nothing but angry water all around him. Too dreadful to dwell on.

She liked the farm. Elijah Springly had plenty of people working for him, and now it was coming on hay-making time there were casual labourers in the fields. She and Martha took fourses out to them of an afternoon, staying to share the snack if there was time, and it was good to laugh and forget her worries. The farmhouse was very old, though new bits had been added down the years. There was a new porch in the middle of the front with a bedroom above, but creeper already disguised the different bricks. The dairy was an extension on the side with a window which didn't match, and a rowan tree had been planted close by it to ward off evil.

Martha was looking out of that same window when the day's work was done.

'There's a bloke just come,' she said. 'Looks like he's got a new strouter for that waggon what half-collapsed last week. Good-looking he is, an' all.'

Hannah heaved a churn up on the freshly scrubbed shelf, then leaned forward to peer through the rowan leaves and saw a young man walking his horse beside the round-topped wall of local brick which surrounded the farm. He had a heavy iron strut for the side framework of a waggon balanced across the saddle, and he wore a green felt hat tilted well over his eyes to shield them from the brightness of the setting sun. It was Shem Whitfield.

'Oh, no,' Hannah breathed.

Last night he had taunted her yet again and it was fortunate neither her mother nor Jonathan Whitfield had been in earshot when she had rounded on him for his impertinence. Shem Whitfield seemed intent on making her life as difficult as possible, never missing an opportunity to test her patience or rouse her temper.

'I like the way you move,' he'd said, following her into the backhouse after supper. 'I know a lot of girls, but when you swing your hips there ain't one as can compare. If you're a virgin then I'm an inexperienced yokel, and I ain't been that since I was twelve. How old were *you* when a man first took you?'

'Mind your tongue,' Hannah had shouted. 'And get out of my way. I hate you near me.'

It was the silliest thing to have said. Straight away he'd drawn her back against him so that she could feel the wanting in him. She'd kicked his shins and scratched the hands which encircled her waist, but he was the stronger and he wouldn't give up easily.

'You only fire me when you get angry,' he'd said.

'Then go to blazes!'

'I'll have you before much longer.'

'Never!' She'd managed to struggle free, and as she'd whipped round she'd brought her knee up to his groin so that pain had made him recoil.

'I'll get you for that,' he'd threatened. 'See if I don't. I've scores to settle.'

He had stomped out to the yard and she'd heard him drawing water from the well. She'd succeeded in cooling his ardour for that moment, but as she'd stood at the sink washing dishes she wished she'd repelled him with more dignity. Truth to tell, she was a mite afraid.

And now he had come over to Five Elms.

'D'you know him, then?' Martha asked.

'He's Mr Whitfield's high-and-mighty son. I'll have to dodge away so he doesn't see me.'

'Why? Maybe he'll give you a ride home.'

'Up behind him on a horse! Never. I ain't giving him that kind of a chance.'

Martha sighed. 'Reckon I'd give him a chance and a half.' She had a broad, homely face, a plump body and a good sense of humour. 'But then, the poor horse wouldn't think much of it, I suppose.'

'You'd be welcome to him.'

As soon as the clearing up was done Hannah took off her apron, and with permission from the housekeeper to leave she made a furtive exit. Hannah thought Shem would return via the lane from Five Elms so she felt safe once she reached the low meadow she always crossed to get to the river path which was a short cut. But he had sharp eyes and hadn't missed his opportunity. There was nowhere to hide when he came galloping across the field, flattening the dry grass which was due to be scythed, and she walked on with her head held proud.

'What's the hurry?' he asked, reining the horse sharply. Dust and seed flew in the air. 'I know you saw me but you made off like a scared rabbit.'

'I ain't scared of you.'

He dismounted. 'No, I reckon you're not.' His tone was aggressive. They were on the reed-edged path before he said anything more, and he took her by surprise. 'Could be I misjudged you when I first came home. I said things about you and me father I'd no right saying. Well, not about you anyhow. Likely you ain't the sort of girl I thought you were, but that only makes me want you more.'

'I don't reckon your father deserved the things you said about him either,' said Hannah, desperate to take his mind off herself.

They reached a narrow wooden bridge over the river just west of Nunscorn and Shem led the horse over first. At the other side he dropped the reins and let it loose in the pasture, then barred Hannah's way, trapping her on the rotting planks.

'I want to tell you about my father,' he said. He had a hand on each rail and was leaning forward so that their faces were level. She could only avoid him if she turned and went back, but he would be bound to follow so she stayed put and returned his stare. 'My father never wanted me. My ma died when I was born and he dumped me on his sister and went off to be an army farrier. Forgot I existed until my grandfather in Nunscorn died and left him the forge. Then I was old enough to be cheap labour so he came and got me.'

'What's that to do with me?'

'Reckon he had as many women as he wanted in them foreign places the army sent him, but things were different when he came home. He always attracted women, that I knew, but the only way he could get a girl in his bed here was to marry her. Since Susan had a legacy from her old aunt it looked like he were on to a good thing.'

'And then she died and I came along, and you thought he was up to his tricks again. Well, *I* ain't got a brass farthing, more's the pity, and I don't please your father any more than he pleases me.'

'No. Likely not.' Shem put on his irritatingly smug half-smile. 'I thought once things was straightened out you'd be nicer to me. C'mon, Hannah, let's be friends.'

'Friends maybe, since we have to live in the same house,' she conceded, reluctantly. 'But nothing more.'

His gaze dropped and he was suddenly sheepish. 'I could love you.'

Hannah was taken aback, and she almost fell into the trap of believing him. Yet even if the confession was not just another ploy to coerce her she could see the danger.

'You'll need to treat me differently before I'll believe that. And you can start by letting me get home.'

'You can ride with me. My father's nag'll stand the weight of two.' He swung her up in his arms before she realised his intention and was about to carry her over to the horse, but Hannah kicked and struggled until he was forced to put her down. His hat had gone sailing into the river and he was red in the face.

'That'll teach you not to take liberties with me,' she cried. It was time Shem Whitfield was taken down a peg.

He flung away angrily, climbing down the bank to retrieve his hat. Her temper dissolved and she laughed when he tipped the water out of it, but Shem wasn't amused.

'Walk then,' he shouted, as he went after the horse. It, too, was now in a capricious mood and kept darting away before he could grab the reins, leading him a dance across the pasture until he finally managed to mount.

'Talk about your father fancying himself with women!' she called out. 'It must run in the family. Well, you don't impress me one bit.' If she had left it there he might have ridden off with his ill-humour, but thinking she had got the better of him she dared to taunt him further. 'My brother Luke would tear you to pieces for pestering me, that he would.'

Shem pulled the horse up sharp, sat tall in the saddle, then charged towards her. Hoofs pounded the dry earth as if the animal were being forced into battle. When he reached her once more he jumped down and caught her in a brutal grasp.

'I wondered when you'd own up to being Luke Jerram's sister. I've a score to settle with him, and you can thank your lucky stars I ain't done it sooner.' He twisted her arm until it was behind her back and she was held immovably against him. His features contorted with rage. 'Nice little business we had going in Ipswich till Luke got greedy. Went off with money belonging to me and set the law sniffing round. Ain't that why I'm lying low?'

'It's got nothing to do with me. Take your dirty hands off my arm.'

'You should try being nice to me.'

'Never!' She spat in his face and stamped on his foot. 'I ain't got no time for you, nor ever will have. You're no more than a stupid boy.' Fear and anger made her reckless, driving her to say things she knew were risky, and she provoked him beyond endurance.

'A boy, am I!' he yelled. 'A boy? We'll see, shall we, whether I'm boy or man.'

He forced her to the ground and she screamed, terrified. This time her strength was no match for his and she couldn't escape. She fought him and begged for mercy, but Shem Whitfield took savage pleasure in giving vent to his fury on her innocent body.

The raping that followed was witnessed out there in the meadow between Five Elms and Nunscorn.

Mosquitoes hovered in clouds over the river. A little way upstream an old man was working outside his eel-hut hanging out

112

bundles of reeds he had tied and trimmed to make liggers for catching pike. Tomorrow he would roll his line round a ligger and bait the double hook with roach before setting it in shallow water to attract his catch. Life was simple and uncomplicated. The problems of youth were far behind him and he didn't envy the young couple near the bridge. He recognised the fellow, the blacksmith's son from Nunscorn. He'd seen him in the Plough and Plover over the last week or two and hadn't been over-taken with him. A braggart, always trying to prove himself. Well, he'd taken on more than he bargained for with that pretty wench, and he was glad.

It wasn't until screams filled the air that he realised it was rape, but he knew his arthritic feet wouldn't get him to the scene quickly enough to prevent the act. He watched helplessly from a distance as Shem Whitfield forced himself on the struggling girl, pinioning her to the ground as he abused her unwilling body. It was criminal. When he had finished the wretch got up and adjusted his clothing, then swung into the saddle and rode his horse at speed in the direction of Nunscorn, leaving his victim sobbing on the dry earth.

Hannah couldn't get up. Her skirt was torn and she was so sore she felt as if she had been ripped apart, but worse than these things was the degradation. Her sobbing became so intense it was like a baying sound and she thumped her fists against the ground until her knuckles bled. She hated Shem Whitfield, loathed him, feared him. She never wanted to see him again and she prayed he wouldn't be home tonight.

She didn't know how long she had been lying there when someone came and stood beside her. There was a smell of river slime and fish, and she saw trousers tied with twine at the ankles above a pair of ancient, gaping-soled boots.

'Can you get up, miss?'

She struggled to a sitting position and saw the old man from upstream. His crinkled face was full of concern.

'Reckon I'm all right,' she said.

'I saw what happened. Weren't nothin' I could do, though.' He had rheumy eyes, faded with age, and they were awash with tears. 'Do you want to come down to my hut and clean up? There's water and a bowl. I won't look.'

Hannah dried her eyes on her petticoat and stood up. 'Thank you, but I'd rather get going.'

She set off towards home, dragging her feet. There was no one she could tell about the violation she had suffered. Ma would never believe her, and even if she had the courage to tell Jonathan Whitfield it wasn't likely he would take her word against his son's. Tears blinded her eyes and ran down her cheeks as she stumbled along.

Most of all she yearned for Ben, but with terrible shame she realised that if he were here now she wouldn't be able to face him. Shem had destroyed her.

Chapter Ten

Jonathan Whitfield was happier than he had been since losing Susan. Mrs Jerram was a good woman, and a good cook. Every evening there was a meal on the table that was almost too much even for his healthy appetite and it was never burnt or under-cooked as Susan's offering had been. He felt disloyal comparing them, but there was no denying that his temper was better when his stomach was full, and his housekeeper could be relied on to ply him with plenty of plain, wholesome food. It was very fortunate he had come across her at just the right time.

His greatest satisfaction was that his son Shem seemed set to stay for good. He was not blind to the fact that Hannah Jerram was a major reason for his decision to stay, but the girl was hard-working and she wasn't flighty. Jonathan liked her well enough and would be well-disposed to accepting her as his son's wife, though she gave no sign of being partial to the boy at the moment. The opposite in fact. It was plain she avoided him.

What disappointed him was that Shem showed little aptitude for working with iron. He didn't like the heat, complaining that it made his hair smell of smoke and his skin erupt in an unpleasant rash. The repairs he attempted on farm implements invariably had to be done again before they could be charged. But he did have a way with horses.

'It takes a strong man to handle the bellows and a sympathetic one to shoe a horse, so I reckon the two of us will make out just fine in time,' Jonathan said, trying to curb his impatience after two frustrating weeks. 'Always hoped you'd join me, boy. The forge'll be yours one day. Time you learnt the trade properly.'

Shem grimaced. 'I'd get on much better if you didn't keep interfering. Reckon I could shoe a horse blindfold.'

'Don't try to be clever.' Jonathan had difficulty keeping a civil tongue. 'Be grateful I'm teaching you. There's a lot who would be glad of an apprenticeship and you're getting yours for nothing.'

He looked at the conglomeration of items strewn over the green in front of the shed, all fashioned to order and awaiting collection. There were parts of ploughs and waggon-wheel rims, pump handles, door fastenings, and whippletrees for a horse's harness to which traces would be attached. Being both farrier and blacksmith he could turn his hand to anything, and hoped that one day Shem would be able to do the same. The boy had to learn, and it wasn't a craft that could be picked up in a day. He set him to making nails first from a long length of heated iron which he had to cut to size. The pieces had to be inserted in the nail-heading tool, then placed over the anvil opening to hammer the heads into shape, repetition which bored Shem, and he grumbled all the time he was pointing each one. By the time he was adept there was a supply of nails to last for months, but he had made progress and was ready to attempt more complicated items.

'You must have the metal hotter,' his father said to him. Shem was fitfully hammering a piece of red-hot iron to try to bend it, but Jonathan made him put it back in the fire until the end of the rod was white from the heat. 'Now you can shape it easily, but you must bend over the anvil further. If you stand back you can't get a good swing with the hammer. Here, let me show you.'

He took the tool from his son and began wielding it from a curved position so that it swung well back over his shoulder before coming down accurately on the iron with perfect balance and far more force. Shem tried again, but the weight of the hammer controlled the movement rather than the strength of his arm.

'Aw, this ain't no good.'

'Try a lighter hammer,' said Jonathan. He looked along the racks of tools on the smoke-blackened wall and found one, then demonstrated once again. 'You have to set up a rhythm. See – up and over, hit the iron, then the anvil. One, two, three, four, then up and over again. You'll soon get the hang of it.'

Shem improved gradually. The trouble was he wouldn't stick at any job long enough and Jonathan was afraid to chastise him too much in case he upped and left like he'd done before when life wasn't going his way. He had an independent spirit and if he wasn't happy in a place he didn't stay. An ungrateful wretch, Jonathan's sister Ellen had called him. As a small boy without a mother Shem had roamed the streets of Ipswich rather than settle with Ellen and her family, sometimes going missing for weeks, and he would re-appear without a word as to where he had been. This time there'd been no word from him since he had walked out on the day his father married Susan, and he'd said nothing about those three years in between.

At the end of another week Jonathan made a renewed attempt to gain his confidence.

'Won't you tell me what you've bin doing since you was here before, son? Have you bin working with horses?'

'Something like that,' Shem said. 'Buying and selling mostly.'

'So you'll've made some money.'

'Reckon not.' They were labouring together at tyring a wheel and the red-hot iron was levered on to the wooden wheel rim. The tyre now had to be hammered into place. 'I can finish this meself,' said the boy. 'Time you let me work on me own.'

Since they were virtually strangers, Jonathan didn't feel he had the right to probe into matters Shem was unwilling to discuss so he didn't try to force the issue. His son's upbringing had been lonely and he was the first to admit that he ought to have given him security instead of blaming the innocent child for the death of its mother.

He sympathised with his son's restless spirit. He had been the same when he was young. His father had taught him how to forge iron and shoe horses from the time he could hold a hammer, but the monotony had got on his nerves and he had moved from Nunscorn to Ipswich in search of adventure. He had been eighteen when he had met and immediately fallen in love with Maria Worthing at a fairground. She had been a workhouse child with nobody to call her own, and she'd jumped at the chance of having a husband, even one with few prospects. Maria produced Shem after the first nine months of marriage and forfeited her life in the process. The experience had left Jonathan so bitter and disillusioned he had packed his bags and offered the only talent he possessed to a cavalry regiment, leaving the baby with Ellen who already had more children of her own than she could manage and didn't deserve to be lumbered with another. So Shem had been unwanted for most of his life. He hadn't been ill-treated but there had been little love to spare in a house where a new child was born every year, and he had learnt early to fend for himself.

117

There just hadn't been time to think of Shem while he had been travelling abroad with his regiment. No time at Meerut during the Indian Mutiny, no time at Lucknow. No time on the Gold Coast of Africa when troops were ordered to move against the Ashantees in a pestilential climate. He had almost died there, though not from wounds. As a blacksmith he was not in combat, but fever claimed so many victims and he had suffered from it along with the rest. He was lucky to be alive.

When his father had died some years later no one had expected there to be any money, but the old man had been thrifty and even after sharing with his sister there had been enough for Jonathan to buy himself out of the army. It meant he was left with no money to run the forge but he'd had no worries about being able to make it pay. He was as good a craftsman as his father had been and he wasn't afraid of hard work. What was more, he had a fourteen-year-old son he took with him to Nunscorn to help restore his now impoverished inheritance. He'd thought it would be good for the boy, but Shem had been like a nervous colt, ready to take off at the slightest disturbance, and disturbance had come in the form of Susan Melby.

Susan had been very young, only just of marriageable age, but Jonathan had fallen for her as suddenly as he had fallen for Maria, and the fact that she had a legacy to help him re-establish the business had made the thought of marriage to her even more attractive. He'd realised too late that in marrying Susan he was putting the fragile new relationship between himself and his son in jeopardy. Shem had accused him of madness, lechery, deception, betrayal, greed and many other things in a quarrel he would never forget, but he'd been too blind to see that Shem was jealous. Susan had taken the place in his father's heart that he had only recently found for himself and he had refused to stay in what he had scathingly called the 'love-nest'.

But now he had returned.

Inevitably, perhaps, there came an evening when good food was not enough to satisfy Jonathan. He always looked forward now to returning to the warm kitchen, anticipating the pleasure of seeing his neatly-dressed housekeeper with her ready smile. He liked her more and more. She was comfortable to have around, and she was very

118

appealing. He recognized the throbbing in his loins as a sign that he had been too long without a woman, but he was an honourable man and would take nothing which wasn't offered willingly. Mrs Jerram never spoke out of turn or looked at him with any sign of invitation, yet he was sensitive enough to know that she would not be displeased if he made a gentle overture.

Luck was with him that evening, though there would come a time when he would see it as the devil's own. Hannah had taken Clemmy out, and Shem had gone riding off the way he did sometimes, so there was only himself and Lilianne at supper. She seemed pleased, too. It was a companionable meal and she took interest in the things he talked about, giving a warm encompassing smile which drew him into her sphere and made him feel wanted.

After supper she picked up her sewing basket and started to mend one of his shirts. He sat near her, watching every movement of her hands, every shadow flitting across her face in the firelight. The quiet intimacy was soothing and it awoke a tenderness in him.

He was surprised he had never noticed until now that she had nice skin. There was a faint down on her cheeks, like the bloom of a peach. He didn't know precisely how old she was. She must be approaching his own age since she had a grown-up family, but she looked much younger, and tendrils of hair escaping from a knot at the crown of her head curled about her neck with a prettiness of which she was quite unaware. Her mouth was generous and the way she lifted her chin showed strength of character. His eyes moved downwards and his heartbeats quickened as he became conscious of the firm roundness of her breasts. He drew in his breath sharply.

'Is something bothering you, Mr Whitfield?' she asked, looking up.

'It's nothing,' he said.

But it was not nothing. It was six months now since he had touched a woman intimately. Suddenly he had an urgent need to gratify his sexual drive and he wanted to kiss and fondle her.

He broke out in a sweat. What of his promise, the vow of celibacy he had taken for Susan's sake? It had been easy to do when she was dying, and he would have done anything to ease her pain. The vow had been just to pacify her, but she had made him swear to it on the Bible. An ordinary promise could have been broken, but swearing on the Bible was different. The enormity of what he had done struck him now with the force of one of his own hammers: in one weak moment he had denied himself physical pleasures forever more.

Jonathan gave himself a mental shake. He ought to have gone outside then to cool his ardour but his housekeeper had stopped sewing and gazed at him with a caring expression which weakened him further.

'You're good to me, Mrs Jerram,' he said, his voice not quite steady. 'Cooking and cleaning and mending as well as looking after my child.'

'It's what I'm paid for.'

'You do more than most women would do.'

'That's because you're good to me too. You've given me and Hannah a roof over our heads. You've allowed me to feel it's my home.'

He swallowed hard. 'I don't know what I'd do without you.'

'Reckon you won't have to, not unless I displease you,' she said. 'I'm right happy here and I ain't bothered what the gossips say if you aren't.'

So folk were talking. The warmth of her voice and the unexpected, scarcely veiled invitation made him ache with desire. He felt like a starving man being shown a banquet.

For a few seconds longer he struggled half-heartedly against temptation. This had been Susan's home and her influence was still strong, but she was dead while Lilianne Jerram was very much alive and plainly willing to do more for him than she did already. He stood up. As if drawn by an invisible thread she too got to her feet. He kissed her experimentally, and she moved closer and put her arms round his neck, offering her mouth to be savoured more deeply. He didn't need any further encouragement.

'You're a very desirable woman, Mrs Jerram,' he said. 'I noticed it the first day we met.'

'I was right taken with you too, Mr Whitfield,' she answered.

He touched her breast and felt the thudding of her heart. 'Then you won't object if we go upstairs. I've a great hankering for you and I ain't strong on patience.'

She was as good as he had anticipated. In fact she was the best woman he'd made love to in a long while. He'd loved Susan dearly, but she had been frightened and immature, too tense for enjoyment, and he'd grown tired of her excuses when he'd wanted her. But

Lilianne was older and experienced. There was nothing like a strong woman to meet up with one's body and share the pleasure. He reckoned she'd made Matt Jerram a good wife in every sense.

One morning at the end of May, a month after the rape of Hannah Jerram, an outlying farmer brought a temperamental colt to be shod for the first time. First-shoeing was always something of an event in the village, usually celebrated later in one of the two inns when the owner, his cronies, and the farrier got together to 'wet the horse's shoes', and word had got round. But Jonathan had been delayed and Shem was alone in the forge. By the time the animal reached the forge quite a crowd had gathered and it pranced and shied, its eyes wide with fear. The old man had a job to keep hold of the rope and shouts from onlookers only made matters worse.

'Can't you see the poor hoss is scared silly?' Shem left the shed and went out to it, a piece of leather doubled over his belt to form an apron and the green felt hat on his head. 'Stand back, all of you while I bring 'im inside.'

'Where's Jon Whitfield?' asked the man, peering in the door.

'He ain't here, but that's no matter. I can shoe a horse as well as me father.'

'Not this one, bor. Needs someone experienced to handle a colt like this 'un.'

'Don't worry. Pa says I've got a way with horses.'

Shem was full of youthful confidence. He'd had a little practice at shoeing in the last few weeks and thought his understanding of animals was all that was needed to make him a good farrier. Sure enough, he soothed the young horse and was able to lead it inside.

'He'll have to be fettered,' someone said. 'You'll have to tie 'is legs and get him over on 'is back. It's the only way.'

'No need of that,' said Shem.

He grasped the colt's right foreleg firmly between his knees the way he'd been shown and measured across the hoof while the crowd beyond the door held its breath. He used the rasp and hoof parers, all the time murmuring soft words to the animal, then while it stood amazingly still he heated and shaped the first of the shoes with a heavy catshead and filed off the sharp edges. But when he held the shoe in place to seat it a cloud of smoke rose up, and though burning the horny hoof didn't cause pain the acrid smell and the hissing

121

noise frightened the horse again. It shied just as he was ready to put in the nails.

'Take care them nails point outwards or you're gonna have trouble,' the owner warned, watching closely.

'I know what I'm doing,' said Shem.

The first nail was inserted and the shoeing hammer came down hard. At that moment Jonathan returned.

'What the hell do you think you're doing?' he demanded, elbowing through the crowd round the door.

The hammer hit the nail at the wrong angle and drove it into the animal's foot where the flesh was sensitive. Pandemonium followed. Shem was no longer able to control the horse and everyone scattered, fearing it would rush outside, but it reared up on its hind legs and knocked down a row of horseshoes and farm tools that had been hanging on a beam. Jonathan was thrown against a bench where he cut his hand badly on a hoof-cleaning knife and Shem backed into a corner with fright. If his father hadn't managed to grab the rope in time he would have been trampled on, maybe even killed.

'You bloody young fool!' Jonathan yelled, tying the rope to a ring in the wall. 'What possessed you? You think yerself so bloody clever, don't you, but you're a stupid oaf. Only an idiot would try first-shoeing a frisky animal like that without fettering it. And you ain't even shoed a nag on yer own yet.' He pressed the bones of his damaged hand together to try and close the gaping wound, and he managed to calm down. 'Now we'll do it my way. Come here.'

'It was your fault. You scared him.' Shem stayed where he was, visibly trembling. 'I ain't going near that animal again.'

'You'll learn to do things properly. Now help me to fetter 'im and I'll show you how to nail a colt's first set of shoes.'

'Go to hell,' shouted Shem. 'I hate you and I wish to God you weren't my father. You never wanted me.'

Jonathan snatched up a whip and lashed out with it in fury, stinging his son's thigh as he skidded round behind the horse which was still agitated. Shem left the smithy at a run as soon as he was clear, but the villagers tried to stop him, as excited now as spectators at a cock-fight.

'Aw, let him go,' said Jonathan, in exasperation.

He was white-faced and in pain. Blood was dripping from his

122

hand. A strenuous pull on the rope to quieten the colt again taxed his strength but he held on, making the cut worse. The crowd closed ranks after Shem's escape and pressed nearer to the door so as not to miss anything.

The animal was fettered and turned on its back, and in due course the shoeing was done. The crowd drifted away, likely to the Plough and Plover, but Jonathan didn't join them. His hand was bleeding through the wad of dirty rag he had tied round it and the wound needed washing. He was just going indoors, more angry and humiliated than he could ever remember being before, when an old man called him.

'Yew got a load of trouble there, bor.'

'I can handle horses,' Jonathan said. 'Don't think I can't.' He reached for a jug of ale meant for drinking with his dinner and downed half the contents without pausing for breath.

'Seems you can't handle that son of yours, though. Right heathen he be. Needs that whip taking to him proper if you ask me.'

Jonathan's face was fiery-red and his eyes glinted. 'I ain't asking you anything, so get out off my property before I take the whip to you an' all.'

'Fair enough,' said the old man. He was bent with arthritis and the few steps he took were obviously painful. He hadn't hobbled far before he stopped, straightened his crooked back and added more fuel to his remarks. 'Likely you ought to know I saw that boy of yours take a girl against her will nigh on four weeks since. Down by the river it were. I saw it from my hut. That were rape, I says to myself. Rape. Seems he ain't fit to be loose.'

'Mercy on us, what *have* you been doing?' cried Mrs Jerram, when she saw Jonathan's hand. 'I'll get a kettle of hot water.'

'No need,' he snapped. 'There's bracken root that Susan boiled in hog's fat last year. It'll be all right if I slap some of that on it.'

'You'll let me bathe it first.'

She made him sit at the whitewood table and saw that he kept his hand submerged in a bowl of hot water until the deep gash across his palm was clean, and while doing so he used his good hand to tip back the rest of the ale he had brought indoors with him.

'How did I come to breed such a son?' he ranted. 'I ought to disown him.'

'Sons can be difficult. I know because I've been through a terrible time with my own.' Lilianne was an understanding woman. She asked few questions. 'Whatever the trouble, in a little time when you've both cooled down it won't seem so bad.'

He didn't tell her that it could only get worse. Clearly the girl Shem had molested was Hannah. Her changed manner verified it. He had watched her avoid the boy whenever she could and she never spoke to him unless it was absolutely necessary, then only in monosyllables.

He had thought it a pity Hannah was so unresponsive. Maybe Shem had found her coolness more than his patience could stand, but that didn't excuse his wicked behaviour. If she had appeared to be capricious there might have been some excuse, but there'd been no sign of a teasing nature. The Jerrams were good people and Hannah was loyal, too. Not a word had she breathed of Shem's treatment of her.

He wondered if Lilianne knew. He couldn't ask her.

She had found a cotton sheet which wouldn't stand another mending and she tore it into strips, then applied some bracken root and set to work dressing the wound as soon as the bleeding stopped. He studied her, affected by the ale he had drunk too quickly. Her touch was confident. Since the evening before last when they had lain together briefly she had become a mite more familiar, and her concern for him now was like that of a wife. He flinched with shame at the memory of what he had allowed to happen.

'I ain't hurting you, am I?' she asked, gently.

She was standing on a level with him as she bound the cotton strips and he could have put an arm round her neat waist. And when she touched against him with apparent innocence to secure the ends of the bandage he was terribly tempted to draw her against him. He needed the comfort of her body close to his, but God alone knew that he must never touch her again.

What a hypocrite he was, condemning his son for his indulgence when he was equally guilty himself of using a woman. He rocked back and forth to try and rid himself of the spectre of Susan rising up to confront him with the breaking of his vow, and in his drink-befuddled mind his sin became greater than his son's. He had put God to the test and already he was being punished.

The bandage was in place and Lilianne picked up the bowl to empty it.

'Take care now, Mr Whitfield. Don't go letting dirt get in that cut,' she said. 'Blood poisoning ain't a nice way to die.'

'It's what I deserve, Mrs Jerram,' he said.

'Mercy on us! What can you have done to have such a poor opinion of yourself?'

He looked at her keenly. Her soft voice was luring him further into the trap, and with renewed anger he saw her as a siren. All women were alike, true descendants of Eve, and he hated them. His clenched fist, iron-hard, struck the bowl of water from her hands and sent it flying. Lilianne Jerram screamed with shock, and the water, red with his blood, spread over the floor. His foot slipped in it as he staggered to the door.

The same day that Shem and his father fell out over the shoeing of the colt Hannah walked home in the evening with Martha Croppit, who was staying temporarily with her grandmother in Nunscorn.

A patch of grease stained Martha's apron and she dipped deep into the pocket, bringing out a squashed pat of butter wrapped in muslin. 'He'd have a fit if he knew I'd pinched this, but my Gran needs it more than he does. Now I'll have to wash my apron before tomorrow.' She sighed. 'Reckon I'll have to find me a rich man to marry so I don't have to go on working for old Springly. Lazy, that's me. I want a cottage of my own with a little garden and enough money to pay someone to cook and clean while I tend the flowers. Now that's not much to ask, is it?'

Hannah shrugged. 'I suppose we'll have to be thankful for what we get,' she said. 'There ain't no prince likely to come after me on a white horse, that's for sure.'

'Me neither. Elijah Springly ain't even got a son I can set my cap at.' The lament lingered a moment, then Martha nudged Hannah's elbow mischievously. 'There's always Shem Whitfield. Now I'd not be moaning if it was *me* he'd got his eye on.'

'Don't talk to me about Shem Whitfield.'

Hannah walked proud and tall, but she ached with worry. Though she showed no sign of it there was no doubt in her mind that she carried a child inside her, and hatred for Shem was like a disease eating at her soul. Her body felt different, as if it were making room for the seed to grow, and her breasts felt strangely heavy. She was three weeks late, and this morning she'd had to rush down the

125

garden to the privy to be sick. By Christmas, then, she would be giving birth. Oh, my, what a scandal there was going to be. If she could be absolutely sure the child she was expecting was Ben's maybe she would have the courage to toss her head and not care, but she was robbed of all certainty. Like as not it would be Shem's bastard.

She had never been able to speak of the raping. Ma was always too busy or too tired, and as the days passed Hannah began to feel it was better kept to herself. Shem hadn't come home that night and since it had happened she had been too ashamed to look at him, afraid of intercepting an insolent expression. Walking home from Springlys had become a daily ordeal. She had stopped taking the short cut across the fields and kept to the lane where someone might come along if ever she needed help.

Shem had tried to apologise. 'Hannah, I never meant to hurt you . . .'

But she hurried away whenever he tried to make amends. She loathed him. He spoke words which were not reflected in his eyes and she would never trust him. Never.

But now it wouldn't be long before Ma became suspicious about her condition, and then life wouldn't be worth living. She had tried several times. 'Ma, there's something I must tell you . . . '

'There ain't no ale for Mr Whitfield's supper, Hannah. Take a jug and get some fresh.'

It was always the same. Ma was deaf these days to everything except what was best for Mr Whitfield, and when they went to bed she turned over and went straight to sleep from exhaustion. Hannah would lie awake, watching the rise and fall of her mother's breast as she slept, wishing she could rest her head there and pour out the grief which was robbing her of appetite and energy. Maybe she would understand. But maybe she wouldn't.

Hannah so desperately needed to confide in someone she was tempted to speak of her dilemma to Martha, but that would be a mistake. Martha was a good friend, but she had a wagging tongue and anything told to her in confidence would be all over the district in next to no time. She thought of Emily. Prim, gentle Emily would be shocked, of course, but surely she would listen and likely she would be wise enough to know what was best to do. Yes, she would ask for Sunday off and walk to Seggenham to see her sister.

It was almost dark when the two girls reached Nunscorn, and Martha's grandmother's cottage already had a candle burning in the window. A long garden path lay between banks of lupins and lavender bushes, and at the gate a cat was keeping vigil in the hedgerow for mice.

'I'll see you tomorrow,' said Martha. Her hand was on the gate latch and she was about to go in when the peace of the summer evening was disturbed by the sound of loud voices coming from the Plough and Plover. She paused. 'You best wait. Or come in with me until it's quiet again.'

Hannah wanted to get home. 'No, I'll be all right.'

'I'll walk with you then,' Martha insisted.

She took Hannah's arm and they turned the corner cautiously. An angry group of men was clustered round the inn door, one of them holding a youth by the collar of his jacket and shaking him like a dog with a rabbit.

'Don't you ever go near my woman again, d'you hear,' the man snarled. 'Some friend you turned out ter be. Git orf 'ome before I kill yer.'

'Yer're too big for yer boots, bor, too big by 'alf.'

'Big-mouthed and no morals,' shouted another. 'Get on back to them loose women you and yer father keep over at the smithy.'

The doors of the nine houses opposite the inn all came open and square patches of light stained the rutted lane. Women appeared and watched the free show with hands on hips, joining in the abuse.

'It's Shem,' breathed Hannah. 'Reckon he's drunk and showing off.' She marched towards the group, her head high and her eyes flashing. 'Take your hands off 'im,' she commanded. 'You're all too drunk to know what you're doing and you can just apologise for saying things about me and my ma that ain't true. You're all as bad as each other.'

Shem was still being held upright by his coat but his legs kept buckling and he was grinning foolishly. The men closed their mouths and glared at her in sullen silence, too surprised to retort; then they let go of him and he crumpled to the ground.

Someone kicked him. Another spat. Hannah bent down and tried to get him on his feet, but he was too heavy, and it wasn't until a pair of willing hands took the other side of him that she managed it. Martha had come to help.

127

'That's right, take 'im off to bed,' someone jeered. 'Not that he'll be much use to you in that state.'

'Take no notice,' said Martha. 'I'll help you with him.'

They draped Shem's arms across their shoulders and dragged him away. His eyes were glazed and he whimpered now like a puppy. Both girls needed all their breath to manoeuvre the incapable Shem in the right direction. They skirted the green and when they were within sight of the forge they propped him against an oak tree for a minute.

'I can manage him now,' Hannah gasped. 'I'll pretend he's been walking me home so his father doesn't see him like this.'

Shem started to sing and she hauled him to his feet again. Luckily he seemed to sober slightly and started to walk a few weaving steps on his own, but she made him put an arm round her.

'Naughty Hannah,' teased Martha. 'Reckon there's more to you than we all know about.'

'You get on back to your grandmother. I'll be fine.' Hannah kissed the other girl's cheek. 'You're a good friend, Martha. I'll see you in the morning.'

Hannah guided Shem round the side of the forge to the stable as quickly and quietly as she could, covering his mouth when he kept singing, and she ignored his swearing as she heaved him inside. The only reason she had helped him was to stop any further revelations issuing from his foul mouth. He'd done her enough harm.

'Han-nah,' he murmured. He fell backwards into the stall and lay helpless on the straw. 'Come here, Han-nah. I want you.'

'Get up! And don't you ever try anything with me again. I hate you.'

He became maudlin, crying like a child, but she made him get back on his feet and guided him to the ladder leading up to his room. It wouldn't do to leave him where Jonathan would find him when he stabled his horse. His feet slithered on the rungs and she had to keep behind him to make sure he didn't fall. When he got to the top he spoke fearfully.

'Promise you won't tell my father. He'd half-kill me.'

'Reckon that's what you need. There's a lot of things I could be telling your father.'

He hiccoughed and staggered to his bed where he flopped down with such force the sagging springs of the old mattress dragged against the boards. He covered his face with his hands.

'I used to be so proud of my father,' he babbled. 'When he was a soldier and he came home on leave all the boys envied me. He looked right smart in 'is uniform and he'd take me out and give me a good time. Then he'd disappear back to his regiment and it was maybe a couple of years before I'd see him again.' His eyes were dull with pain. 'So I'd go off on my own. Roughed it with tramps and the like. I was taken in a workhouse once but that was worse than Aunt Ellen's. Then Pa came back for good and brought me to Nunscorn. I loved him. Reckon I'd never been so happy in my life as I was then. But he didn't want me, 'cept to work. Nobody's ever wanted me.'

'Surely that ain't true.'

'All he could see was Susan Welby. And her not more'n two years older than myself!' His mouth hardened and he clenched his fists. 'She was more artful than an organ-grinder's monkey but he couldn't see it. She wanted Pa, but she didn't want me, so she kept making out I was trouble. The day Pa married her I left home again. Better company on the roads than in a house where she was.'

She let him ramble on and tried to find pity for him, but none would come. He was a lonely youth who hid a load of unhappiness and insecurity behind that brash exterior, but he didn't deserve anything from her after what he'd done. A bat, fresh from hibernation, emerged from the rafters and glided slowly towards the narrow window. It made a faint, high-pitched noise, and without any hesitation it flew out into the dusk through a broken pane, guided only by reflected sounds. Hannah had no fear of bats. They were creatures of instinct.

Shem was breathing through his mouth and alcohol fumes drifted towards her.

'Get into bed,' she said. She pulled the blanket over him and was about to leave when he caught her hand in an unexpectedly firm grasp.

'Love me, Hannah,' he begged. He stared up at her pathetically, pleading with her. 'I want somebody to love me.'

'Love *you*?' she scoffed. 'I'd see you dead first, that I would.'

She descended the ladder and closed her ears and her heart to the sound of his crying.

Chapter Eleven

Hannah was refused time off to visit Emily. Elijah Springly had become wealthy by exacting the most out of everyone he employed, and it being midsummer she was told she couldn't be spared for a whole day.

Two more weeks went by. She was quite sure now that she was pregnant, but the time had passed when she could speak of it to her mother. So Hannah began to plan how she could leave Nunscorn. The best thing would be to pose as a widow somewhere where she wasn't known, but she would need money and she'd rashly given it all to Ben. There was nowhere she could turn for help. Had there been no doubt it was Shem's child she would have been praying for a miscarriage, but she had the strongest feeling that the baby was Ben's, and for that reason she had to protect it.

The situation affected the way she thought about Ben. It seemed like half a lifetime since she had watched him set off for America, and the love she had declared then was now a confused mixture of emotions. Her memories of their loving should have been very precious, but Shem had robbed her of them. In her darkest moments she doubted if Ben would come back, even though he'd promised. Perhaps it would be for the best. She was desperately unhappy, without hope and unsure of everything.

There were two bedrooms in the cottage. The main one was at the top of the stairs where Jonathan slept in a four-poster bed that had been left to his late wife by her aunt. The other led off from it at the back and Hannah and Lilianne shared it with Clemmy, who slept in a basketwork cot she was fast outgrowing. It meant that they had to go to bed before Jonathan. If he retired early they would lie silent on the lumpy mattress, but when he was late they were able to talk in whispers.

On one such night Hannah could no longer stand the worry which was robbing her of both sleep and appetite. She had to risk everything in an effort to get away.

130

'You're happy here, ain't you, Ma?' she said.

She had been so concerned with her own problems that she'd scarcely looked at her mother recently. Suddenly it seemed as if Lilianne had shed several years. She looked like a girl with her hair loose, and it was extraordinary how well she had adapted to the move from home, blossoming in spite of all the hard work she did. There was a bright moon and it caused tree shadows to dance over the whitewashed bedroom walls. Hannah stood in a pool of light and stripped off her skirt and blouse.

'Yes, I'm very happy,' said Ma. She was already in bed, sitting with her knees drawn up and her arms encircling them. 'And so should *you* be. I never thought we could be so lucky after all that happened.'

'It suits you. It don't suit me. I ain't happy one bit and I want to leave.'

'Are you mad, girl? There's plenty as would give their eye teeth to have work and a home like you've got. What brought this on?'

'I've never liked it here.'

Ma gave a long sigh. 'Blow out the candle and get into bed. It's time we talked. Now, tell me what's worrying you. Something's on yer mind, I know it.'

'I just want to get away.'

Lilianne was silent for several seconds. Moonlight shone on her face, showing a tightening of the muscles. Then she challenged her daughter. 'You're expecting Ben Rutherford's child, ain't that so?'

'No, Ma.' Hannah denied it on impulse. Her mouth was dry and her heart was beating so fast she felt dizzy.

'You can't hide it from me,' Ma said. 'I've borne eight children and I know the earliest symptoms. You and I live too close for there to be secrets.' Clemmy stirred and gave a small whimper, but she didn't wake up. Ma leaned over to the cot and tucked the cover round her more securely. 'I've had me suspicions. A baby's a precious thing, a gift from God. But only if it's born in wedlock.'

'I know that.'

'Did you lie with Ben that last night before he left?'

Hannah began to weep, her body shaking. Surprisingly Ma reached out and drew her into the bed. After a moment she caressed her thick honey-coloured hair which spread out like a shawl across the cover and looked silver in the moonlight. She stroked her

131

temple, then leaned over and kissed her cheek which was wet with tears.

Then: 'Hush now. If it'll make you feel better I'll tell you something I've never spoke of before. I *had* to marry your father. I was carrying Luke at the time and we got wed quick, but I never regretted it. I came to love him, see. Maybe we can work something out for you.'

'But Luke was Pa's child.'

'Oh, he was that all right. Never a cause to doubt it.'

'Then it ain't the same. I can't marry Ben, and I sure ain't getting wed to anyone else.'

There was the sound of a horse outside. The blacksmith was coming home, but neither of them heard.

Ma gripped her daughter's shoulders. 'There's only me knows the truth and I'll have no trouble keeping it to myself. All that matters is to get you hitched to Shem as quick as possible.' She smiled, and her tone became surprisingly warm. 'It won't be a bad thing, you marrying Shem. Reckon it'll bond us all together, the Jerrams and the Whitfields. We'll be family and no one can say another word against us being here.'

'No.' Hannah snatched up her skirt and pulled it on again. 'I hate him. He's cruel. I know what he's really like and I ain't staying under this roof another night.'

The stairs creaked beneath Jonathan's heavy tread.

Her mother jumped out of bed and tried to stop her. 'You're lying, you ungrateful mawther.'

'I'm speaking the truth and if you loved me you'd believe me.' She wrenched herself free and backed towards the door which was black with repeated coats of varnish. 'Likely it's Shem Whitfield's baby I'm expecting. He raped me. Would I lie about a thing like that? He raped me, Ma, and I tried to tell you but you were always too busy to listen.'

Lilianne's face lost all its colour and she sank down again on the edge of the bed, pulling her nightgown close round her throat.

'Take care, Hannah. That's a terrible accusation to make. Are you sure you ain't covering up yer own waywardness?'

'He raped me. I've never been more sure of anything.'

The door opened and Jonathan came through to the room with the sloping ceiling behind his own. His powerful body looked ag-

132

gressive in the confined space and Hannah tensed with fear. He was too tall to stand straight and with his head bent the greying beard touched the top button of his blue shirt, covering his thick neck like a mat. The black eyebrows twisted towards each other as he scowled at first one woman and then the other.

'Mr Whitfield . . .' Lilianne began, nervously.

'I heard what was said.' He was not near enough to the window for the moon to illuminate his features, but no light was needed for Hannah to be aware of the intensity of his eyes. 'We will all go downstairs and I'll call my son. Seems we have a serious matter to discuss.' The blacksmith left, grunting as he banged his head against the low lintel.

'Now see what you've done,' hissed Ma.

Ten minutes later Hannah, Lilianne, Jonathan and Shem were together in the parlour, a sure indication of the seriousness of the situation since the meeting was not being held in the kitchen. No one sat down. Hannah stood very straight, her chin lifted high and hands clasped loosely in front of her so that the Whitfields wouldn't think she had any reason to take back what she had said. Shem had been drinking again but apart from a slight stagger when he first came in there was nothing to signify that he might be incapable of defending himself. It was obvious that he had no idea why his father had dragged him indoors and he looked hard at Hannah. She shuddered. Her stomach felt queasy and she prayed the outcome wouldn't mean dismissal for Ma. This job meant so much to her.

'Now,' said Jonathan. His clenched hands rested on the polished mahogany table; a lamp was lit and positioned in the middle of it so that the light shone equally on all four faces. 'There's been an accusation made against my son and there ain't nobody going to bed tonight until the truth of it's admitted. Seems Hannah's with child and she says it's yours, son. What've you to say?'

'It's a lie,' cried Shem. 'Likely she's lying to shield someone else.'

Hannah didn't hesitate. 'Your son raped me, Mr Whitfield, and now I'm expecting a baby.'

'Don't listen to her, Pa.'

Lilianne moved closer to Hannah. 'I ain't ever known my girl to be untruthful.'

'Did you touch her, Shem?'

Shem remained defiant, tilting his head so that his eyes glittered in the flickering glow. 'What if I did, Pa? She was more than willing so don't let her fool you into thinking otherwise.'

'That's a wicked lie,' cried Hannah. 'You did nothing but plague me and it hurt yer pride that I wanted nothing to do with you.' She faced him boldly. 'But if you don't want it known about the baby I'm willing to go away, providing I have enough money.'

They all began talking at once, shouting back and forth across the table until Jonathan thumped it with his fist. The lamp shook and a thin column of smoke spiralled up to the ceiling, giving off fumes which stung their noses.

'Enough!' he commanded. There was a fierceness about him to cause a quaking in the stoutest heart, and as his eyes rested on each one in turn they challenged anyone to deceive him. He turned to Hannah. 'Will you swear on the Bible it was rape?'

'Ain't no other word for it, sir.'

'And where and when did it take place?'

'By the bridge over the river between Nunscorn and Five Elms six weeks ago. I was walking through the meadow home one evening. Shem came after me and I couldn't get away.' She spoke with courage but she was shaking, and her mother held her arm.

Jonathan Whitfield took a deep breath, letting it back with a noise through his nostrils like an angry bull.

'I believe you,' he said.

'You bloody traitor!' yelled Shem. He was trembling with anger. 'I'm your son, Pa. Why don't you believe *me*? Why do you never put me first?'

'I believe Hannah because I know she spoke the truth.' Jonathan caught the hand which would have struck him and held his son in an iron grip with his arm above his head. 'There was a witness to what you did, bor. I was told about it, but I tried to pretend the old man had exaggerated. I didn't want to know what you are.' He flung the boy from him and didn't try to halt him when he made for the door. Then he addressed Lilianne. 'Seems like neither of us should object to our children being wed, Mrs Jerram. For my part I'm glad Shem will have a sensible, hard-working girl for a wife who'll likely be a good influence on him. Tomorrow I'll see Reverend Mitchell and arrange for the sybbits to be called next Sunday. Goodnight to you all.'

Jonathan Whitfield strode away, having settled the matter to his satisfaction.

Marriage. To Shem. It wasn't what she wanted at all and panic took hold of her. She threw her arms around her mother in desperation, gulping back sobs. She was trapped. And she was afraid.

'I can't go through with it, Ma. I'd rather die than marry Shem Whitfield.'

Lilianne kissed her temple and tucked strands of long golden hair behind her ear. 'Hush now, it won't be all that bad. Maybe the boy did something wrong and hurt you once, but he won't do it any more. There's a real nice side to him and likely he'll make you a good husband.'

'I'll never let him touch me again.'

'Reckon you will.' Ma lifted her daughter's head and looked shrewdly into her eyes. 'Just be grateful Shem'll be a father to the baby you're expecting. Some girls ain't so lucky.'

Chapter Twelve

Mrs Girling came to Nunscorn again the second Sunday evening in July, a few days before the wedding of Hannah and Shem was to take place.

A riot of dog-roses covered the hedgerows with a pink and white mantle and their scent drifted through the lanes and over the hay-fields, but the weather had turned blustery. Petals were scattering in the wind, rising on currents of air and then settling like snow-flakes on the heads of church-goers who intended to sit dutifully in the hard pews listening to the Reverend Mitchell expound loud and long on the outcome of sin. But whatever sermon he had prepared was destined to remain unsaid until another occasion. His congregation was waylaid at the church hall by the woman who had stirred them with her preaching three months earlier.

Lilianne was late, having had to wait for the girl across the green to take Clemmy for an hour or two while she and Hannah went together to hear the banns read. She would have liked Shem to come too but he had refused adamantly. Nunscorn had no chapel. The nearest was in a village five miles away and as that was on a circuit there was no knowing which Minister would be preaching each Sunday, so she had reluctantly joined the Reverend Mitchell's congregation. She heard the clamour of voices before reaching the hall and her heart swelled. She guessed who was causing the disturbance and a feeling of exultation made her urge Hannah to hurry.

'Praise be, the woman's here. Quickly, we mustn't miss a word.'

Hannah hung back. 'I ain't that keen. Reckon I'll go on home.'

'You'll do no such thing. Mrs Girling's a marvel and we're privileged she's come.'

Things were going well for Lilianne and she felt as if the Lord was smiling on her at last. Shem Whitfield had grudgingly abided by his father's order to marry her daughter and since the night when everything had come into the open he had been making an effort to please Hannah, although the girl had yet to respond. Offers of help with food came daily, likely no one wanting to miss out on the celebrations, and Lilianne gratefully accepted. As she had foreseen, her status in the Whitfield household no longer seemed to cause gossip and she did all she could to make Jonathan feel it was going to be a joyous, family occasion.

Her feelings for Jonathan were hard to hide. They deepened every day and she was busily sowing seeds which she hoped would bear fruit once the children were married and out of the way. There wouldn't be room for Shem and Hannah to live in the cottage so the upper part of the stable was being made bigger to accommodate bits and pieces of furniture they were being given. Not that Lilianne anticipated occupying the back bedroom alone for long once Hannah had left. She hoped to be able to move into the four-poster bed with Jonathan when she had persuaded him that marriage between their families was a wonderful thing and shouldn't be confined only to the young ones. A double wedding would have been ideal, but she couldn't overstep the mark and she was mindful that Jonathan had only recently become a widower. All she needed was patience.

The raised voices coming from the church hall were heated. Lilianne hurried inside and saw William Mitchell standing on a platform, his face red and arms waving as he objected to the presence of Mrs Girling and her few followers.

'I will not have this blasphemous woman airing her views in my parish,' he was shouting. 'Get out of here, madam, and don't come back.'

'Aye, you ain't welcome,' said a man in a shepherd's smock.

Another shook a fist at her. 'I ain't forgot last time you came. Nigh on ruined my marriage you did with talk of celibacy and I had to beat me wife into seeing sense.'

They were all farm labourers, angry men giving vent to feelings on a subject Lilianne hadn't heard discussed, since she hadn't been in Nunscorn the first time Mrs Girling came. She couldn't understand why they were all so passionate, why they were all condemning her when before she had attracted such enthusiastic crowds.

'Come away, Ma,' urged Hannah. 'I don't like the sound of it.'

'That I won't,' said Lilianne. 'My place is beside her.'

The tall woman in purple merino was unmoved. She stood with her hands folded and a smile on her wide mouth. Her eyes flashed.

137

'What're you all afraid of?' she asked. 'Brothers, if you've been following what I said then you're on yer way to being sinless and there ain't no better state than that. You're ready for the return of our Saviour, and He's coming sooner than you think.'

Lilianne tried to get to her but the tight gathering of men formed an impenetrable barrier. The few who wanted to hear her preach again tried to cry them down. A scuffle broke out and blows were exchanged. The shouting increased.

'Stop!' cried the Reverend Mitchell. 'I won't have trouble here like there's been in Stratford and St Andrew's.'

'I've not caused the trouble,' shouted Mrs Girling. 'It's them as won't listen to the truth that disturb a peaceful meeting for the others.'

'Only last May you were brought before the magistrate for causing a disturbance at the Lecture Hall in Woodbridge. You can't deny it.'

'I don't deny I was taken to court. But it won't stop me preaching the Word.'

'Well, you can't preach here. Be on your way, woman.'

Lilianne at last managed to reach her. 'Come with me,' she urged, pulling Mrs Girling's skirt. 'You can hold a meeting in our parlour. It ain't very big but it's peaceful.'

'Ma, she can't.' Hannah was aghast. 'The house ain't ours to offer.'

'It's what the late Mrs Whitfield would want.'

'Sister, you put these feeble men to shame. Your goodness will be recorded in the Great Book, never fear. Thank you, I accept your invitation.' The woman stretched out her arms as if she were Moses about to part the waves, and a path was made for her. 'Come, all you who genuinely seek the Lord.'

A small procession left the church hall and set off down the lane to the blacksmith's cottage, to the accompaniment of jeers and ridicule; others would have followed to continue the baiting if William Mitchell hadn't pleaded with them to have nothing more to do with it.

'I remember you,' Mrs Girling said, as they walked along. 'You were living in Seggenham and your son was injured from a fall. Tell me what's been happening to you.'

Lilianne Jerram was flattered, and she spoke joyfully of the changes in her life. 'I owe it all to you,' she said. 'You made my faith strong. I can never thank you enough.'

'Like I always say, it's God you should be thanking. I'm only His messenger.' She touched Lilianne's arm and a strange warmth seemed to penetrate the cotton sleeve. 'Call me sister. We all belong to the family of Christ.'

'It'll be a privilege, ma'am.'

Jonathan was out. He had left home early that morning to deliver and fit the hinges Timothy Berger had ordered ten weeks earlier, and he intended to call at Seggenham Manor to make sure Emily would have time off to attend her sister's wedding which was to take place on Wednesday. He'd set out in the best of moods with his rifle strapped across his back, and he'd promised not to return without a hare for the pot tomorrow, so it wasn't likely he would be back for an hour or two yet. Lilianne opened the door and a dozen people trooped into Susan Whitfield's cluttered parlour, including the man with the squeeze-box and a young peasant woman in a shabby dress who had also become a regular follower. There was hardly room to move, but Mary Ann Girling wasted no time getting started and those who couldn't get near had to listen from the kitchen.

'First let's sing a hymn and say a prayer of thanksgiving. Let's raise our voices.'

The music started and at once the cottage was filled with cheerful sound, Mary Ann Girling's voice above all the others, and when she lifted her arms and started the now familiar rhythmic swaying most of those present did the same. Lilianne was entranced. She moved ecstatically, and she was filled with the strange sensation of belonging in mind and body to this powerful woman who could attract people with a single stare from her piercing eyes. There was no holding back.

After the prayer, which was fiery and down-to-earth, she stood on a footstool and towered above everyone.

'Children of God,' she addressed them. 'Since you've had courage to go against the general opinion and you've joined me here I reckon I can speak to you freely of the great divine mission I've been called to give my life to. When I've finished I hope you'll want to stay with me and take up Christ's banner.' She paused and plucked a vase from the mantelpiece, holding it aloft for all to see.

139

'There ain't no need for useless things in our lives. This pretty bit of china ain't useful for anything except for putting flowers in, and flowers look better growing. If I were to drop it, it would break. I tell you, we should all be storing up our treasures in Heaven what'll last forever.'

'How do we do that?' someone asked.

'By sharing everything and living together as brothers and sisters with love in our hearts.'

'Surely that ain't possible.'

Mrs Girling drew the peasant girl and the man with the squeeze-box close to her. 'These two dear people have joined me. Harry Bourne and Miriam Rawlings here have given up their homes and families to follow me and we don't call anything our own. And there are others even now selling up what they've got so they can share in our spiritual joy and live the way Our Lord intends we should, serving Him first, and then each other.'

'Where be your home, then?' asked the wheelwright, who was the most sceptical of the gathering.

'My home, brother, is in Christ Jesus, but I take my body to Victoria Street, Ipswich for the present, until there are enough of us to form a community of our own. That's why I'm asking who'll join me.' There was no immediate reaction, so she leaned forward and stretched out her arms, and when she spoke again her voice was even more persuasive. 'The disciples followed our Lord without question, and they never regretted it. Now I'm asking you, in His name, to follow me and serve that same Lord. *You* won't regret it neither.'

Lilianne looked round the parlour at all Susan Whitfield's knick-knacks and the nice furniture that she had begun to enjoy using. It would be a mite hard, but she reckoned she could live without any of these things. She'd given up everything when she left Seggenham and not minded too much, so it would be easy to leave here and share the few bits and pieces she still owned with Mrs Girling. The thought caused a great upsurge of feeling and she drew herself tall with spontaneous joy. The woman had such strength of character, such sureness of purpose, and she could inspire the same kind of dedication in others. Look at her now. She was like a light in the dim room, her eyes burning with the conviction that she spoke with holy authority. Yes, Lilianne would gladly share her possessions, but she couldn't leave Jonathan.

'No disrespect, ma'am, but how is it you're privileged to know so much about the Lord?' she dared to ask.

'Aye, that's right,' agreed the wheelwright.

Mary Ann Girling was silent for several seconds and Lilianne was afraid she had offended her. But even in silence she held them captive. It was as if no one dared to breathe. She looked at each person in turn until every pair of eyes had met hers, and the only sound in the room was the laboured ticking of the grandfather clock in the corner. An illusion of things ethereal seemed to fill the air.

'Jesus spoke in parables,' she said. The preaching tone was replaced by confidentiality and the change signalled revelations none had dreamed of hearing. 'He spoke in parables because the world wasn't able to understand the truth if He told it any other way. And so it's been with me. But I reckon you're all ready for what I'm going to tell you.' She paused. Then: 'I am the Second Coming of the Messiah. My body contains the celestial life which comes from God in Heaven. Jesus came in the form of a man, but He was both male and female. His body has been in Heaven since He ascended, the God-father and the God-mother, but now is the time for the mother part to come in flesh and blood. It pleased Jesus to take my body to be the earthly habitation for the celestial God-mother to dwell in, that I might live as He lived himself, his bride. I bear the marks of His crucified body to prove I am the same Jesus. The Lord waits for His bride to be accepted on earth.'

She waited, but no one questioned her. Lilianne's mouth was dry and she couldn't swallow.

'*You* are Jesus?' someone said, with awe.

'I am His second appearing, the bride, the Lamb's wife, and there won't be another.'

There was a moment of stunned quietness in which the reaction of the group could be felt strongly. Then a wave of contention swept through the room like a river bore washing over them and drawing them into fierce argument.

'That's blasphemy!' cried the wheelwright. 'That's downright blasphemy and I won't listen to no more.'

But Lilianne Jerram believed.

Hannah was horrified at her mother's involvement with Mrs Girling. She couldn't believe she really intended taking her to Jonathan's

141

house and she stared, wide-eyed, as the little procession set off towards the forge. There was no hesitancy. Ma was intent on providing accommodation for those who saw the Girling woman as some kind of new apostle, and was blind to propriety. Hannah was torn between loyalty to her mother and her aversion to the woman. She looked around. Surprise was equally evident in those who had been loud in their abuse.

'Ring the church bell,' said the Reverend Mitchell. 'Pull hard on the rope so the village will know we have no time for the woman, or anyone foolish enough to listen to her.'

The people who were left filed into church behind the vicar like docile lambs, but Hannah fled.

Shem would be at the Plough and Plover. She dreaded seeking him out but he was the one who must break up the extraordinary meeting in the cottage before his father came home. The late Susan Whitfield might have approved, but she felt sure Jonathan would not. Sweat collected under her hair and trickled down her back as she ran, making an ugly wet stain on her blouse. She was afraid Shem would refuse to be prised away from his ale, but it was early yet and he wouldn't have downed enough to make him belligerent. An inward shuddering started up at the thought of having to approach him.

Since the banns for their wedding had been called there was a difference in public attitude towards Shem Whitfield. He had become respectable, though whether he would remain so after the celebrations would depend on how he conducted himself once he had a wife. Food and drink at the blacksmith's expense were not to be missed, so much could be temporarily forgiven, but Hannah could neither forgive nor forget for a single second. She hated him with such intensity it frightened her, and nothing would ever change the way she felt.

She reached the door of the inn and had to lean against the wall to recover her breath. The window was open. Men were grouped round the fire which glowed red with wood shavings even though it was summer, and the heat shimmered. Through the haze she saw Shem, a clay pipe in his mouth, tankard in his hand, and she could hear his bragging voice quite clearly.

'Three more days and she'll be me wife. Reckon we'll make a handsome pair an' all.'

'Pity she never smiles,' an old man said. 'She don't look over happy to be marrying you.'

'She'll soon know how lucky she is,' Shem boasted.

Her hands slid down over her breast to her stomach where the child nestled. She knew in her heart that it didn't come from Shem Whitfield's seed, and for all his boasting he was a fool. He was going to give his name to a child that likely was not his, and he would have to support it until it was grown. The years stretched bleakly ahead and she felt ill at the prospect of sharing them with a man she detested. For the child's sake she must learn to live again, but nothing would ever blot out the searing memory of Shem raping her.

The dizziness passed and she went boldly inside the Plough and Plover for the first time, catching her breath as a surge of smoke stung her nose. All eyes turned to her.

'Three days to the wedding and already she's come to check on you, bor,' the landlord said with a laugh.

Shem rose from a bench and by his expression he was none too pleased to see her.

'What're you doing in here?' he demanded.

Hannah pulled his sleeve urgently. 'You've got to come, Shem. Mrs Girling's back and Ma's taken her home to hold a service at the cottage. There'll be trouble.'

'Who's Mrs Girling? Ain't never heard of her.'

'The preacher woman,' someone said.

'We've got to get her out before your father comes home.'

There were five other men in the bar and now she had their attention. All had either seen or been told about the woman.

'Gone to Jonathan Whitfield's you say? Best see to it then.' The man who spoke got to his feet.

Another wiped his hands on his breeches. 'Trouble, you reckon?' He slapped Shem on the shoulder. 'Likely you'll need help, bor. We'll come with you.'

'No, not all of you,' shouted Hannah, her fears increasing. 'Shem, I just want you to come with me to tell the woman to get out.' She dragged him by the hand, but he downed the contents of an almost full tankard before she could move him.

'Right, I'm ready,' he said at last, and strode to the door. The other men followed, and from the nine cottages opposite their womenfolk were quick to see something exciting might be afoot.

'The preacher woman's back,' one man called to his wife.

'I'll tell her what I think of *her*,' said the woman. 'No more sleeping with your husband! She must be barmy. What sort of teaching's that?'

The matter was taken out of Hannah's hands. Shem, strutting like a pheasant, led the procession down the lane to the smithy with a collection of heathens following behind, all spoiling for a fight. None, she was sure, would want to join in the form of worship peculiar to Mary Ann Girling. Likely the inside of church or chapel hadn't seen one of them since baptism.

She was in a panic. 'There's no need for all this lot to come,' she cried. 'Make them go back, Shem. Please.'

'What *do* you want, girl? First you drag me from my drinking, then you object to my friends coming with me.'

'Get rid of the woman on your own. It's *your* home she's gone to.'

As soon as they turned the corner the sound of singing could be heard. Shem stopped abruptly and his face went pale. The evening sun slanting through the chestnut leaves lit the parlour window through which strange swaying movements could be seen inside, arms lifted, bodies contorted.

'Witchcraft,' he gasped. His face was white and beads of perspiration collected on his forehead. 'I ain't going in there. Let's leave 'em to it.'

The men grouped round him, their mouths falling open, and the women clutched at coat-tails. Music from a squeezebox wailed and whined. When it stopped they picked up sticks. All but Shem.

'Where are your guts?' Hannah taunted. 'She won't hurt you.'

But Shem was trembling. 'You can if you like. I ain't going anywhere near her. Reckon with all them weird things going on in there she must be in league with the devil.'

Hannah looked round at the gawping faces, and angry impatience replaced her fears. She waited a moment and when no one moved forward any further she marched on ahead. 'I can see I shall have to do the job myself, and I don't need any of you to help me so you can all go home.'

The front door which led straight into the parlour was slightly ajar and she pushed it open wider. The woman held her audience spellbound and no one turned to see who had come in. It was the first time Hannah had seen her since the day Luke broke his leg, but she remembered her vividly. She spoke in authoritative tones and her eyes singled out each one in turn, resting just long enough for their strange, hypnotic power to be absorbed. Hannah's nerves tingled and she dare not interrupt.

Shem had followed her after all, and the others drifted nearer. It was then that Mary Ann Girling declared that she was Jesus. After that there was bedlam. The crowd from the Plough and Plover piled inside and a great argument started with voices raised and fists used to express enraged feelings. There were those who believed, and those who didn't, and a fight broke out before many minutes had passed. This was something Shem understood better.

'If you don't get out, all of you, you'll be sorry!' he cried, bellowing to make himself heard above the noise. 'My friends and me mean business.'

'Don't let him annoy you, brothers and sisters, and don't put up any resistance to these unbelievers,' said Mrs Girling. In the midst of the disturbance she stood calmly, braced to resist the buffeting from dissenters and converts jostling all around her in spite of her plea. 'We suffer persecution gladly, young man.'

Hannah struggled to reach her mother who was pinned against the back wall in the small, packed room.

'Come away, Ma. You shouldn't be mixed up in things like this.'

But nothing would persuade Ma to desert the woman she was responsible for bringing to the cottage. 'I ain't going anywhere without Mrs Girling. It's terrible them speaking to her like that. It's sacrilege, that's what it is. They don't know what they're doing.'

Shem took up a poker and stood on a chair to rally support. 'Down with heretics. Throw them out. We don't want the likes of them here.'

A china vase crashed to the floor and broke. Someone fell over a stool and another knocked a picture from the wall. The tiny parlour seethed with men and women provoked into taking sides against each other and they spilled out into the front garden. Such chaos had never been seen in Nunscorn within living memory. While the trouble was at its height the girl who had been minding Clemmy came across the green with her. And Jonathan Whitfield returned home.

145

The blacksmith stayed on his horse. 'What the hell's going on? Stop the racket this instant! Who's responsible for all this?'

Those outside backed away. He looked formidable as he towered above them, eyes fiery and greying locks flying wild from fast riding. He reached over his shoulder for the barrel of the shotgun he'd taken with him to kill hares which hung in a bag from the saddle. The horse pawed the ground in agitation at the noise and the whites of its eyes gleamed in the evening light.

'Stop, or I'll fire,' the blacksmith roared.

He was facing the doorway. He dismounted, drew the gun and cocked it ready for discharging.

'Don't be a fool, man!' someone behind him yelled. 'It's your son in there. And the preacher woman.'

'I'll put the fear of God in them,' shouted Jonathan. He pointed the gun skywards. 'I won't have fighting in my house, d'you hear.'

Hannah was nearest the door and she saw with horror what was happening. She knew, of course, that Jonathan wouldn't fire the gun, but she had to put a stop to it before someone got hurt. She rushed out and confronted him.

'What do you think you're doing, Mr Whitfield! Shame on you. Put that gun down.'

'Out of my way, girl,' said Jonathan. 'I won't have my home turned into a battleground by anyone.'

He was about to fire a shot in the air, but at that moment someone careered into Hannah and sent her thudding against Jonathan's arm. The gun went off. The sudden jerk discharged the shot through the parlour window where it narrowly missed hitting the gesticulating figure of Shem standing tall on a chair, and made a hole in the opposite wall. Screams echoed all round as he fell to the ground with shock, but he quickly picked himself up again, his face chalk-white.

The fighting stopped. Jonathan, it seemed, was more shaken than anyone. He put the gun down and went indoors, followed nervously by Hannah. All eyes were on him.

'You tried to kill me,' Shem breathed. He was trembling violently, his teeth clicking together and his lips bloodless. 'What've I ever done to you that you want to kill me?'

'Son, that just ain't so. I'd never forgive myself if anything had happened to you. I only meant to scare the lot of you.'

'You've never wanted me. No one wants me. Hannah ain't got a good word neither. You're all against me.'

Jonathan remembered his anger. 'You brought trouble to my house. Did you expect me to overlook it?'

But he was speaking to his son's back. Shem rushed past him with tears coursing down his pale cheeks and he made for the stable. 'Don't worry, you won't have to put up with me any longer.'

'Mr Whitfield, it wasn't his fault,' said Lilianne.

Jonathan didn't listen. He was busy herding the crowd out through his door with harsh words and a heavy hand. One by one they trickled away into the approaching twilight.

'Get on home,' he shouted. 'There won't be any more free entertainment tonight.'

Mrs Girling was the only one to have stayed calm throughout the disturbance, but her hawk eyes missed nothing. Harry Bourne was at her side, where he had been all along, and Lilianne didn't leave her.

'And *you*, woman, what have you got to say?' Jonathan faced her, his anger bringing high colour to his cheeks.

'I was invited here, brother, as an accepted stewardess of God, to peacefully bring the words of Christ Jesus and to sing His praises.'

'You brought fighting.'

'No, brother, I brought love. It was sinners and unbelievers who broke up our happy meeting because they're afraid of the truth.'

Hannah took Clemmy from the girl who was cowering in a corner with the child's face pressed against her shoulder in fright. Poor Clemmy. She was crying pitifully and tried to resist the move to other arms, but the girl was anxious to get away.

'Hush now,' Hannah said, rocking the little girl in her arms and smoothing the tousled head. She took her outside. 'There ain't nothing to be afraid of.' But she was saying it to convince herself as much as the child.

She disliked Mrs Girling intensely and was alarmed at the hold she had taken on Ma. Hannah was pretty sure there was nothing in the Bible to say that when Christ appeared again He would take on a woman's form. She remembered the sacred picture in Seggenham Church of Jesus talking to little children, and the man with the beautiful face and halo of light round his head bore no resemblance at all to Mrs Girling. It was all made up, a means of getting known

147

and seizing power, and Hannah had no wish to associate with such impiety. She wanted none of it.

A cricket accompanied the background voices and a toad appeared from a hole under the steps to the stable. Shem was a long time saddling his horse, if that was what he had intended doing. She ought to go in there and try to comfort him since they were soon to be man and wife, but she didn't know what to say. It was her fault there had been so much trouble. In all fairness it must have seemed as though his father had meant to harm him, and he had every right to put distance between them until the anger had cooled, but what of the wedding plans? If he left now there was no certainty that he would be back to honour the agreement they had made.

Hannah took a few steps towards the stable. Clemmy was getting heavy in her arms but she protested at any attempt to put her down and Hannah murmured soft, meaningless words to soothe her.

She hoped Shem would leave for good. Over the last three weeks she had grown more confident and less afraid of him as she realised just how weak he was underneath. He hadn't attempted to talk his way out of marriage or tried to take privileges prior to the ceremony, but his better behaviour had done nothing to improve her opinion of him. Yes, she prayed he had gone for good.

Clemmy's sobs stopped, sleep making her head loll weightily, and Hannah hovered a moment longer to compose herself and prepare suitable words of comfort for Shem. The evening had settled into tranquility after the storm and not a breath of wind disturbed the leaves of the chestnut tree. Even the voices behind her in the cottage had ceased. Into that peaceful stillness came a squeaking sound, high-pitched and regular, as if a child was playing on a swing inside the stable. Back and forth. Back and forth.

Hannah lifted her skirt with her free hand and hurried towards the sound, drawn to it by a sudden, unreasonable fear of something unknown. It was almost dark within the old walls, but Shem hadn't lit the lantern. His body was hanging from a rope suspended from a beam across the roof and it was still swinging gently to and fro, lifeless and grotesque in the dim light.

Though Hannah's screams rent the air they would never awaken the dead.

Chapter Thirteen

Word of Shem Whitfield's suicide spread like fire through a timber yard, and those who had been fighting earlier returned to the smithy that same night to express deep feelings, few of them charitable. One or two knocked on the door to give sympathy, but Jonathan Whitfield bawled at them all.

'Clear off! Leave me in peace, can't you. Ain't you seen enough!'

The majority gathered round the stable to stand and stare with morbid curiosity, and they remembered the shot Jonathan had fired. There was a shattered pane in the parlour window to bear witness to the fact that it had almost been murder. A chanting started up and increased in volume as people aired their disapproval, urging him to leave before anything else bad happened in the village. Suddenly they were blaming him for the death of poor little Susan Welby who'd been too well brought up for the likes of a blacksmith old enough to be her father. There'd been nought but trouble since he'd come to Nunscorn.

When there was no more response they gradually wandered away and night descended like a cloak to cover the smithy's cottage where Jonathan was alone with the body of his son. He had banished everyone else, including his housekeeper and her daughter. Mrs Girling, the woman at the root of the trouble, had tried to provide reasons for the tragedy which had triggered his anger to the point of dementia, but before he'd got rid of her she had prayed for Shem's soul with real sincerity, which was more than the Reverend Mitchell had done shortly afterwards.

'The boy took his own life and that's sinful,' the vicar told the grieving father. 'He can't be interred amongst decent folk.'

'What right have you to forbid my son a peaceful resting place?' Jonathan demanded. '*I* killed him as sure as if I'd aimed at his heart. I should have seen he wasn't happy and given him more of my time. It's me who should be buried outside the graveyard wall. Don't punish the boy further.'

'The decision isn't mine,' said Reverend Mitchell. 'Shem chose to die by his own hand and there's no way you can exonerate him. The sin is his alone.'

Jonathan was inconsolable, rejecting every attempt to pacify him. But in truth there were others who had to take a portion of the blame, and each had confessed it.

'Reckon it was me who drove him to it,' Hannah had said. 'I failed him when he needed someone, and tonight I showed him up in front of his friends.'

'I shouldn't have brought Mrs Girling here without your permission,' said Lilianne. 'It were wrong of me.'

'And I shouldn't have come, not even to worship, when you were not here to say we were welcome,' said Mary Ann Girling.

Jonathan had alternately cursed his own insensitivity and ranted at God's unfairness. Then he had voiced anger at Shem for doing such a terrible thing.

'That boy never considered anyone but himself. Never! How could he do this to me?' He had thumped his fist against his temple, then lapsed into mournful self-pity. 'He was my son. My son, d'you hear. And now he's gone and I don't know what to do.'

'Search your conscience, Brother Whitfield,' Mrs Girling had said. 'Then do what you know is right. God will help you.'

'Don't try yer preacher ways with me, woman. No one can help me.'

Jonathan had taken up the gun and made them leave, threatening and cursing the three women until they feared what he would do if they stayed.

When he was alone he went into the parlour and shut the door, taking the gun with him. He sat down in the same chair he had used only two months ago to spend a night beside Susan's coffin, and the futility of what Shem had done appalled him. It seemed like only yesterday his infant son had lain for the briefest time against the breast of the sweet girl who had given him birth.

'I always liked the story of Noah,' Maria had murmured, her voice almost too weak to hear. 'All them little creatures God wanted saved.' Even then she had been chill with the approach of death, but she had smiled at her child and kissed him. 'Let's call him Noah.'

'What sort of name's that?' Jonathan had scoffed.

'Shem then. Shem was one of Noah's sons and he survived.'

She had left this world believing that her son would live and that her husband would take good care of him. After she had gone Jonathan hadn't been able to look at the baby and he had left him to grow up among Ellen's brood. He should have been there throughout Shem's childhood, guiding and instructing him, and most of all showing him love. So many failures, he saw in retrospect. So many things he could have done differently to spare his son heartbreak. Now it was too late.

There was a wound round the boy's throat where the rope had cut into it. He looked so young lying there, a youth who had put an end to his life just when it was starting, and it was such a cruel waste. Jonathan wept as he looked down at the still figure and his regrets weighed so heavily he would have given anything to change places with him.

The gun at his side was loaded. Only one shot had been fired and there was another waiting to bring him release from a pain he could tell would never cease as long as he drew breath. He rested the barrel against the spot between his eyes where the ache was worst and his fingers caressed the trigger.

He didn't hear the door latch. Nor did he see that he was no longer alone in the room. He was cocooned in his own private agony, blinded by pain and anger and resentment. The woman stood beside him in silence until she judged the moment right to gently uncurl his fingers and take the gun from him. He didn't resist.

'We've all got regrets, Brother Whitfield, but they ain't going to solve anything unless we put them in the hands of the Lord,' said Mary Ann Girling. 'Killing yerself won't bring him back. Reckon it would do more good if we pray.'

Jonathan clenched his fists but didn't look at her. 'Pray! What's the good of praying to a God Who's taken away everyone I ever cared about. He ain't got no love for me and I ain't got none for Him. Oh, no, woman, I ain't praying. Didn't I tell you to get out of my house?'

'I've come back. We're put on this earth to help one another, and seems you need strength right now, so let's talk about what's right and what's wrong, and not take the name of the Lord in vain.'

She put a hand on his forearm and he felt a strange warmth penetrate the strong cotton of his shirtsleeve. The abuse he had been about to utter stuck in his throat, and his gaze was drawn to that work-roughened hand which touched him so lightly yet possessed a power he didn't understand, and he saw the mystic white mark, like a scar left after a nail had been driven between the bones.

'There's a lot of things for you to do yet in this life, brother. Don't let the devil rule you, but trust in the Lord Jesus. He's healing you already, I can feel it.'

Her hand moved up to his head and rested on the thick mass of grey-black hair until the roots tingled with renewed life. He closed his eyes as an extraordinary heat made him burn inside, and his temper withered away.

'Aye, I can feel it an' all,' he said.

'Now repent, Brother Jonathan, and you'll be forgiven.'

He pushed her from him. 'It ain't up to you to say whether I'll be forgiven or not.'

'Tell the Lord you repent of your sins. Say it, brother. Say it out loud and mean it.'

But he couldn't. He raked his fingers through his hair, and there were furrows across his brow deep enough to plant as he scowled at his tormentor.

'There ain't nothing for me to live for. Why didn't you let me do what I wanted without interfering.'

She didn't touch him, yet he was aware even more of a spiritual force emanating from her.

'Have you forgotten the Jerram girl?' she asked. 'Her Ma told me she was to have been wed on Tuesday. She's expecting Shem's child. Now ain't that enough to make you stop and realise there are people who need you? And what of your daughter – had you forgotten her? Repent, Jonathan Whitfield, and the Lord will help you, take my word for it. I'll pray for you mightily till you're able to do it for yourself.'

She was the most remarkable woman he had ever met. He remembered the ecstasy in her face when he had seen her dancing, the way it had changed her from plain to radiant, and the good in her was so potent he could feel it warming him once more.

He clasped his hands together and said: 'Oh, Lord, I do repent of my sins.'

After he had said it there was an eerie silence in the parlour, as if the dead and the living were waiting together for a sign. But though none came Jonathan felt the blackness giving way to light in his mind and he breathed easier.

Mrs Girling spoke quietly. 'There are many ways the Lord calls us to service. You've a lot of talent that could be put to good use. Think on it, brother. If ever you've a mind to follow me you'd be bringing practical help to God's Children. Perhaps what's befallen you this night will bring you to serve the Lord. I pray so.'

He stayed in the parlour until the sky showed the first flush of dawn, long after the woman had gone, and he heard Lilianne and Hannah creep back indoors and upstairs to bed. By morning he had searched his conscience and knew exactly what he had to do.

Hannah didn't want to go to work on Monday morning. She felt ill and said she was quite unable to walk to Springly's, but Lilianne made light of it.

'If you don't go you'll lose your job,' she said. 'Pull yourself together, girl, and act normal. There ain't nothing can be done here.'

'Reckon I'll lose my job anyway. I can't see Mr Whitfield letting us stay after what's happened.'

'He'll need us all the more. We've got to help him. It wouldn't be right for him to be on his own.'

A terrible gloom hung over everywhere. The weather had turned dull and there was rain in the air which made the windows damp. Lilianne had covered the broken one with a piece of wood, and the parlour door was firmly closed so that Shem could rest in solitude. Not that anyone would want to go in. There wasn't likely to be any caller anxious to pay last respects to a young man who had taken his own life.

Jonathan's bed hadn't been slept in and he had left the house at first light without saying where he was going or when he would be back. She knew he had been in the parlour all night and she had longed to bring him out, but he had a right to privacy and he would have resented the intrusion. She'd thought there would be a chance to talk to him this morning once they were alone and she had planned words of comfort, but he hadn't even waited for any food before setting off.

After Hannah had left Lilianne was alone with Clemmy and it was difficult to have patience with a small child when once again life was dealing out a bitter blow. She had sounded confident when she had said Jonathan would still want them, but there was no knowing what the blacksmith would do in the face of last night's tragedy. In all probability they would be homeless again before long, and with Hannah expecting it wouldn't be so easy to find fresh work.

She paced up and down with Clemmy dragging at her skirt, idle for the first time since she had come here to live. 'Yer father should have told me where he was going,' she said, and Clemmy whimpered, sensing the day was all wrong.

But Jonathan didn't have to tell her anything. She didn't have any hold on him. She couldn't break through that great lonely pride which isolated him, and she was no nearer knowing his thoughts than on the day they had met. Yet she loved him.

Tears could no longer be held in check as she dwelt on the trouble she had brought to his house. She had invited Mrs Girling here impetuously and without a qualm, mesmerised by the woman's words. Shem's suicide had detracted nothing from the strength of her faith in Mary Ann Girling, but she bitterly regretted having allowed a meeting to take place in Jonathan's parlour. If she hadn't done that, maybe Shem would have been alive now.

The shadows were long across the yard when Jonathan came home. The horse clopped through puddles left by rain which had now cleared, and when Clemmy ran across the cobbles to greet him he scooped her into his arms, holding her against his chest with an unusual ferocity which made her cry. There was rabbit stew on the stove. Usually he lifted the lid and took an appreciative sniff at his supper, but today he walked past the pot and went straight into the parlour without a word, closing the door behind him. He remained there so long Lilianne was afraid the supper would spoil, and she hovered near, not knowing what to do. When he came out his face was granite hard.

'I've sold everything to buy peace for my son,' he said. 'There'll be no proper funeral but at least he'll lie in the churchyard.'

'Sold everything,' Lilianne echoed, shivering. Seemed like her worst fears were coming true.

'I needed the money so I sold my inheritance.' He pushed away the plate of supper she had put in front of him. 'The Reverend Mitchell was a hard man to bribe but he had his price same as everyone else. When it's dark I'll be getting help to take the coffin to the cemetery.'

'But did you have to sell everything? What will you do? Where will you go?'

154

'Move on. There ain't no way I could stay here.' The lines on his face were etched deeper than yesterday, and his drawn expression was matched by the harsh timbre of his voice. 'Likely I'll not rest easy, Mrs Jerram, until I'm in the grave myself, and maybe not even then. I kill the people I love, you see.'

She crumpled her apron with agitated fingers and pressed one corner up to her mouth to stop her lips trembling. 'Don't speak like that, Mr Whitfield. Don't even think it. It's wicked to slander yourself and it hurts the people who care about you.'

'There ain't no one cares about me.'

'*I* care about you.' Her hands itched to reach out and caress him, but she feared his reaction. She wanted to draw his great shaggy head against her breast and ease away the remorse that was eating into him like a canker. 'And what about Clemmy? What about about my daughter and Shem's child she's expecting? What about me? May the good Lord forgive you if you desert us all.'

He lifted his head and looked at her keenly. Something in those dark eyes made her quiver with sudden expectation. Perhaps the hopes she had secretly cherished were about to be fulfilled. She returned his gaze unashamedly.

'I know my responsibilities, Mrs Jerram,' he said. 'And you can be sure I'll not walk out on them.'

Chapter Fourteen

No one had thought to send word to Emily Jerram that there would be no wedding on the Tuesday after all, so she was given some hours off for the first time since she had been working at Seggen-ham Manor. The bailiff, Joseph Nelson, had business in Wickham Market and when he heard she was going to Nunscorn he offered to take her part of the way in the gig. He hitched it early and she settled herself next to him on the seat, aching with longing to see her mother and sister again.

Emily had become very thin. Her bones were too prominent, forming hollows at the base of her neck and from cheek to jaw, and her eyes seemed too large for her wan little face. Consequently her energy dwindled. Cook tried to make her eat more, but Emily had no appetite. She worked from dawn till dark helping to prepare enormous meals for the Keans, then having to clear up afterwards, and the sight of food sickened her. Yet as soon as she was on the road that morning she began to feel hungry just thinking of Ma's cooking.

'It's very kind of you to give me a lift, Mr Nelson,' she said, as they bowled along. 'I'm really grateful.'

The man grunted. 'By the looks of you I don't reckon you'd have made it to Nunscorn on foot.' There was a bluff kindness about him. He'd been keeping an eye on the waif-like girl since the Squire had taken unnecessarily harsh revenge on the Jerrrams. Poor, innocent little creature. It'd been like uprooting a poppy from a cornfield and expecting it to survive in a hothouse. He'd watched her wilt and it saddened him. 'Reckon it'll do you good to see yer ma.'

'Oh, yes.' Emily's eyes shone. 'I've missed her so much.'

She loved travelling in the gig. From her high seat she could see into fields where the hay was being cut and the smell of it brought memories of summer days last year when Luke and Ben had been out with the scythes. In silence they drove alongside a dyke edged with charlock and mallow. The hogweed had buds waiting to burst at the top of stiff, straight stalks, and dog-roses were running riot over the hedgerows, the first delicate pink and white flowers opening in the sun. A slight breeze sent their faint perfume wafting towards her. She hadn't realised how much she needed to be outdoors instead of shut away in a hot kitchen all day.

'Tell you what,' said Joseph Nelson, when the rosy rooftops of Wickham Market appeared in the distance. 'I'll take you all the way to Nunscorn and pick you up later. How's that sound?'

'Just wonderful,' said Emily. 'You're very kind to me, Mr Nelson.'

'Ain't difficult.'

The road through Wickham Market was crowded but Emily didn't mind the delay. She enjoyed seeing so many people. When they were on the open road again the air brought a bit of colour to her cheeks, and she passed the time telling Mr Nelson about the wedding.

'I'm that looking forward to it. I'll have me a brother-in-law that's right handsome, so I'm told. Ma wrote Shem Whitfield's real nice and she hopes we'll be a family again.' She paused, and a small, worried crease appeared on her smooth brow. 'Mark you, I'm surprised at Hannah deciding to get hitched so soon, but maybe it was love at first sight, and I'm glad.'

He dropped her at the edge of the village, not far from the spot where Lilianne and Hannah had first met up with the Reverend Mitchell, and he told her to be back there at four on the dot. That would give her time to join in some of the celebrations after the ceremony.

'Not a minute later than four, mind, unless you want to walk.'

'I'll be here. Thank you, Mr Nelson.'

She walked along the lane carrying a canvas bag containing a few fancy tit-bits of food Mrs Cotton had given her which Ma wouldn't be able to provide, and two pillow cases she had made and embroidered herself as a wedding present for the bride and groom. She was nervous of meeting Shem, but would try to like him if he pleased Ma. It was amazing how delighted she had been to have news of the coming marriage. She wanted Hannah's happiness of course, but more than that Emily's hopes had been raised. Someday Ben would come home, and when he found that Hannah hadn't been prepared to wait even three months before finding herself another man he would at last see which sister would make him the better wife. Emily intended to console him in ways he would find irresistible.

157

There was no sound of festivities like there would have been in Seggenham on the day of a wedding. Even though it was still early there would have been children with posies chasing from garden to garden, and women trailing back and forth like ants from their own homes to the bride's with food and flowers, laughing as they went. The air would be buzzing with excitement at the prospect of a day of celebration going on until well after dark, everyone joining in. Nunscorn was sombre and silent, and when the church clock sounded the hour it was more like a funeral toll. Emily came to the end of the lane and looked anxiously across the green. The only person she could see was an old woman leaning on her garden gate.

'I'm looking for the blacksmith's cottage,' Emily said to her.

The woman sniffed, then pointed. 'Over there, beyond the chestnut tree. What would you be wanting with him?'

'My sister's getting married to his son today. I've come for the wedding.'

She was wearing a dress of white cotton patterned with cherries, and it had pink bows to decorate the ruched hem, lifting the skirt just enough to show the petticoat underneath. It had belonged to Mrs Kean's personal maid before she got too fat for it, and Cook had made it fit by taking tucks in at the waist and lifting the shoulder seams so that the sleeves sat comfortably on her thin shoulders. The bonnet had been passed down from the coachman's wife who said it was too young for her, being made of white straw and decorated with pink ribbon and lace. It suited Emily. It framed her little pointed elfin face to perfection and showed she had a wistful beauty which wasn't noticeable when she wore her working clothes. She looked pretty enough to have been a bride herself.

The old lady's demeanour changed. She opened the gate. 'You'll not've heard then,' she said sympathetically. 'There ain't going to be a wedding. Shem Whitfield went and hanged 'imself on Sunday night after his father tried to shoot him.'

What little colour there was in Emily's face ebbed away and she grasped the fence for support. She swallowed hard and tried to ask why it had happened, but the words wouldn't come.

'Come in and sit down, miss,' the woman said.

Emily shook her head. 'I must find Hannah and Ma. Oh, this is *awful*.'

She started to run across the green towards the chestnut tree, but

158

her legs were weak with shock and she stumbled, almost falling just before she reached it. The forge door stood open but there was no light inside. The fire was dead, the hammer silent, and there were no horses to be shod. But standing in the yard at the side was a roan mare harnessed to an ancient carriage. She went across the yard to the cottage which was as dark and mournful-looking as the forge. Raised voices could be heard inside.

Emily knocked loudly on the door and the shouting stopped. Hannah came. She was dressed in black and her hair was knotted at the crown of her head, drawing the skin tight at her temples. Signs of recent weeping could be seen in her eyes, the lids blue-tinged and puffy, dark rings beneath them. She stared at Emily, almost as if she didn't instantly recognise her, and then she gave a cry and stretched out her arms.

'Oh, Emily, I'm so glad to see you. So glad, so glad!'

Ma came rushing. 'I'd forgotten you were coming. Sweet mawther, how could I have done that?'

'I've just heard there ain't going to be a wedding,' said Emily, trying to embrace her mother and sister both at the same time.

They babbled incoherently, kissing and crying and not making sense. Ma drew her inside. The kitchen was hot and flies buzzed round a flitch of pork hanging from a beam. The shelf above the range was cluttered with pewter pots, a bowl of clay pipes, tobacco tins and a flatiron. A clock on the wall had a pendulum which glinted every time it swung to the left and caught the light. The hands pointed to nigh on ten o'clock. All these things Emily noticed because she didn't want to look at the big man with long greying hair and a beard who stood with his back to the window so that she couldn't see his expression. He held a child in his arms and his posture was formidable.

'They was wrong, whoever told you there ain't going to be a wedding,' the man said. He transferred the child to Ma's arms and came out of the shadows. 'Time we got ready. Go and put on yer best dress, Mrs Jerram. And you, Hannah, can wear what you would have worn for Shem.'

On Monday evening, after a day's work which had left her exhausted, Hannah took the short cut home across the meadows and the bridge by the river bank. She didn't have to be afraid any more.

Shem would never accost her again, never ride his horse in angry style or try to impress her with his masculine strength. She would never have to lie beside him in a bed, or wash his clothes, or cook his meals. All day she had performed her daily tasks automatically, hardly answering when Martha spoke until she could no longer stand the anguish of her own thoughts.

'But *why* did he do it?' Martha had asked several times. She was always greedy for gossip and couldn't get Hannah to satisfy her curiosity. 'Why would he kill 'imself when he was going to get married tomorrow? Don't make sense.'

'There was a fight,' Hannah said at last, breaking her silence.

Martha pursued the opening eagerly. 'Was he drunk again? I've seen 'im drunk, remember. Reckon the drink had addled his brain.'

'He wasn't drunk. Maybe if he had been he wouldn't have got in such a state.' Hannah clapped her hands at a farm cat which ventured into the dairy, and then she took pity on it because it was close to giving birth to a litter of kittens. She let it have a dish of cream. The poor thing looked so pitiful that the sight of it brought easy tears to her eyes and she had a strong feeling of empathy. Her own hunger was in the soul. A lack of love and comfort caused an emptiness which nothing else could relieve and she was cold inside. But Martha was a good friend, and once the tale had started flowing in the late afternoon Hannah found it such a relief to talk she couldn't stem the scalding stream of words. 'It were all the woman's fault, Mrs Girling. She's a powerful body, strange as a witch I reckon, and I never want to see her again. If she hadn't got Ma so befuddled with her clever talk she would never have been preaching in Mr Whitfield's cottage, and then Mr Whitfield wouldn't have fired the gun that so near killed Shem it sent him demented.'

The garbled story was told erratically, and long after the two girls had finished work they remained huddled together at the foot of a hayrick, questioning the workings of Fate. So the shadows which had lengthened on Jonathan Whitfield's return home were even longer when Hannah finally set out to walk across the meadows.

She felt a lot better, having cast her fears on the willing ears of Martha Croppit, and the rest against the rick had restored her energy. She supposed she would be taking the same path tomorrow morning now, since there was no bridegroom to make it a wedding day, and she trailed her fingers through the tallest buttercup stems, staining them gold with pollen. She was desperately sorry for what had happened to Shem, but there was no denying his death had saved her from a marriage she'd been dreading. And now, when it became obvious she was with child, likely there would be sympathy from people who knew she ought, by rights, to have been a bride.

She had crossed the bridge and was approaching the road when she saw a horseman riding towards her. Even at a distance and in fading light there was something familiar about the way the horse pranced. It was the same one Shem had used, but the rider was Jonathan Whitfield.

'You're late,' he said, reining in and turning the horse. 'I came to see that you were all right.'

'I had a lot to do.'

'Yer ma said you weren't feeling well when you left home this morning. I was worried.'

His concern took her by surprise. He seemed to have recovered well from the desperate mood of last night when he had alternated between bouts of shouting and hopeless muttering, and she couldn't doubt that he was genuine. She was grateful.

'That was kind of you, Mr Whitfield.'

'You're carrying my son's child,' he said. 'I'll be seeing you're looked after right well till it's born.'

'Mercy on you,' she cried. The unexpected comfort of having someone concerned for her own welfare had been short-lived. It was only the baby he cared about. She was provoked into terse comment. 'So my child is now precious enough to be protected, is it?'

'Get up on the horse. It's still a mile to home and it'll be better for you to ride.'

She didn't argue. His manner didn't invite it, and since she was very tired it would have been silly to refuse. She put her foot in the stirrup and he helped her up. The smell of horses was strong on his clothes, and there was mud on the leather buskins buttoned over his trouser legs, as though he'd been riding hard and got splashed earlier when the rain had been heavy. Hannah viewed the top of his head and marvelled at the thickness of his hair. When it had been wholly black he must have been devilish-looking. He was awesome enough now with his bushy brows and mouth that seldom smiled. In build and features Shem had resembled his father but his colouring had been much fairer, so likely in that respect he'd taken after his mother. Shem hadn't possessed his father's resilience either, that was for sure.

Not another word was said as Jonathan led the horse through the Debenham road, and folk looked away as they passed the Plough and Plover. He didn't stay once he had seen Hannah home. He watched her go indoors, then mounted his horse and went off somewhere at a fair pace without having put his foot over the step himself.

She and Ma sat up late talking in the kitchen. When it was pitch dark they heard Jonathan come in the front door with some other men. They went in the parlour, and left again with measured steps as if they were carrying something heavy.

'They've taken the coffin,' Ma whispered. Then, 'Poor, dear man.'

Hannah peeped through the curtain and saw shadowy figures supporting on their shoulders the box containing the body of the man she should have married the next day. She hadn't liked Shem, but she couldn't bear the furtive manner of his burial, whether it was in hallowed ground or not, and her shoulders shook with sobs.

'Hush, child,' said Ma, drawing her into her arms. 'I'm full of sorrow for you, and for him, but there ain't nothing we can do.'

They heard Jonathan stumble up the stairs long after they had gone to bed. It sounded as if he flung his boots against the wall after he had taken them off.

'He's been drinking,' Ma said. 'Maybe I should see if he's all right. He's been through so much today, what with selling everything to bury his son an' all.'

'It ain't our business,' said Hannah.

They were both sitting up in bed when the knock came at the door. Ma hastily rose and drew her shawl round her to hide her nightgown before bidding him come in. He stood in the doorway, a lighted candle held close to his chest making the strong contours of his face appear more pronounced and his eyes brilliant.

'I forgot to tell Hannah she won't be going to work in the morning,' he said.

'But we thought as there's to be no wedding . . .'

'There will be a wedding, Mrs Jerram. I obtained a special licence when I was in Ipswich today. I'll be marrying Hannah myself so that my son's child will bear his name.'

It would be hard to say which of the two women was the most

162

shocked by Jonathan Whitfield's extraordinary announcement. Likely it was Hannah; though she protested and cried until her eyes were so painful she could hardly close them there was no hope of making him change his mind.

'I've prayed over the matter and I believe it to be God's will,' Jonathan said. 'You should be grateful, girl. I'm offering you respectability.'

'I want to leave. I'll go away and have the baby somewhere where no one knows me.'

'Shem's child will be born a Whitfield.' He was adamant. When she tried to push past him and make for the stairs he stopped her with one hand, holding her with such strength she could do nothing except back towards the bed where he forced her to sit down. 'I'll have no more arguments, do you hear? My mind's made up.' He looked down at her for what seemed an interminable time. 'I'll be kind to you, Hannah, I give you my promise. We'll be going to the church at eleven o'clock tomorrow. The Reverend Mitchell's expecting us.'

He went out, and after dropping the latch firmly in place he moved a piece of furniture against the door. Hannah hammered on it with clenched fists, shouting at him to let them out, but he had no intention of doing so even though she continued the onslaught until she collapsed with exhaustion.

Lilianne had said very little. She stood against the window like a cold, carved figure, the only movement being a rapid rise and fall of her breast.

'How could he do this to me?' she said, after time had elapsed. The words fell into a strained silence. 'How could he do it?'

Hannah got up and went to her mother, draping her arms around the unbending shoulders. 'I'll be all right, Ma. I'm strong and you don't have to worry about me.' When there was no response she tried to give the comfort she was being denied for herself. 'If I have to marry him I'll insist you'll stay with us. We won't go anywhere without you. I couldn't bear it if you was sent away.'

After a while Lilianne's taut body relaxed a little, and her voice became warmer. She said: 'Aye, you'll have to marry him. Reckon he's a saint. There ain't many men who would sacrifice everything the way he's doing for the sake of a son who failed him. You just count yourself lucky, my girl.'

163

So it was that just before eleven the following morning a horse and an ancient carriage with four people in it left the blacksmith's forge and headed at a regular pace for the church. On the back seat were Lilianne Jerram and her older daughter Emily. On the front one Hannah Jerram sat straight and resigned beside Jonathan Whitfield who held the reins. Less than an hour later he had become Hannah's husband.

PART TWO
London
1870–72

Chapter Fifteen

In August 1870, two months after the wedding of Hannah and Jonathan Whitfield, the woman arrived in London. Some weeks later she was joined by a small band of followers from Suffolk who had sold all their possessions. The proceeds were pooled to provide for the community she established and the woman took charge of everything. They now called her Mother Girling.

Her preaching had a new forcefulness.

'I am here, brothers and sisters, to proclaim the love of God. I bring you good news, wonderful news. Give up your sinful ways and follow me, for I can lead you into God's love. *The Lord Jesus lives in me.*' Her strong voice reached every corner of the place where she was holding a meeting in Sutherland Street off London's Walworth Road. Henry Irving in his finest acting performance couldn't have bettered Mother Girling when she was in full flood. She made her audience hang on every word. 'The penalty for sin is death, and death happens when we are in the midst of life if we don't heed the words of the Scriptures. Our bodies may live on, but our souls are destroyed. But I can save your souls. Follow me and you will never die.'

New converts joined the congregation every week. It was not a conventional chapel. Often she had to pause in mid-sentence to let a train pass overhead – the building being constructed under an arch of the London, Chatham and Dover Railway. And there were other interruptions, of course. Large crowds began to gather on the three evenings a week that she preached, mostly seeking admission to the hall, but some of the young rowdies were refused entrance and they would shout and whistle outside.

'It is written, "Whoever he be of you that forsaketh not all that he hath, he cannot be my disciple." Do you think I haven't made sacrifices for the Lord's sake? I tell you, my dears, I have given up my husband and children because that was God's will. Give up your earthly pleasures and learn to serve the Lord. You'll not regret it. I tell you with authority because I am the Second Coming of the Messiah.'

She didn't often speak of George Girling, the man she had married when she was twenty. He remained in Ipswich, working in an iron foundry and setting up as a general machine-fitter, and there were those who said that he was a sensible man to let such a strange wife go her own way. Few knew that she had borne George Girling ten children, though only two had survived. Her son William was sometimes seen at meetings, but not her daughter or her husband.

Curiosity brought most of the gathering to the meetings in Walworth. Prophetic utterances and the way in which the believers danced affected people strongly. Such bizarre rituals had not been seen publicly in London, and the way the participants shook from head to toe with religious fervour soon had the newspapers referring to them as Shakers. The nickname stuck, much to Mrs Girling's annoyance. She preferred her flock to be known as The Children of God.

The Shaker name annoyed others too, especially an American gentleman visiting the city to lecture on Shakerism.

'You are an imposter, ma'am,' the gentleman declared, standing up one evening amidst the witnessing of converts. 'You've no right to call yourself the Second Coming. The Messiah returned in our dear Mother Ann when she came to America a hundred years ago to found the United Society of Believers in Christ's Second Appearing.'

'I know of Ann Lee, brother,' said Mary Ann. 'She was a good Quaker woman and she understood the dual personality of God. I don't deny she believed in what she preached. All I know is God called me ... *me*, Mary Ann Girling. I am no imposter.'

'You've copied our ways. You dance the way we do. You practise celibacy.'

'Sexual union is the root of all evil.'

'It is indeed, ma'am, as Mother Ann was told by God in a vision of Adam and Eve carnally entwined. The celibate are without sin and therefore will not die. I agree with your teaching, but I cannot accept your claim.' The American thumped a balled fist into the palm of his hand. 'Acknowledge Mother Ann and be one with us.'

'Sir, I'll not go against God's calling. We are Children of God, and through Him I declare Christ lives in me. He has marked me as His own.'

Doubters had to be put in their place so she held her hands aloft with great show for those near enough to see for themselves.

Mother Girling's conviction that she was the new Messiah was perhaps the issue which had provoked most trouble and controversy among the farm labourers who had come either to worship or heckle at her meetings in Suffolk, and she'd been arrested many times along with troublemakers and brought before the Justices of the Peace for being the cause of disturbances. She had no fear. She quoted the Bible in her defence and out-stared them with her hypnotic gaze. She had been dealt with fairly because she gave the impression of speaking the truth and she could make even the keenest doubters of her divinity shiver.

She had accepted an invitation to preach at a revival meeting in south London earlier in the year. When disturbances became more frequent and country chapels refused to let her use their premises she had seen it as a sign that she should move permanently to the city. Her two most faithful converts, Harry Bourne and Miriam Rawlings, were the first to vow their allegiance and their willingness to go wherever she felt called to lead them. Among the rest were Lilianne Jerram and her daughter Emily, and Jonathan Whitfield with his pregnant wife and his child. In all they numbered twelve. There were others who would have come if husband or wife had been of like mind, but few were prepared to give up all they owned, and divisions among families brought many excuses.

Possibly she would have been supported by far greater numbers if it hadn't been for her call for celibacy. This was the issue which brought more dissent than any other. Some would have been willing to give credence to a new doctrine which promised salvation for their souls, but when it included rules on what must be done with their bodies it was a different matter. Families were split over it. A threat to Mother Girling's life was made by a man whose wife, like the late Susan Whitfield, had seen the proclamation as a gift from God, a legitimate way of denying her husband his conjugal rights.

Many people believed that by practising chastity they would be granted eternal life. For Jonathan Whitfield, the vow of celibacy was a main factor in his conversion. He had a countryman's superstitious fear of retribution, and had convinced himself that the manner of Shem's death was entirely attributable to his own failure to keep the oath he had sworn on the Bible. Having lapsed once and suffered terrible punishment he knew it must never happen again.

Legally he was entitled to sleep with Hannah, and might yearn to do so after the baby was born, but that would be once more tempting fate. The only way to prevent it was to live the kind of life Mother Girling stipulated, in a community where the men were segregated from the women, and all lived as brothers and sisters.

When the American gentleman returned to his own country he was accompanied by four converts to Shakerism. One was a wealthy lady by the name of Miss Kitty Long. Miss Long's stay in America was brief, but when she came back she made herself known to Mother Girling, whom she had heard was genuinely Shaker-like. Finding that what she had heard was indeed true, Miss Long rented a house in Battersea Bridge Road, and the property was made available to the Walworth Shakers. Several moved in.

It was in this house that Hannah Whitfield gave birth to her son. Hannah thought she would never get used to the noise and smell of London. Her first sight of so much traffic, the densely packed buildings and the crowds had made her feel so insignificant she had wanted to turn round and go back to Nunscorn, or better still to Seggenham. In her pregnant state she felt weak with longing for Ben, but she was no longer free to indulge in such thoughts. It was safer to yearn for the security of the farm and Luke's teasing, the friends of her childhood and the wide, endless skies above flat Suffolk marshes. None of these things would be hers any more. Instead she had to share a bed with Emily in a cramped room where mice ran around brazenly with the equal rights of permanent occupants.

Ma was different. From the day of the wedding she had changed, just as if a light had been extinguished inside her, and each day she was so occupied with the work Mother Girling organized that there was no time left to talk about the strangeness of their new life. Hannah tried, but Lilianne spoilt every opportunity by saying that she was either too busy or too tired.

'Be grateful we've kept together as a family, girl,' she said. 'You've a good husband to thank the Lord for, a child on the way, and you'll never go hungry. That's more than a lot can say, especially here in the city.'

Emily clung to Ma and received the comfort denied to Hannah. There had never been any question of her not being part of the company who set out for London. When it came to the question of whether or not she believed in the teaching of Mother Girling, however, she always answered carefully so that no one could tell what her true feelings were.

'Mother Girling does what she thinks best for everyone,' Emily would say. Or: 'Reckon if Ma and Mr Whitfield have no doubts about her then she must be a good woman.'

No one called Hannah's husband by his first name. He was not the sort to encourage familiarity, and when he walked with the three women who had become his responsibility he was sternly aloof. At first Hannah had feared him. He was strong-willed and had given her no chance to refuse to marry him, so she had expected he would require her to be a wife in every respect from the first night after the ceremony. That evening he had gone out, but Ma had said she must be ready to share his bed when he returned. She had waited dutifully and with miserable resignation long after Ma had shut the door of the room they had previously slept in together. Yet when he came home he'd been surprised to find her waiting up, and had been full of concern.

'Why aren't you in bed? It's been a tiring day for you and you'll be needing yer rest.'

'I . . . didn't know where you'd want me to sleep, Mr Whitfield,' she had stammered, her face as hot as the fire in the grate.

He had looked at her kindly. 'You can have my bed to yerself tonight. I'll stay down here. No sense in disturbing yer mother now, but from tomorrow you can bed with her same as you've always done. There ain't nothing for you to fear from me, Hannah. I'll not be troubling you.'

Not once since then had he approached her, and at first she had thought it was out of respect for her pregnancy. But when Susan's things were sold and Jonathan declared his intention of working for Mary Ann Girling in her moral crusade, Hannah knew there was more to her husband's abstention than mere care for her well-being. Lilianne was consulted about them becoming converts, Emily was sent for, and they left Nunscorn to live in Ipswich until preparations for the move to London had been completed.

Hannah was the only one who had protested.

'Do I have no say, Mr Whitfield? The woman's a charlatan and I ain't taken in like the rest of you. I don't want to be part of a

171

community. I don't want to bring up a child in such unnatural surroundings, and I certainly don't want to listen to her blasphemies all me life.'

She had never been so outspoken. She'd had no conversation with Jonathan at all, unlike her mother who seemed much more at ease in his company. To Hannah he was still a stranger, and if things hadn't happened so fast while she was incapable of thinking clearly, she would never have married him.

He said: 'I'll overlook what you've told me, but I'll thank you not to repeat your views ever again. Mrs Girling is kind and charitable. We're very fortunate she's offering us a new life free from sin, and we will all work for God. From now on our days will be given over to work and worship, and our child will be taught the same principles.'

'It isn't your child.'

'My blood will run through his veins and I shall care as much for him as I do for Clemmy. He will be mine, and you will never again say otherwise, d'yer hear?'

He was convinced the baby was going to be a boy. Hannah pressed her hands to her stomach where the embryo was growing, and she pictured Ben Rutherford's grey, grey eyes condemning her for letting this man be so presumptuous.

She remained rebellious until after the family were installed in the house in Marbro Terrace, Battersea Bridge Road. She refused to attend Shaker meetings, saying it was too far for her to walk to Walworth, and she looked after Clemmy while Ma took sweet, docile Emily along with her to dance and sing to the music of Harry Bourne's squeezebox. But she couldn't get out of prayers. Three times a day everything stopped for them and she was expected to leave whatever she was doing to go down on her knees in the room set aside for communal assembly. Her days were spent learning to cook substantial meals mainly from vegetables grown in a nearby allotment, and if there were no men to harvest them for her she had to do that too.

She was happiest when she could leave the house, and on fine days she frequently took Clemmy to Battersea Park. It was a relief to find an open space after the mean, ugly streets and she would sit on the grass gazing up at the sky. The riverside, too, appealed to her. She liked the smell of pitch and tar, and it excited her to see vessels negotiating the abrupt curve of the river under sails of orange or brown. Big black barges were drawn up high on the foreshore for repair, and she would watch the men at work, envying them their skill.

She hardly saw her husband at all. Each morning he crossed the old wooden bridge which shook alarmingly under the growing weight of traffic, to do work for a farrier across the river in Chelsea. The money he earned was given to Mother Girling who used it to feed her flock and keep the house going. It was a house divided; the men were segregated from the women and kept to their own quarters except for meals and prayers. At the beginning there were three men and five women. More came later.

The prayers, for Hannah, were a ritual from which she couldn't escape, but she said them with a closed mind, determined not to let the Shaker influence invade her soul. None knew that she went alone to sit in the parish church when she was sent to do shopping. The sight of the brick building with its square tower and spire brought a sense of normality into her changed existence and she would stay as long as she dared in the quietness, seeking an answer to the questions she found so confusing. No answers came. She was tempted to speak to the vicar one day, but he was bent with age, and pain from arthritis twisted his features. He had looked at her and walked by without seeing that she suffered mental pain which tortured her equally as much.

Chapter Sixteen

Two weeks before Christmas Hannah went into labour. It was on a frosty night when two in a bed was better than one for keeping warm, and Emily shivered and sneezed when she had to move out so that things could be made ready. Being young and healthy Hannah had few difficulties and after six hours she gave birth to a lusty boy-child, with only Ma and Miriam Rawlings to assist her. Miriam was a young country girl who had trusted Mother Girling enough to leave her parents and home to follow her. She had a natural gift for midwifery, and she delivered the baby as easily as if she had been doing it all her life. Hannah held her son in her arms soon after the cord was cut, and she gazed in awe at the tiny mite who had kicked inside her only minutes before.

'He's a fine boy, Hannah,' Ma said as she washed him in a washstand basin. 'Just like you or Luke when you was born. Reckon he's a Jerram if ever I saw one.'

He was quite perfect. Not a blemish marked his skin, and since he weighed a good eight pounds he was smooth and pink. Hannah studied every detail of his features and saw that he was almost a replica of herself, with a mouth that was full, a short, straight nose and wide forehead. The downy hair was golden and the chin firm. Long, minute fingers fluttered over her breast, and as she held him there she was filled with the kind of love that had previously been beyond her understanding. Her lips rested against the baby's head, lingered until she felt a tiny pulse tingling under them, and a surge of emotion brought tears to her eyes. He was the most precious thing she had ever held.

Hannah slept for most of the day and dreamt that Ben Rutherford came to demand why the boy didn't have black hair like his. When she awoke she had been crying in her sleep.

Mother Girling was Hannah's first visitor. She sailed into the room and took the child in her arms, making a sign of the cross over him.

'Praise the Lord,' she cried. 'Here's the youngest addition to our community. Long may he live to serve God.'

'Not as a Shaker,' said Hannah, her skin creeping with anxiety the way it always did when the woman was near. She wanted to snatch her son away from her but she didn't have the strength. 'I won't have him brought up in this mad-house. I want him to become a man, not a dancing puppet.'

A shadow passed over Mother Girling's face and she flinched. Then she replaced the baby in Hannah's arms and sat on the edge of the bed, smoothing the skirt of the red merino gown she always wore for meetings. Sadness clouded her usually hawk-like eyes.

'Why do you fight the Lord, Sister Hannah? Why do you resist every effort He makes to reach you through me? I long to bring you God's peace.'

'You've bewitched my mother and my husband and maybe my sister, but you'll not convert me.'

'The Children of God come to me of their own accord, because they believe the Lord has sent me to help them. They have the wisdom to see that I speak the truth.'

Hannah ached from the birthing but it was that physical weakness which gave her strength to question the woman, knowing that while she was lying helpless in bed she could expect a more compassionate hearing.

'By what right do you call yourself the Second Coming of Jesus?' she asked, drawing herself up higher on the pillow. 'Ain't it wrong to claim such a powerful thing? I'd be afraid, that I would.'

'Three times the Lord came to me in visions before I took notice,' said Mother Girling, with unusual humility. 'Once should have been enough but to my shame I had to be sure. I was directed to the Book of Revelation where it says, "There appeared a great wonder in heaven, a woman clothed with the sun, and the moon under her feet, and upon her head a crown of twelve stars." I knew God was telling me I'd been chosen. He wanted me to give up everything for Him, so I could spread the Word.' She paused, breathing in deeply. 'I tell you this, sister, I shall never die.'

Hannah went cold. 'I don't believe you. No one can know that, and you ain't any different to the rest of us.'

The woman took one of her hands in both of hers and held it gently. The brown skin with the strange white marks was roughened

175

by an outdoor life, but her touch was so tender it felt to Hannah as if a warm, maternal caress was soothing her in mind and body.

'My dear, do you believe in Jesus?'

'Of course I do.'

'Then He'll tell you who I am in His good time. Just let love for Him and love for everyone you meet be more important than anything else in life and you'll be forgiven your sins, I promise.'

'And what of my husband? How am I to feel about him since it seems you've forbidden him ever to come to my bed?'

'Do you love him?'

'I hardly know him.' Hannah tried to draw her hand free, but though there was no pressure she couldn't seem to get away. 'You've trapped me, you and Mr Whitfield. I'm a prisoner, ain't I, tied to a man who's sold everything, even his soul, to follow you. Why should he be giving you everything? Why? It ain't right that you should take from us the way you do.'

'Do you still not understand?' the woman countered. 'I take nothing. We share everything for the good of each other, like it says in the Bible. Ain't I quoted it often enough? The Apostles said, "And all that believed were together, and had all things common; And sold their possessions and goods, and parted with them to all men, as every man had need." That's the way we live, sister, firstly for God, and then for each other.'

'Well, one day I'll be leaving here. I'll take my baby and go to America if ever I get the chance and you'll not be able to stop me.'

Mother Girling sighed. 'Sister, don't be blind to all the good things around you. Don't be fooled by the false promises of the outside world. I'm going to say prayers with you now and we'll ask God together to help you give your life to Him.'

She stayed with Hannah for more than an hour, mostly on her knees beside the bed as she beseeched the Lord to have mercy and to send the Holy Spirit to guide and enlighten this wayward child in her care. The eyes of piercing blue fixed on Hannah with a hypnotic intensity which she managed to resist. Perhaps Mrs Girling was all the things she said she was, and indeed she was being kind, but that didn't make her likeable. If anything Hannah's anxiety increased. She cradled her newborn son against her breast and

176

covered his little head with her hand as if to close his ears to the confusing philosophies of the Shaker woman.

After she had gone Hannah tried to sleep again, but her mind was too disturbed. She felt completely alone, an island in this sea of religious fervour, and there was no one in the house she could talk to who would have sympathy for her objections. Ma wouldn't let anything stop her from attending the Walworth meetings, and her daily life now consisted solely of work and prayer. Emily seemed to have no mind of her own, and her husband was unapproachable.

Jonathan was allowed to visit her that same evening. Ma had been in to wash her so she was fresh and sweet-smelling, but smarting still from the coldness of the water that had tinged her cheeks with a blueness which made her look fragile. The baby nestled against her for warmth and was hidden by the blanket. Jonathan came in the room cautiously. The floorboards groaned under his weight even though he trod on the balls of his feet, and he looked as nervous as if he were a first-time father.

'Where's my son?' he asked.

'He ain't your son.'

'Well, from this moment he's my son and I'll let no one say otherwise.' He pulled back the blanket. 'Let me see him.'

When he took the child in his arms the hard lines of his face softened. For several minutes he stared at the baby in silence and Hannah wondered if he was saying prayers like Mother Girling had done, until she realised that he was studying every detail of the tiny features just as she had done herself.

'I could wish he was more like Shem,' he said. 'The colouring could be his but it's you he looks like.' He handed back the blanket-wrapped bundle and tucked the covers in place. Then, to her surprise, he touched her hair, smoothing it away from her temple with the gentleness of a loving husband. 'And you, Hannah? How have you fared?'

'I'm tired,' she said. 'But I reckon I'll be on my feet in a day or two.'

She saw relief sweep across his face like a breeze rippling over corn, and she was stirred by it. He actually cared.

'That's fine. I'd not want anything to happen to you. It's been my experience that a man can easy lose a wife in childbirth.'

'Would you care if you lost me, then?'

'You're the mother of my son and I'll expect you to bring him up so we can be proud of him.'

'So that's all I mean to you.' The stirring hadn't lasted long. Likely she would be expendable if she didn't do the job properly. She bristled with indignation. 'I'm just the means of providing you with a substitute for the son you lost. A salve for your conscience. Not that I want to be anything else.'

He wrestled with annoyance at her impudence, clenching his fists until his knuckles showed white. 'I'll forgive you for that, Hannah, since you're in a delicate state right now, but don't ever say such things again. I ain't a cruel man. I know my responsibilities, and when I married you I aimed to see that you were looked after. I'll go on doing that the best I can, and all I ask in return is that you're a good mother to our son.'

Hannah was ashamed. 'I'm sorry, Mr Whitfield.'

'I want this boy to know his family,' he went on. 'He'll never doubt that he belongs with us, and we won't be parted. He's in a good family here and I'll be teaching him the things I should have taught Shem instead of trying to make him wield a hammer properly. Things that matter, like respect and loyalty. And love. Aye, I'll love him, Hannah, and he'll know it.'

She ought to have welcomed the declaration, but the vehemence of his words had the opposite effect. They seemed almost like a threat, and she held the baby so tightly he whimpered.

'D'you think I won't love him, then?' she asked. 'D'you think I ain't got feelings too?'

Jonathan's frown cleared away and he smiled gently. The black hair covering his upper lip lifted slightly to show the firm, handsome line of his mouth. 'Of course I know you care. I ain't forgotten the way you snatched Clemmy from the geese.'

Hannah broached another subject that had to be settled. 'Mr Whitfield, if it's all right with you I'd like to call the baby Matthew after my father.'

'It can be his second name,' he said. He bent over and opened the blanket to look again at the boy with intense satisfaction. 'I've already decided he'll be christened Aram, after the son of Shem in the Bible.' He repeated it. 'Aye, he'll be Aram, son of Shem. It's the one admission I'll make to the identity of his true father.'

'No!' Hannah cried, revulsion making her sit forward. 'He's mine and I've a right to call him what *I* want.'

Jonathan lost patience. 'My mind's made up. There'll be no argument.'

She stared at the door he shut firmly as he went out. Her teeth clenched to stop her helplessness being expressed in either anger or tears, and she fell back against the pillow exhausted. The months of mental and physical anguish had been submerged by the pain she had endured giving birth, but now she was tortured again. She would never be able to love a child of Shem Whitfield's, never.

The baby gave a little cry and opened his eyes wide. They were as grey as the first clear colour in the sky on a bright new morning. Grey as steel. Grey as the eyes of Ben Rutherford. Hannah gazed into them a moment, then cradled Aram to her breast with a fierce, protective instinct which told her she was holding a baby conceived in love, not rape. It didn't matter what name he was given.

Chapter Seventeen

Ben Rutherford didn't stay in Billingsgate longer than a week. The only lodging house he could afford for Amos Hanberry and himself was so filthy it made him retch, and he feared they would both be ill. There was no sanitation, broken windows, and when he drew water from a pump in the alley he had to straddle an open gutter which ran with garbage and slops. He hated the constant smell of fish and incessant noise, and he didn't have the Cockney sharpness or the local knowledge necessary to earn a living there. Amos wasn't happy either. He feared the workhouse more than anything and played on Ben's good nature, beseeching him not to go off and leave him on his own.

'I ain't cut out for city life. I'm too old for it,' the old man wailed. 'It were a mistake coming here.'

'Reckon it was,' Ben agreed.

'Then let's go back to peddling round the country.'

Ben was tempted to set Amos up with a new cart and send him on his way, but he'd grown fond of him and felt responsible. He'd almost decided not to give way to sentimentality when by a stroke of luck he met a man who knew of someone called Titus Hanberry. Likely it could be Amos's son.

'If it's the Hanberry I'm thinking of he moved from here years back and did well for himself over at Bermondsey. A clever bloke he was. Too bright to stay round the fishmarket.'

Ben went back to Amos with the news and they lost no time following it up. That same day they asked directions to Bermondsey and a market porter pointed across the river with a grubby finger coated in fish-scales.

'Watch yer backs and yer pockets if you ain't been there before,' he said.

In spite of the dire warning they packed their belongings the next morning and cheerfully left the lodging house where they'd to share a filthy room with three others, making for the river landings where

180

watermen vied for trade. Ben stared across at the opposite bank and saw a church spire rising bravely above a confusion of roofs and walls, like a lily in a bed of weeds, and he kept his eyes fixed on it to keep up his hopes. If Amos could be left in his son's care it would leave him free to pursue his original plans. Though since coming to London he'd scarcely had time to think of America and the idea no longer appealed so strongly.

Ben had never been on the water. He stepped warily into the rowing boat, and disliked the unstable feeling so much he was quite unable to help Amos. Several labourers scrambled in after them and by the time the waterman cast off into the tide the river was lapping at the gunwale. The motion made his stomach lurch as the little boat took a weaving course across the river to avoid larger vessels, and he pictured the misery of a long voyage lasting weeks. That was when he decided he definitely didn't want to cross the Atlantic.

The afternoon tide was low and there were steps to climb to the landing slip on the Bermondsey side. Barges were grounded on mudflats where wrecks of older vessels lay exposed like skeletal ribs, and there was a smell of rotting vegetation and slime. The labourers pushed their way ashore, and Ben and Amos followed, despondent at the sight of so many warehouses, stores, granaries and manufactories. Hopes of finding Titus receded once more as they looked up at the tall, close-packed buildings which almost seemed to meet above their heads and made them feel insignificant. In Billingsgate there had been people to ask. Here the men were grim and evil-looking, and Ben could tell the warning to be watchful had been given with good reason. They went up one of the Thames stairs and through a narrow opening between the warehouses to get to Pickle Herring Street which suggested that they hadn't left the fishmarket so very far behind, and Ben approached a seaman who looked more upright than most.

'Good day to you,' he said. 'We're looking for a man by the name of Titus Hanberry. Maybe you can tell us where to find 'im.'

'Nar. Never 'eard of 'im,' was the reply.

He tried again a couple of times and got the same answer.

'T'ain't no good,' said Amos. 'Reckon me heart's crying out for the sight of green fields. I hate it here.'

The bright day had dimmed. The air was thick with fumes from tallow chandleries and tanneries away to their right, and the sun scarcely penetrated. But Ben didn't give up. He stopped a small man in a ragged jacket, trousers that looked as though they were held together with grease, and a dirty hat several sizes too big.

'Ever hear of a bloke called Titus Hanberry?' he asked, considering politeness to be a waste of time.

The man straightened his stooping shoulders, as if out of respect. It brought on a fit of coughing. 'Mr 'anberry now – 'im as makes rope? 'E'll be at the works at this time of day, 'im being a stickler for keeping an eye on them as works for 'im. He ain't a bad bloke, though. I was there meself till me cough got too bad.'

'And where is the ropemaker's?'

'I'll show you, guv'nor.' Despite his bent body the little man walked fast ahead of them, turning furtively every now and then to beckon with his thumb. He stopped at a gate by the top of a straight passage, all of quarter of a mile long by the looks of it. On either side were high walls, and between them a man was walking slowly backwards, drawing out fibres to make a taut thread which he spun with the dexterity of a spider making a web. A young boy turned the crank-handle of a three-foot spinning wheel.

'That's the rope walk,' said their grimy friend. 'Mr 'anberry'll be inside the building behind the wall.'

His dirty hand turned palm upwards and he looked around as if there were villains ready to come to his aid if money wasn't forthcoming. Ben thanked him and dug deep in his pocket to find a coin which seemed to satisfy, for he touched the brim of his grease-black hat and disappeared into the shadows.

Ben was anxious now to trace the elusive Titus Hanberry and he found himself quite excited, as if he were about to meet up with someone of his own after years of absence. It seemed too good to hope for that Amos might be related to a wealthy man.

'What do you reckon then, Amos?' he asked. 'Could it be your son?'

'Could be right enough,' Amos said. 'He always were a clever 'un.'

Entrance to the long building was reached through an arched gate over which was an emblem of St Catherine, the patron saint of ropemakers. Ben looked up at it with interest, and it was almost as if she was welcoming him in.

They gave their names and were shown into a room at the top of a flight of iron stairs where sunlight filtered through a high window which was above the level of the wall outside. It faced a narrow street, at the bottom of which the river could be glimpsed like a slither of silver patched to the dark, dank warehouses. Papers were piled on shelves and overflowed on to a pitted wood desk. Behind it sat a balding man who peered at them over his round, gold-rimmed spectacles for several seconds.

'You old codger,' the man said, getting up and holding out his arms. He was short like Amos and had the same smile. When they embraced there were tears in both men's eyes. 'Damned if I ain't glad to see you. I thought you must have snuffed it years ago. How did you find me?'

'Wouldn't have done if it hadn't been for Ben Rutherford here. Been better than a son to me these weeks he has.'

'I'm indebted to you, Mr Rutherford. There ain't many as would look after a crafty old devil like me father.'

'I enjoyed his company,' said Ben. 'We were travelling the same way.'

'He was going to America to find 'is brother,' said Amos. 'But reckon I've talked him out of it.'

A clerk in a rusty black suit brought in a tray of tea, and cleared coils of fine rope off a chair for Amos to sit on. Ben perched on a pile of boxes. He liked the smell of the place. The hemp had a warm, country tang which made his nose twitch pleasantly, and when he fingered a lock of it hanging from a nail he had an urge to work with the tough fibres.

'How can I repay you?' Titus asked, after his father had recounted their adventures in detail over the tea. He was a good man and a fair one. 'Seems we owe you a great deal.'

Ben didn't hesitate. 'You can teach me to make rope,' he said.

The money which Hannah had given Ben went to pay for his apprenticeship at the Hanberry Ropemakers. There was nowhere near enough for the full amount, but Titus was willing to waive the rest provided Ben showed an aptitude for the work, especially as he was much older than the other apprentices. After a few weeks there was no doubt that Ben Rutherford was going to be an asset to the firm.

By day he laboured in the ropeyard, and at night he stayed in a room the Hanberrys had found in Rotherhithe, close to where they lived themselves. It was not far to walk, and the area was considerably

183

better. The only trouble was that he still had Amos for company, part of the bargain being that the old man must share his accommodation. Titus's wife was a woman who ruled her husband and family, and she had made it clear that she wouldn't have her father-in-law under her roof. It was no great hardship. If looking after his old friend was the only condition to him learning a trade, then Ben decided he was very lucky.

He learnt quickly. He entered the yard and started at the beginning, cranking the wheel-handle the way he'd seen a boy doing that first day, and he soon progressed to cleaning the fibres and seeing they were straight and of equal thickness. At night he studied illustrated books showing how hemp was grown, and taught himself to read better so that he could understand the text. He discovered that fibres were found under the skin of the hemp-plant stalks, and that after the crop was cut it had to be soaked in water then beaten to remove the pithy core so that the fibre could be separated from the stems. The whole subject intrigued him and he was hungry to find out everything about the industry that had been going on since Noah built his ark.

By Christmas 1871 Ben was adept at using the hackle boards, even though it was a job normally done by women. Faster than anyone he could wrap a streak of hemp round his hand, oil it with whale oil and draw it through the steel pins studding the hackle boards until all the fibres were parallel. The streaks he had done were never tangled, and he waited impatiently for the day when he would be spinning them in the rope walk.

He got on well with all the men, but quickly made a friend of one in particular. His name was Alfred Thornton and though he was a year younger than Ben he was already a spinner. Alfred had started at the ropeworks when he was fourteen, and though he had a slight deformity of the leg it didn't stop him walking back and forth along the rope walk endless times a day. He was good-humoured, generous, and always had an ear open for talk of some new entertainment. This led him to hear of something which promised an evening's amusement, and it was two months after Christmas when he spoke of it to Ben.

'There's a place in Walworth where crowds go to hear a rum woman holding religious meetings three times a week,' he said. 'What say we go?'

184

'Sounds dull,' objected Ben. It wasn't one of Alfred's better suggestions.

'There ain't nothing dull about Mother Girling, apparently. She hypnotises everybody then gets 'em dancing. Shakers they're called.'

Girling . . . the name was familiar. With a start Ben recalled where he had heard it. The kitchen at Kean's Farm and Hannah working in it were memories he cherished, but that terrible day more than a year and half ago when Luke had fallen off the barn roof there had been a stranger there. Hannah, Emily and Ma had stood round the table while he was putting splints on Luke's broken leg. The other person had been a woman called Mrs Girling, and she had applied comfrey to the wound before saying prayers. It had upset Hannah because there were strange marks on her hands, as if nails had been driven through them. He would never forget Hannah's fear.

'Where does this woman come from?' he asked Alfred.

'Heaven, she'd have you believe.' Alfred laughed and punched his friend's arm. 'Let's go and be saved, brother. Half an hour's walk and we'll be there. If the New Cut swells get bawdy we might be able to join in a scrimmage.'

Ben was not so sure about the scrimmage, but Mother Girling's name suddenly made him homesick for Seggenham and the family he called his own. Hannah was always in his mind. There was just a chance that if it was the Suffolk woman she might have news of her, and he prayed for even the smallest tit-bit. His heart longed for her; his body ached for her. He went to public-houses with Alfred, and there were girls to ease the pain in his body for a night, but the heartache was different. Nothing could take that away. He had loved her so long and so deeply.

Where was she now? She'd said Ma was taking her to Nunscorn where a blacksmith was giving them work. Pray God the blacksmith was honourable, and the local men too dull to tempt her.

He was learning his new trade partly for Hannah. As soon as he was earning good money he planned to risk a journey to Nunscorn so that he could marry her and bring her to London – though it was impossible to picture his beautiful, bright, wilful girl cooped up in the kind of place he shared with Amos. It would be like caging a wild bird. He wanted a better life for Hannah than the women had who lived in Bermondsey and Rotherhithe where poverty and dirt and child-bearing made them look old before they were thirty. He wanted to provide a good home for her, and it was this determination that made him work all the harder.

It was frosty the evening Ben and Alfred set off for Walworth, and a three-quarter moon gilded the streets with silver. They paid for baked potatoes from a huckster in the Old Kent Road who had polished his potato can until it shone and produced butter and salt from a compartment at one end to put on them. It was warm by the fire-pot and steam rose from a pipe above the boiler, forming a bluish vapour in the frosty air. The potatoes were followed by hot codling apples bought from a ragged woman who was tipsy from swigging gin to keep out the cold, and when they had eaten enough they downed a quantity of ale at a nearby tavern. Thus fortified they arrived at Walworth Road.

The meetings, they discovered, were held under a railway arch in Sutherland Street, and they had only to follow the crowd to find the venue. Ben had expected to see a chapel, but the building was almost derelict, the doors no more than rough pieces of wood coated with tar. A host of hooligans had congregated outside and, sure enough, toffs from the New Cut were trying to gain admittance by unkind flattery. None of them were allowed in.

The Shakers began to arrive. They were simple folk in plain garments that had seen better days, but they were clean and wholesome. Ben stood well back as they greeted each other exuberantly with loud kisses.

'Ain't it naice,' called out the swells. With lips well-pursed they imitated the kissing sounds, hugging each other and dancing in profane mockery of the form of worship that would soon go on inside the building.

Alfred found it all a huge lark. 'Come on, let's go in. I've got to see what they do.'

But he and Ben were classed with the jostling mob and were refused entry by the doorkeeper.

'This is a house of God,' the man thundered, which brought a roar of laughter. He was burly enough to have been a Billingsgate porter and had no trouble barring the way. 'Have you no respect? We ain't a travelling circus.'

'Could have fooled us,' called a girl in clogs which she clattered on the cobbles.

Ben felt uncomfortable. It wasn't that he had sympathy for the Shakers, but they were entitled to their beliefs and ought to be allowed to conduct their meetings with dignity. He began to wish he hadn't drunk so much ale, then maybe he would have been able to go inside, if only to see the Girling woman. After all, it had been his prime purpose in coming.

He was about to tell Alfred he'd seen enough when a big, handsome man came upon the scene and was greeted effusively by the other Shakers. He had a black, wide-brimmed felt hat pulled well down over his head, but locks of thick greying hair curled below it at the back of his neck and a beard covered the collar of his coat. A girl had her hand tucked loosely through his arm, and she seemed to hang back as if reluctant to go inside. She was tall and thin, and the shawl over her head was held across the lower part of her face to protect it from the cold. When they were beneath a gaslight the girl turned and glanced across the road. Her eyes rested on Ben momentarily, and he saw her body jerk with shock. He turned icy cold, then hot. It was quite ridiculous to suppose the girl was Hannah, yet even at a distance and in poor light he felt sure it was her. She didn't remove the shawl from her face but her gaze locked with his briefly until her companion smiled at her and she responded by drawing closer to his side. Ben's heart leapt and he darted across the road. Too late. The man had spirited her away through the tarred door and he was forbidden to follow.

'The girl and the man who just went in . . . who are they?' he demanded of the doorman.

'Why d'you want to know?'

'Who are they?' Ben persisted.

'It was Brother Whitfield and 'is wife, if it's any concern of yours. Good, honest, God-fearing folk. Not like you lot. Now will you clear off.'

So it couldn't have been Hannah. A vast disappointment swamped Ben and he let Alfred drag him back into the crowd, refusing to answer when his friend wanted to know what had come over him.

'Looked like you'd seen a ghost,' Alfred said.

Ben felt a fool. He had almost convinced himself that a complete stranger was Hannah, and he was thankful he hadn't called out her name. Likely the man would have taken exception to someone trying to get his wife's attention and there could easily have been a brush with the Law. That was the last thing he wanted now that he was well in with Titus Hanberry. He recalled Ipswich jail, and the horror of it sent a prickling fear through him from his scalp to his toes.

'Let's go home,' he said.

That night he lay awake while Amos snored. Whenever he closed his eyes he kept seeing again the eyes of the tall girl who was a Mrs Whitfield. He remembered the way she had reacted: at the sight of him she had definitely been disturbed, and he was not vain enough to think that it was because of his good looks. She was a Shaker, a follower of the Girling woman who had come from Suffolk. He cursed himself for not having waited until after the meeting had finished, to make quite sure who she was. He had to see her again – he had to be certain.

Meetings were held three times a week, which meant he would have to wait until the evening after next, and that would be Sunday. His nerves were on edge. Uncertainty made him irritable at work and impatient with Amos, and he wished he knew where the Shakers lived so that he could investigate the sooner. Luckily Alfred Thornton was with his family on the Sabbath and Ben was able to set out alone. He didn't want company.

The weather had changed and it was raining, making the roads muddy. Ben was wearing his better trousers, a second-hand pair of moleskin ones he'd bought which didn't look so countrified as his old corduroys, and he didn't want them splashed so he kept to the inside of the pavement as he hurried to Walworth. He arrived at the railway arch early, a clean cap on his head and a shine on his boots. This time he intended to gain entrance, so he helped a man to lay planks over a muddy patch which had to be crossed to get inside the building and was rewarded for his efforts by pious words of thanks.

'God bless you, brother. I hope you'll join us in worship when Mother arrives.'

'I'll be honoured, brother,' said Ben, in like manner.

He went in before the rabble arrived to chant ridicule outside. His nerves were tense and he was worried he might not see her in the dimness, since there were only two meagre gaslights to illuminate the room. A piece of green baize covered a carpenter's table which he guessed would serve either as an altar or pulpit, and there was a

188

collecting box ready to be handed round. He sat on a bench where the maximum light would fall on her face as she came through the door. Supposing she didn't come. He tried not to think of the possibility, but should it happen then he would corner Mother Girling and find out the girl's true identity. Not knowing was torture.

The faithful came in a few at a time and Ben found himself being welcomed with such enthusiasm he had to get up from the bench in order to be polite. Older women kissed him warmly and the men shook him by the hand. He had been there twenty minutes when he came face to face with Emily Jerram. It was hard to tell who suffered the greater shock.

'Ben Rutherford!' she gasped. Her face, even in the poor light, could be seen to lose its colour. 'Why ain't you in America?'

'So it *was* Hannah I saw.' He hadn't even heard her question. 'She's here, ain't she? I must see her.'

She quickly regained her composure and voiced disappointment. 'It would've been nice if you'd said you was pleased to see me.'

'Of course I'm pleased. I ain't never been so surprised.'

'But you'd rather I was Hannah. Well, she's got herself a husband and she won't be here tonight.'

'Where can I find her?'

'She won't want to see you, Ben. Ma neither since you went off with her money which I'm sure you'll have spent by now.'

'I intend to repay it.'

'Pshh,' she scoffed.

Ben didn't want to talk about money. He tried again to get his adopted sister to tell him where Hannah was living, and frustration made him want to shake her when she refused to say.

'Why did she marry the man? Tell me that.'

'For love, why else? Mr Whitfield's wonderful. Reckon he swept her off her feet.'

'I'll not believe it till I hear it from her own mouth.' He couldn't accept that Hannah had cared so little about their promises to each other that she'd been able to turn to someone else so soon. 'And why did you all come here with Mrs Girling? Seems there's been a lot going on since I left the farm.'

A sigh escaped her. 'It's been a difficult time,' she said, and he thought she was going to cry. Her hands fluttered as she debated whether to touch him, and the tone of her voice changed. 'I'm real

189

glad to see you, Ben. Reckon it's the best thing that's happened since we came to London, that I do.' She reached up and kissed him without further embarrassment, seeing as it was the fashion among Shakers. Her lips were cool and quivering. He was taken by surprise and his arms enfolded her for the sheer joy of being reunited with his family, but she quickly broke free. 'No, not here. It ain't allowed. I'll have to meet you somewhere where we can be alone.'

'I'll visit you all,' he said. 'I'll come tomorrow night.'

But she hastily discouraged him. 'No, you can't.'

'Why not? Tell me where you live.'

Two more people came in. He recognized the big man. It was Hannah's husband, and he was old. Ben's muscles became taut and his fists clenched as he imagined the satisfaction of knocking the brute to the floor. He looked to be ox-strong; there was no questioning his appeal, but surely he was more than twice Hannah's age. There was something wrong. Ben knew Hannah better than anyone and he couldn't credit her falling in love with someone who didn't share her youth or her sense of fun. At first sight there seemed to be nothing light-hearted about Mr Whitfield.

Behind the man came Ma, thinner than he remembered and more subdued.

'Don't let them see you,' Emily warned. She trembled with nervousness. 'Ma'll make a fuss about the money, and if there's trouble the police get called. We ain't popular round here.' She guided him to the shadows at the back of the room.

'Why ain't Hannah here?'

Emily hesitated. 'Because . . . well . . . someone always stays behind to cook supper. It was her turn.'

Ben gripped her arm until he must have pinched the skin, but she didn't protest. 'Where do you all live?'

At that moment Mother Girling arrived. He had no difficulty recognizing the gaunt figure dressed in red merino, and when she displayed her prominent teeth in a wide smile he remembered feeling uneasy in her presence, resentful that she had come as a stranger into the kitchen at Kean's Farm that terrible day and taken charge. She had charisma, no one would dispute it. But the right or wrong of it depended on the measure of faith her teaching instilled, and Ben was far too practical to be influenced.

The woman immediately claimed everyone's attention and the joyful mood in that dim sanctuary was dangerously contagious. She went to the baize-covered table and lifted her hands for silence. Her hawk's eyes flicked from side to side as she surveyed her flock and it was as if a yoke had been thrown over the assembly to bring it within her power. A flickering oil lamp behind her threw grim shadows. Hands stretched towards her.

She spoke: 'Some of you dear folk may be new to our meetings. I'm sorry for the ill-convenience of our premises, but I welcome you whole-heartedly in the name of the Lord, and if you can't stay till the end of the service at nine o'clock will you please leave now before we lock the doors.'

No one moved. Ben stayed beside Emily. He would have preferred to leave but it would have meant attracting attention to himself so he pulled his cap well down over his eyes and turned up the collar of his coat, hoping that Ma Jerram wouldn't look his way. He needn't have worried. It amazed him to see that she hung on to every word the woman uttered and he doubted if she would have been interested if Queen Victoria herself had joined them.

The service began. A girl with a Suffolk accent launched into an impassioned prayer which lasted almost a quarter of the first hour and was followed by another intoned by an elderly man. Mother Girling offered the third prayer, and by this time Ben was beginning to wonder why the Shaker nickname had been coined. He had to wait until after the collection box had been handed round and she had delivered a lengthy sermon before the reason was revealed. The final part of the meeting was the strangest display of dancing he had ever seen. Men and women began performing extraordinary gyrations which seemed to have a hypnotic effect on them. Some moved with closed eyes and bumped into others; the huge man who had been doorkeeper stamped and whirled with his arms extended; another was about as graceful as a bear. One young girl became excited and started chanting that she could see the Devil fleeing from their midst, taking a child with him.

'Save the child!' the girl cried. Her eyes were glassy. 'Save the child from the Devil.'

Ben didn't like it. He drew his muscles tight and kept a clear mind while those around him slipped into a trance-like state which made them slaves to Mother Girling's ideals. It pained him to see Ma

191

Jerram mesmerised like the rest, and his only consolation was that Emily showed no inclination to take part. She stood beside him in silence, her small face tight with worry.

'If you ever want me I'm at Hanberry Ropemakers in Bermondsey,' Ben said, under cover of the chanting and prophecies. 'This ain't the place for you, or for Hannah.'

'Hannah's taken to it the same as Ma. I only came to London because Mr Whitfield was right kind and said I shouldn't stay in Seggenham on me own.'

Their whispers brought a look of disapproval from Mother Girling, and even Ben felt the strength of those piercing eyes as they probed every dark corner in search of suspected dissenters.

When the dancing stopped he turned to speak to Emily again, but she had slipped away and he couldn't see her. A train rattled overhead, and when the doors were opened a barrage of bawdy remarks burst from the crowd still waiting outside. He daren't stay. He left while effusive farewells were being exchanged, but on his way he managed a few words with the man who had played the squeezebox.

'Wonderful meeting, brother,' Ben said. 'Where can I find Mother Girling if I want to join the Shakers?'

'We're Children of God, brother. Mother doesn't like us being called Shakers.'

'I'm sorry.'

'Marbro Terrace is where you'll find us. A hundred and seven, Battersea Bridge Road.'

Ben thanked him, and stepped out into the winter night. He was far more disturbed than he had been on his previous excursion to Walworth. For a moment he stood alone on the cobbles of Sutherland Street and looked back at the railway arch where Mother Girling's faithful children still lingered. Hannah's husband and Ma Jerram hadn't emerged yet. Likely they had plenty to talk about, and after that they would walk home.

Ben turned out his pocket. He had a bit of money on him, enough to call a cab to take him to Battersea Bridge Road.

Hannah didn't go to Shaker meetings if she could get out of it. She hated them and was thankful she had the excuse of looking after the baby. Sometimes Jonathan insisted that she accompany him, and then Ma would stay behind with Aram, but she knew that when the weather turned warmer she would be expected to take him with her, and then there would be no precious time to herself.

These last two days she had been unsettled, imagining things. It had started with that fellow outside the Meeting Hall who had looked so much like Ben Rutherford. The sight of him had made her heart quicken and she had wanted to run across the road on winged feet. At the time only Jonathan's firm hold of her arm had stopped her and she'd been angry at the restriction, but she had been glad since that he had saved her from making a fool of herself. Ben was in America.

Imagining. Surely there was no foundation for the uneasiness she felt lately when she saw Ma looking at Jonathan. Her expression was complicated – a mixture of sadness and anger and disappointment, and an unmistakable yearning which ought never to be there. Ma had been right taken with Jonathan when they first went to Nunscorn, and at that time she had been a widow for three years. Likely she had built up hopes for herself which her daughter had thwarted, and that would account for any apparent lack of compassion. It was the first time Hannah had thought of her mother in such a personal way and it worried her.

She wondered if Jonathan had any idea of Lilianne's interest in him. He was a man dedicated to what he saw as his duty and in his way he was kind, but Hannah knew he was not happy either. The life they were leading wasn't natural and he wasn't cut out for it. His rightful place was at the blacksmith's forge in Nunscorn and he deserved a wife he could love. Instead, all his emotions were lavished on Clemmy and Aram, particularly Aram. The boy he believed to be his grandson now dominated his life.

'Reckon this boy saved my sanity, Hannah,' he said one morning. He rubbed his beard against the tiny face and Aram smiled up at him like an angel. 'Ain't nothing I wouldn't do for him. I'd give me life if it was necessary.'

'Would you leave Mother Girling?'

It was very early and they were alone in the kitchen for a few brief minutes. Hannah looked at the burly man holding her child and found it hard to accept that he was her husband. She felt sorry for him. Guilt had altered his life, dictating every action, and it was making him a slave to Mother Girling whom he saw as his salvation. In some ways Hannah was relieved since it saved her from having to share his bed, but she felt like a prisoner and would put up with anything, even wifely duties, if he could be persuaded to leave the community.

He was slow to answer. 'There ain't no reason to leave,' he said. 'It's a good Christian house and sharing everything means we'll not go hungry. We'll see when Aram's older. I'll decide what's best for the boy then.'

The house was dark and damp and there was never enough fuel to make a decent fire. Mother Girling took the spartan attitude that being cold toughened the system and strengthened the spirit, so she had no sympathy with anyone who complained. Hannah didn't mind so much for herself, but she worried about Aram and she carried him strapped against her breast with a shawl so that her own body heat would keep him warm. He wasn't growing very fast and had hardly put on any weight so that at two and half months he still looked to be newborn. But he had strong lungs and cried lustily when she didn't have enough milk to satisfy him.

She loved her son deeply and with growing fascination. Though small he was perfectly formed and she could have kissed and cuddled him all day long. She loved the nape of his neck where tendrils of golden hair curled, and she touched his minute toes and fingers as if they were jewels she was hoarding. She cradled him with utmost tenderness, and when Jonathan took the baby from her to shower him with his own gruff expressions of love she was desperate to have him back in her arms again. There was something about the intensity of Jonathan's devotion which sounded an alarm in Hannah's heart.

The evening that Ben attended the meeting in Walworth Hannah was making potato soup ready for when everyone came back. Aram was asleep in the wooden cradle Jonathan had made and she had to resist the temptation to wake him just for the pleasure of holding him. The occasions when they were alone were so rare that she had to make the most of them, and it was at these times she would whisper secrets into his tiny ears.

'Your real dadda would love you, my son. That he would. Reckon it's a good thing he's in America. Likely Mr Whitfield would kill us both if he found out you ain't his precious Shem's baby.'

She stirred the soup in a large iron pot on the range and gently rocked the cradle with her foot. It was a surprise to hear a cab stop outside. There was always heavy traffic along Battersea Bridge Road but none of it stopped at night after costers' carts and the street-traders had trundled home. Hannah balanced the spoon across the top of the pot and went to the window, keeping well hidden behind the faded plush curtains. A tall man paid off the cabbie and turned to look up at the house. Hannah's heart seemed to stop: this time there was no question that it was Ben.

When he knocked, conflicting emotions made her reluctant to move and she trembled like a hover-fly not knowing in which direction to dart. Once it would have been natural to run to his arms, but not any more. She daren't let him in for fear Jonathan would return.

He knocked again.

Her pulses throbbed and she could scarcely draw breath. She couldn't let him go away without a word, though. Quickly, before anyone came back, she must find out why he was still in London.

She opened the door a little way and came face to face with him. He said nothing. Neither did she. But their eyes met and the months of separation melted away.

'Let me in, Hannah. I must talk to you.' He tried to push the door open further but she came outside and shut it, barring his way.

'You can't come in,' she said breathlessly. 'I've a husband and he'll be back soon.'

'I know – I've seen him at the Meeting Hall.' His expression grew hard and his voice was like gravel. 'Why did you marry? Why didn't you wait for me? Didn't our promises mean anything?'

'What did they mean to you? If you weren't going to America you could have sent word. I thought you were thousands of miles away.'

The cold winter air was full of drizzling rain and it settled on their clothes like shiny beads in the gaslight. She hadn't remembered the strength of their attraction, or quite how desirable he was. She longed to put her arms round his neck, to draw his head down and press her lips to his, but likely there were watching eyes at neighbouring windows. And once she touched him there would be no going back. She would belong to him again.

Unwisely her hopes soared. 'Are you still waiting to get a passage?' She visualised them setting sail with Aram to start a new life together in another land.

'I'm not going to America,' he said. 'Reckon I'm safe in London.'

195

'What about the money I gave you?'

'It's gone. But I'm aiming to make some more.'

'Gone! Ma's money.' She stepped back into the doorway, finding relief in anger. 'If that ain't just like you, Ben Rutherford. Squandering what was given to you, on women and drink no doubt, with no thought for the hardship it meant to us. That money would have made Ma independent and things would've been different. I'm thankful I've found myself a good husband who'll provide for me, because it's a sure thing you would never be able to.'

'It weren't like that. I brought an old man called Amos Hanberry to Billingsgate . . . '

'I don't want to see you ever again, you sinner, so don't come round looking for me.'

'If that's how you feel.'

'Yes, that's how I feel.'

They argued back and forth with accusations and excuses, hurting each other while the precious time of reunion was wasted. It wasn't what Hannah wanted, but she took refuge in it.

'Reckon it was a mistake thinking you ever cared for me then,' said Ben.

'It was,' said she. And all the while her heart was beating crazily in contradiction.

He looked down into her glittering eyes. 'Tell me one thing. Are you happy with the man you married?'

'Of course I'm happy.'

'Do you love him?'

'I'm his wife. He's good and kind and I wouldn't do anything to hurt him. Of course I love him. It weren't anything but a roll in the hay between you and me. Now, if you'll excuse me I've got to finish getting supper. Goodbye, Ben.'

She went inside and closed the door quickly. It would have been disastrous if she had broken down and sobbed in his arms. After a few minutes she heard his footsteps die away, and Aram began to cry. She picked up the baby as if in a daze and went once more to the window, soothing him automatically.

'There, there, my love. You do the crying for both of us. I sent yer dadda away and he doesn't even know you exist.'

Her body ached as she peered into the wet night. She didn't know where he had gone or where he lived and he wasn't likely to come back after the roasting she'd given him, but it was for the best. Ben was a waster. Tears blurred her eyes, and she clung to the lie she had told about loving Jonathan Whitfield. The only person she loved was Ben, whatever his faults, but she had been right to send him away.

A group of people came into view, a tall man with a woman on either side of him, and another woman leading the way. They were still singing hymns. Hannah held Aram against her shoulder and went back to stir the soup which had stuck to the bottom of the pan.

Chapter Eighteen

Neither Hannah nor Emily spoke of seeing Ben. The evening he called at Marbro Terrace Hannah successfully hid her emotions by concentrating on the supper she had nearly spoilt, blaming poor Aram who continued to cry and wouldn't be pacified.

Emily hugged the secret to herself and was more cheerful than she had been for weeks as she started to plan her escape from the Shaker community. She'd been careful not to tell Ben where they lived, but she knew where *he* could be found and she was going visiting right soon. It was urgent that she should give more credence to the story she had told of Hannah's happy marriage and she must make him see it would be useless to try and become part of the Jerram family again, unless it was to be through herself.

That night she dreamed of Ben. She saw him riding a white horse across the Suffolk marshes, galloping through the water meadows with spray flying up in his wake like gossamer wings, but two black devil dogs were chasing him and they had the faces of Luke and Hannah. They were trying to bring him down and destroy him. Emily flung open the farm gate for him to ride through and when he was safe inside with her the gate became a wall to shut the dogs out. It was a vivid dream which didn't fade and it gave her added incentive to find an excuse to leave the house long enough to go to Bermondsey, which she learnt through careful questioning was only thirty minutes' walk away.

'You've been gone an hour, Sister Emily,' Mother said, when Emily's enquiries about Bermondsey made her late for prayers. 'It doesn't take that long to buy milk. Where else have you been?'

'I got lost, Mother,' she lied.

'Then we must pray together so that you're not lost again, my dear.'

Mother had assumed the role of protector and guardian. She owned them, body and soul, having purchased them with visions and promises, and she imposed impossible restrictions. No decisions were made without referring to her, no money was spent without her consent, segregation was strictly observed and the celibacy rule was absolute.

Fear of being on her own had made Emily a Shaker. She pretended obedience and joined in the prayers, but she would never acknowledge that Mother Girling was the next Messiah. It embarrassed her that the Shakers were becoming objects of ridicule and were pelted with rotten eggs and tomatoes when they arrived for meetings.

'And now we're being made fun of in music-hall songs,' said Ma. 'It's wicked, that's what it is.'

Emily had heard one of the songs and she hummed it softly when no one was listening. It gave her a certain satisfaction, as if she was getting back at the Girling woman, and at Ma for being so stupidly devoted to her. Her mother had taken charge of the communal laundry, cooked and cleaned and prayed with equal fervour, and was never without Jonathan's daughter Clemmy clinging to her apron. Clemmy was demanding and cried petulantly when she couldn't get what she wanted. Emily couldn't understand Ma spoiling her so. She played with the little girl, brushed her hair and petted her as if she were her own.

She tried to talk to her sister about it. 'Why does Ma make such a fuss of Clemmy Whitfield?' she asked. 'She never takes notice of Aram like that. I'd be hurt if I was you.'

'Ma was paid to look after Clemmy. Guess she got to love the poor little motherless thing.'

'More than her grandson? That's what it looks like.'

'Maybe it's hard for her to accept Aram,' Hannah said, but wouldn't add to the surmise.

Sometimes Emily suffered pangs of suspicion. Aram had been born nine months after Ben's escape from prison – surely he hadn't risked going back to see Hannah? She had changed from a carefree, hoydenish girl into a solemn young woman, and she was always agitated when Jonathan Whitfield displayed excessive devotion to her child. It was a mystery.

Aram wasn't Jonathan's, Emily knew. On the day of Hannah's wedding she had walked into a nest of intrigue concerning Shem Whitfield, the raping, and the boy's suicide which had led Jonathan to sacrifice everything for the sake of the unborn baby. The first time Emily had picked up Aram she'd studied the tiny features. He was like Hannah, except for the eyes. They were the colour of Ben Rutherford's, and it was this which had made Emily suspicious. She had instinctively refrained from telling Ben that Hannah had a son.

Men and women ate separately in the kitchen. Mother Girling sat like a matriarch at the head of the women's table and was always served first as soon as prayers had been said. At supper the following night Mother had found need to chastise one of her flock. Her jutting jaw moved up and down like a machine as she tried to eat and speak at the same time.

'I must remind you all of the two verses in the Acts of the Apostles by which we live,' she said. Her light blue eyes raked the assembled group and settled on a girl called Ruth, who had recently arrived to join them. '"Neither said any of them that ought of the things which he possessed was his own; but they had all things in common." Sister Ruth, it has been brought to my notice that you have kept a piece of jewellery, a brooch which hangs on a cord round your neck. Is it true?'

The poor girl hung her head in confusion and Emily pitied her.

'I'm sorry, Mother. I can't part with it. 'It was the present my husband gave me on our wedding day.'

'Your husband is dead, sister, but the Lord lives. To whom are you giving your allegiance, the living or the dead?'

'To the Lord, Mother. To the Lord.'

'Praise be. Then I will take charge of the brooch, if you please, and we will ask God together to forgive you and to rid you of the need for earthly reminders.'

Eating stopped while more prayers were offered, and Emily grieved for the girl as she handed over the precious gift, knowing she would never see it again. It was then that Aram started to cry. Hannah got up to see to him, but Mother Girling stopped her.

'Leave the child where he is, Sister Hannah. He won't hurt if he cries for a few minutes.'

'But it ain't good for him,' protested Hannah. 'He gets hot and feverish.'

'Sit down and finish your supper, my dear. That baby ain't putting on enough weight. Get plenty of nourishment inside yourself then maybe the young 'un will thrive.'

'He's *my* baby,' cried Hannah. 'I'll not be told what to do.'

Mother Girling folded her hands on the table and pushed away her empty plate. 'Sister, haven't you learnt yet that we're a family, and as head of that family the management of children must always be referred to me. Ain't that so, Sister Lilianne?'

'That's so, Mother,' said Lilianne, putting her arm round Clemmy who had a high chair next to her at table.

'Our little ones will learn obedience and patience from the earliest age. Since there's to be no marriages here, and no intimacy, there'll be no babies born to swell our ranks, so we must treasure the ones who come to us through the great mercy of the Lord Jesus Christ. I shall instruct them as they grow older, my dear, and they will become faithful Children of God.'

Emily watched her sister in silence, saw the way her mouth set in a stubborn line and knew that her independent spirit would never be broken. Hannah was biding her time. She was no more a willing convert than Emily herself, but was tied to the community by her marriage to Jonathan Whitfield and her child. There was nothing she could do but accept the decrees of Mother Girling, and Aram had to wait for attention until she had finished every spoonful of her supper.

That night when Emily was about to go up to bed she heard muted voices in the yard. The back door was open an inch and she flattened herself against the wall so that she could see through the crack and hear what was being said. A cold draught stung her face but that was nothing to the icy exchange going on in the only private place where a man and a woman could meet. It was Hannah and her husband.

'Why didn't you tell me what you planned to do before you married me?' Hannah was saying. She was almost spitting with anger. 'I hate this place and I'll not be letting that woman have charge of my baby. I'll leave, I tell yer.'

'That's up to you. Go where the hell you like, but my son stays here with me.'

'He ain't your son and I won't be parted from him.'

'Aram is my flesh and blood so don't ever say that he ain't. Git back in the house and don't defy Mother again.'

'What a weak fool you are, Jonathan Whitfield. You shut your eyes to the truth and you're taken in by a madwoman who thinks she can change the world.'

Jonathan slapped her. His huge right hand dealt a stinging blow to her face from which she recoiled in pain, and Emily flinched in sympathy. But he repented immediately.

'Hannah, I'm sorry.' He caught her arms and held her when she would have escaped. His face was raised in misery and he searched the sky as if in fear of retribution. 'Say you'll forgive me. Sometimes I'm driven by the Devil. What will Mother say if she sees a bruise on you?'

Hannah gently released herself and stepped back. 'Don't worry. I'll make sure she doesn't see if I'm marked.' She smiled up at him and touched his hand. 'I'm sorry, too. You're a kind man and you do what you think's best for us.'

She turned towards the door and Emily ran upstairs quickly. She'd seen that particular smile of Hannah's before and knew it meant a scheme would soon be brewing for her to get revenge.

'Emily, are you awake?'

Hannah nudged her sister, put a light finger over her lips to make sure she didn't call out, and whispered in her ear. It was three o'clock in the morning and she was lying next to her in the bed they shared. She wore all her clothes.

'What's the matter?' Emily opened her eyes.

'Come downstairs with me.'

Ma was sleeping soundly in the next bed with Clemmy curled up in her arms. The child was cutting a back tooth and had been fractious all day, but Mother Girling had made a herbal concoction to soothe her so she didn't stir either as the two girls slipped out of the room. They went down the stairs carefully, testing each one for creaks before stepping on it, and didn't feel safe until they reached the kitchen where grey ash smoked in the grate. Hannah closed the door and they stood in the dark, two shadowy figures afraid of being discovered.

'Where d'you think you're going?' Emily hissed. 'You ain't leaving, are you?'

Hannah went over to the window where starlight gave a faint glimmer. She opened her shawl and showed Aram nestling like a sleeping kitten against her breast. 'I'm taking him away from that woman's clutches. There was a drop of stuff left she made for Clemmy's toothache and I gave it to him so he'll not wake up till we're safe away.'

'But Mr Whitfield . . .'

'Mr Whitfield hit me because I said things he didn't like.'

'You can't leave him. He's your husband. Plenty of women have to put up with a beating from the man they married.'

'I'll not have any man beating me, that's for sure.' Hannah leaned forward. 'There's something I must tell you, Emily, but it must be absolutely secret. Give me your promise not to say a word.'

Emily crossed her heart the way she'd done when they were children.

Still Hannah hesitated. Then: 'Ben Rutherford's in London. He didn't go to America.' She heard her sister gasp but it was too dark to see her expression. 'I'm telling you because I'm going to find him, but Ma mustn't know. He's got rid of all her money I gave him for his passage. She'd be livid and she might tell the police.'

'How do you know all this?'

'He came here last night while you were at the meeting. I wouldn't let him in and we nearly had a fight, but oh, it was good to see him. I was a right fool to send him away.'

'Did he tell you where he's living?' Emily gripped her wrist and sounded so anxious it was tempting to give her a reassuring hug, but it would have disturbed Aram. 'And how did he know where to come to see us?'

'He'd been to the Meeting Hall so someone must have told him. I knew it couldn't have been you, because you would have said something. Seems he brought an old man to Billingsgate so likely that's where he'll be.'

Emily's grip tightened painfully, her nails digging into Hannah's skin. 'You can't go. You've no money.'

'Mother Girling left her purse on the kitchen table for a few minutes after supper. I helped myself to a few coppers and I don't count it as stealing since she takes everything from us. I've got a bit of food, too.' Hannah prised the biting fingers from her wrist. 'Now you're not to worry. I can take care of myself and I ain't afraid.'

'You're being very selfish,' Emily accused. In the silvery light she looked ethereal. Her tangled hair hung over her shoulders like thistledown, and her piquant face had a pale beauty. Tears glistened in her eyes, but there was something else – a strange light which gave them the appearance of stones glistening. She had always been the timid one, but there was a spiteful side to her nature of which Hannah had been made aware in the past. Emily's hands were now tightly clasped and she was wringing them. Her voice was hard. 'If you leave us all here I hope you get lost. London's a very big place.'

'That's an unkind thing to say.'

'I want to leave as much as you.'

'Then come with me.'

'I can't. Someone has to look after Ma.'

Hannah's nerves were so taut she wanted to shake her sister. 'I've been through a lot, Emily, while you were safely in a job at the Manor, and I can't take any more. It ain't going to be a picnic looking for Ben so I'd be obliged if you'd wish me well instead of making out I'm off to a life of pleasure. It's for all our sakes I'm doing it. When I find him I'll make Ben understand he's head of the family with Luke gone, and he's responsible for us. We'll get no sense out of Ma – her head's been turned, and something's got to be done about it.'

It was difficult to keep their voices low. Emily looked as if she wanted to argue, but had to be content with showing her disapproval in the set of her mouth and shoulders.

'What'll I tell Mr Whitfield in the morning?' she asked.

'Nothing. You didn't even hear me leave.' Hannah crossed the shawl tightly over her chest and tied the ends behind her back so that Aram was in a safe sling. 'Don't lock the door after me, then it won't seem like someone let me out.'

Emily's hand was on the latch when she asked the last urgent question. 'Did you tell Ben about the baby?'

'No. There was no need.'

The pale features softened a little and Emily stood aside to let her sister go out into the night. 'Take care,' she said. She didn't attempt to kiss her or offer good wishes to help her on her way.

'I will. God bless you, Emily.' Hannah, too, withheld any sign of affection.

She set off towards Battersea Bridge and crossed the Thames with a fairly light step, trying to put Emily's attitude out of her mind. Though the night was raw and fog cloaked the river she didn't notice the cold as she hurried along. Even at this early hour there were a few people about, mostly asleep in doorways or padding furtively along the pavement away from whatever mischief they'd perpetrated. London's heart seemed to beat in unison with her own and she felt free for the first time since Jonathan Whitfield had pressured her into accepting him as husband in a loveless marriage.

Chapter Nineteen

The house in Marbro Terrace shook with the ferocity of Jonathan's shouting. He swore like a heathen and stamped from one room to another as if Hannah would be found skulking in some dark corner. The Children of God pleaded in vain for him to be calm.

'How could she have left without you knowing?' he demanded of Emily. 'You share a bed. You must have heard something, damn you!'

'I was real tired, Mr Whitfield,' said Emily nervously. 'Hannah gets up regular to feed the baby so if she moves around I take no notice.'

'And you, woman.' He faced Lilianne. 'Surely *you* heard something?'

'Not a sound. Clemmy slept all night so I wasn't disturbed.' Lilianne touched his arm sympathetically. 'The girl's wilful but she wouldn't go off on her own in the city. She'll be back in no time.'

When Mother Girling was told of Hannah's disappearance she blamed herself. 'I should have been gentler with her. Sister Hannah's always found it hard to accept our ways and I ought to have had more patience.'

'You've no need to reproach yourself, Mother,' said Lilianne. 'My daughter's always been a great trial and when she comes back I hope as how you'll punish her for being so ungrateful.'

The woman fixed her eyes on Lilianne, staring at her for several seconds with an unblinking gaze. 'There is no punishment here, sister. Love binds us together and we share our troubles as well as our devotion to the Lord. What we will do now is pray for Sister Hannah's safe return and when she comes back we will welcome her with open arms.'

'I must find my son,' said Jonathan, taking his coat from a hook behind the door. 'I'll not rest till he's safe.'

'You'll not go anywhere, brother, until we have said prayers.'

The Shakers all knelt down obediently. The prayers lasted half an hour and Jonathan could hardly contain his impatience. He had no idea where to start looking for Hannah, but inactivity would drive him mad and he itched to start out on the road.

His conscience gave him hell. He'd treated her badly last night. Since Shem's death he had been tormented by a sense of failure. Some days he didn't know what he was doing here and longed to go back to the country where he could work for himself and provide for his wife and child from his own pocket, but he had pledged himself to Mother Girling and the setting up of a Christian community. He was paying for his sins, but he hadn't learnt from them. There were nights when his body ached for a woman. He'd thought that once he gave up normal life to serve God he would not be troubled by the cravings of the flesh, that God would reward him for his service by making him immune to earthly desires, but it hadn't happened. He was living in purgatory. Dreams disturbed him most nights and he would wake up in great discomfort which couldn't be eased even secretively in the close confines of the room he shared with other men. It was never Susan he dreamt about, nor his present wife. It was Lilianne. Each time he looked at her he guiltily remembered the pleasure she could give, and he was ashamed of his disloyalty to Susan's memory. Perhaps it had been a mistake to marry an innocent young girl when it was a strong woman he needed.

His wife was as much a stranger to him now as the day she had entered his house, and he was beginning to blame her for his present situation. If she hadn't come to Nunscorn Shem would never have acted so wickedly and he would have been alive today. They would have been working together, he and Shem, in the forge that should have been kept in the family for future generations, but Hannah had brought disruption. Because of her he had lost his son and been forced to sell his living and his property. Because of her he was no longer in control of his own destiny. It had felt good to strike her. For one terrible moment he had been tempted to beat her savagely, but it was the Devil who had prompted him and he had been given the strength to resist. He had to remind himself that Hannah had given him Aram.

Aram was all that made life worth living. The days when he felt as if he were going mad he had only to pick up the baby and meaning would return to his life immediately. He felt guilty because he loved the boy more than he loved Clemmy, his dear Susan's child, but there was nothing he could do about it. Aram hadn't taken the place of Shem, but he had come so that a new start could be made, and in him Jonathan would make up for all the neglect that Shem had suffered. Aram was his second chance, the sign of God's mercy. And now Hannah had taken him away.

Every morning Jonathan set out early to walk the streets of London in search of his missing wife and child, and every evening he returned to Marbro Terrace without word of them. Mother Girling began by having sympathy, but as the days went by and their prayers continued to be unanswered her patience wore thin.

'Brother Jonathan, your wife doesn't want to be found, and her wickedness is destroying you. We all want to help and we urge you to keep faith with the Lord. In His good time He will show her the light and she will repent and come back of her own accord. Meanwhile the farrier across the river is still willing to pay for the work you do, and if we are to eat we can't rely on the collecting boxes bringing in enough money.'

Mother Girling was an imposing figure. She had rescued him from death, for what it was worth, and he remembered the power of her persuasion. But he was doing no good here.

'Reckon I'd best leave,' he said. 'Seems there's too much bitterness in me and I ain't worthy to sit at your table.'

'*Our* table, brother. We share everything, and we help each other. You're taking on the burden of your wife's failings, but there's no need for that. Each of us is responsible for our own sins. The Lord knows the good you've done, the sacrifices you've made. Your reward will be in Heaven, but there's still plenty of work for you here on earth. He needs you, and so do we. If you was to slip back now it would be as if you'd never repented and the Lord would wash His hands of you.'

Jonathan sighed. 'You're my conscience, Mother.'

He believed in every word she uttered because he needed direction. He accepted her as the Messiah because she believed it herself and could back up her conviction with visions and physical signs. Like everyone else, at the meetings she held he became carried away with religious fervour, and until Hannah's desertion he had done everything he could to spread the good news of her coming. He longed for the world to see Mother as the great saviour he knew her to be, and when he was inclined to question God's slowness in revealing the truth he had to remind himself that at the first coming of Jesus in male form very few had believed at the start.

So Jonathan went back to work with the farrier and tried to rely on the power of prayer to restore Aram to him, but when a week had gone by without any word from Hannah he became more and more depressed. The only person who could penetrate his gloom was Lilianne Jerram. He wished it were possible to be alone with her. There'd been no chance to talk privately since they had become Shakers, but the conventional words exchanged in public were enhanced by a special tone, and sometimes there seemed to be a message in her eyes.

At the beginning of March a fever spread through the house, not too serious, but debilitating enough for the sufferers to be excused attendance at evening meetings in Walworth. One by one the Shakers went down with it, with the exception of Mother Girling who brewed them herbal remedies and prayed for their speedy recovery. Jonathan was among the first victims and he sweated on his bed for two days before he could struggle to his feet. Lilianne was one of the last, and she took the infection worse than any of the others. Mother took Clemmy to her own bed where there was less risk of her becoming ill, and the door of the women's room was kept closed so that Lilianne could sleep.

On the Sunday evening when everyone except Lilianne was fit once more, Clemmy threw a tantrum.

'I want Ma Lily,' she cried. It was the name she had called Lilianne from the time she learnt to talk. 'No, no, no. Go away,' she screamed at anyone attempting to calm her. 'I want Ma Lily.'

Jonathan picked up his daughter and tried to pacify her with games and cajoling, but the child was out of control. He carried her round the house, promising that the next day she would see Ma Lily, but Clemmy cried with heartbreaking persistence and he was left with her after everyone else had departed for Walworth. So there was no one else about when Lilianne opened the bedroom door and called.

'Bring her to me, Jonathan. I'm better and she won't take the fever from me now.'

Thankfully Jonathan climbed the stairs and entered the women's room for the first time. Lilianne looked like Emily with her pale

face and hair loose about her shoulders, and his heart quickened to
see her in her petticoat with a shawl pulled close across her chest.
Clemmy struggled out of his arms and ran to her, the sobs subsiding
into hiccoughing gulps as she grasped Lilianne's legs and begged
to be picked up.

'She's been missing you,' Jonathan said. 'Reckon you're the nearest she's had to a mother since Susan died.'

The house was so quiet now the crying had stopped. The timbers
cracked and downstairs the clock he had brought from his cottage
chimed seven.

'You look tired,' said Lilianne. 'Sit down for a minute while I
rock Clemmy to sleep.'

He watched her with the child and her soft crooning relaxed him.
Clemmy's thumb went into her mouth. She buried her head against
the soft breast of the woman she loved more than anyone else, and
within minutes she was asleep. The sight brought a lump to his throat.

Lilianne put the little girl in Emily's bed and tucked a cover round
her, then gave all her attention to Jonathan.

She said, 'I wish I could comfort you same as I did the little one.
And reckon I need comfort myself.' She sank down on the bed,
drawn and pale from the illness. It didn't make her any less desirable. 'There's love all around us but it ain't the same as lying close
to someone.'

He protested. 'It's forbidden.'

'No one will know if you lie down just for a minute, and no
harm'll be done.' Still he was reluctant. 'Please, Jonathan.'

He took off his boots and lay down. Lilianne came to his side
under the blanket. His arm encircled her and she rested her head
against his shoulder, the length of her body touching his in quiet
companionship.

'How is it with you?' she asked gently. 'You've made so many
sacrifices.'

'I'm paying for my sins.'

'What nonsense. You ain't a sinner.'

'Maybe I am – maybe I ain't. All I know is the Lord was more
good to me than I deserved when He gave me Aram, and now He's
taken him away.'

She kissed his cheek and her mouth moved down over the smooth
hair of his beard. He closed his eyes and sweet sensations stole

210

through him. The presence of someone so near had a wonderful soothing effect and his mind eased.

'You've got Clemmy,' she said. 'And you've got me, Jonathan. I love you. I always have.'

The sensations became prickly, like stinging nettles making his skin hot, and they all suddenly surged to his genitals.

'You're a generous woman. I've got real strong feelings for you – wrong feelings.'

She put her hand inside his shirt and caressed him. 'I love Mother,' she said. 'I'll devote me life to her, but I can't believe she's right in saying a man and a woman shouldn't be joined, else where would the next generation be if everyone listened? Take me, my love, if that's what you want.'

Her body was warm. He breathed in the smell of her and his senses reeled. After months of celibacy nothing could have made him refuse the release she offered. Their union was ecstatic.

The following morning Clemmy developed the fever she'd been sickening for all the previous day. By mid-afternoon she was so ill it was impossible to feed her the herbal concoction Mother Girling had directed Lilianne to spoon through her dry lips, and everyone in the house came to the bedroom to pray. Jonathan mopped the little face of his child and unmanly tears added to the sweat that lay in beads on her forehead.

Just before midnight Clemmy Whitfield died.

Chapter Twenty

Ben was in the rope walk with one of the spinners who was showing him how to load his waist with streaks of hackled hemp before he could start learning to spin. The ends had to be at the back and he had to be able to draw out fibres from the middle of the streak, twisting them between his finger and thumb so that the resulting thread could be attached to one of four hooks on the big spinning-wheel.

'You're doing well,' his tutor said. 'You're taking to the work like you was born to it.'

'Reckon I've got to make up for lost time. I don't want to be the oldest apprentice in the business for longer than I can help.'

'You won't be. Never knew anyone learn so quick.'

Ben was pleased with his progress, and he knew Titus Hanberry was impressed. Sometimes the older man would take him into his confidence.

'You remind me of myself when I was young,' Titus said. 'I came to London with a load of fish and an even bigger load of ambitions. Never one to waste an opportunity, I wasn't. It was an accident I came into this business, but I had a feel for it straight away, same as you've got, and I made up my mind to be a master ropemaker before I was thirty.'

'Sounds like the way I've been thinking too,' said Ben.

Titus smiled. 'I'd best see you don't try to buy me out.'

'No fear of that. I ain't got a penny to my name.'

'But you will have, son. You will have.'

Ben liked Titus Hanberry. The man was a fair boss and would have made a good friend if their circumstances had been more equal. As it was, Titus saw to it Ben received expert guidance and all the help he needed to succeed, in gratitude for the care he had taken of Amos.

Ben attached the whirls of fibre to the wheel the way he was shown and a boy cranked it slowly so that he had to start walking backwards. But he wasn't drawing the hemp out in the right quantity and it began to tangle.

'You have to make sure the same amount of fibre comes from both sides of the bundle,' said the spinner. 'Not bad for a first attempt, though. Use yer left hand to smooth it.'

Ben tried again and improved, but he had a long way to go before he would get a piece of thread long enough to throw over even the first of the stakes driven into the ground at intervals along the walk. He had spent days watching the competence of his tutor with envy. Once sufficient length had been spun the man would direct the boy at the wheel to unhook it and fix it to a winding reel, then he would walk slowly forward with the end of the thread taut in his hands to stop it unravelling. Backwards and forwards he would walk, repeating the process until the reel was full. This was the most skilled job in the yard, the one which would take Ben the longest to learn, and until he had mastered it he wouldn't be able to progress to the next step, which was strand-making. Others might think him a fast learner, but Ben was impatient to be proficient in the whole business.

He was engrossed in his third attempt to twist the fibres correctly when the youngest apprentice ambled up to him in the ropeyard.

'Ben Rutherford, there's a young woman asking for you at the gate.'

His cold fingers suddenly refused to respond and the thread tangled round the hooks on the wheel. He didn't know any local women. It had to be Hannah. 'What does she look like?'

'Dun ask me,' said the youth. Ben was not a favourite with the apprentices, being older and shown preference.

'Best go an' see,' said the spinner. 'But don't make a habit of it.'

Ben unwound the hemp from his middle and tried to brush the pieces off his trousers. He was bursting with joy. Over two weeks had passed since he'd called at the house in Marbro Terrace and in that time Hannah had never been far from his thoughts. He had wanted to snatch her up and make off with her, bring her to his lodgings and tell Amos to find a bed elsewhere, but he'd had to respect the fact she had a husband. He'd gone over every word of hers a hundred times, trying to read things which might lie behind them, but he was always left with the painful truth that she hadn't cared enough to wait for him so much as a month or two before getting hitched to a stranger. She'd been angry with him for not using Ma Jerram's money to go to America. She'd railed at him just like the old Hannah in the farmyard, as if the wonderful thing that had happened to them in the barn on the night he left was wiped from her mind. She had shut the door in his face and it had seemed clear she didn't want to see him again. It had taken all of sixteen days for her to think better of the way she had treated him, but after as many weeks or months he would still have been glad.

He hurried to the gate, full of eager anticipation, and saw a girl with a shawl over her head waiting against the wall. The afternoon sunlight had strengthened with the approach of spring. It shone on a window opposite and reflected across the narrow street, touching the girl second-hand, like an afterthought. Her pale, elfin face was lifted to the light, as though to warm herself, and she was oblivious to urchins who came running from an alleyway with an irate vagabond in noisy pursuit. It was Emily.

Disappointment swamped Ben. He ought to have guessed. It was Emily he had told where to find him, not Hannah, and it wasn't really likely that Hannah would leave her husband and come looking for him after all she had said. He sucked in his frustration and fixed a smile in place.

'Emily,' he called. She turned quickly. Her big eyes were very blue and her lips curved with pleasure. In the city street she was as out of place as a rose would have been growing in the gutter, and a great tenderness welled up in him. 'What are you doing here?'

'Oh Ben, I'm so glad I've found you.' There was a catch in her voice. 'I've left the Shakers. I can't stay with them any longer. You've got to help me.'

'What's happened?' He thought immediately of Hannah, fearing something dreadful.

Her eyes filled with tears. 'I ain't one of them like Ma and Hannah. I hate it there. I really hate it.'

So it was only Emily's problem. He breathed easier. 'Are they unkind to you?'

'No.' She used the corner of her shawl to wipe away the tears. 'But with Hannah and Jonathan so happy and Ma so wrapped up in Mother Girling there ain't no one to care about me. And I don't hold with all the things Mother says and does.' With great effort she gulped back a sob. 'The woman frightens me with her talk of sin and repentance. She reckons she's the Second Coming of Jesus, but

214

when He came the first time He was gentle, wasn't He, and He didn't scare people.' She pressed her lips together to stop them quivering. 'I can't go back there, Ben. I can't.'

She was so distressed that Ben knew he had to do something. He was very fond of her and he couldn't bear to think of her purity being threatened by the forced acceptance of a doctrine which went against her own Christian beliefs. It was wrong.

'Ma'll be worried where you are,' he said.

'No, she won't. I told her about finding out you was still in London and I said I was coming to you. She said the money ain't important any more since she owns nothing and she wishes you well, just as long as you'll look after me.' She touched his hand. 'I've never stopped thinking about you since that terrible day the constables took you off.'

'That night of the meeting someone told me where you lived. I went there but I didn't go in. Hannah was angry I hadn't let you all know I didn't go to America. Seems she doesn't want to see any more of me.'

'That's because she's got Jonathan.' Emily's expression softened a little, but there was a hint of envy in her tone. 'Reckon they loved each other from the minute they met. Wish I could have someone love me like that.'

She was quite enchanting in the March sunshine which now bathed her in a peach glow, so delicate and timid and in need of cherishing. City life might agree with her if she could be established in a decent home. Maybe Titus Hanberry's wife could do with an extra maid? He rejoiced that she had come to him, even while Hannah's fickleness lay in wait to torment him when he was alone. He felt very protective towards Emily; Hannah had always been able to take good care of herself.

'I must get back to work or I'll be in trouble,' he said, 'but I'll give you my address to go to. You'll find an old man there called Amos Hanberry. I look after him. Tell him who you are and likely he'll be pleased to have company till I get home.'

'Thank you. Oh, thank you, Ben.' Emily stood on tiptoe and kissed him. Her brow cleared. Her relief was evident. 'I love you, Ben. I knew you'd help me.'

He gave her directions and watched her set off. All around were sounds of cranking and hammering in neighbouring yards, iron-rimmed wheels trundling over cobbles, barking dogs and street-traders' cries. A gang of mudlarks came up from the river, a sign that the tide was high. Their grimy little bodies stank of river filth and their ragged clothes were as stiff as boards with an accumulation of dried dirt. They shouted and squabbled over a copper nail one of them had found while foraging through the mire. Such a nail was very valuable, and the disputed ownership of this one looked like ending in a fight. There was never any peace in Bermondsey.

Ben wished he could have sent someone with Emily to make sure she was safe; she looked too frail to be walking the streets of London without an escort. She was as sweet as a breath of clean Suffolk air.

Emily's love for Ben Rutherford had always been a strong, jealous emotion, but she hadn't fully realised the depth of it until she saw him so unexpectedly at the Meeting Hall in Walworth. She was shaken by it, frightened even, and the experience made her devious.

She didn't feel she had told any real lies. In the beginning she had only exaggerated a little about Hannah's marriage being so blissful, and clearly Hannah must have given the same impression to Ben since she'd sent him packing without explaining that marriage had been forced upon her. Ben would never have tolerated that – any hint of the truth and he would have forced his way in and caused trouble. It was better for everyone's sake that he'd been led to believe in Hannah's willing union with Jonathan Whitfield, and Emily congratulated herself on saving a lot of heartache. Every word and action was fully justified.

It was the greatest relief that Ben didn't know about Aram, for he wouldn't have accepted Hannah's rebuff with such resignation. And now he mustn't find out that she had left home and was wandering about London alone. Emily felt no guilt at not having told her sister where she could find Ben. She had to look after her own interests. Anyway, Hannah was a survivor and when she was unlucky in her search she would soon return to the Shakers. It was more important to make Ben realise that his future could lie with Emily now that Hannah was unobtainable.

'Tell me how Hannah met the man she married.' Ben wasted no time before asking questions. They followed hot on each other for the whole of the first evening. 'He ain't from Seggenham.'

She answered patiently. 'I only know what Hannah's told me. I was made to go and work for Squire Kean after the farm had to be left. Ma and Hannah went to Nunscorn without me. It were awful.' It hurt that he showed no sympathy for her own hard time. 'Ma met Jonathan Whitfield in Seggenham and he offered her a job looking after his house and his little girl.'

'The blacksmith. I thought he had a sickly wife.'

'She died before they got there.' Emily quaked with worry. He knew so much.

'And Ma didn't mind him paying attention to Hannah so soon?'

'No. The poor man had been starved of love. It must have been touching the way he and Hannah got to love each other straight away.'

'This man Whitfield, he didn't force himself on her, did he?' Ben's fists were clenching and unclenching.

Emily laughed. 'Oh Ben, I never knew you were such a worrier. Jonathan was a perfect gentleman. You see, Hannah saved his little girl from getting killed by geese the first day she got there.'

'So he married her out of gratitude.'

'No, of course he didn't. They fell in love, I tell you!'

He wanted to know of Jonathan's background, about which she could truthfully say she knew very little, and about the wedding which she painted in rosy hues. The more she made up the easier it became to believe in the romantic story of Hannah's marriage, and Ben's brow grew darker.

'Likely she fell in love with a pretty cottage and the money to run it,' he said. 'Hannah always had ambitions.' He reached for a jug of ale, tipping it to his mouth and swallowing more than was healthy for him in one go. 'The bitch! Serves her right the old man turned out to be a religious bedlamite.'

Emily said nothing more. There was no need.

Sharing a room with two men was not an ideal situation, but she was determined not to be dislodged from the haven she had found and so she didn't complain. A curtain was threaded on string and drawn round the bed which she occupied in solitary comfort that night while Ben and Amos slept as well as they could on the floor. She didn't even feel guilty about denying the comfort to Amos Hanberry who could have done with it, considering his advanced age. Amos hadn't taken to her. The next morning, as soon as Ben

217

had set off for the ropeyard, he was asking how long she meant to stay.

'I'll stay as long as Ben lets me,' Emily said.

'Reckon you should be going back to your Ma. You can't stay here forever. There ain't room, and it'll spoil Ben's chances with women having his sister around.'

'I ain't his sister!'

'Near as.'

Talk of other women frightened Emily. She wanted Ben for herself, always had done, and no one was going to steal him from under her nose now, not after all the trouble she was taking to get Hannah out of his mind. Amos looked at her shrewdly, and she knew he resented her. She wished he would go out and suggested he might enjoy the music she'd heard coming from a pub round the corner, but he remained obstinately in his chair.

She spent the day cleaning the room and washing clothes for the two men. A meal would be ready for Ben when he came home, and he would see how good it was to have a woman about the place to look after him instead of having to be responsible for a grumpy old man.

It was wonderful to be free of the Shakers and she would never go back. Likely she wouldn't be missed all that much. When Ma wasn't dancing attendance on Mother Girling she was worrying about Jonathan Whitfield who had sunk into a silence bordering on madness since the death of his daughter Clemmy. It was Ma who should have married Jonathan. There could be little doubt that she had an unhealthy affection for the man who was her son-in-law, and Emily wouldn't hesitate to use it if Ma ever tried to break up her own association with Ben.

That evening Ben came home with an invitation.

'I've spoken to Mr Hanberry about you maybe working for him at the house,' he said. 'I'm to take you there later to meet Mrs Hanberry. Seems they've needed a new housemaid for a while now, and they're real interested in a nice girl from the country.'

The Hanberrys lived in a tall house in a reasonably pleasant street in Rotherhithe. It had a bow window looking on to the street and two steps up to the front door. A posh house, Emily thought. She and Ben were shown into the parlour which was illuminated by gas-mantles, and little popping noises came from the white cones covering the flames. There was a horsehair sofa in the window recess, two armchairs beside the fire, and a round table in the middle of the room, covered with a chenille cloth. The large sideboard against the far wall had the biggest mirror at the back of it that Emily had seen since leaving Seggenham Manor, and her reflection showed a nervous girl biting her bottom lip. She hastily forced a smile as Mrs Hanberry got up from one of the armchairs.

'How d'you do, Emily,' the lady said. Emily bobbed a curtsey. 'I understand from Ben you have been living with those strange people known as Shakers.'

'Yes, ma'am. But I wasn't happy. Ben's been real good to me and he doesn't want me to go back. That's why he's anxious for me to get a post.'

'And are you a good Christian?'

'Oh yes, ma'am. I'm rightly a Methodist.'

'Hmm, well, that's some improvement I suppose.' In the pause which followed Emily was subjected to close scrutiny. Then: 'As it happens I do need a new maid. Tell me about your last employment so that I can judge if you'll be suitable. Have you ever looked after a house such as this?'

Isobel Hanberry was a short woman, but lack of height was unimportant. She held herself well, her dark head tilted at a confident angle and her back as straight as a column. Likely she was about Ma's age. Ben had said there were three daughters. Her eyes were keen and intelligent and she spoke with the quickness of someone with a sharp mind who wouldn't tolerate incompetence, so Emily was careful with her answers. She owned up truthfully to only having had experience of kitchen work and went into details of what she had done at the Manor, but with touching humility she confessed to always wanting the chance to be a housemaid.

'I know I can suit you, ma'am. I'll work very hard,' she said.

'She'll do that,' said Ben, who had been standing behind her like a guardian. 'At home it was mostly Emily who kept house and did the cooking while Ma and Hannah worked outside.'

After a few more thoughtful moments Mrs Hanberry smiled, and kindness softened her rather plain, serious face. 'Well then, seeing as my husband is full of praise for your brother and trusts him completely I think I can offer you the post of maid here. I'm afraid we haven't room for you to live in, as Cook occupies the only spare bedroom but I shall be quite satisfied if you get here by six each morning to light the fires, and you can leave at nine o'clock in the evening. You'll take your orders mostly from Cook. I do charity work to help women in prison and I don't want to be worried by trivialities. I shall expect you to see what wants doing and to use your own initiative.'

'Yes, ma'am. Thank you, ma'am.'

Her new employer studied her again. 'You don't look much like your brother.'

'Oh, we ain't truly brother and sister, ma'am. Ben were adopted, and I love him more than anyone in the world. I'd do anything for him.' Emily turned to Ben with a radiance which made her beautiful. 'Why, I'd marry him if he wanted me to.'

'That sounds like an excellent idea, especially if you're to continue sharing his lodgings,' said Mrs Hanberry. 'My husband will agree. He has very high moral standards. And Ben, you need a wife if you're going to be as successful as Mr Hanberry assures me you are. Who better than a girl you've known all your life and who thinks so highly of you?'

Ben gave a start of surprise and his eyebrows shot up. It was the first time Emily had made him aware of her feelings. If he'd been a stranger she would have observed propriety and kept them hidden, but she had known him most of her life and felt no embarrassment.

'I'll give the matter thought,' he said, politely and without enthusiasm.

'Best not wait too long,' Mrs Hanberry advised. 'Otherwise she'll be snapped up by some other suitor, I'm sure of it.'

On the way home Ben hardly spoke. It was very dark so she kept as close to his side as she could and tucked her arm through the crook of his. She felt his resistance immediately.

'Ain't it lucky you know such nice people,' she said, tightening her hold a little. 'Wouldn't it be awful if they ever found out about you being a horse-thief.'

Chapter Twenty-One

Hannah had no idea that finding someone in London was nigh on impossible without having an address. She set out with a prayer in her heart and high hopes of putting Aram in Ben's arms before the day was out, but that vision waned with the moon soon after daylight came. The streets on the north side of the river became more congested the further she walked, and from the sound of it Billingsgate was a rough area where she would need all her wits about her.

'What d'yer want to go there for, ducks?' asked the man at the coffee stall where she stopped for some breakfast. 'T'ain't for the likes of you to be going there on yer own.'

'I've got to find someone.'

'Yer're better orf without 'im by the looks of you.' Her shawl had slipped and the bruise on the side of her face showed up angrily where Jonathan had hit her the night before. 'Take my advice, ducks, and go on 'ome. They're a rough lot what lives round Billingsgate.'

She sat in the shelter of an old clothes-horse with a sheet thrown over it to protect her from the wind which had sprung up. There she fed Aram, and spent an extra copper on some pea soup to warm herself. An old woman tried to beg some of it. She had black whiskers sticking out of her chin and ragged clothes were piled on her body in torn layers, the bottom ones likely to have been there for years. When there was still an inch of the thick soup left in the bottom of the bowl Hannah gave it to her out of sympathy.

She didn't turn back. Her spirits were high now that she had quitted Marbro Terrace for good, and she felt no guilt at having left her husband. She kept on walking, always with the river to the right of her, until her feet were sore and Aram's weight dragged her shoulders down and made her back ache. The time had come to spend some of her precious money on a ride on one of the omnibuses which raced along at top speed. But it was then that things started to go wrong. She found herself snatched on board the omnibus by a conductor keen not to let a rival company get the trade, and there was only room for her to squeeze into the seat between a large gentleman in a voluminous coat and a woman sitting up next to the horses. The woman shuffled to make more room and the edge of her cape covered Hannah's lap, but she got up quickly at the next stop, hurriedly paid the conductor and stepped into the street.

'Hey,' the conductor called. 'Yer've paid me too much.'

The woman didn't seem to care. She stepped down and mingled straight away with the crowd on the pavement.

'Hey!' called the conductor again. Then he addressed his passengers. 'Anyone lost any money?'

Hannah went to feel in her pocket and found it had been slashed with a pocket-knife where the woman's cape had covered it. Her purse was gone.

'I have.' She stood up in consternation. 'She took my purse.'

The conductor jumped from the vehicle and chased after the culprit but there were too many people around and she had successfully made off with her spoils. The poor man came back panting.

'Sorry, miss. You'll 'ave to get orf, less you've got the fare tucked away somewhere.'

'I've nothing else at all,' she cried. 'What am I going to do?'

'I'll pay what she owes,' said the man in the voluminous coat, producing a coin which he held out in the palm of his hand. The conductor took it, and Hannah was dumped on the pavement with Aram now crying lustily. She had no idea where she was.

There were a great many people about, all hurrying here or there and it was hard to find anyone with time to ask directions. She finally spoke to a young woman wearing a shabby crinoline and a blue jacket.

'Please can you tell me how to get to Billingsgate.' Better to approach a female.

The young woman wore her hair in a net. A jewelled ornament brightened the mousy curls clustered at the crown of her head, and when she lifted the crinoline there was a glimpse of striped petticoat beneath it. She looked keenly at Hannah.

'You look tired,' she said.

'I am. I've been walking since before it was light, and now I've had me purse stolen.'

'Would you like a cup of tea?'

222

'Oh, wouldn't I,' said Hannah, with fervour. Aram wouldn't be pacified. 'I need to feed me baby, too.'

'Come with me then.'

It seemed a long way to the promised refreshment. Along several streets Hannah followed a step behind the girl so as not to trip over the hem of her skirt and the people they passed grew more villain-ous-looking. Labourers loitered suspiciously on corners; boys dressed in black frock-coats and with an eye for a likely pocket to pick stood in the middle of the path; drunken women, most of them elderly, hugged doorways in abject misery. There were old-clothes stores with second-hand articles hanging outside, a druggist with coloured jars of blue and green and purple liquid brightening the window, provision shops bulging with customers, and a baker's advertising wheaten bread at sixpence a loaf. An old man carried an advertising board which by the looks of it was more than his strength could stand, a ballad singer tried to make himself heard above the noise of an endless stream of traffic, and a band of filthy children darted out of a passage to beg for a crust. The girl thrust them aside with the confidence of someone used to such surround-ings, and stopped at a lodging-house door.

'Here we are,' she said, turning the handle. 'You'll be able to rest here.'

She took Hannah inside. The kitchen was large and seemed full of people – twenty at least. There were tables littered with jugs and bottles, baskets and bonnets and an array of articles which looked as if they belonged in a broker's shop. On one side of the room women sat eating bread and herrings. Men were at a long table at the other side. A huge fire burned cheerfully in the grate which had a boiler on either side of it, and a row of brightly painted tea and coffee pots lined the mantelpiece. Coat pegs on the wall were all in use.

The girl who had befriended Hannah went and spoke to an old woman with gold rings on her fingers and a striped apron over a silk gown which must once have graced a gentlewoman.

'Come over 'ere, my pretty one,' said the old woman in a wheezy voice. When she smiled it showed she had teeth missing. 'A nice cup 'o tea's what you want and a bed for the night, ain't that so?'

'I'd like some tea, but I want to get to Billingsgate before dark,' said Hannah.

'Billingsgate? Nar, you rest up 'ere a while. Termorrer yer'll feel more like going there. See to the babe first whilst I get you a cuppa.'

They were so kind. Who would have thought such rough-looking people would care that she was tired and a mite frightened after what had happened on the omnibus? Hannah gladly accepted the tea and a share of the bread and herrings. No one would hear of her leaving.

'My name's Lottie Beck,' said the girl in the crinoline. 'Mrs Humby owns the house.'

As darkness fell Hannah began to feel uneasy. Some of the better-looking, better-dressed young women left the kitchen. Soon the men extinguished their pipes and crept out one at a time, pulling on black caps and putting on shabby jackets removed from the coat pegs. One wore tartan trousers, and to her horror he opened a cupboard and brought out a rusty iron cage full of rats.

'Dan catches 'em for the rat matches down at Bucks Tavern,' said Lottie, seeing Hannah's expression. 'They has a pit where they tip the rats in and then let a terrier loose amongst 'em and take bets on how many it can kill in five minutes. They reckon as one dog killed five hundred rats in five minutes once.'

'That's awful,' gasped Hannah. 'I hate rats, but I couldn't bear to see them killed like that.'

She wished she was back in Marbro Terrace. The events of last night no longer seemed worthy of the rash step she had taken, and the Meeting Hall in Walworth would have been infinitely preferable to the big kitchen where menacing shadows appeared once the candles were lit. The bedroom where she was to sleep was no better. It was full of beds, each one with a flock mattress, two rugs, two sheets and a pillow, but even in the candle-light it was possible to see that they were alive with lice. All night she lay on her back with Aram against her breast to try to keep the creatures off him.

So much for her hopes of reaching Ben. In the morning she knelt by the bed and prayed, as Mother Girling had taught her, and earned the scorn of her companions.

'T'ain't no use expecting anyone up there to hear you,' said one woman. She had occupied the next bed from about four o'clock onwards.

'D'yer reckon God ever smiles on the likes of us?' asked another.

'Where's religion ever got you then?'

Hannah took no notice. One night among a roomful of prostitutes was not going to shake her faith in the least. It hadn't taken her long to realise the nature of their profession.

'Maybe you should give the Lord a chance,' she said. 'He looks after you if you believe hard enough.' She was surprised to find herself sounding like Mother Girling.

'G'on!' scoffed a girl who had disturbed everyone with drunken singing when she'd returned in the early hours. 'Where've *you* bin hiding yer head? If you don't look after yerself there ain't no one else going to do it.'

Hannah went down to the water-closet in an out-house, found there was a place where she could wash, and she was able to clean Aram. In the kitchen there was tea and a bowl of gruel for her.

'That'll be threepence you owe me for the night's lodging,' said Mrs Humby, when she had finished. She was holding out one of her beringed hands.

Hannah stared at her. 'You know I haven't any money. Lottie told you yesterday I had me purse stolen.'

'I never heard it said, ducks. I'm a bit deaf, see.'

'It's been real kind of you to take me in, Mrs Humby, but I can't pay you till I find who I'm looking for in Billingsgate.'

'Now ain't that a shame,' the woman said. She turned to the girls who were closing round. The air in the kitchen became menacing. 'The young lady can't pay me. Best see she earns the money, don't yer think?'

There was a chorus of assent. Fear stabbed like a knife into Hannah's heart and she clutched Aram so tightly he began to cry. But she knew instinctively there would be no pity, particularly if she lacked courage.

'I ain't going out on the streets for you or anybody,' she declared.

'Too good to work, are yer?'

'No. Honest work ain't never killed anyone and I do me share.'

'What makes you think what we do is dishonest?'

'I ain't selling me body.' Hannah stood up to them fiercely and no one would have guessed that nightmare memories of Shem Whitfield were making her tremble inwardly. She couldn't think of anything worse than having to oblige some of the dreadful men she had seen yesterday round the neighbourhood.

Mrs Humby smiled. The gaps where teeth should have been made the change of expression evil. 'For the babe's sake we'll not be expecting you to please the gentlemen just yet. Lottie'll take yer out and show yer how not to come home empty-handed. Seeing as yer was done by someone with skill you ought to be pleased to get yer own back. Lottie! Give the girl a few lessons before you go out, then see to it she brings back a purse before dark.'

What a fool she had been. She ought to have known such a woman wouldn't do anything out of the kindness of her heart – likely she didn't *have* a heart. Hannah cursed herself for being so naive, and searched desperately for a way out of the trouble she had invited by her gullibility.

'Best do what she says,' Lottie advised.

Noise above caused further disruption. A man with his trousers gaping came hurtling down the stairs ahead of a half-naked girl who pushed her booted foot in his back and yelled abuse.

'Drunken sod! I'll teach you to expect favours for nothing. Next time I'll have me money first.'

The wretch vomited, spewing foul matter as far as Hannah's skirt. She recoiled in horror. The women laughed derisively.

'You'll have to get used to that, ducks.'

'Never!' cried Hannah, too revolted to touch the evil-smelling stuff on her clothes. Lottie produced a slimy dishcloth for her to rub it with, but the stench affected her nose and eyes as she rubbed at the filth feverishly. The man who had produced it slunk away.

She had to get out of this terrible hole. Listening to Lottie was going to be the only way. So she paid attention to the girl's instructions on how to pick pockets. After an hour she was able to 'fan' the pocket of one of the other girls without being detected so that she could tell if there was a purse inside. The purse then had to be extracted with even more care. It was difficult but she was quick to learn the knack. And all the while she was making plans. She had to show growing enthusiasm and pretend a keenness for the business, then as soon as she was in a crowded street she would give Lottie Beck the slip and head once more for Billingsgate.

'Do you make much money?' she asked.

'I can make twenty quid or more on a good day, but I 'ave to give it to Mrs Humby and she shares it out.'

In this respect there was a similarity between Mrs Humby and Mother Girling, but there it ended. Mother Girling was a saint by comparison. She wondered why Lottie didn't leave the lodging house, keep the money she made and find a place of her own to live. She could afford somewhere nice if she was as successful as she said.

It was not long before Mrs Humby demonstrated her cleverness. 'This afternoon you can go out with Lottie and we'll see what you bring back,' she said to Hannah. 'I've been watching. You're light-fingered. You've got the gift, I reckon.'

'What if I get caught?'

'You'll be entertained by 'er Majesty for a month or two, ducks.' The woman gave a raucous laugh. 'But I know you'll be careful. There's meat and some bread before you go, and tea to warm you up. Give the babe to me while you eat.'

She took Aram and danced him on her ample lap until he gave a real smile. Hannah ate the meat with enjoyment, but watched anxiously as her child responded to the wicked old woman. Men had been coming in and out of the brothel, led up the stairs by the tousled-headed women with skirts torn from rough handling, and vulgar sounds had carried to the kitchen. She couldn't wait to escape.

'Come on,' said Lottie at last, handing Hannah her shawl.

'I'm ready,' Hannah said. 'I'll take my baby now.'

She went to take Aram, but Mrs Humby had stood up and moved near to the fire. 'Nar,' she said. 'You'll not be taking the babe anywhere. I'll be keeping him until you come back with enough money for your lodgings.'

'You can't do that!' Hannah screamed at the woman and tried to snatch Aram from her arms, but there were men in the kitchen who restrained her when she became frantic. She kicked out at their shins and struggled violently, but they shoved her out into the street where Lottie Beck was waiting, and slammed the door so that she couldn't get back inside.

'No sense fighting,' Lottie said. 'She always wins.'

Chapter Twenty-Two

For a few days after Clemmy's death Jonathan scarcely moved from a chair in the kitchen where he sat for hours blaming himself that she had died. Lilianne was desperate to know what to do. Everyone tried to convince him that since the fever had affected them all it couldn't have been his fault, but still he sat in deep depression.

'Jonathan, let me help you,' begged Lilianne. 'Let's talk about it.' She knew his conscience was tormenting him. It was terribly unfortunate that Clemmy had died so soon after Mother Girling's celibacy rule had been broken, but the little girl would have died anyway, and Lilianne was equally heart-broken, having loved her as if she'd been one of her own. And though she loved Jonathan she didn't know how to cope with his state of mind.

Thankfully the morning after Clemmy's funeral, which had been an ordeal, he came downstairs looking more like his usual self. His eyes were brighter. He had groomed his hair and beard, his shoulders no longer sagged, and he wore his outdoor coat.

'I'm leaving,' he said, standing in the doorway.

The segregated assembly was already eating breakfast which Lilianne had prepared. Mother Girling finished chewing her bread and her tongue travelled over her prominent teeth after she had swallowed it.

'Come and eat, Brother Jonathan. You can't go anywhere on an empty stomach.'

He eyed the food, and when nothing else was said he sat down in his usual place, helped himself to bread and meat and filled his mouth.

'You've forgotten to give thanks to the Lord, brother,' Mother Girling reminded him.

Jonathan had his back to her. 'I ain't got nothing to thank Him for.'

Mother Girling went to his side. She put a hand on his shoulder and waited until he looked up aggressively.

'I'm finished with God,' he muttered. 'Reckon I'd best take myself off before I drag any more of you down in the pit with me. Since I'm headed for Hell I'll be better off joining others going the same way.'

'You may have finished with God, but He hasn't finished with you, brother. If you've reason to think God is punishing you, remember that He only disciplines those He loves,' she told him. 'It's written, "whom the Lord loveth he correcteth; even as a father the son in whom he delighteth." And in the Book of Matthew Jesus says: "I am not come to call the righteous, but sinners to repentance." Maybe you should begin to rejoice.'

'He's taken my little innocent Clemmy. What's she done to deserve it, I ask you? She was sweet and good. If you're the Second Coming of Jesus you ought to know it, Mother.'

'God only tells me what He wants me to know, and what He wants me to tell you. Right now He wants you to know He loves you, whatever you've done wrong. He ain't against you for your sins. It's the sins themselves He wants to help you work against.'

Jonathan pondered over it, then dropped his head into his hands. 'There's a limit to what a man can suffer.'

'Remember Job. No man has ever suffered more than he did. He complained bitterly but he never lost his faith in God's love and he was well rewarded.' The woman's hand moved over his rough hair until her index finger rested on his forehead. With gentle pressure she made him look up again. 'Stay with us, Brother Jonathan. We need you here.'

Seeing another woman of her own age touching him affected Lilianne strongly, though she was loath to admit to jealousy. She held her breath until Jonathan finally agreed to stay.

The exchange of words brought normality back to the community for a short time. Jonathan returned to work for the farrier and Lilianne went daily to a local workhouse where she did the laundry in return for vegetables grown in the garden. But her spirits had never been lower.

If Jonathan had insisted on leaving the Shakers she would have gone with him. She would have sacrificed everything to be with him, and knew that her own sin was greater than his since it was her daughter's husband she coveted. Jonathan didn't love her in the same way. He had merely used her, as he would have used a whore, to relieve the ache in his body.

Nightly she prayed that Hannah would come back with her child, for Aram's return would give Jonathan new hope. She deplored her younger daughter's desertion. Of course she'd always been aware of Hannah's unhappiness but her own hurt and disappointment at not being able to marry Jonathan herself had prevented her from showing sympathy. In all fairness, Hannah had adapted to the situation with admirable courage. She had borne her child and accepted her husband, but she was not cut out to be a Shaker. She was too strong-willed, and it had been inevitable that she would clash with Mother Girling.

What worried Lilianne most was the total silence following her disappearance. Whatever her faults in the past, Hannah had never been one to cause deliberate hurt. She would have sent word if she was safe and well, knowing how her husband and mother would worry. Something dreadful must have happened to her, Lilianne felt it strongly. Mother Girling had enlisted the help of people attending her meetings, Londoners who might know where to look for a missing girl, but still there was no news and the verdict was always pessimistic.

'She'll've starved,' they said, or, 'The lung sickness takes 'em quick in the slums.'

Jonathan had been round to hospitals and workhouses without success, but it was impossible to walk every street or knock on every lodging-house door in the hope of finding her. The other suggestion, that her daughter might be making a living as a prostitute, appalled Lilianne and she rejected it angrily. There was one last awful possibility: that she could have been attacked and left for dead.

Lilianne tried to talk of her fears to Emily, but the subject seemed to frighten her. However, Lilianne was desperate for a sympathetic ear and so she persevered.

'I can't stand not knowing what's happened to her,' she said one night, after going over things yet another time. 'I feel as if I'll go mad. Reckon I never knew how much Hannah meant to me.'

'You've got me, Ma,' Emily said.

'But I want Hannah.' Lilianne broke down and cried, which was something of a phenomenon for she rarely gave way to emotion.

The following morning Emily was waiting outside the workhouse gate for Lilianne when she went to collect the laundry. Her piquant face was half hidden by her shawl, but her eyes sought her mother's.

'Ma, I love you,' she said. 'I can't bear it when you're unhappy, so I'm going to look for Hannah and bring her back.'

Lilianne's face blanched. 'What're you saying, child?'

'You're not to worry about me. The Lord'll be with me, and I'll let you know where I am, I promise.'

'Emily, you can't do this. You dear, wonderful girl, please spare me more worry I beg you.' This was terrible.

'I prayed over it last night after we talked and I know what God wants me to do.'

'But you don't know where to look for Hannah!'

Emily clung to her for a moment, then broke free and hurried away before anything else could be said.

'Stop, child! Please don't leave me.' Lilianne started to run after her, but it was no use. She collapsed with shock against the work-house wall and sobbed as Emily ran light of foot down the road and turned the corner without looking back. 'I didn't mean it when I said it was Hannah I wanted. I want you both.'

Hannah alone in London was one thing, Emily was another. She was such an innocent.

'Oh God, *please* take care of her,' she begged. 'Now all my children have gone.'

Chapter Twenty-Three

Emily had a lot for which to thank Amos Hanberry. The old man was sometimes a mite difficult but he had become appreciative of what she did for him and generous in his praise when his son Titus came to visit. In gratitude Titus Hanberry made Ben and Emily an offer.

'Tell you what I'll do,' Titus said. 'If you two good people become man and wife and are willing to go on caring for my father I'll buy a small house you can all live in rent-free until Ben's apprenticeship is finished. Emily will of course continue to work for Mrs Hanberry. How does that sound?'

'It sounds wonderful,' cried Emily, clapping her hands.

Ben was disappointingly slow to agree. He was satisfied with arrangements as they were.

'It's too big a step to take,' he said, when they were alone. 'I'm very fond of you, Emily, but that ain't the same as loving.'

'How many people marry for love?' Emily asked. Her hopes were high, but she knew she had to be very careful with words. 'I'm willing to sacrifice my freedom so you can better yourself. Lots of people would commit a crime to get what we'd be getting out of it.'

'I'd not planned to settle down with a wife.'

'You could do worse than me,' she teased him. 'I'll be good to you.'

'I know that.'

'Then what's so terrible about getting married?' She didn't give him a minute's peace until he had been talked into it. And then he had to be persuaded not to get in touch with her mother to let her know about the wedding.

'Ma wouldn't approve, Ben, you know that. She'd make a fuss and say we're too much like kin. I'll write to her afterwards.'

Thankfully he didn't mention Hannah and Jonathan, but then she'd not expected it, knowing how he still felt about Hannah. The less said about her sister the better. She would soon make him forget her altogether.

The wedding was arranged to take place in the Methodist Chapel in Bermondsey. The Hanberrys were church people and had been willing for it to be at St James's Church near Jamaica Road, but Emily had been brought up in the Methodist tradition and said she wouldn't feel comfortable in such a big new building with columns at the entrance which made it look like some kind of temple. So plans were quickly made for the Methodist Minister to conduct the marriage service.

On the day before the wedding Emily had just returned from work when there was a knock at the door. A short, stout gentleman stood awkwardly on the step with his hat in his hand.

'I'm from the chapel, Miss Jerram. I've very sad news, I'm afraid. Our dear Reverend Wilkins took ill and died of a heart attack this morning.'

'Oh, no. Poor man.' She was genuinely sorry. Then: 'But what about my wedding?'

'I regret it must be postponed, my dear, until a circuit minister is available. It may be a week or two.'

Emily was distraught. By then Ben might have changed his mind. Besides, the Hanberrys had set the day aside to attend and she didn't want to upset them. The three daughters, Jane, Maria and Elizabeth, had bought new clothes, and Jane had kindly turned out one of her old dresses for Emily to wear. It was to be the happiest day of her life, even if Ben was a reluctant bridegroom.

She left Amos complaining that his tea was late, and ran to the chapel which was two streets away. She knew some of the circuit ministers. They were kindly men who responded to a sweet smile and an air of fragility. She would look at the list in the chapel and see which one lived near enough for her to go now and plead for an hour of his time tomorrow morning.

The chapel door was never locked. It creaked as she opened it and she went inside expecting the hall to be empty, but to her surprise a young man was at an open cupboard. Three Bibles were in his hands. For a moment they eyed each other warily, then the young man smiled.

'Ah, gracious lady, what can I do for you? You have caught me at a busy moment.'

'So I see,' said Emily. She was immediately suspicious. 'I can't recall having seen you here before. What're you doing with our Bibles?'

He put them back in the cupboard reverently, tipping them off the palms of his hands so that they slid into place on the shelf. His hands were white, his nails well cared for.

'Allow me to introduce myself. I am the Reverend Michael Playfair from the – er – Rotherhithe parish.' His voice was surprisingly loud for a smallish man.

'Are you a circuit minister, then?' Emily asked. What luck if he was!

'In a manner of speaking,' he said.

He had a black moustache which twitched up towards his right nostril then the left as he tried to make up his mind which parish to call his own. His shoes were well-polished. His shirt was immaculately white but frayed at the collar from which his neck stretched up like a stalk to support his small head. Dark, well-brushed hair smelt strongly of oil. He wore a black suit which had seen better days, and a red and blue cravat held in place by a pearl-headed pin.

Emily lifted the edge of her apron to her eyes, and by thinking of her plight she managed to squeeze a tear or two on to her lashes.

'I was getting married tomorrow, Reverend Playfair, but now I can't because our Minister died this morning. I wonder . . .' She pressed her lips together as if to gain control of her emotions. 'I wonder if you could possibly come here at eleven o'clock tomorrow and perform the ceremony. Me and my Intended would be eternally grateful.'

The Minister put his hands together and raised them high. They were slightly unsteady. 'The Lord knows my life is dedicated to spreading His joy, and what happiness there is in joining two young people in holy matrimony.' He looked at Emily with a rakish expression which was contrary to his calling. 'I envy the lucky gentleman. It would give me the greatest pleasure to help you if I could, my dear, but alas I shall not be this way tomorrow.'

'Couldn't you please spare us even a few minutes of your time?'

'I wish that I could.'

Emily turned aside, her tears now genuine. It was then that she looked out of the side window which faced on to a small yard at the rear of the chapel, and she saw a large horse-drawn waggon. The horse was tethered to the fence. She hurried to the window.

'You're not a circuit minister,' she accused him. 'You're only a travelling Gospel preacher.'

He came after her. 'I take the Word of God to those who can't get to chapel,' he declared. 'I travel from place to place as God wills me. Since my ordination I've seen the great need for preaching in the streets where I can reach people starved of spiritual comfort and knowledge.' The waggon had religious texts painted over the sides, and in large letters were the words METHODIST HOME MISSIONS CHAPEL CAR. At the front, under an overhanging roof canopy, was a door with an etched glass window, and in front of that a waist-high barrier which gave the impression of a pulpit. 'My church is out there,' he said. 'Blessed is the Lord! He has provided me with the means to bring Jesus Christ to every man and woman who hears my voice. Through *my* voice the Word is spread.'

She faced him. 'And through *our* Bibles. You were going to take them away, weren't you?'

He ran a finger round the inside of his collar, and beads of perspiration trickled off the oiled hair.

'Dear lady, I only wanted one. It was to be for a workhouse where God has seen fit to teach a man to read so that the scriptures can be heard by the poor destitute inmates who need hope more than anything else. Would you deny that's a worthy cause?'

'Yes, I would,' said Emily. 'The governors of the workhouse should provide a Bible.' She stood straight and raised her eyes to his. 'I caught you stealing, but I'll not tell anyone if you'll agree to come back tomorrow to conduct my marriage.'

He shifted uneasily under her stare. 'Would it be worth my while?'

'I'll give you a guinea if you'll do it. Only no one must know you're a travelling man, and you must make it quick. I don't know when the Reverend Wilkins's funeral will be.'

Michael Playfair tugged at his moustache. She could almost see the guinea swinging in front of his nose like a carrot before a donkey. He was unlike any Minister she'd met, but he had the authority to make her Ben's wife and that was all that mattered.

'Very well,' he said. 'I'll do it, not for the money you understand, but because I couldn't bear such a lovely young lady to be disappointed.'

*

Ben took no interest in the wedding arrangements. In spite of her unfaithfulness he still loved Hannah with an overwhelming strength. No other woman could match her, and marriage to anyone else was bound to be nothing more than a convenience, to improve his prospects. Better perhaps to settle for Emily, whom he knew so well, rather than a girl who only appealed to him sexually.

The bride looked very pretty in the pink-checked taffeta dress Jane Hanberry had given her. It was a crinoline, the first Emily had ever worn, but she walked in it as if she belonged to the middle-class. She was very nervous. All through the ceremony she kept glancing behind her, as if expecting someone to raise an objection, and her thin hands trembled so much Ben had difficulty slipping on the ring.

The Minister was in a hurry.

'Dear people, I must apologise for making this a brief ceremony,' he said. He smelt of pomander and looked more like a music-hall entertainer than a clergyman, but his manner was suitably clerical except for the speed with which he dispensed with formalities. 'As you know, our revered Reverend Wilkins passed away suddenly yesterday and I'm asked to fill in for him. Consequently I am much needed to minister to the sick and needy, but I feel privileged to be at this joyous occasion and I hope it will be memorable for the happy couple. Yes, I hope so indeed.'

He rattled through some prayers and hurried them through their vows. The marriage certificate was signed and handed over, and in no time at all he was shaking Ben by the hand. Emily was overcome with gratitude. She dipped into her reticule and gave him a coin, though it was not her place to do so.

'Please use this to help someone in need,' she said. 'It's the least I can do to thank you for coming.'

'My dear Mrs Rutherford, you are the soul of generosity. Be sure the Lord will bless you,' the Reverend Playfair said, patting an oiled wave of hair into place. 'I wish you both a long and happy life together. Now, if you will excuse me, I must be going to my next appointment.'

His hasty departure left everyone breathless.

When the wedding party emerged from the chapel there was a little cloud of dust down the road. Years of scanning the Suffolk marshes had given Ben keen eyesight and he could read the words

Christ Died for the Ungodly written on the back of a mission car fast disappearing. The Minister's method of transport surprised him, but Emily was demanding his attention so he thought no more of it.

After the wedding Isobel Hanberry very kindly provided tea at her house for the newly-married couple, Cook having been asked to make a special cake for the occasion. Emily felt awkward being treated so royally by her employers, but Ben adapted to it as if he had always been used to mixing with people higher up the social scale. Titus Hanberry spoke to him almost as an equal, and she was proud of her new husband. She could tell it wouldn't be too many years before he was capable of employing people himself provided he could find the money, and then she would be able to have a servant of her own. It was such a glorious prospect that she began to copy some of Mrs Hanberry's gracious little mannerisms in preparation.

Their new home was ready for them to occupy straight away. It was furnished with unwanted bits and pieces from the Rotherhithe house and Amos had come back early and lit a fire so that it was warm when they arrived. He'd also brought in a large jug of ale which he persuaded Ben to help him drink. It took such a long time to empty the contents that Emily was left to retire to the marriage bed alone, and when Ben eventually joined her he was too drunk to do anything except sleep. So Emily's wedding night, which she had anticipated with excitement and a certain amount of fear, slipped away without consummation.

Two more nights passed before he finally made her his wife in more than name. She felt a strange sweetness in the lower region of her stomach as soon as he was lying beside her, and when he leaned over to kiss her cheek, as he had done on the previous nights, she dared to press her thin body close. Ben put his arms round her and slid his fingers through her fine, silky hair.

'I don't want to hurt you,' he murmured.

'I don't mind, Ben.'

'It don't seem right somehow. I still think of you as a sister.'

'Silly,' she said, nestling against him. The warmth of his body stirred her further. 'We're married.'

He was very gentle with her. But Emily discovered she had an unexpected sensuality, and after the initial pain which caused her muscles to tighten against him she found the careful rhythm of his movement within her becoming very pleasurable. So much so that after he was spent she kept her slender legs twined about him and he had to disentangle himself before he could roll over on to his back.

'That was . . . very nice,' she whispered. Her nightdress was bunched up uncomfortably under her arms. She removed it instead of pulling it down, and her small, almost non-existent breasts brushed against his arm. 'You can do it again if you like, Ben.'

He laughed. It was a most welcome sound, the first indication of any gladness since they'd left the chapel.

'What a surprising girl you are,' he said.

Ten minutes later he took her again with more force, and she responded energetically, surprising herself when the ecstatic sensation in her body built up to a pitch where it culminated in a series of convulsive shudders which made her moan.

Oh yes, she promised, she would soon make him forget about Hannah.

Chapter Twenty-Four

The days dragged by for Lilianne after Emily had left The Children of God, and she worried unceasingly in spite of Mother Girling's insistence on putting everything in the hands of the Lord.

'Sister Emily is full of goodness,' Mother said. 'Jesus loves her. She'll be guided by Him and come to no harm.'

A week passed. Two weeks. April came and the light evenings brought larger crowds to Sutherland Street to jeer at the Shakers and mimic their dancing. A new nickname, 'the Walworth Jumpers', was given to these Children of God who asked only to practise their religion in peace, and it was shouted derisively by the New Cut swells who set up a wailing noise outside the door of the Meeting Hall and performed gyrations bordering on the obscene which caused ribald laughter. Eggs were thrown at the Shakers when they arrived and the road became congested with sightseers. The result was that Mother Girling had notice to quit the Walworth hall.

Newspaper reports likened The Children of God to the American sect also known as Shakers but who called themselves Believers. There was talk of a connection between the two. Mother Girling was quick to deny it publicly.

'*I* am the only chosen one,' she declared vehemently. 'I am the Messiah.'

Nevertheless, The Children of God were anxious to hear how their counterparts were faring after a hundred faithful years, and Miss Kitty Long, the wealthy spinster who regularly attended the Walworth meetings and had been to America herself, was able to tell them first-hand about the good people of New Lebanon. She sat in the kitchen of the house in Battersea for which she paid the rent, and gathered Mother Girling's many converts around her that they might hear her experiences.

'Like us the Believers receive spiritual gifts from on high which makes them dance and sing with great fervour,' she said.

'No more than the brothers and sisters here,' said Mother Girling. She sounded indignant.

'And they're so clever at making things.'

'Do they sell them?'

'Oh, no. It would be immoral. They make things to use. The chairs, I was told, have to be beautiful enough for an angel to sit on.'

The farm labourers and lowly city workmen who toiled equally hard for perfection listened with avid interest. They pressed Miss Long for as many details of Shaker life in America as she could remember and she told of their work and study and prayer, their Quaker-like way of dressing and their belief in celibacy.

'If a man and woman form ... er ... an attachment they must return to the World,' she said.

Lilianne did not dare look in Jonathan's direction.

Miss Long described their chapels and the plain houses they lived in with separate dormitories for men and women, and she talked of Mother Ann, who in earlier times had apparently had visions similar to the ones seen by Mother Girling.

'I regret to say, Mother, that our colonial cousins think of you as an imposter,' Miss Long told her, diffidently.

Mother Girling sat with her spine straight against the back of a well-worn chair which no discerning angel would have appreciated, and her piercing gaze settled on the other woman with powerful command.

'Sister, do you sincerely believe that I am the Second Coming of the Messiah, chosen by the Lord God to bring new hope to the world?' she asked.

'I do, Mother,' answered the spinster, without hesitation.

'I am the *only* terrestrial habitation chosen by the Lord God to reveal the female side of Him. At His First Coming in Jesus He was seen as a man and He was destroyed because He said He was God. After the crucifixion God the Spirit raised His body to Heaven and glorified it, and from that time there's only been a few who have seen Him. Twelve years ago the time had come to give out the mother part of Himself. The celestial God-mother came as a bride, a great light out of Heaven, the female part of God adorned as a glorious bride yet having no substance. She had to have a terrestrial body in the shape of a woman, and it pleased the Lord God to call

Mary Ann Girling by name. He has taken my body, and mine alone, to dwell in. I am filled with the celestial life and I live the same life that Jesus lived.'

There was silence. Lilianne gazed at Mother Girling and expected her to be surrounded by an aura of great light, but nothing changed. The dull room was just the same as always, except that the occupants were drawn together by a strong bonding of minds concentrating on the words they had just heard.

'Does that mean you'll be crucified?' one man dared to ask.

Mother Girling smiled, and those she called brothers and sisters saw only the beauty of it, not her large teeth and plain, angular features.

'I shall never die,' she said. 'And neither will you, my dears, now you've been fully accepted into the faith. Do you all believe what I've just said?'

With one voice they said that they did.

She might have convinced her devoted followers that she had no connection with the American sect, but that same month a woman whose husband was committed to the Walworth Shakers took him to court in the belief that he was about to desert her and leave for America with them. Nothing could have been further from the truth. Mother Girling had no reason to leave London, but Lilianne thought of her son Luke and would have gone willingly to America if Mother had decreed it.

When Emily had been gone for four weeks Lilianne received a letter from her. She tore it open hurriedly and looked at the signature before reading the spidery writing which covered the page. Relief flooded through her in a warm wave and her eyes smarted with tears which made the words dance, but her relief quickly turned to disappointment and anger.

'*Dear Ma,*' she read. '*I haven't found Hannah but I've found Ben. I have a post in Rotherhithe with Mrs Hanberry. I am her maid. Ben works for Mr Hanberry.*

'*I love you, but I won't be coming back. Yesterday Ben and me were married. I am very happy.*

'*Your loving daughter, Emily Rutherford.*'

Lilianne tucked the letter away in her bodice and said nothing to anyone. She needed time to think about the news it contained.

At least she knew that one of her daughters was safe, but the reappearance of Ben Rutherford here in London was bad news indeed. Not only had he taken her money, he had taken Hannah and in all probability given her the child on which poor Jonathan doted. Now he had taken Emily as well. Lilianne hated him.

As her mother had known, Hannah was not cut out to be a Shaker. She was even less suited to be a pick-pocket.

The shock of Aram being held hostage filled her with fear. It would have been enough to make a less spirited girl collapse in despair, but Hannah was now well-practised in surviving life's hard knocks and after the initial panic had subsided she knew that temporarily she had to become a thief. But once Aram was in her arms again she would never relinquish him. She would leave the lodging house immediately and chance finding somewhere else to sleep. Maybe she would return to Battersea. The problems she'd been facing there were nothing compared to the trouble she was in now.

That afternoon as she walked beside Lottie she took note of the way they were going. The house, she discovered, was in Queen Street which led in turn to the place where seven streets met, and Hannah recognised the druggist's shop with the coloured jars in the window. Seven Dials, Lottie said the central space was called. From here they went northwards, as near as she could tell by the direction of the sun, and all the time Lottie was telling her what they would do.

'It's too risky for you to lift anything yet,' she said. 'You ain't had any experience. So we'll work together. When we get to the end here it'll be crowded and we'll stand about like we're lost till we see a lie-dy who'll likely be worth stopping.' Ladies were always to be their victims. It was harder to rob a man without being caught. 'I want you to ask 'er the way to Holborn, looking straight in 'er eyes, and while she tells yer I'll be relieving 'er of 'er purse.'

It sounded less frightening than having to actually do the pocket-picking herself and Hannah breathed a little more easily. They didn't stop until they came to a main thoroughfare which was bustling with people and traffic, vehicles thundering by in a continual stream.

'Where's this, then?' Hannah asked.

'New Oxford Street.' Lottie took hold of Hannah's arm. 'Since we're both respectably dressed we ain't likely to arouse suspicion, and there's enough folk about to lose ourselves quick if things go wrong. Now . . .' She stopped and looked about her, eyes raised as if to gauge her whereabouts but flickering sideways every few seconds to watch a well-dressed woman in a flounced green satin gown who was coming towards them. 'P'raps this lie-dy can 'elp us.'

Lottie's Cockney accent was more common than her appearance, and Hannah's Suffolk burr was the one likely to convince someone that they really were lost. They stood in front of the woman, and with a nervousness which made her stutter, Hannah did the talking.

'Excuse me, ma'am, can you tell me . . . us . . . the way to Holborn?'

The lady had a kind face and she took trouble explaining. Hannah thanked her gratefully and almost forgot that it had been but a ploy to rob her. A few minutes later, as they walked arm-in-arm towards Holborn, Lottie pressed a gold watch into Hannah's hand and told her to put it somewhere safe.

'But . . . how did you get it?' Hannah was astounded.

'She 'ad a pocket under one of the flounces. Had to break the ring it was attached to but that weren't difficult. It'll fetch four quid if we're lucky.'

The trick was tried again and yielded a purse containing ten sovereigns which were also transferred to Hannah's keeping. After that their luck ran out. The next lady they approached was also alone and Lottie had said they would walk each side of her on the crowded pavement. Hannah had gained confidence and she repeated her request for directions more easily. But the hooked handle of a walking cane came round her forearm just as she was being told that Holborn was but a few yards further on, and she was drawn back against a powerful chest. Lottie disappeared as swiftly as a snuffed-out candle-flame.

'I've been watching you, young woman, and I've alerted the police.' A deep, masculine voice rumbled above Hannah's head and she shook with fright. A policeman joined them and she was given over to his firm grip. The intended victim was suffering an attack of the vapours and had to be helped to a shop doorway where someone produced a chair for her to sit down.

'Turn out yer pockets,' said the policeman.

'They made me do it,' cried Hannah. 'They've got my baby and won't let me have him back.'

She had never been so frightened in her life. Her hands were sweating yet she was so cold her teeth chattered, and her eyes were wide in her desperate appeal to be believed. But the gold watch and the ten sovereigns were all the evidence needed to convict her.

No privileges were allowed, though she sobbed and pleaded for Aram to be found, and she was taken straight to Marylebone police court where she was committed for trial. All night she lay in the police cell with a leaden heart, her arms aching to hold her baby, her breasts aching to feed him, but no one had any compassion. Her case was all too familiar. She asked for her husband, told them that she was a Shaker and begged for someone to take a message to Walworth, but there was no response except for jibes about the antics of the Girlingites as one policeman called them.

'I ain't surprised yer in trouble if yer one o' them,' the man scoffed. 'I'm allus being called to restore law and order at Shaker meetings.'

At her brief trial the next day there was no one to pay for counsel to plead for her, no one to speak in her defence, and the magistrate had no hesitation in sentencing her to two months in Newgate prison. It was a lenient sentence as hers was a first offence. She could easily have been given six months.

From the moment the heavy oak gate studded with iron nails closed behind her Hannah's spirits sank to their lowest ebb. The smell and feel and sounds of Newgate almost suffocated her, and she had to be restrained when she attempted to run back and claw at the wood. She was taken first to a receiving room where she suffered the indignity of being examined by a prison surgeon to make sure she had no infectious disease. The milk from her breasts had soaked her bodice and the smell was growing stale and so unpleasant she felt sick, but no comment was made, and when she tried to get the doctor's sympathy he gave none.

A turnkey without a sign of compassion in his granite features then took her along a stone passage where several gates had to be unlocked and locked again, and as she went through them she gave up hope. Through a door composed of wooden bars she could see women walking to and fro in a narrow yard, on one side of which was what looked to be a cage roofed in at the top where visitors and prisoners could talk through iron bars. The women were pathetic creatures, mostly haggard and ill-clad, though there was one with a man's silk handkerchief tied over her flowing hair who didn't have such a dejected set to her shoulders.

It was so cold Hannah anchored her shawl more tightly round her arms. Up some stairs now to a ward which was a slight improvement. The windows faced the interior of the prison, but whitewashed walls gave a lightness to the large, bare room. There was a fire burning at one end and about a dozen women were seated on wooden forms at a deal table in front of it. A shelf ran along both side walls from which sleeping mats were hanging on hooks, a rug and a blanket neatly folded above each one. The women here were quite decently dressed and some were doing needlework. They looked up at Hannah's entrance, but no one spoke other than the wardswoman who asked her name.

Later, stewed beef and brown bread was served on pewter dishes. A girl in a cap and a dirty white apron moved along one of the forms nearer to Hannah.

'My name's Eva Brown. What was you done for, ducks?' she asked.

'Nothing,' said Hannah. 'I was tricked by a wicked woman in a lodging house who stole my baby.'

The girl sniffed. 'High and mighty, ain't yer.' She wiped her nose on the back of her hand. 'Well, we're all the same 'ere.'

Hannah could see that she was scarcely more than a child, and when she remembered her own carefree days on the farm she felt great pity for her.

'I'm sorry,' she said. 'I ain't any different either. All I want is me baby back.'

'Better orf without the little bleeder I'd say.' The harsh words were accompanied by another sniff, but then the girl's eyes filled with tears. 'Mine died.'

When night came Hannah was given a sleeping mat and a space on the floor farthest away from the fireplace. Texts from scripture were pasted to a board on the wall and when she couldn't sleep she tried to concentrate on them. '*Be not overcome of evil, but overcome evil with good,*' she read. She turned to Eva Brown who was lying beside her, and clasped her hand. After an initial stiffening of the fingers Eva silently returned the gesture of friendship.

Mother Girling's teaching helped her to get through the night. She prayed for strength to survive this new ordeal, prayed for it to be over quickly. But six weeks later, when her sister Emily married Ben Rutherford, Hannah was still shut away in Newgate prison.

Chapter Twenty-Five

Two days after the wedding of Ben and Emily, Amos was taken ill with a bad chest. He coughed all that night, bringing up unpleasant phlegm, and Emily had to sit with him, afraid to go to bed in case he couldn't get his breath. Early the next day Ben thought it best to tell Titus of his father's illness.

Isobel Hanberry came at once and made a poultice of vinegar and onions and oatmeal which she put on the old man's back and chest as hot as he could stand it. She also had a bottle of liquorice and chlorodyne mixture for him to take by the spoonful and she scolded him for trying to spit it out.

'You'll soon recover if you take your medicine and stay in bed,' she said. 'Emily, I wish I could tell you to stay here and see that he does but it's my day to go to Newgate prison so I need you at the house.'

'You risk infections yourself going there, ma'am, I shouldn't wonder,' said Ben.

'It's a risk I have to take. Those poor girls need someone to try and turn them from their evil ways. Some are lured into crime through no fault of their own and they're the ones I hope to persuade to make a better life for themselves once they've done their time.' She drew her wide skirt round her to negotiate the stairs. 'I'm concerned about one such girl I met last week who was made to take up thieving because her baby is being held to ransom. She seems quite decent, though she foolishly left her husband. I promised to try and contact him but apparently he belongs to that strange sect they call Shakers.'

Mrs Hanberry's clipped way of speaking made the words very plain to hear. Ben had preceded her down the stairs and was standing ready to hand her down the bottom ones. Emily followed behind. She almost stumbled at mention of the Shakers and the word vibrated like a gong in her ears. Ben lifted his eyebrows sharply.

'Now, I must hurry.' Isobel pulled on her gloves and smoothed them up her wrist.

'No, wait,' gasped Emily. She forgot her manners and dashed to the door in front of her, barring her way. 'The girl from the Shakers . . . did she tell you her name?'

'Er . . . Ann I believe. Ann Whitfield. No, I think it was Hannah. Why, what's the matter, child?'

Emily's legs would hardly hold her and she had to cling to the doorpost. All the colour left her face and her mouth fell open. It was Ben who stayed calm, though the shock to him must have been even greater since he hadn't known that Hannah was no longer with Jonathan and Mother Girling. He went straight to Emily and helped her to a chair while addressing Isobel Hanberry over his shoulder.

'Hannah Whitfield is my wife's sister, ma'am. When I've got her a glass of water I'll be grateful if you can tell us all you know.'

It seemed that Hannah had been in prison for six weeks, practically the whole of the time since she had left Marbro Terrace, but Aram was still in some dirty lodging house. Emily felt faint. In her eagerness to win Ben she hadn't cared about her sister. Her disappearance had made it easier to slip away herself and make up stories to soothe away any suspicions Ben might have had that Hannah had been coerced into a loveless marriage. She sipped the water her husband held to her lips.

'Pull yourself together, Emily,' he was saying. 'You must go and tell your mother and Jonathan Whitfield. What can they have been thinking about to let this happen to her.' He turned respectfully to his employer's wife. 'I'm going to Newgate myself, Mrs Hanberry. Emily and I will make up the time we owe.'

'We'll go to the prison together,' decided Isobel. 'I'll send word to the ropeyard. But I can't spare you for more than two hours, Emily. Hurry back as soon as you've spoken to your mother. There's a lot of housework to be done this morning.'

Amos started coughing again, but Emily didn't go and make him take his medicine. She had too many other worries on her mind.

Ben had thought that Newgate would be much like the prison in Ipswich where he had been detained pending his trial for horse-thieving, but like everything else in London it was bigger and dirtier and noisier than he could have imagined. With a sinking feeling in his stomach he entered the cage-like area facing the women's exercise yard. His nerves were tense and he wanted to breathe deeply to steady them but that meant inhaling a stench of unwashed females, garbage and drains. He looked through the iron bars and a prostitute sidled over, lifting her skirt and eyeing him provocatively as she offered him a good time for free if he would get her out of the place. Mrs Hanberry was at his side and Ben's face reddened. There was no sign of Hannah.

'I'll go and make enquiries,' Mrs Hanberry said. 'You stay here.'

She was hardly out of sight before Hannah came through a gate opposite. Ben's heart almost stopped. Her hair was matted and dirty, so dark with grease no one would have known it was honey-gold. Her grubby dress hung like a rag on her emaciated body, her feet dragged, and even at a distance he could see her eyes were as dull as stone. He hung back in the shadows to collect himself. He hadn't been prepared for such a change in her and he couldn't face her until he was able to do so without revealing his shock.

Ever since Isobel Hanberry had said her name this morning he had been choked with anxiety, and he continued to curse himself for not having checked that Hannah's life was as idyllic as Emily had painted it. He remembered how she had been in a hurry to close the door when he had called, and saw now it could have been that she was afraid of her husband returning to find him there. She had left him, according to Mrs Hanberry. It wasn't surprising. He ought to have known that a young, vital girl with Hannah's wayward temperament wouldn't fall for a man old enough to be her father. The more he thought about it the more he blamed himself for not having questioned Emily thoroughly instead of accepting her word. He had been so jealous, so angry, and so disillusioned.

He hadn't forgotten Mrs Hanberry's other revelation. There was a baby. The girl's baby was being held to ransom, she had said. He couldn't think why Emily had never told him that Hannah had a child, or why Hannah hadn't told him herself. There was mystery attached to it, that was for sure, and Ben played with the possibility that it was his. But then he dismissed the idea. Emily would have behaved differently. She wouldn't have been so keen to marry him knowing he had fathered her sister's child.

His thoughts were chaotic as he looked at what Hannah had become, but one thing was absolutely certain. He loved her more than ever.

He moved forward and she saw him. Her forehead creased and she blinked hard as if afraid she was imagining what she saw. Then her dragging feet were released from the weight of despair and she pushed aside the women in her path so that she could run to him. Her hands grasped the iron bars.

'Ben! Tell me it's really you and I'm not going mad.'

He bent his head and rested his lips against the cold, outstretched fingers. He couldn't speak for the lump in his throat.

'How did you know I was here? How did you find me?' She was crying.

'Emily works for Mrs Hanberry,' he said. He caressed her arm. 'My questions are more important. How am I going to get you out of here? And how the hell do you come to be *in* here? Oh, Hannah, I never could trust you out of my sight.'

'After you came to Battersea I couldn't stay with Jonathan any longer. I told Emily I was going to try to find you.'

'You told Emily!'

'She was the only one. I didn't tell anyone else.'

'You didn't tell me you've got a baby.'

Tears were running down her cheeks unchecked, etching lines through the grime on their journey to the down-turned corners of her mouth. 'I've lost him, Ben. A terrible woman called Mrs Humby took him from me and said I had to pick pockets and take her the money before she'd let me have him back. But I got caught.' She was so distressed she couldn't stop shaking and he wished he had the strength to tear down the bars keeping them apart. 'Please, *please* get him back for me. I want him.'

'Where does the woman live?'

'A lodging house in Queen Street. Lottie Beck lives there as well and she told me it was in Seven Dials.'

She was being harassed by the prostitute, who kept giving her small, cunning nudges to get her away from the best-looking man to visit the prison in a long while. An old woman in a tattered dress kept uttering anguished cries nearby. There was so much to say, so many things to ask. Ben wanted to warn Hannah that the baby could be dead by now, but it was impossible to hold a conversation.

Mrs Hanberry came back, and a waft of lavender water was as welcome as a breath of fresh air. She smiled warmly at Hannah. 'Good morning, my dear.'

'Good morning, Mrs Hanberry,' said Hannah. Then her eyes widened. 'Hanberry. Now I know why your name was familiar! It were an Amos Hanberry I was to ask for when I was looking for Ben.'

'Amos is my father-in-law,' she explained. 'Now, how pleased you must be to see your sister's husband. Wasn't it fortunate I mentioned your name this morning.' Isobel saw another of her needy chicks. 'Oh, there's Maggie. Will you excuse me while I have a word with her.'

Hannah withdrew her hands. A look of disbelief was replaced almost immediately by pain, and she stepped back just as Ben pressed himself against the bars in a futile attempt to shield her.

'You married Emily!'

'Three days ago.'

'And did she have any trouble getting you to marry her?' Hannah asked, in a tight and bitter tone. 'Or are you using her to hurt me?'

'You told me you were happy with the man Whitfield. Emily said repeatedly that you and he had fallen for each other right off. Did you expect me to wait around hoping you'd grow sick of him, or he'd conveniently leave you a widow?'

'You're cruel, Ben.'

'You said you didn't want to see me again.'

'I didn't mean it.'

'Then why did you say it? You know how I feel about you. If I'd thought anything was wrong I'd have moved heaven and earth to help you, but you sent me away.'

Hannah closed her eyes and swayed. 'If it's true you still feel something for me then please get Aram back. I'll never ask for anything else.'

'Whose baby is he, Hannah?'

Her lids lifted slowly and the stone coldness was there again. 'He's my husband's child, of course. Jonathan worships him.'

When he was outside on the pavement once more he looked up at the walls of Newgate and clenched his fists into tight balls. It wasn't the prison he wanted to strike. It was women. For the life of him he'd never understand their way of thinking. He didn't know why Hannah had spoken to him so angrily that night in Battersea, why she hadn't told him about her son, why she had made out she was happy with Jonathan Whitfield if she wasn't. He didn't know why Emily had never told him that Hannah had left the Shakers

250

before she did so herself, or why she had echoed Hannah's declaration that the marriage was a happy one, unless it was to be deliberately misleading so that he wouldn't be tempted to interfere in Hannah's affairs.

He was angry with his wife. She had cheated to get him to the altar and he wouldn't forgive her in a hurry.

Suddenly Hannah Whitfield was having more visitors than anyone else in the women's ward at Newgate. Her husband came not long after Ben Rutherford had left, but he didn't cause the prostitute to be so attentive, and he didn't bring tears to the eyes of his wife, though they glistened in his own. He left after about ten minutes and followed a similar route to the one Ben had taken.

He came out of the prison by Old Bailey, turned right into Ludgate Hill and kept on walking, oblivious to the jostling crowds on the pavement and the congestion of omnibuses, carts and carriages which moved through a pall of smoke from a train crossing the railway bridge. He rubbed shoulders with city men in black coats and top-hats, costermongers sporting silk neckerchiefs and long cord waistcoats decorated with numerous buttons, women in crushed straw bonnets, rich Jews, poor Irishmen, and a dustman with a leather flap hanging down from his hooded cap as he led his horse and box-cart in the same direction. People from all walks of life passed Jonathan by. Likely they were all weighed down with problems. Likely few of them were prepared to take such desperate measures to solve them. Jonathan vowed that he would kill if it was necessary to get Hannah's child back.

Having asked the way to Seven Dials he strode along at a pace which made other pedestrians get out of his way. Meaning had returned to his life and he thanked the Lord for it. This morning he'd been about to leave the house when Emily had arrived. He'd never taken to Lilianne's older daughter, never quite trusted her or wanted to know her better. He hadn't been particularly welcoming. It had been left to Lilianne to give him the news that Hannah was in prison, and dreadful though it was, his heart had lifted miraculously and he had felt ten years younger at once. Their prayers had been heard.

Seeing Hannah had almost reduced him to tears. The pitiful change in her affected him deeply, and he wanted to pick her up and remove her from such a terrible place. But that was impossible. She had another week of her sentence yet to serve. Her agonised cries for Aram still echoed through his mind, and he felt ill with fear for the baby's safety. He'd vowed that nothing would prevent him from restoring the child to her, but a baby's life was held cheaply in the slum areas of London.

And yet he had hope. As he hurried along he spoke to God and it seemed as if he was walking in light for the first time in weeks. The darkness was behind him, along with his sins for which he had been forgiven by God's grace.

Seven Dials was the poorest quarter he had ever visited and he didn't linger, though had he been set upon he would have had the advantage of size and strength. The men and youths he passed were thin, sickly-looking specimens, and he kept his hands in his pockets even though he carried nothing worth pinching. He found Queen Street without too much trouble, but the terraced houses with steps down to basement kitchens all looked much the same and he didn't fancy knocking on every door to find the woman he wanted. He decided to stop a young man coming from the opposite direction who looked surprisingly honest.

'Can you tell me which house belongs to a Mrs Humby?' he asked.

The young man eyed him gravely, and countered with a most surprising question. 'Would you be Jonathan Whitfield?'

'Aye, I would. How in the world do you know me?'

'I'm married to Hannah's sister Emily. The name's Ben Rutherford. I sent my wife to say we'd found out about Hannah being in prison.'

Two days ago Lilianne had shown him a letter from Emily saying she had married the boy her mother had brought up as an adopted son. Hurt and unhappy about it Lilianne had been. The unfeeling way Emily had treated her was the main reason why he hadn't wanted to talk to the girl himself this morning, a fact he'd afterwards regretted. Seemed there was much more he could have learnt. And he hadn't listened properly to Hannah's babbling because his mind had been racing ahead, but now he recalled that she had spoken of another visitor called Ben.

'I'm relieved to meet you,' Jonathan said. 'Maybe with there being two of us we'll be able to collect my son without too much trouble. Have you found out where the woman lives?'

252

'You've passed it. It's nearer the Dials.'

Jonathan turned to retrace his steps and the two men who minutes later rang the bell of Mrs Humby's lodging house looked a formidable pair. They were of similar height, being over six feet, and both had powerful shoulders and muscular arms. The girl who came to the door was immediately suspicious.

'We want to see Mrs Humby,' said Ben.

'If you're copper's narks she ain't here.'

'We ain't the police.' He pushed her aside and went in, closely followed by Jonathan.

When they got to the kitchen their way was barred by a burly fellow with a ruddy countenance obviously resulting from liquor consumption, for he leered at them from the doorway with his feet against one side and his head against the other.

'Mrs 'Umby ain't in,' he said, brandishing a gin bottle. 'Git orf the premises before I make yer sorry yer came.'

Ben had no trouble dislodging him from his diagonal position and he fell in a heap on the floorboards, swearing profusely. The occupants of the kitchen, a dozen or more of both sexes, looked up at the intrusion but at that stage no one else felt obliged to make a fuss.

'Which of you is Mrs Humby?' Ben asked. He had taken the initiative and so far Jonathan had let him do the talking.

Steam rose from a galvanized bath of near-boiling water in which a fat woman near to the fire was soaking her swollen feet. She was dressed in purple satin, and the gold rings on her fingers glinted in the glow from banked-up coal. Her hair had traces of red in the grey and it was brushed into ringlets, some of which were held incongruously in place at the crown of her head with a comb studded with jewels.

'State yer business,' she said. 'I'm Mrs Humby.'

Jonathan stepped forward. 'I've come for my son, madam.'

'Don't know what yer talking about.'

'You kept my son hostage while you sent my wife out to thieve for you. I want him back.'

The woman looked him up and down, her lips parting to show the gaps where teeth were missing. 'Wife, yer say? You're married to that ungrateful young baggage I was so kind to? Couldn't trust 'er to do anything proper.'

'Where's the child?' Ben demanded.

She licked her thick lips. 'Now if you'd said *you* was 'er husband

253

I wouldn't 'ave bin surprised.' She got up and stepped out of the water on to a towel thick enough to have been stolen from gentry. Her feet were as red as raw meat and sore places on her toes oozed pus, but she thrust them into a pair of men's shoes and dropped her skirt over them before going to a door behind her. She called up some stairs, 'Lottie! Bring the kid down 'ere.'

A child began to cry and Jonathan's relief was so great he would have followed her, but Ben stopped him. The men who'd been sitting at a long table were now closing in behind them, and the women moved into a menacing bunch. Sweat gathered on his forehead and he could feel his shirt sticking to his back in the kitchen heat. The woman's bulk filled the doorway and she took something from a girl who could only be glimpsed. When she turned again she had Aram in her arms, wrapped in a filthy blanket, his small fair head just visible. Jonathan's patience could no longer be curbed and he lunged forward, but the men behind him were quicker. His arms were seized and he was dragged back.

Ben bided his time.

'You've got Lottie 'ere to thank he's still alive,' said Mrs Humby. 'Right taken with the little bleeder she is. Gawd knows why.'

The girl came into the room. She had a kind face. With a little trouble taken she could have been attractive, but years of being dominated by Mrs Humby had robbed her of all youthful zest and she looked tired and drawn. Her eyes flickered over Jonathan, but stayed longer on Ben.

'I'm glad 'e's got a father,' she said.

'Give him to me!' shouted Jonathan, struggling to free himself. His strength was insufficient to succeed against the sheer weight of numbers.

'Not so fast.' The woman was back beside the bath and the rising steam made the baby cry more persistently. 'I said 'e'd be returned for a price.'

The women pressed forward, half a dozen harpies who looked evil enough to be pawns of the Devil. They saw that Ben was about to make a grab for the baby and they set about him, clawing and scratching like vicious birds so that he had to protect his face.

'Try to get 'im by force and I'll drown 'im in hot water.' Mrs Humby held Aram over the bath, and the girl called Lottie screamed. 'Let me 'ave yer money.'

254

It was no idle threat. Jonathan was desperate. 'Have mercy, ma'am. I ain't got a farthing.'

'Then say goodbye to yer orfspring.'

Another second and likely she would have been as good as her word, but Ben shouted an offer. 'You can have me watch. It's all I've got.'

They'd already taken it from him. It was passed to Mrs Humby so deftly he didn't know he'd been relieved of it until it appeared in her hand. She held it to her ear, and then she nodded.

'Better'n nowt.' She dropped the simple timepiece down the front of her bodice, and gave the men a signal to release Jonathan. ''Ere, take the kid and go. Good riddance to it.'

Aram was handed over, his screams proclaiming there was nothing wrong with his lungs, and Lottie cried.

When the two men and the child were thankfully outside in the street they hurried towards the Dials, anxious to put distance between themselves and the lodging house, though it was unlikely the occupants would have thought them worth following. Long strides brought them quickly back to the Strand, and from there they parted to go their different ways.

'I'm in your debt,' Jonathan said. 'I'd give my life for the child, but reckon his would have been forfeited first in there. I'll replace the watch somehow.'

'You can't replace it,' said Ben. 'It was given me by Matt Jerram just before he died and I treasured it. But since it was for Hannah I lost it there'll be no regrets.'

He pulled aside the blanket to look closely at the baby which was quiet now in the security of loving arms. Aram's soulful grey eyes briefly gazed back at Ben Rutherford.

Chapter Twenty-Six

Seven more days and Hannah was free to leave Newgate. Early in the morning she was escorted by a turnkey in a black suit and broad-brimmed hat to a small bare room near the main door, where Jonathan was waiting for her.

'My dear, I've been praying for this moment,' he said. He kissed her on both cheeks and his beard was rough against her skin. 'Mother's given me money for an omnibus to take us home. Come.'

She didn't speak. The air outside was heavy with mist which promised a bright day later. She filled her lungs with it. Jonathan took her arm and she accepted the support gratefully since her legs were weak and two months of prison food had sapped her strength. Her mind, too, was numb. She heard her husband's voice but nothing he said seemed to register. The dress she was wearing was the same one she'd had on when she left Marbro Terrace, though dirt made it almost unrecognisable, and the knife-slit in the pocket through which her purse had been stolen had torn so far it almost split her skirt in two. Now she was to ride again on an omnibus, and Mother had graciously provided money for the fare. Nothing had changed: Jonathan was still subservient to Mary Ann Girling, and Hannah cringed inwardly at his dependence on her.

It didn't matter that she was being taken back to the Shakers. She was past caring where she went as long as she was out of Newgate, and the only thing to lift her spirits was the thought of having Aram in her arms again. Jonathan had come to tell her he was safe but, sensibly, he hadn't brought him to the prison for fear of infection. She had seen a baby die there. No compassion had accompanied its passing and the little body had been taken away from the grieving mother like a bundle of old clothes for disposal. Hannah had wept.

Her joy and relief at being free was marred by the news of Ben's marriage to Emily. It was treachery. Yet they'd both been free. She hoped Emily would never know that she and Ben had been lovers, but sometimes there'd been a thoughtful expression in her eyes when she was holding Aram. Hannah tormented herself by longing afresh for the man she loved and couldn't have. Ben would have sent her back to her husband anyway if she had managed to find him in the labyrinth of London's streets. Seeing him briefly through prison bars had brought her close to breaking point, so great was her love. But in marrying her sister he had distanced himself further from her than if, as first planned, he had boarded a ship and gone to America.

Jonathan was very concerned about her. 'Some rest and good food'll make a difference,' he was saying. 'We'll soon have you strong again.'

He didn't ask why she had left him two months ago. He didn't rebuke her, or blame her for what had happened to Aram. He was more caring than he had ever been, which made her feel worse, and she wished she could respond instead of keeping silent by his side.

She looked at him on the omnibus. His face was thinner, his hair greyer, and the lines between his eyebrows were deeper, but he was still a handsome man. She was not vain enough to presume that her escapade alone was responsible for these new signs of aging, but it must be partly the reason. She had put his adored grandchild in the greatest danger. He caught her eye and their gaze locked for several seconds.

'I missed you very much, Hannah,' he said. 'So did yer Ma, and all of us.'

'How are they all?' She found a voice at last. 'Is Ma well?'

'Aye. She can't wait to see you.'

'And Clemmy?'

He looked away and she saw by the hunching of his shoulders that something was wrong. Then: 'My little Clemmy died of a fever. There was no way we could save her. I've been distraught.'

The ice round Hannah's heart suddenly started to melt, and the pain was like warming frost-bitten fingers before a fire on a snowy morning. She caught his hand in hers and clung to him with a compassion which welled up from the very core of her. Tears stung her eyes.

'Oh, Jonathan, I'm so sorry.' It was the first time she had addressed him by his given name. It came naturally, as did the urge to give comfort. 'How dreadful. Ma must be heart-broken too.'

'I was all for giving up and going to the Devil, but Mother Girling saved me once more. Reckon she's the only one who thinks me worth it.'

'You're a good man, Jonathan. You did right by me though likely I didn't deserve it, and you were good to Ma, giving her a job. Don't think badly of yerself. You've no reason.'

'If that were only true.'

She tucked her arm through his to walk across Battersea Bridge and he allowed it until they came within sight of Marbro Terrace. She was feeling stronger now. The air had revived her and the exercise was restoring some of her lost energy. But as she approached the house she became fearful once more, and the thought of going inside produced an attack of panic which almost paralysed her. She stopped in the middle of the pavement and couldn't go any further.

'What's the matter?' Jonathan went a few more steps before turning.

'I can't go in there. I don't want to be a Shaker.'

'What nonsense is this? Are you afraid you're going to be punished for running away? No one will say anything about it. We're all too pleased to have you back.'

The trembling which had started in her legs progressed through her body and she couldn't move from the spot.

'I want to lead a normal life with my husband and child.' Her voice was quivering. 'Let's get Aram and leave, Jonathan. Let's make a life for ourselves somewhere else, away from Mother Girling.'

For a moment his eyes shone. Then a shadow obliterated any sign of happiness from his face and his expression became set like a mask. 'We're needed here to do God's work,' he said. 'Come, girl, they'll be waiting for us.'

He had to drag her the last few yards.

The years ahead stretched before her bleakly. She was married, yet not married. There would be no more children, and she would never again know what it was to have a man. Her husband had never taken her as his wife, and as long as he put Mother Girling's teaching first they would never belong together in body. Some women would envy her and call it good fortune, but Hannah was a sensual girl and she had a lot of love to give. Maybe now that Ben was married she would have been able to devote herself to Jonathan and make a good life for them, something she could have sworn he

258

wanted himself, but he was too greatly influenced by the Shakers. There was no reason now for her to shirk her duty. She had to be beside him and honour his decisions.

Her return to the fold was an occasion for rejoicing. She was treated like a prodigal daughter, and the meal her mother had prepared was a feast compared to the food she'd been forced to eat in prison. Ma was there with Aram bouncing against her shoulder, Mother Girling opened her arms to her, Miriam Rawlings and Harry Bourne had made simple gifts, and Miss Kitty Long gave her a new Bible with her name inscribed on the front page. Hannah was overwhelmed. She took her child and pressed her cheek against his, smothering him with kisses until he gurgled and smiled. He'd grown much bigger in two months in spite of his ordeal and it was clear that Lottie Beck had been a friend. Though likely she would never see her again Hannah wished there was some way she could rescue her from Mrs Humby's clutches.

'You need rest, child,' said Ma, hugging her as soon as the greetings were over and they were alone. It was a long time since she had shown such concern for her and weak tears again pricked Hannah's eyes. There were no reproaches, no cutting words or criticism. 'I'm real glad to have you back safe, that I am.'

She was allowed to sleep for most of the day in the bed she shared with her mother, and Aram lay in the crook of her arm, his golden head soft and warm against her face. She loved him so much it hurt. And she knew she ought to count herself lucky that she had a safe haven. Her experiences in Seven Dials and in Newgate had shown her a side of life beyond imagining, and she pitied the poor girls who had no hope of knowing anything better. Yet a rebellious part of her wondered if their freedom wasn't preferable in some ways: the show of love and forgiveness by everyone in the house was like being bound with a silken thread and she could see there was going to be no escape.

'We must praise God, sister, for your safe return,' said Mother Girling, when Hannah was encouraged to talk later. 'Open your heart to the Lord and He will show you what you must do to repay Him for His goodness.'

But Hannah was not one to fall on her knees and believe that all she had to do was utter words and everything would come right. She would rather get on and *do* things, make things happen.

That evening she was expected to be rested enough to go to the prayer meeting.

'We've a new Meeting Hall now,' said Ma. 'We had to leave Walworth, but Miss Long knows a gentleman who's part manager of a hall in Chelsea and likely he'll join us as a convert one day soon. Seems he has contact with the Believers in America and he's very sympathetic. He's allowed Mother to use the Ebenezer Hall for worship – ain't that wonderful?'

It was quite a long walk to Little College Street in Chelsea, across the river from Battersea, and now no one stayed behind, not even Aram. Jonathan carried the child and Hannah walked beside him. The Shakers attracted a lot of interest as they went in the hall, but there were no rotten eggs thrown and jeering was more restrained without the New Cut mob to instigate it. Inside there were chairs to sit on, and room had been left on the floor for self-expression when the hymns were sung. By the time the meeting started and the doors were closed the hall was full, and Mother Girling stood on a daïs in front of the same baize-covered table she had used in Walworth. She held up her hands and there was silence.

'Today, brethren, we have the greatest reason to rejoice and give the Lord our thanks. We remember the parable of the shepherd who brought back the lost sheep across his shoulders and said to his friends, "Rejoice with me; for I have found my sheep which was lost". Our dear Sister Hannah is returned to us and we praise God for keeping her safe in the midst of her trials.'

Hannah wanted to sink out of sight. She had never been so embarrassed, and Mother Girling's long discourse seemed as if it would never end.

But at last there was music. People got up one by one as the spirit entered them and they began to shake from head to toe with ecstasy. Bizarre dancing commenced. Worshippers twisted and turned with slow, ungraceful movements, arms waving and bodies contorting strangely. The sight of them repelled Hannah. Then she looked across the hall and Mother Girling's eyes were fixed on her, burning with a fire which scorched her senses, and she couldn't look away. It was as if the woman was drawing her into a different dimension where time and place disappeared.

Hannah began to dance.

PART THREE
Hampshire
1872–86

Chapter Twenty-Seven

At the end of the year Miss Kitty Long bought a house for the Shakers in a Hampshire village called Hordle on the edge of the New Forest, and before Christmas Jonathan Whitfield, Harry Bourne and a third man went to take possession of it. The house, known as New Forest Lodge, was situated in a quiet road called Vaggs Lane. Thirty-one acres of land surrounded it, together with some small barns which could be used for crops and animals. Miss Long also provided money for the livestock and farming implements.

Mother Girling and five of her disciples travelled to the New Forest in January 1872, and when they saw the house they could hardly contain their joy. Hannah and Lilianne clasped each other, their relief at arriving in such a pleasant spot making them forget their tiredness from the journey.

'It's lovely,' said Hannah.

'So pretty,' Lilianne agreed. 'Think of the plants we can grow in the conservatory.'

The lodge was a very old red-brick house, the glass conservatory with a door in the middle stretching between small gabled wings at each end of the front aspect. A weeping willow tree graced the front lawn and a stable with a ladder leading to a hayloft lay to the left. The inside was equally pleasing.

Hannah laughed. 'We'll rattle about like a handful of peas in a jar.'

'Not for long,' said Mother Girling. 'New friends will join us as soon as we spread the news. The Lord will direct them to us. If we're to be self-supporting we shall need many willing hands.'

Sunday worship started immediately and the sound of music and singing brought curious neighbours to see what kind of people had moved in. Likely they were astounded. The heckling and the need to convince a sharper-witted audience in London had heightened Mother Girling's gift for oratory and she held forth at length in the stable which was to be turned into a chapel. Many listened to her sympathetically and came again the following week. Others were sceptical, but they came again anyway because the meetings provided such comical entertainment.

In some ways Hannah was sorry to leave London. Since her release from Newgate she had been going with her mother to the local workhouse in Battersea, staying to prepare food for the children who had little hope of a brighter future. Initially, the work had helped to take her mind off her own problems, but as the weeks went by she ached to do more for the destitute women there, and she missed the children she had befriended.

Aram was now over a year old and as lively as a puppy since he had found his feet were for standing on. Within days of leaving the city his cheeks gained a rosy colour and he was outside with Jonathan at every opportunity. His golden hair was growing long and curly like a girl's, but his features were already developing a masculinity which promised he would one day be a very handsome man, and by the size of his hands and feet he was going to grow tall. Hannah marvelled over him daily.

She saw very little of Jonathan once they were in the country. He worked outdoors all day even when the weather was cold enough for snow, and nearly the only time they met was at the evening services Mother Girling now held. At meals they sat at different tables, and at night they retired to separate rooms at either end of the house. Sometimes Hannah twisted the wedding ring on her finger and thought how little it meant. In a community where love was taught and practised all the time she craved for something more.

Once, on a rare occasion in London when they'd been alone, Hannah had tried to tempt Jonathan. It was brazen of her, but she had always favoured plain speaking.

'Don't you ever want me as a wife, Jonathan? Am I not attractive enough to make you want to live a normal married life? You made me marry you, but you've condemned me to live like a nun, and that ain't what I was born for.'

He'd frowned, but she had sensed a longing in him and couldn't understand why he persistently denied her.

'We have repented of our sins and been saved, Hannah. Would you go back on that? The way to everlasting life is to renounce earthly temptation and be pure in body as well as in heart.'

'Reckon I'd rather let the next life take care of itself,' she had said.

Jonathan had clasped her hand unexpectedly, and a wave of warm feeling had stolen through her at the touch of his strong, male fingers. She'd felt ashamed. She didn't love him, yet his masculinity affected her.

'There are things I wish I could tell you so as you'd understand.' He had kept hold of her hand for several minutes, risking being seen by other Shakers. 'Likely it's wrong you should be tied to me, but I believe it's part of the Lord's plan. I've a great affection for you, girl, and I would have been sorely broken if you'd never come back.'

'It was Aram you wanted.'

'I wanted you.'

She'd gone a step further, testing him. 'Then take me. Don't I mean more to you than Mother Girling?'

It was a step too far. He had left abruptly and she hadn't dared to question him so closely again. They had moved to the country now, but her husband was still not her husband, and release for her yearnings had to be found in hard manual work. There were no luxuries, but money was provided from the common fund for food and clothes and warmth, and though frugality was necessary there was no hardship.

'The Lord has been good to you, Sister Hannah,' Mother said. Her powerful eyes constantly pierced Hannah's resistance. 'Now it's time for you to devote your life completely to His service. Don't be afraid. I'll show you the way.'

Gradually she was caught up in the power of Mother Girling's persuasion. Soon after the move to Hordle she was as much under the woman's spell as the other converts and she never missed a prayer meeting. Maybe there were times when Mother's eloquence didn't touch her and the words meant nothing, but as soon as the music commenced and she started to dance it was as if her spirit was taken over. She would move sensuously, stepping and swaying to the rhythm with her eyes closed, and a surge of sheer joy would course up through her body as if she were being caressed. If it was a spiritual reaction she welcomed it as a sign that it was worth seeking a life in Heaven, but she feared the feeling was more a result of her own sensuality.

Since leaving London she had tried not to think of Ben and Emily. It was too painful. She wouldn't have believed that her sister could be so deceitful, and for a while she had seethed with futile anger at the callous manner in which Emily had won Ben for herself. The couple had been to visit Ma in Battersea on two occasions. The second time, just before Christmas, Emily was heavy with child and she had seemed to flaunt her condition instead of discreetly trying to hide it. Hannah's only compensation was that Ben had not acted like a devoted husband. He had shown concern for his wife's comfort, but it had been done with unsmiling courtesy, not with a look of love.

In early spring there came a letter from Emily to say that she and Ben had had a daughter whom they named Selena.

Word of the Shaker community spread throughout the area and it wasn't long before Mother Girling's flock had vastly increased. Over the next year more people gave up their worldly possessions to live in harmony with those who had already discovered the gratification of sharing everything, and their contributions, together with what was collected in the boxes each Sunday ensured there was always enough money to provide for everyone. In all, they numbered a hundred and sixty, most of them from the farming community, and all drawn to New Forest Lodge by Mother Girling's magnetism and the power of her oratory. There were slightly more women than men, and almost fifty children made up the number, many left by parents who deserted them soon after joining the society.

'The little ones are very precious,' Mother Girling said. 'Jesus taught us to love them and try to be like them. We'll continue looking after as many as need us, and since there'll be none born to us we must care doubly for the ones God sends.'

Rumours of loose-living among the Shakers began to circulate in the neighbourhood after a while, and scathing remarks could be heard in pubs and village stores for miles around.

'Heard tell the Shaker women ain't no better than they should be,' said one gossip to another. 'They have babies secretly and if they die they bury 'em in the garden.'

'I believe it. Men and women don't live together without sharing beds.'

266

'All that pious talk covers up a right den of sin, I reckon.'

Mother Girling heard all the rumours and laughed at them. No immorality existed among her people, a fact which she stressed at every meeting, and the wagging tongues were mostly silenced except for those with evil minds who didn't want to believe in the rewards she promised for celibate living. She drew up a set of rules which every member of the community had to sign, and failure to live by them meant expulsion.

All persons joining this community must give evidence of new life or belief in Christ as the way of life, according as the Gospel sayeth. Here she quoted from the Bible, Acts IV. 32–4, the passage she gave to all newcomers to read.

On entering the community every person must willingly give up to M. A. Girling, the accepted Stewardess, all they possess – gold, silver, goods, and all clothing except what they are wearing, without the expectation of ever having them again. Articles so given up are not to be asked for again, nor will any article be allowed to be taken off the place without M. A. Girling's permission.

No parent will be allowed to inflict any punishment on their children, nor to interfere in any way with their management; and no person under the age of fourteen to be left by their parents in the community. This rule was perhaps most frequently broken because usually the guilty parents had disappeared, and the children couldn't be left to fend for themselves.

No marrying or undue intimacy between man and woman allowed.

No teaching or doctrine to be introduced into this community different to what has been observed and advocated by M. A. Girling, her teaching being in strict harmony with the Apostles order and Gospels of Christ.

All disputes, either temporal or spiritual, to be submitted to M. A. Girling, and her decision to be final.

No masters. All to do what is appointed them as under God.

No wages paid.

No one allowed on the premises without leave. No one to sell anything off the place, or to take anything off the premises.

No goods to be secretly brought on to the premises, or to be concealed; all to be given up for equal distribution.

Men to rise from 6.30 to 7.0 am.

Women to rise from 7.0 to 7.30 am. Breakfast at 8.0.

There followed the words of a hymn she had written herself, in which she said she was armed with Gospel power, and at the foot of the document was Mary Ann Girling's signature.

Hannah signed reluctantly. The rules gave too much authority to one woman, but if she didn't accept the conditions she would be turned out, and Jonathan had made it quite clear that if she left it would be without Aram. She wrote her name under his, but even as she did so she was aware of putting comfort before her principles. New Forest Lodge was an agreeable place to live, and without Aram she couldn't be happy anywhere.

She took to reading. She found books in the house and since she was no good at sewing she decided to improve her knowledge. As her fluency increased she read aloud in the evening to the women busy with needles and thread. Mother Girling stipulated that it should be passages from the Bible, but in addition she got through the whole of *Pilgrim's Progress* and *Fox's Book of Martyrs*, both of which had influenced Mother in her youth. As a result of her studies she was asked to teach the children, with Miriam Rawlings to help keep them in order. It was a job she enjoyed and it took up most of the day, leaving other young women free to carry out household duties.

The menfolk were good workers who kept the house in prime condition, tended the land, and produced fine crops. At summer's end and haymaking time Mother Girling lent the men to local farmers to help bring in the harvest but they were not allowed to receive a wage for what they did, although they were allowed to accept any contribution their employers cared to give to the common fund. The group prospered those first two years. The good years. But they were not destined to last.

At the beginning of 1874 there were so many mouths to feed it was becoming more difficult to provide for them. Contributions from the public had fallen off and there'd been no new converts bringing in money and animals. Those who came now were more often young people who had left home and needed shelter. Mother took them all in, influencing them strongly, and again there were outcries from the clergy. One local vicar, the Reverend John Pollins, accused her of practising hypnosis, and a gentleman by the name of Andrew

Peterson, who had been a High Court Barrister and had lived many years in India, stood up at a meeting and publicly denounced her.

'The woman is using mesmeric powers to convince innocent people that she is the reincarnation of the Deity,' Mr Peterson said. He was not a tall man but he had the air of a patriarch. Long white hair fell on his broad shoulders and life in India had given him a weathered complexion. 'She makes them perform like circus animals for entertainment, and accepts money for it. I challenge her to prove her authenticity.'

The Reverend Pollins went so far as to persuade Mr Peterson to hire a hall and bring a professional mesmerist over from the Isle of Wight to show that the extraordinary behaviour of the Shakers, their dancing, their beliefs and other curious antics, resulted from the hypnotic power of one woman. Mother Girling was not present, but Lilianne, Hannah and two other Shaker girls, Mary Glaser and Beth Page, went to the meeting and sat at the back.

The mesmerist was small and thin, with little to commend him in the way of looks. At first glance he might have been dismissed as a nonentity, but like Mary Ann Girling he had power in his eyes and used it to good effect. His visit attracted a crowd of villagers to the hall and when he looked around there were downcast glances as all feared being picked upon to take part in the experiment. One old hag dared to speak up.

'There's the ones you want, mister, them at the back,' she cried, pointing to the Shaker women. 'They're the ones what's touched.'

Hannah and her mother refused to take part, but Mary and Beth were brought forward. To Hannah's consternation the mesmerist was able to make them perform silly tricks such as climbing on each other's backs to charge around like horses. And he made them try to stand on their heads, an exercise they attempted with no thought for the unseemly spectacle they presented with their legs in the air.

'See!' the audience cried.

'Just shows it's true the woman's a fraud.'

'If you've got the gift you can make people believe anything.'

A youth with a red face jumped up on a chair to see better. 'They wear drawers, though,' he shouted. 'Must be protection against them poor blokes what ain't getting any oats.'

Everyone joined in the ribald laughter, and even coarser jokes followed as the two girls remained upside down with their feet against the wall. It was too much for Hannah. She was in such a temper she marched to the front of the crowd and confronted them like an enraged politician.

'Stop it this minute! Stop your wickedness, I say! How dare you make fun of our friends. And how dare you ridicule and doubt the goodness of Mother Girling.' She turned her fury on the mesmerist. 'Release them. You've no right to use your talent so unkindly and I'll thank you to be merciful and not comment on the indecency you've forced on them.'

Her tirade had the required effect. Somewhat shamefaced the little man ordered the two girls to stand up, then he snapped his fingers and brought them out of the trance which had robbed them of all dignity.

'Go back to your seats,' Hannah directed them. She was afraid they would be harassed as they passed between the people, but likely most felt guilty about the sport they'd had at their expense. The laughter died down to a rumbling and there were a few fidgeting feet to signal embarrassment. Hannah addressed the crowd with a surprising boldness. 'How many of you have been to a meeting of The Children of God?' she asked. 'How many have witnessed the form of worship we hold?' A hand went up slowly, followed by another. Gradually about half the number present admitted to having watched a Shaker meeting, though not to taking part. Hannah got to the point. 'And have you ever known Mother Girling to make anyone behave like the spectacle we've just seen? No, I say!'

Lilianne pushed her way through to join her daughter on the platform.

'Our dear Mother inspires us with faith in God through her goodness and her teaching,' Lilianne declared. 'If you read your Bibles you'll know it tells us in the Psalms to dance. Jesus said: "I have piped unto you, and ye have not danced." We dance, good people, because through Mother we feel the spirit of God in us and we want to express our joy. This man is just a music-hall turn.'

'I object,' cried the mesmerist. But his audience was fickle and he was shouted down.

Mr Peterson, who had been sitting quietly at the side, came forward and help up his hands for silence.

'Friends, this has been an enlightening evening,' he said. 'These brave ladies do much to persuade me that Mrs Girling's claim to have direct communication with God may after all be true. But that doesn't lessen my interest in the power of hypnosis. The gentleman from the Isle of Wight is *not* a music-hall turn. Wonderful things can be accomplished through mesmerism, as I have seen for myself at the mesmeric hospital in Calcutta where a Dr Esdaile helps a great many people to live better lives.'

'Your doctor friend may be fine, sir, but this man set out to ridicule us,' said Hannah. 'We would like an apology.'

'I was asked to prove a point.' The mesmerist was ruffled. 'And I think I succeeded.'

'You proved only that you can make people do absurd things that you decide in your own head,' Hannah persisted.

'Mother Girling has never forced her will on anyone or tried to win converts by false means,' said Lilianne. 'She is filled with the Holy Spirit Who inspires her to speak the word of God, and it's her goodness that draws us to her.'

'You speak blasphemy,' cried the Reverend John Pollins. 'The woman who controls you is a fraud. She holds innocent people against their will.'

'No one is forced to stay with us.'

'I've had a young man, a Shaker, in my house who begged me to shelter him because he wanted to get married and was afraid of Mrs Girling's wrath. He was afraid she would drag him back and make him give up the girl he loved. The woman is a cruel hypocrite, giving people hopes for eternal life which she can't possibly prove are right.'

'Mother Girling was chosen by God,' Lilianne cried. Then she left the platform proudly, followed by Hannah.

Heated argument developed, but the Shaker women slipped away before they could be drawn further into the controversy. The evening had been an ordeal and Hannah felt quite weak. To her surprise her mother took her arm as they walked back to Vaggs Lane, and a rare warmth flowed between them.

'I'm proud of you, Hannah,' Lilianne said, 'that I am. How I wish Mother could have heard you speak up.'

Hannah's chin lifted defiantly. 'I did what I did because that nasty little man was ridiculing us and it got my temper up. I don't believe in Mother Girling any more than I've ever done.'

271

Chapter Twenty-Eight

By the second summer at Hordle Mary Ann Girling had taken complete control of her ever-growing family. She decided daily what work had to be done and who should do it, dividing the jobs so that no one did more than his or her fair share and no one was given a task greater than his or her capability. She always took charge of the money, though it worried Jonathan Whitfield that she kept no books or records.

'There are rates and taxes to be met,' he said to Lilianne. 'If she doesn't write down what money she's got to cover them she'll be getting in a fine pickle and likely there won't be enough to meet the bills.'

He sometimes drove Mother Girling in the pony and trap to Lymington, a nearby town where she did shopping for things that couldn't be grown or made, but on this occasion it was Lilianne who had been entrusted with the task.

As she sat up beside him in the cart on a glorious summer day the last thing she wanted to talk about was rates and taxes.

'Let Mother worry about it,' she said. 'She won't let anyone else handle the money so she must know what she's doing.'

'I ain't so sure. She took me into her confidence when the house was first bought. Seems it cost two thousand two hundred and fifty pounds, but Miss Long only paid one thousand two hundred and fifty, so the rest is on mortgage. Mother has to pay the interest twice a year. She should be keeping accounts.'

It was a privilege to be taken into his confidence, but she felt obliged to curtail any further revelations. 'I don't think you should be telling me this, Jonathan. Mother's confidences will be safe with me, but I reckon she'd not thank you for discussing them.'

'Aye, maybe you're right. But it worries me.'

Lilianne liked Lymington. Its wide shopping street was on a steep hill leading down from St Thomas's ivy-covered church, and at the bottom of the hill was the river. She liked to watch the rowing ferries cross the water, and wished she could sail down the estuary out into the Solent, and set foot on the land opposite, which she was told was the Isle of Wight. When she had bought the material Mother wanted for the children's clothes she begged Jonathan to take her down to the quay.

'I like it by the water,' she said. 'Makes me think of home in Suffolk. Matt used to take me to Woodbridge when we was courting, and sometimes to Orford. I loved it there.'

Her voice was soft and friendly. Marriage to Matt seemed a lifetime away now and it was difficult even to remember what he had looked like. Whenever she thought of him, images of Jonathan intruded. Since Clemmy's death he seemed to avoid her; this was the first time they had been alone for months and the way he had opened up was the most encouraging sign she'd had in a long while.

Standing in the sun with Jonathan beside her was idyllic and she moved so that their arms touched in a companionable gesture. His presence gladdened her heart and she wished the morning could last forever. She loved him with a longing which was at odds with her faith, and it cut so deep she didn't even feel shame.

'Jonathan, are you really happy being a Shaker?' It was a question she had been awaiting an opportunity to ask.

He smiled. 'Reckon I've been reasonably peaceful,' he said.

They walked in silence past the Bethel chapel behind the wharves where sailors could attend religious services, and when she tucked her arm through the crook of his he allowed it to remain there, though such intimacy would have been forbidden at New Forest Lodge. They reached the place where he had tethered the pony and he helped her up into the trap. When she was seated he looked up at her and sighed.

'Aye, I'm happy, Lilianne, so long as I can keep the Devil behind me,' he said, as if there'd been no break in the conversation. He climbed up beside her and took the reins. 'There's leather to collect on the way back. It's amazing how the Lord's sending us men with so many talents. Even a shoemaker now.'

'Is it difficult?' she asked, with a boldness that made her skin tingle. 'Keeping the Devil behind you, I mean.'

They travelled a short distance while he gave the matter thought. Then: 'Aye, sometimes I think it's more than me body can stand.'

The sun was warm on her back and she lifted her head to breathe in the scent of a beanfield they were passing. Excitement was coursing through her, though she tried to quell it.

'Since we're speaking frankly I must tell you that you still mean more to me than you ought, you being my son-in-law,' she said.

The road was rough and the cart gave a lurch which sent her sliding along the seat towards him. He gave the horse a flick with the whip as if it was to blame, and elbowed Lilianne back to her place.

'Brother and sister is what we are now,' he said, and his tone became harsh. 'Twice I've taken advantage of you and I've paid the price for me sin, as well you know. There'll be no more of it.'

'I've blamed meself for what happened in London and I'll not tempt you again.' Her heart was beating uncomfortably hard. 'But you'll not stop me loving you.'

'Enough, woman. Shame on you.'

She was upset and didn't know what to do. He had never spoken to her like this before and she couldn't be sure whether it was his way of covering his true feelings, or if he really meant what he said. Likely he was afraid of the kind of love she'd offered in the past, but she would settle for anything that would bring them closer together. Surely he must know that.

'I've been thinking lately I might take Hannah and Aram and leave the community,' he said, when they were clear of the ruts.

This was the last thing she had expected and she stared at him open-mouthed. 'You don't mean it.'

'I do, but I'll thank you not to tell anyone else.'

'And would you leave me behind?'

'I need my wife.'

Lilianne felt sick. She couldn't believe that she'd made a fool of herself by exposing the way she cared when all the time he was hankering after Hannah. More than his body could stand, was it? She'd thought he was referring to his need of herself.

'Does Hannah know?' she asked in a small voice.

'I've not told her yet.'

'Then I'd advise you not to. It'll get you nowhere.'

He negotiated a corner and they had to wait for a herd of cows to pass. The animals trundled by in leisurely fashion, making Lilianne think of the ones she'd owned before Jonathan had come into her life. In those days she'd not known the meaning of jealousy, but she knew it now.

'Hannah is strong and obedient,' he said. 'I watch her often and I owe her a proper life. I'm too old for her, but we'll be happy together with our son.'

'Aram ain't your son.'

'Near as. He's my own flesh and blood.'

'How can you be sure?' Lilianne was so angry and disillusioned she wanted to strike him but didn't have the strength. The only way to hurt him was with words. With the truth. She wouldn't be spurned and let him get away with it. 'Hannah's only ever loved one man and that's Ben Rutherford.'

'What're you saying? What's that to do with Aram?'

'The day we came to Nunscorn she'd just helped Ben escape from jail for horse-thieving. Likely she'd lain with him before he went, so who's to know if Aram wasn't planted before your Shem had his way with her.'

As soon as the words were out she knew it had been a mistake to bait him. His temper had been lying dormant since he had become a Shaker but she had just provided the spark necessary to cause a new eruption.

'Shut your mouth, woman!' He lashed out, the back of his hand catching her squarely on the jaw, and as she reeled backwards she almost fell off the cart. 'If you ever provoke me with such lies again I'll not be responsible for my actions.'

He whipped the horse with such fury the poor animal charged up the lane as if demons were after it, and the cart threatened to fall apart. Lilianne clung on for dear life, and long before they reached New Forest Lodge every bone in her body felt shattered.

Nothing more was said about him leaving with Aram and Hannah.

On Sundays Mother Girling ruled that all the women must be dressed alike to attend meetings, and plain white dresses in a simple style were made. The hair had to be worn loose, hanging down the back in long ringlets. Mother did not count herself an exception. She had her hair brushed by one of the girls until it obligingly twisted into long curls which fell past her shoulders, still dark in colour but threaded with grey. The sight of so many whirling white-robed figures added to the rumours of occult influence, but mainly it was a question of economy: the fabric was cheap to buy.

As the year progressed, Jonathan's prediction of financial trouble proved correct. There was less variety of food, and the adults were expected to let the children have the best of it. Ways of making money were suggested to her but Mother Girling turned them down indignantly.

'We are in the hands of the Lord and He will provide,' she said. 'This is only a temporary setback which can be overcome with more fervent prayer.'

'But Mother, I can make shoes and sell them!' said the cobbler. 'I'm always being asked.'

Mother Girling withered him with an icy glance. 'Have you learnt nothing since you've been here? We live like Christ, and He never sold anything. Neither shall we.'

Miss Kitty Long, no longer wealthy, had taken up residence with the Shaker family in the house which she had provided. Like all the other converts she had given her money to Mary Ann Girling, but it was on Miss Long that a writ was served in May 1874. The interest was overdue on the mortgage for the first half of that year, and when it was still not paid a sheriff's officer arrived with about forty men to take possession of some of their livestock.

Jonathan was very angry. 'Did they need to send an army? What do they think we are, a bunch of brigands?'

The men took two horses and three cows which raised over a hundred and thirty pounds when sold, though they were worth more. The amount of money owing had been just twenty-five pounds, but when Miss Long wrote a letter to her solicitor with a request for the return of the extra money, it was refused. She was told curtly that in future the interest must be paid regularly or they would foreclose.

It was December that same year when the blow fell. On the fifteenth of the month the weather turned extremely cold and a keen east wind carried rain which turned to sleet. In these conditions another army of bailiffs arrived mid-morning to evict Mother Girling and her 'family' from their home.

'The Law requires us to remove you and all your possessions from this property,' said the sheriff's officer, having pushed his way in through the front door. 'Non-payment of the mortgage is a serious

276

offence, madam, and you were warned of the consequences if the money was not forthcoming.'

Mary Ann Girling stood tall and proud. 'There is still money owing to us from the sale of our cattle in the summer.'

'I came to the Lodge with the money and asked for Miss Long. Two of your men said she was away.'

'That's a lie,' she said. 'Miss Long hasn't left the community for a single day since she came here nearly two years ago.'

The man squirmed slightly, but quickly recovered and continued in an increasingly aggressive manner.

'Miss Long has defaulted on the payment for this half year. I therefore have no choice but to authorise my men to evict you. I suggest you don't put up any opposition to their entering the house and doing their work.'

'We never refuse anyone, or turn anyone away.'

The Shakers gathered in the chapel to pray and sing while their possessions were carried out into Vaggs Lane where they were quickly dusted with a damp white covering of snow. Seventy-seven beds were taken outside, the bedding heaped in a pile nearby, and the Shakers sang with deep feeling. Tables and chairs, cupboards and a piano followed, but still they sang. They danced devoutly, whirling and gyrating with endless energy to the music of the harmonium, until that too was removed, and they continued dancing to hymns which they sang unaccompanied.

A large crowd of local people began to gather, filling the lane from either end as they pressed to see what was happening. Farm produce and equipment was thrown into neighbouring fields, and by late afternoon, when at last the house and barns were empty, it was time for the Shakers themselves to be ejected.

'It's a shame,' people murmured. Sympathy for them was almost tangible but there was nothing anyone could do, faced with about thirty bailiffs, to reverse the situation.

'They may be queer but they don't deserve to be treated this bad.' The sentiment was echoed by nearly all the bystanders.

Mother Girling was the first to be turned off the property. She walked with her head held high and was soon joined by the rest of her flock which gathered at the roadside. When the last one had left, the gate was shut and fastened with a padlock and chain. Snow stung her cheeks and settled on her lashes, making her blink rapidly, though anyone might have been forgiven for thinking tears were the cause. The good home she had been blessed with for her Children had been taken away and now she would have to start rebuilding. Dark windows made New Forest Lodge a dead place now, the silent rooms a shell from which the Spirit had departed, but out here in the lane lanterns were being lit, and she could feel the power of God's presence. He seemed to be telling her that bricks and mortar were no more important to man's survival than was the body which housed the soul. All that mattered was love and faith.

There had to be a reason for the eviction, apart from the one given by the sheriff. God had given with one hand, but it was not His way to take back with the other unless it was because they were capable of achieving something better. She knew He hadn't deserted them. Her prayers for fresh deliverance would be heard without a doubt.

'Trust in the Lord,' she entreated those around her. 'He is testing our faith and we mustn't be found wanting.'

In a little while she would find a place to be alone to pray, like Jesus had done. She knew how to preach, but she also knew the need for silence so that she could listen for God's voice.

'Reckon you should take the matter to court,' said Jonathan. 'They owe you money from the sale of the animals and it ain't a valid excuse to say Miss Long weren't here to give it to.'

'I don't hold with the law,' Mary Ann answered. 'The only law I obey is the one taught by Jesus.'

'But Mother . . .'

'We will stay here until God tells us what He has in mind for us next.' She raised her hands in supplication and lifted her eyes to the heavens from whence came the driving sleet which filled the ruts in the lane and turned them into miniature dykes. 'We'll hold our evening service in the open. Come, let's sing to the Lord and rejoice that He has given us voices to praise Him. Dance, my children, dance.'

She rallied them all into a group and the singing started once more, but the intense cold made their voices sound reed-thin, and women and children trembled in their light clothes which were quite unsuitable for the winter weather. Mary Ann's feet pained her. It was dark by now and most of the onlookers had left to go to their warm cottages, though a few still lingered, moved with pity for the plight of these innocent people.

The Reverend Pollins, who had no doubt rejoiced at the misfortune of those he called heretics, came to offer the use of a barn to any who would leave Mary Ann Girling, but not one of the Shakers deserted her.

Hannah had never been so cold. Hay was being tossed about in the icy wind, catching in her hair, and when she ran to gather up Aram she slipped on beans which were strewn across the lane. The wicked waste of food made her angry and she wanted to shout at the sheriff's officer who surely didn't have an ounce of compassion in him. They ought to have been given warning so that alternative accommodation could have been found. She was determined not to give way to an underlying fear which clawed at her stomach. She had overcome worse trials, alone and without any hope, so she wouldn't let this new calamity sap her morale. Singing and dancing and praying were all very well, but she felt sure God was not going to help them unless they started helping themselves.

'Jonathan, get some of the men and start making a shelter out of the bedsteads,' she commanded her husband, who along with everyone else seemed too stunned to act. 'The children must be kept warm.'

Her entreaty brought a response and several of the men went to help Jonathan Whitfield spread some of the bedding across the furniture to make a crude shelter which would at least shield them from the wind and keep off the worst of the snow. It was coming on harder and everyone huddled together, but it was clear the children needed more protection. Mother Girling finally swallowed her pride and allowed the little ones to be taken to a nearby cottage for the night.

There was hardly anything to eat, certainly nothing warming, but no one complained. The voices of the Shakers could be heard all through the dark hours as they kept up their prayers and hymns. Hannah sat between her mother and Jonathan.

'Put your arm round me,' she begged him. 'There can be no objection if we're to survive in this weather.'

He was slow to comply, but when his strong arm finally provided her with comfort she relaxed against him and closed her eyes to shut out the hideous scene. She could feel him trembling, yet there was warmth emanating from his body which took a little of the chill out

279

of her own. And in spite of everything she was conscious that after four years of marriage it was the first time they had been this close. He was breathing strangely, a deep intake of breath released in short, gasping sounds. More than once during the night his hold of her tightened, almost with cruelty, and she thought her ribs would be crushed. Over the last few months she'd sensed a change in his attitude towards her; sometimes he'd give a calculating look or a sharp word, and sometimes a hint of desperation, as if he wanted to be done with the restrictions imposed by Mother Girling. For a while she'd taken heart. If he'd come to her with plans to make a new life away from the Shakers she would have fallen in with them willingly, but he remained as distant as ever.

In the morning the snow had stopped but it was still bitterly cold, and pinched blue faces told the effects of their terrible privation. Hannah felt that her toes would drop off if she bent them and there was pain in her hands and feet. She was so cold she couldn't even think properly, but she remembered that Aram was somewhere warm and felt grateful.

Kind people brought them bread and milk and cheese as soon as it was light, and when they had eaten Mother Girling assembled them for prayers. There was a great stamping of feet and slapping of arms across the chest to restore circulation, but they had been sitting too long in the freezing cold for there to be much improvement. Hannah looked across at the empty house where they ought to have been setting about their daily duties, and she shook with anger. It was so grossly unfair, so wicked to turn people out in temperatures cold enough to kill. She longed to see the back of Vaggs Lane, but Mother Girling obstinately refused to let them move.

'We're not going anywhere,' Mother declared, 'not until we're able to go back to the Lodge. We'll wait for the Lord's instructions. He knows what's best for us.'

The day was long and the easterly wind continued to blow, threatening more snow before nightfall. The children were returned to them, shivering violently as they encountered the cold after the warmth of their lodging place, and Aram struggled from Hannah's arms to try and run towards the gate of New Forest Lodge.

'I want to go home,' he wept. He was a sturdy little boy of nearly four now and he was showing signs of inheriting his mother's wilfulness in spite of Mother Girling's strict training. 'I don't want to stay out here. It's cold and I hurt.'

Hannah restrained the boy and nursed him until he fell asleep for a short while. It wasn't often she got the chance these days. Jonathan had become possessive of him since the summer and took him everywhere, even insisting that he was old enough to sleep with the men rather than suffer mollycoddling in the women's quarters. Mother Girling had backed up Jonathan's claim and Aram was becoming grown-up before he had hardly been a baby.

Curious spectators gathered once more to witness the plight of the Shakers, some bringing more food, but others inclined to ridicule the faith of a group of people who believed God would work a miracle for them. Newspaper reporters came armed with paper and pencil to record the strange sight in Vaggs Lane, and one man spent time drawing a picture of the scene.

It was midday when Hannah became aware of a young man with a bundle over his shoulder and a pipe in his mouth. He wore a black cap pulled well down, a seaman's jersey, wide-cut breeches and strong boots. She watched him come down the lane from the direction of Milton as if he was looking for someone, and his gait drew her attention. He walked with a swaying motion which could have been the result of a life at sea, but more likely it was because he appeared to have one leg slightly shorter than the other. She drew in her breath, gathered her wet skirt round her and took a few faltering steps towards the man.

'Luke,' she breathed. '*Luke*.' She spoke his name louder. He looked in the direction of her voice, tipping back the cap with his forefinger to see more clearly. He was clean-shaven and his hair was golden-fair like her own. 'Luke, it *is* you!'

'My God,' he exclaimed. 'Hannah! I'd a feeling I might find Ma, but not *you*.'

He dropped his bundle in the slush and held out his arms for her to rush into them.

Chapter Twenty-Nine

Being married to Ben was not the fulfilment of all Emily's dreams. She'd thought that once they were man and wife she could make him love her with a passionate devotion that would bind them together in everlasting happiness. Ben was a good husband, kind and hard-working, but from the moment Mrs Hanberry had given them the news of Hannah's imprisonment it was as if a cloud had descended, and after more than three years of marriage it still showed no sign of lifting.

They had two daughters now, Selena who was nearly three, and eighteen-month-old Patience, but the doctor had warned that another pregnancy could prove fatal. Ben had said it would be better if he didn't come to her bed any more, and the dreadful truth was he had seemed to welcome the necessity. From then on he had slept downstairs, the second bedroom being occupied by Amos, and Emily had been left with only hard work and the babies for company day and night. It made her irritable and impatient, and her face was showing a network of very fine lines because she continually fretted and frowned.

Ben's apprenticeship at the ropeworks lasted two years and by the end of it he was able to take on responsibility. There was murmuring, of course, that he was given preference. Titus Hanberry treated him like a son, often asked his opinion, and gave him a plum job inside dealing with orders, all because he had saved old Amos, Titus's father, from going to the workhouse.

'Worth looking after the old beggar, ain't it,' was the general comment. 'If that ain't sucking up to the master, what is?'

Nevertheless, Ben was popular with everyone. He was a fair go-between in a dispute, and he could do any of the jobs in the yard from the most menial to the very skilled. If one of the boys was ill in winter he could be seen turning the wheel in his place, and if an extra spinner was needed he was pleased to step in. And the office work he was doing was more like a continuation of his apprenticeship. Mr Hanberry was training him to understand management so that there would be someone he could rely on in an emergency. In fact, Ben's privileges had very little to do with repayment for his kindness to Amos. Titus liked him as a man, admired his intelligence and enjoyed his company. They got on well together.

It wasn't easy looking after Amos, and Emily had to put up with him and do the work. The old man was becoming more difficult with age and it was a fight to make him keep himself clean. He was often belligerent. His appetite increased and he ate greedily, devouring everything put before him and then demanding more, which was a strain on the meagre household budget. However, Emily was well aware that without him they would not be living in their nice little house. She still worked for Mrs Hanberry, having to take the children with her, but payment was considered to be in lieu of rent, so there was only Ben's small wage to live on. The days were long and trying, and she was so tired she sometimes looked back wistfully on her time with the Shakers.

Just when it seemed her routine could only become more arduous, two things happened which were to change the lives of Ben and Emily completely. The first occurred on a very wintry day in January 1875. Emily had a cough which was making her feel unwell and Mrs Hanberry had kindly said she could leave early, as long as the table was set for the evening meal and there was enough coal indoors to last until morning; hence it was only four o'clock when she hung up her apron. She usually left at six now, in time to get supper for Amos, and for Ben who got home before her. Today the children were fractious. She had to carry Patience balanced on her hip and drag Selena along, so by the time she reached home she was exhausted.

'Get on inside and be quiet,' she said to Selena when they arrived, giving her a little shove so that she could shut the door quickly before too much cold air rushed in. She set Patience down. 'You too. I'll get some milk for you when I've seen to Mr Hanberry.'

She was chilled to the bone, and the house felt only a few degrees warmer than the street outside. Shivering and coughing she went straight to the kitchen and found Amos asleep in his chair with his feet in the hearth, but there was no fire to warm them. The grate was grey and cold and no coal had been shovelled from the box beside it since she had left this morning.

'Amos, you lazy old man, what do you think you're doing letting the fire go out?' she cried. No use stoking it. She would have to empty the ashes and remake it before she could start cooking. 'Wake up and help me, can't you.'

Amos didn't stir.

The children began to grizzle.

Emily looked with distaste at the old man's dirty shirt and his waistcoat caked with spilt food. His trousers were stained and the kitchen stank of urine. She shuddered, hating the thought of touching him, and dreading even more the washing she would have to do. Revulsion made her shout at him again, but he didn't wake up, and suddenly she realised that he wasn't breathing. She touched his hand and found it stone cold. Amos was dead.

The terrible shock made Emily ill. She didn't know what to do, never having been near a dead body before except to look briefly at Pa after he'd been laid out in the parlour. The children couldn't understand why Amos didn't answer when they greeted him as usual, so she shut them upstairs in the bedroom, fearing they might try to climb on his knee.

When Ben got home he found Emily vomiting and almost incoherent, but there was no time to comfort her. He sent her up to be with Selena and Patience while he found a woman who would help to lay the old man out. When the job was done and Amos was lying peacefully in his bed he brought the little girls down and gave them bread and milk. After that there was the unhappy task of going to tell Titus what had happened.

'Don't leave me,' Emily sobbed when he said where he was going. She grabbed his coat and tried to stop him. 'I'm afraid to be alone in the house with him.'

'Pull yourself together, girl. He can't hurt you.' Ben was very distressed at losing his old friend and it made him impatient. 'You're upsetting the children.'

That night Emily went to bed knowing she wouldn't sleep. The thought of a body lying in the next room terrified her, and her cough got worse. At last Ben came upstairs and for the first time in over a year he got into her bed. He drew her into his arms and it was such a wonderful relief she began to cry, pressing herself as close as she could to find the comfort she needed.

'I'm sorry I was sharp,' Ben said. He stroked her hair. 'It was as much of a shock for me.'

'I know.'

'I'll miss him badly.'

'I know.'

He sighed. 'I've been thinking, we shall have to find rent for the house now Amos is gone. It's going to be hard.'

'Maybe we shall have to leave.' Emily snuffled against his shoulder, trying not to cry noisily and wake the children. Selena in particular was a very light sleeper. 'Oh Ben, I couldn't bear it if we have to find another place to live. We could never afford anywhere as nice.'

'Let's worry about it later,' he said. 'I'll stay with you tonight.'

She stayed in his arms and he kissed her temple, but he didn't attempt to extend the affectionate gesture. Her nearness caused him no excitement, apparently. On this occasion she was glad.

After Amos's funeral two days later Ben and Emily were invited back to the Hanberrys' house in Rotherhithe for tea. Titus and Isobel's daughters were there, some members of Isobel's family, and a few close friends. Among the latter group was an elderly man with bushy sideburns and a vast moustache which covered his mouth and made drinking tea a noisy, troublesome business. He was introduced as a solicitor acting on the family's behalf. When the light meal was over he wiped the damp moustache with a handkerchief and positioned himself with his back to the fire so that all could see him.

'Mr Leonard has a few words to say to us now,' said Titus. 'But before he begins I should like to thank you all for coming today. My father was a good man, and also a clever one. During his early life he held a position of some importance in a Suffolk bank, but after the death of my mother he felt he couldn't bear the restrictions of his job and he chose to sell up and take to the road. He was happy as a cheapjack. He had no responsibilities and he made a lot of new friends. Recently he made a will and deposited it with Mr Leonard, who is now going to read the contents to us.'

There was surprised shuffling as the solicitor clipped some pince-nez over the bridge of his nose and took the relevant papers out of a small leather case.

He began to read. 'The last will and testament of our dear relative and friend Amos Henry Hanberry who departed this life on the fifth of January in this year of our Lord eighteen hundred and seventy-five. "To my son Titus I leave the sum of five hundred pounds and my gold Hunter watch he borrowed from me and never returned when he went to London." ' There was a titter of amusement, and Titus put his hand to his waistcoat pocket where the timepiece always stayed. He smiled ruefully, enjoying the joke. The solicitor went on: ' "To my grand-daughters Jane, Elizabeth and Maria I leave the sum of one hundred pounds each to buy a small amount of independence from their mother and help them to find husbands." ' Oh, that was cruel. Isobel might not have wanted to look after him but she'd been a good daughter-in-law in other ways. ' "Lastly, I leave to my friend Ben Rutherford my pipe and the watch I was forced to buy when I was without one." '

Emily smiled at Ben, knowing how he would treasure the rather battered relic which the old man had wound regularly before retiring each night.

' "And finally," ' the solicitor went on, ' "I leave also to the said Ben Rutherford the residue of my estate. Nothing can repay his kindness to me. For my sake he gave up his intention to go to America and start a new life and I, in my selfishness, allowed him to do it because I had such an affection for him. However, now that I am gone he may wish to think again about it. The money I leave him will ensure he and his wife and family have a comfortable passage to America and enough left over to start a new life better than any he had dreamed of." ' Mr Leonard looked up and cleared his throat. Then: 'The sum Mr Hanberry leaves to Mr Rutherford is five thousand pounds.'

A gasp went up, and Emily fainted.

The return of Luke Jerram to his mother gave Mary Ann Girling new hope. Although there was nothing he could do to make a stand against the sheriff's men, she nevertheless seized the opportunity to rally her destitute flock.

'Brothers and sisters, hear me!' she cried. She stood alone between waterlogged ruts in the lane, the feather in her bonnet drooping but her spirit uplifted. There was nothing like adversity for bringing out the gift of showmanship and she used it to the best effect. 'We are being persecuted, but we will never be broken. Never! The Lord has shown us His great mercy by bringing back to Sister Lilianne the son who was lost. It's a sign of His goodness, a sign that He hasn't forsaken us and never will.'

'Why doesn't He unlock them gates and let us back in the house then?' someone grumbled.

'Why did He make us come out here in the first place?' asked another.

'Children, who are we to understand His ways? It's not up to us to question. We must accept and remain ever hopeful. We have to rise above this calamity and our faith will be rewarded.'

The scene was utterly depressing after another night huddled under hedgerows. Mats and blankets spread over the branches sagged with the weight of rain and sleet and the washtubs balanced on them to stop the wind tearing them free. In the dimness of these pathetic bowers little could be seen of the occupants as they huddled together for warmth.

'Come and pray with me, brothers and sisters,' called Mary Ann. 'Dance for the Lord and He will warm your bodies. Sing for Him and He'll lift your hearts. Nothing will change if we don't pray for deliverance.'

She chivvied them until first one and then another ventured out into the icy lane. Soon all were gathered in response to her powerful appeal. The service she conducted brought back the spectators who had deserted them at nightfall, and hot water and food was handed round to everyone.

Luke was dazed. 'I've been to some strange parts of the world,' he said, 'but this takes some beating. It's terrible.'

'You've come at a bad time,' Ma told him. 'It ain't always like this. We're very happy with Mother.' She quickly changed the subject. 'Where's Sal Radford? I'd hoped she'd changed and was making you a good wife.'

'I left her in America with a gambler who was better-looking than me, and richer. She didn't like it when I was robbed of my money.'

Luke didn't want to talk about Sal. Neither would he join in the singing or the contorting Shaker antics. He was too upset to even watch. Instead he lumbered off to the edge of the encampment and sat on an upturned barrel beside a mangle to try and think what could be done to get his mother and sister away from this band of religious maniacs. It appalled him that they had become involved. He had sometimes feared for his life in storms and mountainous seas, but he had never spent a night on the cold earth beneath a dripping hedge.

'It's good to see you, Luke.' Hannah spoke quietly behind him.

He turned to her with fists clenched in desperation. 'What in Heaven's name are you doing here? I don't understand it.'

'Ma told you last night.'

'About Ben being in prison and the farm gone. The move to Nunscorn and you marrying Jonathan Whitfield after his son died because you were having his baby. Yes, I heard all that but it answers nothing. What possessed you all to give up everything and follow this crazy woman?'

'She helped you once,' Hannah said.

'Physically, maybe. I'd never let her within a mile of my soul.' He looked at Hannah and his heart ached. He'd been carrying the bitterest resentment around for years, imagining his younger sister enjoying her carefree existence. Nothing could have prepared him for the suffering he now saw. He stood up and clasped her by the shoulders. She was so thin he could put his fingers into sockets between the bones. 'Did you love the son who died?'

Hannah took a deep breath. 'Let me tell you about Shem Whitfield, the man I should have married,' she said.

'Shem! *Shem* Whitfield?'

'Ah, so the name means something to you.'

'Yes,' he said. The easterly wind merely added to the coldness suddenly blowing through him.

'You should do because he knew you. Seemed you worked together stealing horses until you got greedy and went off with all the money. Shem never forgot.'

'I had to leave the country in a hurry.'

'Leaving everyone else to pay. Me and Ma, Ben and Shem.' Her thin body quivered. 'Oh, I didn't love Shem, I hated him. He was wicked. But I was going to have to marry him because he raped me and I was pregnant. He raped me, Luke, to pay for what *you* had done to him. You weren't around for him to get revenge so I was the next best thing.'

Pain gnawed at his leg. It plagued him often, especially when the weather was wet. He had learnt to live with it, but that didn't stop him remembering who was responsible, and he had never forgiven Hannah. Now he had to take a fresh look at what had happened. He had gone away from Seggenham nursing a grievance big enough to sink a ship, but by nature he was not vindictive and so he hadn't

288

sought to get revenge. He had gone his own reckless way after the accident, thinking that no one had been hurt but himself, and in truth he had put the horse-stealing episodes to the back of his mind. Never for an instant had he visualized the consequences of his crimes spreading out to include all his family. It brought everything back with sickening clarity.

His eyes were cast down. 'What can I say? Seems I got my own back without knowing it. I'm responsible for what you and Ma have become. I'll never be able to live with myself knowing that.'

'Ma's happy. Honestly she is, Luke. She wouldn't live anywhere else but with Mother Girling.'

'But not you. You can't be happy here in this hell-hole. I've got to do something about it.'

'There's nothing you can do,' Hannah said. 'I'm here because I have a husband and son and I can't leave them. I tried leaving Jonathan once but it nearly ended in disaster. Sometime I'll tell you about it.'

Luke looked over his shoulder at The Children of God who continued to dance and sing with an innocence and faith which touched his heart. They were good people who surely hadn't done anything to deserve this shocking situation and they made him ashamed of his own hard attitude to life.

He moved painfully, his hip grinding with the arthritis that had set in. 'Time somebody stirred up help to find proper shelter anyway,' he said. Then: 'I'm not very good with words, Hannah, but I'm saying sorry. I didn't know what I'd done.'

Hannah put her arms round him and buried her face against his neck to hide her tears. 'I'm sorry too,' she cried. 'It was me who started everything going wrong.'

Ben's inherited fortune made things difficult. Titus and Isobel were understandably upset that such a large sum of money should go to someone outside the family, and to an employee at that, but it wasn't Ben's fault and they tried to be fair. No one had known that Amos had any money. He had contributed nothing for his keep even though it had been a hard job for Emily to make ends meet. He'd allowed Ben to buy drink for him, and he'd scrounged coppers when his tobacco pouch needed refilling. His clothes had been washed and repaired by Emily so many times they would hardly hang together, but never once had he hinted that he could afford new ones. Even his grand-daughters had been known to feel sorry for him and bring an occasional box of sweetmeats, though his son had given nothing, that being part of his bargain with Ben. So Amos had lived like a pauper when all the time the old devil had been a rich man.

Emily no longer needed to be a housemaid, but she didn't stop working for Isobel Hanberry straight away. She said she would stay until someone else was found. Then there was the house which belonged to the Hanberrys. They couldn't go on living in it rent-free. Ben suggested that they might buy it, but Emily had other ideas and she gave him no peace.

'We must go to America, Ben, like Amos said. Likely we can find Luke. Then we can set up a business together, if he hasn't already got too settled. Maybe he's got a wife and children of his own by now, just think of it. Oh, it would be wonderful to travel, and we can afford to buy a much better house than this.'

'I'm happy at the ropeyard,' said Ben. 'I've worked meself up right well and Titus Hanberry has been good to me, training me. I can't let him down.'

She persevered whenever he was at home. 'We've got to think of ourselves now. And our daughters. We can make a new start in America and no one need know we never had anything.'

'You'd like to be a grand lady, wouldn't you, Emily?'

'Reckon I would,' she said.

But Ben had no intention of letting her talk him into making any hasty decisions. 'There's no hurry to go changing things yet.'

Before the end of that same week the second thing happened which was to shape the course of their lives. Instead of them going to look for Luke in America, Luke came in search of them.

Ben was not finding it easy to work with Titus since coming into the money. There was an undercurrent of bad feeling which wasn't expressed, but it made their working relationship prickly, to say the least, and it was praiseworthy that Titus didn't actually voice his resentment. The two men could have been almost strangers as they discussed the merits of hemp from Dorset as opposed to the new imported variety of Manila hemp which they'd been invited to try.

'I think you'd best write to Dorset soon and see if you can get the price down,' Titus said.

'I'll do that,' Ben agreed. 'Maybe I could go down there.'

'Not unless I think it worthwhile.' A week ago Titus would have discussed the advisability of it with him, but now he made it plain that he was still the master. And Ben didn't want it otherwise. He knew how much he owed this man, and it pained him that their relationship had been marred.

It was then that a boy knocked on the office door and came in.

'Beggin' yer pardon, sir, there's someone by the name of Jerram asking for Mr Rutherford.'

Ben thought of Lilianne and his heart almost stopped, fearing she had come with bad news of Hannah. Permission was given for him to see what the visitor wanted and Ben went down almost as fast as the resident black cat which passed him on the stairs like a fleeting shadow. In the yard he found a seaman waiting.

'Glad I found you, Ben. I was afraid I'd got the wrong place.'

The seaman met his eyes, and to his amazement Ben discovered it was Luke. He didn't know whether to be relieved or worried, and finished up being plain overjoyed.

'Luke, by all that's wonderful!' He held out his hand and Luke clasped it firmly. 'We were talking about you only last night – thinking of maybe coming to America to look for you.'

'I've not been there these last four years. Left in seventy-one when I couldn't find work and I've been mostly at sea ever since.' Luke looked around, then back at Ben in his neat moleskin trousers and short black jacket. 'Seems *you've* done well for yerself.'

'I've been lucky in many ways. You'll be surprised to learn I'm married to Emily and we've two little girls.'

'I know about it.'

'Who told you?'

'Look, Ben, before we start catching up on what's been happening I must tell you my reason for coming,' Luke said. 'It's urgent. My last ship docked at Southampton just before Christmas and there wasn't likely to be another one I could sign on with for several days so I went to the Mission. There I saw a newspaper, and I was reading it all unconcerned when a name jumped off the page and made me remember the old days. Mrs Girling, it said, who'd set up a religious community on the edge of the New Forest, was in some money trouble. Well, I didn't think it could be the same woman who came to Seggenham, but when I read further it mentioned some of her

291

followers and Ma's name was amongst them. I couldn't believe it. So I asked where the place was, found I could walk it in a day, and set off to find out what was going on.'

'It's a weird company,' said Ben.

'You know where Ma is, then?'

'Ma and Hannah, yes. They were here in London for a while. That was when I met up with Emily again. It's a long story.'

'Well, if you knew, why didn't you do something to get them out of it?' Luke's tone changed to anger. 'I've never been so upset in my life.'

'Oh come, it ain't that bad. Strange maybe, but they chose to live like it.'

'I'd call it a wicked disgrace and I want you to go back there with me and help do something about it. They won't listen to *me* on my own. When I got to Hordle there'd been a blizzard. It was icy cold with an easterly blowing that was fair crippling, and there they all were camping out in the lane with no food or shelter because the sheriff's men had turned them out of the house. I was horrified, that I was.'

Ben's heart lurched and he grabbed Luke by the arm. 'How was Hannah? And Ma, did you see her?'

'Oh, I saw them. Hannah was blue with cold and so thin there was nothing of her. Ma looked no better. Reckon they'd been half-starved for weeks. Yet they refused to leave that crank of a woman who reckoned the Lord was coming to save them. I tell you, I was livid.'

'That was before Christmas, you say. Where are they now?'

'In a barn. A farmer said they could have the use of it for a few weeks after the police threatened to put them all in the workhouse. I helped move their belongings, but the place ain't half big enough. There ain't room for them all to sit down at one time, and it's cold and unhealthy. I'm begging you, Ben, come with me and try to persuade them to leave before they die of exposure.'

Ben took Amos's second-best watch from his pocket and looked at the time. He couldn't go home for another hour yet, but Emily would be there.

'I can't talk about it now,' he said. 'We'll make plans tonight. Go and give Emily the surprise of her life and I'll join you as soon as I can get away.'

Terrible, terrible news. He needed time to himself to think.

He had been relieved when the Shakers moved to Hampshire. It had meant he couldn't visit Hannah, but that was a good thing since he'd been wishing he could go every five minutes. Relieved, too, that she was back in the countryside. He'd thought it would be better for her there. She had sent letters to Emily once or twice with news and it had sounded as if she was settled and happy. Aram was growing and Ma was contented, she had written. Jonathan Whitfield was scarcely mentioned. Not a day went by when Ben didn't think of Hannah, and her apparent happiness was his only consolation. Now this!

His life with Emily sometimes exasperated him to a point where it was difficult to keep his temper. She had never had a sense of humour, and lack of one had made it harder for her to look after Amos. Ben had loved the old chap and they'd had many a laugh even towards the end when he could be difficult, but Emily had always grumbled about him. Too late she had decided to mourn him openly, when word of his benevolence got round, but it was all show and mostly for the benefit of Isobel Hanberry. Emily minded what people thought of her. Ben had learnt that she loved no one better than herself and would go to great lengths to get what she wanted, even marriage.

When he got home he found Luke in his chair and a child on each knee. Selena and Patience obviously thought it great fun to have an uncle they'd never seen before, while Emily was fluttering round him like a moth at a flame, chattering non-stop in a high, excited little voice.

'. . . so when the will was read I was so overcome I . . .' She broke off when Ben came in, turning to him with happiness shining in her eyes. 'Oh, Ben, what a marvellous surprise! I couldn't believe it when I opened the door and saw who was standing there.'

'You've come into money, then,' said Luke.

'I've been telling Luke we're going to America soon. He says there'll be wonderful opportunities for us. Different to when he got there penniless.'

Ben lifted Patience into his arms and kissed her chubby cheek. She was not so fickle as Selena who stayed with her new uncle.

'Has Luke told you yet why he came looking for us?' he asked. 'Or have you prattled on so much he hasn't been able to get a word in?'

'We've talked about everything.' Emily picked up a cloth and went to the range where a pot was boiling. She lifted the lid and tested the gravy. 'I've been getting supper while he told me about seeing Ma and Hannah, and about the way they're living.'

'And did you care that your Ma and your sister are cold and starving?'

'Of course I care, but what can I do? We didn't say they'd got to be Shakers.' She carried the pot to the table where three places were set. 'Come and have supper. Selena, keep Patience amused and I'll see to you both later.'

Luke got up. 'Smells good. Reminds me of the rabbit stew Ma used to make.'

The children began to cry, Emily shouted at them, and bedlam ensued. No use trying to hold a serious conversation until they were in bed. Ben had made up his mind that they were definitely not going to America, so there would be fireworks when he told his wife, and an argument at the table would mean the meal being spoilt.

While the brother and sister talked of old times he sat quietly watching, surprised at his pleasure in seeing Luke again. By rights he ought to have turned him away after the trouble he had left behind when he'd departed in such a hurry from Seggenham, but Ben was not one to hold a grudge. Luke's accident had changed everything, including his character for a while, and he couldn't be held totally responsible for what had followed. From what he was saying his own life hadn't gone smoothly either. In New York he had been robbed of the money he had made stealing horses so he'd been forced to take whatever menial work he could get to earn enough for board and lodgings in a squalid part of the city. And he'd been lonely.

'Reckon I never appreciated how good life was on the farm until I'd left it,' he said ruefully. 'I missed Ma and all of you, but I thought you'd be glad to get rid of me.'

'Oh Luke, no,' cried Emily. 'Though you've a lot to answer for, what with us having to give up the farm, and Ben landing in jail for horse-thieving, and . . .'

'Emily was telling me you got caught, bor. I didn't mean that to happen. I thought with me out of the way that would be the end of it. I'm real sorry.'

'Let's not talk of it now,' said Ben.

Later, when Emily had taken the little girls up to bed, he told Luke they would go to Hampshire together. He didn't know what could be done, but he couldn't stay in London doing nothing. He would have no peace of mind until he had seen for himself what the situation was like.

'I'm relieved,' Luke said. 'I somehow thought you'd be as worried as me, if not more so. I wasn't blind when we were young. I knew you were besotted with Hannah. It must make you sick knowing how she's been treated by those Whitfield men.'

Ben went cold. 'What're you saying, bor? According to Emily it was love first off when Hannah met Jonathan Whitfield. What others are there?'

'Seems Emily hasn't been straight,' said Luke. 'She must have known about Shem Whitfield raping Hannah then dying before he could marry her. She was at the wedding when his father was decent enough to make an honest woman of her.'

'What! A raping, you say? Why have I never been told?' Ben's muscles tightened and there was a painful constriction round his heart. 'My God, I'll have something to say about this.'

Luke gripped his arm, forcibly stopping him from storming off to confront his wife. 'Don't stir things, bor. Likely Emily didn't want you hurt.'

'Like hell she didn't!'

'And it won't help Hannah none if you let her know you're acquainted with the truth. If she'd wanted you to know she would've told you.'

This new disclosure complicated Ben's feelings a hundredfold and he couldn't think straight. But Luke was right. He must bide his time.

The only thing which eased his heart was knowing at last that Hannah hadn't played him false. She hadn't found a new love the moment he was forced to leave her.

Chapter Thirty

The plight of the Shakers attracted much public sympathy in the area around Hordle, and Mother Girling graciously accepted a sum exceeding sixty pounds collected to help them. Offers of shelter came from different quarters, none to compare with the luxury of New Forest Lodge, but at least they were provided with a roof over their heads when a local farmer offered them his barn. That was at the beginning of January. It was a most unsuitable dwelling for so many people, and for two weeks there had to be a rota allowing half the assembly to lie down at a time while the others stood packed together in corners to keep warm. When their cramped conditions came to the notice of the authorities the farmer, who had acted with the best intentions, found himself in trouble for permitting overcrowding, and once more the Girlingites needed new accommodation. In answer to their prayers a country gentleman in the neighbourhood put a barn on his own land at their disposal, but as there was only room for the women and children Mother Girling took exception.

'We're very grateful, but this can only be a temporary arrangement,' she said, when they left the men in possession of the original accommodation. 'We're a family of God's children and we belong together.'

A condition was imposed on her acceptance. The religious fervour of the Shakers resulted in some discarding their clothes while in the grip of spiritual awareness, and Mother Girling was asked to sign a guarantee that this would not happen any more.

'I'm willing to help all I can,' said her latest benefactor, a good Christian gentleman. 'But I can't have it known that impropriety takes place on my land. There must be no disrobing.'

'The Children of God have no inhibitions when moved to express themselves freely, but there is no indecency,' she answered. She took the request as a slur. 'My lambs are innocent, I assure you.'

'If there is no signed undertaking I'm afraid I must withdraw my offer,' he said.

The immediate need for more shelter left her no option but to comply, but she was not happy about it. Stripping only happened on rare occasions when a few were so greatly moved they were unaware they were doing anything contrary to good taste.

Even though the men and women were now a distance apart Mary Ann made them gather for prayers at least once a day, which meant either party trailing across water-logged fields, and on Sundays meetings were held in the cottages of sympathetic local people. Most of the Shakers were in no fit condition to walk far. There was no hot water, no facility for cooking properly, and lack of decent food was taking its toll of their strength. Mother Girling tightened her belt and set an example in fortitude, urging more prayer for their deliverance, but though her case was taken up legally and she received two hundred pounds in compensation for the wrongful withholding of her money, she was not allowed to take her flock back to New Forest Lodge.

A bailiff came one morning during the first week of February. He arrived towards the end of a prayer meeting and stood at the barn door gazing in with an incredulous expression. The women, all dressed in white, were swaying and dancing like bedraggled angels with their eyes closed and hair floating free. But what was more astounding, instead of skirts they all wore trousers with frills at the bottom, white trousers with a shirt-like garment over the top. It was the new style of dress Mary Ann had decided would be suitable for work and she had kept the women busy sewing to help take their minds off their suffering.

'I've come to see Miss Long,' the bailiff managed to say to Beth Page, who asked what he wanted.

'Miss Long ain't here, but if you wait you can see Mother.'

There was no music, only curiously compelling voices singing hymns, and he had to bide his time until they came to an end.

'Halleluiah! Praise be to God!' cried Mother Girling at last, and a chorus of halleluiahs echoed round the barn.

She was dressed like the other women, incongruous in white trousers with black boots showing underneath, and her hands were hidden in a muff. Bailiffs were to be avoided since the eviction so she kept him waiting a while longer, fearful of another order to move, but to her surprise he was offering more money.

'I'm instructed to give you eighty-eight pounds,' he said. 'I'm afraid it's long overdue. The sale of your animals last spring raised more than the sum owing to us and we are returning the surplus.'

Mary Ann said nothing for several seconds, unsettling him further with a fixed stare. She had no time for bureaucracy. If it had taken all this time to work out a simple piece of arithmetic there was a lot wrong with the system and she wanted no part of it.

'You can take the money back,' she said. 'It's animals I need.'

'We regret it was necessary to deprive you of them, ma'am, but there was a debt to be paid. And now we are honouring our debt to you.'

'Too late to prevent the unbelievable hardship you've caused to my people. I demand you provide me with cows and a horse to replace the ones sequestered and sold so unfairly. They'll be far more useful than money.'

Whether or not the bailiff fell under the spell of Mother Girling's hypnotic gaze, within another week the animals were delivered. This upturn in their circumstances prompted another move, this time to a field in Vaggs Lane almost opposite to New Forest Lodge which was sold at the end of February.

The new settlement was hardly an improvement. The only advantage was that the group was reunited, but some of Mother Girling's followers had returned to their families so the number was now reduced to eighty, not including the children. It was a ramshackle encampment which no self-respecting gypsy would have envied. Tents were made with old carpets draped over poles until something better could be organised. It was no place for the sick or the very young and they were able to stay in the original barn which had recently housed the menfolk.

Snow fell again. It shrouded the ugliness with a pure white covering, and underneath there was still hope.

Luke's return unsettled Hannah. She'd been overjoyed to see him again, but memories of Seggenham came flooding back, and questions about the rightness of her present life surfaced once more. In nightmares she was haunted by the spectre of her brother lying unconscious with his shin-bone piercing the skin of his leg. She dreamt she bent over him and that same bone pierced her heart. When she awoke she tried to find comfort in her reconciliation with Luke, but it was impossible to change the events which had followed

298

his accident. She shivered as she lay on the barn floor where the only warmth generated was from the women huddled together.

Luke had promised to come back to Hordle. He'd been very upset about Ma living so abysmally and hadn't understood her refusal to accept his offer of help. He'd tried to persuade her to go with him to London after she'd told him about Emily and Ben, but Ma had been adamant. Her place, she'd said, was with Mother.

Hannah's guilt had returned to haunt her. In a way she was responsible for the destinies of so many people, and the enormity of her role in what had happened to them struck deeper than ever before. After the move to the Vaggs Lane field she knew it was time to gather some courage and try to salvage something from the apparent disaster.

The conditions in which they were living were affecting the health of the Shakers. Colds and coughs were numerous, and poor diet was causing weakness and various stomach complaints which set the victims rocking with a griping pain. Hannah kept free from infection and helped to nurse the others, but she was perpetually tired. With so many laid low, those who were fit found themselves overloaded with jobs just to keep the company together.

Early one foggy morning she struggled across the field with two buckets of water she had filled at a pump in a nearby farmyard, and felt as if she hadn't strength to go any further. Twice she put the buckets down and rested, but when she looked across at the set of tents which marred the landscape with their wretchedness they seemed as far away as ever. Other folk were stirring. There were signs of activity, but people were moving slowly in the fog-laden air, like shadow figures acting out a drama in slow motion. Hannah stopped again and stared. She closed her eyes, but when she opened them the scene was still there, silent and eerie, and she was filled with disenchantment. The intolerable predicament of these trusting souls gnawed at her more than hunger and she was angry at their suffering. She wanted to shout and scream, wake them up, harass them into action of some sort – but it was useless to think of it. Mother Girling would turn a hypnotic gaze upon her and pray for the demon of rebellion to be driven out.

Jonathan was chopping wood at a distance from the rest, hidden from them by a bank of laurel bushes. She watched him raise the chopper and bring it down with a rhythm he hadn't lost since leaving the forge, and all her anger concentrated itself in the steady movement of his arms. He was wasting his life. They were all wasting precious talents. A barn was no place for over eighty people to live with any dignity, and it was no wonder so many were ill when they were packed together like roosting chickens. She'd had enough of it. Others might be content to wait for the Lord's instructions but Hannah felt it was time to make a personal stand.

She picked up the buckets with renewed energy and carried them over to where Jonathan was working. Aram was shivering beside him, clinging to one of the leather gaiters strapped round his father's big legs, but he ran to her at once and she gathered him into her arms.

'I want us to leave here, Jonathan,' she said, her voice strong with resolution.

He stopped work and surveyed her. 'And where would we go?'

'I don't care. Anywhere as long as it's away from this dreadful place.'

'And where d'you think we'd find shelter when we've no money and nothing to call our own?' He propped the chopper against the fence. 'Aram, come and put the wood in the basket.'

The child scrambled down obediently and did as he was told. Jonathan's hold over Aram angered Hannah further and her nerves tensed with frustration. She wanted to do something to shake his complacency, and suddenly words came tumbling out to express feelings she had always kept hidden.

'It's your fault we have nothing,' she said bitterly. They were far enough away from the rest of the community to be out of earshot. 'If you were a man, Jonathan Whitfield, you'd be providing for us. Reckon I admired you when we first met, for yer strength and the way you took charge and made decisions, but you ain't got a ha'p'orth of guts any more.'

'Have you gone mad, girl?' He shook his tousled head. Her outburst was so unexpected.

'It's you that's mad. Mother Girling's turned you soft in the head. You're no more than a slave, doing things any idiot with muscles could do instead of using the knowledge and talent God gave you. I want a husband who ain't afraid to be a man. Not that I love you, because I don't. You're a lily-livered coward hiding behind Mother Girling's skirt, and don't say it's because you believe her promise of Everlasting Life if you don't touch me. I'd not believe you. You're just afraid.'

His face was turning purple and he reached towards the chopper. 'Bitch!'

'Strike me down,' she goaded him. 'Do something, anything, just as long as you wake up and see what you've done to us – what Mother's doing to us. You're afraid to even touch me. Our lives aren't our own.'

Aram began to cry. Harsh words were almost unknown to him and he tugged first at Hannah's skirt, then Jonathan's coat, but they were too engrossed to pay him attention.

'Afraid, am I?' Jonathan stepped towards her, towering over her, his brow as thunderous as a black storm sky. 'You don't know what trouble you've just stirred up, woman.'

He clasped both her arms above the elbows and forced her against his chest, then one hand clasped the back of her head in a grip of iron so that she couldn't escape the assault of his lips on hers. His beard was unpleasant against her skin, but the touch of his mouth sent a current through her starved body and she responded by pressing herself closer. He used his tongue to open her lips, kneaded them thoroughly and explored within until she was weak with longing for more. Her natural sensuality had built up like a dam over the years of celibacy and at the first touch she could no longer contain her need. She twined her arms round his neck and small moaning sounds of pleasure escaped her.

His hand cupped her breast as his lips became more demanding. She moved so that he could reach inside the neck of her blouse and when his fingers caressed the tender skin it seemed every nerve was tingling. As soon as he lifted his head her back arched to keep him near and she stretched her body against his in a way that couldn't fail to arouse him.

'Slut!' he accused, bruising her breast. 'Is this how you enticed my son?'

'No!' Every pleasurable sensation disappeared instantly. She hated him for reminding her of Shem.

He took her mouth again. She struggled. Then his hand went up her skirt and he touched her intimately. Oh, the treachery of her body. A throbbing started that she couldn't control and she was aflame with physical desire for more. She could tell the effect she

301

was having on her husband was no less potent but she was in no state to consider how inappropriate was the time and place for passion to seek expression. It was he who put a stop to it.

'It was a whore I married,' Jonathan breathed, thrusting her away. 'Devil woman, temptress. I hope you've sought forgiveness for your sins.'

Aram threw himself at him, pounding his thighs with pudgy fists. 'Don't hurt Mama.'

'How can you say such terrible things?' Hannah cried. 'You know I've not been near a man since you married me, and until today you've never touched me, or I you.'

'Cried rape, didn't you, when my poor Shem took you. But what about Ben Rutherford? And likely there were plenty of others before him.'

Fire turned to ice in her veins. She gasped, and every vestige of colour drained from her already pale face. Her eyes grew huge with consternation, her tongue clove to the roof of her mouth, and she took a step backwards. Lack of good food had made Jonathan thinner, but exercise ensured his strength endured. He was still like a bear with his long rough hair and beard, and the anger in him was frightening.

'There were no others,' she managed to say.

'And Rutherford?' She was silent, and after an agonising moment he gave a groan and grabbed her back into his arms, almost crushing her ribs. 'Tell me it ain't true you laid with him before Shem. I've bin going out of my mind.'

'Let me go!' Raw dismay touched every nerve and set alarm signals ringing in her head. She had stirred up trouble for sure. 'Everything I told you about Shem was true.'

'Do you swear it?'

'Yes, I swear it. Why are you accusing me after all these years? I don't understand.'

His grip on her almost stopped her breath. 'If you've lied to me . . . it'll mean you alone are responsible for the life we lead now. Because if you were wicked enough to let my son take the blame for what Rutherford did then you'll know I made sacrifices for nothing.'

He flung her down in the mud where she sprawled with her face in a pool of filthy water. Then he swung Aram up on to his shoulder and strode away.

Chapter Thirty-One

It was March before Ben was able to get to the New Forest with Luke. Emily's cough persisted and he wouldn't leave her on her own to look after the children while she was so low. She'd been forced to stop working for Isobel Hanberry and they now paid rent for their house – a sum in excess of that charged for neighbouring property, but Ben didn't complain. He didn't want to move his family yet, and he had ample money to meet the cost. The atmosphere was still strained between himself and Titus, and his working day had become longer and harder, as if Titus was insidiously punishing him. When he asked for time off to visit Hampshire, an excuse was always found as to why he couldn't be spared.

Emily was no help. Whenever he spoke of trying to get away she coughed more and feigned weakness. He was certain she was not so ill as she made out and he lost patience.

'Don't you *want* me to see if there's anything I can do for your mother? I can't send them money – they'd be made to hand it over to Mrs Girling, and I ain't having that.'

'They chose the life,' Emily said stubbornly. 'I don't see why you need do anything.'

No one knew the frustration Ben was suffering in being denied the chance to travel south. Luke's disclosure about Hannah's rape hadn't killed a growing suspicion that Aram Whitfield could be his son. Instead it was strengthened. Hannah adored the boy. Had he been conceived through rape she wouldn't have loved him the same.

Ben longed to see Aram for himself. He had vivid memories of the day he and Jonathan had rescued Hannah's baby from the Humby woman. He'd looked in the wrappings and likened the child to Hannah, seeing a marked resemblance in the features and colouring. He had given no thought then to the possibility that maybe he had paid Matt Jerram's watch as ransom for his own child. Surely Hannah would have let him know . . . and Jonathan's desperate anxiety to get the baby back had seemed to prove *he* had no doubts it came from Whitfield stock. Only later, counting up the dates, had Ben wondered if Hannah had tricked Jonathan into marriage in a desperate bid for respectability.

There was nothing Luke could do on his own to help Ma, and he had kept on reminding Ben of the urgent need for them both to go down to the New Forest. Ben was no less anxious, but he was a married man with responsibilities and couldn't afford to be reckless. An opportunity finally came by way of a letter to Titus Hanberry from an old friend well advanced in years by the name of George Crummock. Titus asked Ben to stay behind in the office on the day it arrived.

'Sit down, Ben,' he said. He moved a pile of books off the only other chair and blew on them to send the dust flying. 'I'm of the opinion it's time we came to a parting of the ways. My father's will may have been a godsend to you but I must admit it was a thorn in the flesh to me and my wife. It's changed things between you and me and I reckon the only way we can come to a new understanding is for you to be working somewhere else.'

Ben was still standing. 'You're sacking me, then. I didn't think it would come to this.'

'Not the sack – the chance to leave of your own free will.' Titus produced a letter from his pocket and unfolded it. 'Damn it, sit down, bor. You're funny tall and it hurts me neck looking up at you.' When he was anxious the Suffolk accent of his youth became more pronounced. Ben obliged. 'Now, a piece of information came my way this morning which might interest you, since you've got money you ought to be investing in something worthwhile. A friend of mine wrote that he's too old to keep his business going any longer and he's looking for a buyer.'

'What kind of business and where is it?' Ben asked, catching the drift at once. 'I ain't moving back to Suffolk, or to Scotland or anywhere like that.'

'Rope,' Titus said. 'George Crummock taught me how to make it, and I've taught you. Seems the art's been passed on right successfully.'

'He's selling a ropeworks then?'

'That's the sum of it. Nice business in Hampshire near enough to Southampton to corner part of a market in shipbuilding, but out in the country where the air would be good for Emily and the children. How does it sound to you?'

304

It sounded too good to be true and Ben's heart gave an automatic leap of excitement. He remembered Luke saying he had walked from Southampton to the New Forest, so he'd be within easy visiting distance of Hannah. What is more, he would be on his way to becoming a manufacturer of some standing like Titus, a self-made man, and in a few years he might be making enough money to buy the kind of house Emily would like to own, and to give Hannah and Ma Jerram all the help they might need. The prospect was like a rosy dream. And it took but a few seconds to realise that that was all it could be.

'I ain't ready for it,' he said. 'I've only just finished an apprenticeship and I ain't got the experience. It would be too much of a risk.'

'I'd trust you to run this place in me absence.'

Ben grinned. 'That would be *your* money I was gambling with.'

'And you'd make me more. Can't say further than that. You've got a good head for business and you learn quicker'n anyone I've met.'

'You're flattering me to get me to agree. You must want rid of me real bad.'

'Real bad,' Titus agreed. But now he was smiling too, and for the first time in weeks there was a feeling of friendship between them. 'Son, you've amazed me with yer aptitude. I don't want to lose you, but I'll help you get started because I'm certain you've got the ability. You're worth cultivating. Me father knew it, and the old codger was a good judge of character.'

'But I can't run a business on me own.'

'Stop finding arguments. What you do is put up the money and take over, then let the men you employ do the running of it until you get the feel of what you want changing. They'll be experienced men. They'll know what they're doing. And you're too intelligent not to know if they were taking advantage. I'd stake me last shilling on you, Ben. You've got it in you to succeed. So shall I write back to George and tell him to expect you down there to inspect the place?'

Ben took a deep breath. 'Aye. Tell him I'll be there next week . . . if that's all right with you, sir.'

'It's all right with me. If it wasn't leaving the yard with no one in charge I'd come too, but I can tell you George Crummock was always an honest man and he'd built up a fine yard last time I heard. You'll know right enough if it looks a good investment. And if he wants more for it than you can afford and you need a loan, I'll vouch for you at my bank.'

'Thank you.' Ben shook Titus by the hand, his grip so firm the older man winced. 'It feels good to be in favour with you again, and I'll not be wasting the teaching you've given. I owe a lot to the Hanberrys.'

He went home and talked the plan over with Emily, and though she was still hankering for America he was able to convince her that it was worth investigating the chance to buy a ropeyard of his own. They would be taking a big step up in the world, and as long as she was going to be able to play the lady it didn't really matter which side of the Atlantic was the playground.

The following week Ben and Luke travelled by train to Hampshire.

Whenever he thought of leaving the Shakers, as Hannah had begged him, a pain struck Jonathan Whitfield. It started in his temples and circled his head like a length of leather being pulled tighter and tighter until he felt as if his eyes were bulging. At first he didn't connect the pain with the thought. He was busy from morning till night working on the renovation of an old building of unburnt brick which was to be their new chapel, and he assumed the constant hammering affected his balance at the end of the day – though it shouldn't have done, since he'd been wielding a hammer practically all his life without any ill-effects.

The pain didn't come regularly. It happened at night when he considered Hannah's remark that he was wasting his talents. The third time it came he was lying in the dark tent he shared with three other men, and sleep had eluded him for several hours. He was plagued with doubts as to what to do about his wife. Hannah affected him like a fever, bringing heat to his body, torment to his mind, and visions of a new carnal freedom away from the fetters of Shakerism. He needed her physically. He wanted to set up home with her and Aram in some quiet village where he could become a smithy again. He wanted her, but he didn't love her. He loved Lilianne, which made matters even worse.

Fears for Aram had started to grow. If they left the community and he lived a normal life with Hannah he would once more be breaking his vow of celibacy, and he was terrified that Aram would be the sacrifice God would exact from him as punishment. It was too great a risk to take, and for Aram's sake he had to cast aside his own desires. Fear made him over-anxious about the child and he'd kept him close ever since he had been old enough to sleep with the men rather than with his mother. His greatest worry was that Hannah might try to take Aram away as she had done in London.

Jonathan refused to give credence to Lilianne's cruel hint that Aram might not be Shem's son. Though he had taunted Hannah he didn't really believe her capable of such wicked deception, and he closed his mind to Lilianne's insinuations. They were the product of jealousy, and he forgave her. Jonathan knew enough about women to recognise a desperate attempt to erase the threat to herself when he had unwisely talked of leaving with Hannah. Lilianne's attachment to him was a source of guilt and shame because he had used her in times of stress. Sometimes he watched her and knew that if Shem hadn't returned he might have found happiness at last with Lilianne.

The pain had never been so bad as this night in March. He lay awake with his temples throbbing and his head feeling as if it were resting on bricks. When he could stand it no longer he got up quietly and went outside, wrapping his worn coat round him to keep out the cold. He was shaking. There was a bright moon silvering the grass and creating deep shadows, and he stood for a minute gazing at the sky, marvelling at the brightness of the stars. One in particular seemed to hang there like a beacon, so vivid it beckoned him, and he started walking across the field like a blind man. The pain caused lights to flicker at the side of his eyes and zig-zag lines blotted out everything except the light of the star.

He kept walking until he reached a rough stone shelter used by the animals. It wasn't a stable – he saw it as a tomb. Surely there should have been a rock in front of the entrance. He blinked hard to try and clear the haziness but it persisted. The entrance was open to the cold night air and he could see inside. It was empty.

His heart was beating so fiercely it made the throbbing in his temples worse. He could hear voices in his head telling him to go inside the shelter, and he had to bend nearly double to obey. An animal drinking-trough against the back wall looked like a stone slab in his pain-racked state, and with shoulders well bent he went over to it, expecting to see a pile of discarded grave clothes lying near it. There was nothing except the hoof-trodden earth and dried animal dung, and the smell of the place stung his nostrils. After a few moments he backed out again.

He was filled with a terrible disappointment which he couldn't understand. It seemed as if he had been on the point of discovering something of great importance, but it had come to nothing and he was left only with the pain in his head.

And then he saw Mother Girling coming across the field towards him in the moonlight. She was dressed in her white working costume of trousers and smock, and a small white hat covered her flowing hair. The bluish light gave the material a peculiar brightness, and Jonathan started running to her. Disappointment was replaced by an incredible joy.

'Mother, I recognise you,' he cried. He fell at her feet and touched the white frill of her trousers.

Mother Girling put her hand on the top of his head in bewilderment. 'Whatever's the matter, Brother Jonathan? I couldn't sleep and I saw you stumbling over to the hut. Aren't you well?'

'You're alive again, Mother. Thanks be to God.'

'Stand up, man. What're you talking about? Of course I'm alive. Haven't I told you I shall never die?'

He got awkwardly to his feet and pressed balled fists to his eyes. At last the pain began to recede. When he looked around everything was the same as always, the old building half-repaired, the carpet-covered tents, the cows lying by the hedge, the horse standing guard. He looked behind him and the stone shelter no longer resembled a tomb. Mother Girling was as substantial as ever.

He felt such a fool. 'I'm sorry. I had a terrible dream.' He repeated his apologies several times and begged her to forgive him. 'I thought I heard voices but it must have been the wind in the trees.'

Mother faced him with excitement shining in her piercing eyes. Both her hands clasped one of his.

'You've had a vision, brother. Tell me about it. Tell me what you heard and what you saw.'

But Jonathan had returned from the edge of madness and wanted to forget.

'It was nothing.'

He regained his dignity and strode back to the tent where the three other men and Aram still slept on, oblivious.

The morning after Jonathan's strange experience Hannah took a pile of children's washing to a trough behind a shed that was being constructed for the women's sleeping quarters. The shed was four and half paces wide by sixteen long, and the urgent need to get the tarpaulin roof fixed meant a gang of men were shattering the morning quiet with their hammering. She thought Jonathan was one of them, so she was surprised when he came with a bucket of hot water from the stove just as she was loosening the stains with a rub in water not far from freezing.

'I must talk to you,' he said. 'I want to say I'm sorry. I'd no right to say what I did about you and Ben Rutherford. Nor anything else.'

'What brought this on?'

A frown furrowed his brow. It had grown more pronounced of late and was now a mark of permanent sorrow which ought not to be there if he truly believed in the holiness of Mother Girling.

'Last night I thought Mother had died and was risen again,' he said. 'I saw a tomb but it was empty, and then I saw her walking towards me all in white.'

Hannah dried her red, raw hands on her apron and could hardly bear the touch of the material on them. But that was nothing to the sharp pain his words inflicted inwardly. He looked drained and she feared for his sanity.

'This was a dream, wasn't it? You dreamt it.'

'No. I saw the tomb across the field and I went over to it. Then Mother came.'

'Oh, Jonathan.' She was frightened for him, and she felt the stirring of some deeper truth struggling to find voice. 'Jesus was the only one to die and rise again. There ain't never been another, nor will there ever be.'

'Mother is the Second Coming.'

'I don't believe it. What you saw was just in your imagination.'

'How can you say you don't believe? Why are you here?'

She raised her voice a little. 'I'm here because of Aram, and because of you. Legally I'm married to you, Jonathan, and that means my place is with you. I don't like it, but what choice have I got?'

309

'Look to your conscience. We all accept what Mother provides because we believe in her. We have faith. If you don't have that faith you've no right to be counted a disciple. You're a female Judas.'

'Will you stop it! This is worse than what you said about me and Ben.'

'Is it?' His aggressiveness evaporated as quickly as it had come and he went on in hushed tones. 'I was shown last night that Mother *is* the Christ. If I ever had doubts I've none left now.'

Hannah covered her ears. Her husband's declaration strengthened her own conviction that things here were wrong. Mother Girling was a good woman, certainly, and true to her belief in her own divinity. But there were times when she used the Bible to further her own ends, and since she had started reading well herself, Hannah felt sure that sometimes Mother misinterpreted passages. She must try to make Jonathan see the error of trusting in Mother Girling implicitly.

'Why do you think God would let you see a vision of Mother resurrected?' she asked him now. 'What reason would He have?'

'It was to convince me of her reincarnation.'

'No, it ain't true. I know it, and God would never let you think it.' She touched his arm. 'Do you believe in Jesus, Jonathan?'

'Of course I do.'

'Then you can't accept everything Mother Girling claims, because Jesus said no one comes to the Father except through Him. If you believe Jesus you can't believe Mother as well. You had a dream, that's all. Forget it and you'll feel better.'

'Mother *is* Jesus.'

'I won't listen to you!' The hot water he had brought was steaming. She poured it into the trough and plunged her hands in, enduring the pain. 'I must get on with my washing.'

For several minutes he stood behind her while she worked but he didn't say anything else, and neither did she.

The ropeyard was not what Ben had expected. It was in a village called West Borley which was close to the Beaulieu River and on the edge of the New Forest. It was within easy reach of an odd little place called Buckler's Hard where boatbuilding in the second half of the eighteenth century had been a major industry. Nelson's favourite ship HMS *Agamemnon* was one of many famous naval vessels built there, but by 1822 the sons of Henry Adams, a master builder, went bankrupt for the second time and that was the end of an era. A few ships had still been built for a while, but for the last twenty-five years there'd been nothing at all, mainly because iron was successfully replacing wood as the basic raw material for ships commissioned by the Navy.

Lack of government orders had not only put an end to local ship-building, but had also affected small industries nearby which had relied on supplying parts for vessels under construction; among them was George Crummock's ropeyard. Rope was still produced, but not in any quantity, and after the bustle and noise of the yard in Bermondsey it seemed extraordinarily quiet.

'I'll not be misleading you,' said George Crummock, an elderly man with sparse white hair sticking up at right-angles from his head as if he'd had a shock. The fact that he was fat and jovial encouraged Ben to make exhaustive enquiries about the business whereas he might otherwise have dismissed it out of hand. The man looked as if he lived well, and he couldn't do that if there was no money coming in. 'I've been through lean times these past few years I admit, but things have picked up a bit and I'm supplying regular to a yard in Southampton. Steamships still need rope, and so do farmers. Besides that we make a few nets for agriculture, and there's a tidy little profit to be made out of sacks come harvest when farmers want bags for their potatoes.'

'I'd like time to think it over,' Ben said. He was not going to be rushed. Luke was with him and he wanted them to discuss it over a meal at a hostelry in Beaulieu where they'd booked a room for the night.

'Is the house included in the price?' Luke asked, at dinner.

'It has to be. Part of it forms the workshop and the rope walk leads off from the garden. Damned if I'd ever pictured a country alley given over to spinning but it seems to serve the purpose right enough.'

'Emily won't like having to help make nets.'

'Emily will fall in with whatever I choose to do.'

The following morning Ben hired two horses from the landlord of the Beaulieu Arms, and he and Luke set out early to ride from there to Hordle. They had been told it was a distance of seven or eight miles and were directed to take the road to Lymington across Beaulieu Heath. Ben looked forward to breathing in the sharp March air; he hadn't been to the country for five years, and he'd not realised how much he had missed it. In the early days of living in London he had sometimes dreamt of his beloved Suffolk marshes, but there'd been too much occupying his mind of late for fair dreams to intrude.

He knew the Forest stretched for over a hundred square miles and he'd imagined it to be a solid mass of trees. In the train they had passed through dense wooded areas once Southampton had been left behind, but there'd been heathland too, and this morning he looked forward to a good ride to the Shaker encampment. It was satisfying to feel a horse under him again. He led the way out of the village on a frisky animal, leaving Luke to follow, and he had to wait for him when he reached a high point on the edge of the heath.

'Just look at the view,' he called, reining the horse and turning it. 'You can see the river, and I reckon that's the Isle of Wight yonder. Ain't it something!'

The day was clear. Too clear, the locals would say, bringing the certainty of rain later, but the clarity was to be enjoyed while it lasted and it afforded a view that took Ben's breath away. The ancient grey, red-roofed buildings of Beaulieu clustered now at the bottom of the hill between the river and a small sea-loch where wildfowl congregated. Ben picked out the abbey ruins, part of which had been preserved to form the parish church, and Palace House where once the abbot had lived rose in grey majesty from the wide green lawns. He waited for Luke to come alongside. The sun was climbing high over the distant island and shedding gold on the gorse which grew in profusion over the heath. The smell of its blossom was like honey, and already there were a few bees collecting from it.

'Kissing won't never be out of season up here,' Luke laughed, skirting a gorse thicket where two of the forest ponies nibbled tender shoots of new grass.

Ben filled his lungs with the glorious air as they rode side by side. He hadn't felt like this since leaving Seggenham. Up here on the heath the feeling of space reminded him of home, but it was warmer and bluer and more hilly. They had to be careful of bogs, but they were used to that.

'What're you going to do when we get there?' Luke asked. They had covered over a mile in record time with a strong breeze whipping through their hair, and the question came only when they had to slow down at the road leading to Lymington.

'I must talk to Hannah,' said Ben. 'Ain't nobody'll stop me. You were right, I love her.'

Ben tried to be full of confidence. He hadn't come all this way to fail. He imagined the offer of a cottage of her own was all that was needed to persuade Ma Jerram to quit, but he was not so sure about Hannah. Loyalty to her husband kept her there, but if he offered to find work for Jonathan Whitfield, surely she would make him accept. It was quite incomprehensible to Ben how a strong, healthy blacksmith could give up a good living to follow some false prophet with freakish ideas about how to find a perfect life hereafter while having no qualms as to the terrible quality of life she was subjecting them to on earth. If Hannah was taken in by the woman it was serious indeed, but it was Ben's belief that she was far too sensible to be coerced, and it was that which gave him hope.

They dropped down towards Lymington but didn't need to go through the town. Their instructions had been to cut through Lower Buckland and they came out on another stretch of heathland which took them towards a small village called Sway. It was here that Luke lost his sense of direction.

'Damned if I know where we are,' he said, as they came down a steep hill. 'Don't see anything I recognise, but we can't be too far away.'

'We'll ask the next person we see,' said Ben.

Sway was a sleepy hamlet and passing through it they'd not seen anybody, but on the fringe there was a large house by the name of Arnewood Towers, home of Andrew Pet⁻rson, the retired High Court barrister who had brought a mesmerist from the Isle of Wight to challenge Mother Girling. Much building work was being carried out on the estate. The place was alive with labourers and it was here that the travellers stopped.

'We're looking for the New Forest Shakers,' Ben called. 'Can you tell us if we're heading the right way?'

Two of the men came to the gate with tools in their hands, and their attitude was belligerent.

'Are you from the law?' one asked. Both looked up at Ben and Luke astride their horses, and their eyes took in Ben's neat clothes. ''Cause if you are we're telling you them Shakers are decent people and they don't deserve the way they've been treated.'

'We're not law men. We're . . .'

'Strange they may be,' interrupted the second, 'but they've a right to their own thinking and shouldn't be penalized for it. They don't bother no one.'

'My ma and my sister are Shakers,' Luke told them. 'We've come to see how they're doing.'

The men had been balancing heavy hammers across their shoulders like weapons, but Luke's answer seemed to satisfy them and first one then the other lowered the implements.

'Reckon you're all right then. And you ain't got that far to go. Turn right at the end of here into Silver Street and carry on till you get to Vaggs Lane.'

'Ah yes,' said Luke. 'That sounds familiar.'

'Many thanks,' nodded Ben. He was about to draw on the reins to swing away, but his attention was caught by the construction going on inside the gate. 'Tell me, what're you building? Seems different to anything I've seen.'

Labourers were busy mixing a substance on a board platform, powder with gravel and water. Others were ramming the stuff into frames which, when dried, obviously made large slabs of building material, and these were being used to erect a square dwelling of the plainest design.

'Concrete,' he was told. 'Mr Peterson's mighty interested in it. Seems he came back from India with the idea it's better'n bricks for building with, and we ain't arguing since he gives work to many as would otherwise have none. Pays a better wage than the farmers, too.'

'Can I come inside and look?'

'Reckon there ain't no harm. Mr Peterson's in London till the week's end. Usually he's around telling us what to do and how to do it.'

What Ben saw impressed him greatly, and Luke was no less interested. It was a fairly large estate and all the new buildings on it were made of concrete, though the big house which had been altered and enlarged was in traditional style. Mr Peterson was obviously a generous employer, and one who expected to provide work for some time to come as he had a carpenter's shop and a blacksmith's forge in the grounds.

'Is it likely Mr Peterson would take on another blacksmith?' Ben asked.

'Mr Peterson only takes men what have no work. Why, you aimin' to get a job?'

'No. But likely it might help if there was one available for a man I know.'

'You'd have to ask Mr Peterson.'

'Maybe I'll be doing that.'

Ben felt pleased with himself. The day had started out much better than he had expected and he would be going to the Shaker community with a definite proposition to put to Hannah. The thought that in a short time he would be seeing her made his heart flip excitedly and he was impatient to get going again. He had to go in search of Luke who was so fascinated by the revolutionary new methods of construction it was difficult to prise him away.

'For two pins I'd've rolled up me sleeves and got busy,' Luke said, as they rode on towards Hordle after spending nigh on an hour watching the men work and asking questions.

It was but a short distance to Vaggs Lane, and as they approached the field where the Shakers were living there were sounds of industry. A greater comparison was hard to imagine than the labouring of the men at Arnewood Towers and the primitive methods being used here. Ben was appalled. Close to the road and sheltered by the hedge there was one shed presumably finished, and another partway done. The planks used were old and worm-eaten, and the second hut in particular couldn't possibly have been weatherproof judging by the gaps in the wood. Both buildings were roofed with tarpaulin, and it sounded as if floorboards were being laid. The rest of the accommodation was a collection of tents, and in an open space between them was an old stove with a crooked chimney, presumably the only facility for cooking and heating water.

Ben stopped when they were several yards away. 'You told me it was awful, but I never thought it would be this bad,' he said.

'I was just going to say what an improvement there is on the last time I was here,' said Luke. 'If you think this is bad you should have seen where they were before, in a barn with nothing but straw to lie on.'

Several women were toiling on patches of ground which were being well dug, no doubt to produce crops. Children were removing weeds from great clods of earth which could then be broken up and raked over ready for planting, and it seemed the job brought satisfaction because in spite of the effort involved there was breath left for singing. Ben and Luke walked their horses to the gate, and a small boy looked up from his weeding.

'Uncle Luke!' the boy cried. 'Uncle Luke, I knew you'd come back.'

He sped across the rough ground, almost tripping in a pair of boots that were several sizes too big for him, and the women stopped what they were doing to stare. They were wearing the most outlandish garments Ben had ever seen. Never before had he known women in trousers, and the degrading sight sickened him. He was torn between watching the boy and looking for Hannah, but a quick glance was enough to tell him that she wasn't there. Even in those extraordinary clothes he could have picked her out immediately.

The little boy threw himself at Luke, who picked him up with delight and swung him round.

'Aram, you've grown, bor. Where's your ma and your grandmother?'

'They ain't here. They've gone with Mother.'

'*Where* have they gone?' asked Ben. Anxiety put an edge on his voice. Surely he hadn't come all this way only to be thwarted once more by the Shaker woman, and he dreaded some new hold might be exerted over Hannah.

'Dunno,' said Aram, looking at the newcomer with interest. 'Who are you?'

Ben felt a jerk of surprise as he met the child's eyes. Their clarity and colour were a mirror image of his own.

'This is your Uncle Ben,' Luke was saying. 'I've been telling him about you. Say hello to him.' He transferred the boy to Ben. 'You stay here while I go and find someone to ask about Ma and Hannah. The Shakers don't like prowlers and I don't want Mother Girling fixing me with her beady eyes. Scare the life out of me they do.'

He went off in the direction of the women, leaving Ben with the boy in his arms. The strangest stirring affected him. He was used to cuddling his plump and spoilt daughters at bedtime, but this was totally different. Aram's little body was thin but firm and he was heavy to hold, though partly because of the clods of mud sticking to the soles of his boots. Hannah's boy. Oh yes, he was Hannah's boy with his thick golden hair and his sensual mouth, and the likeness brought a tight feeling to Ben's throat. But the grey eyes and the way his hair grew to a peak on his deep forehead were not characteristic of his mother. Ben's finger automatically traced the V-shaped pattern on his own forehead. He could see no likeness to Jonathan Whitfield at all.

'Didn't know I had an Uncle Ben,' Aram said, studying the newcomer.

'Has your ma never spoken of me, then?'

'No.'

He wouldn't have believed it could hurt so much to hear the negative reply.

'Your mother and I grew up together and I love her dearly,' he said. 'Like I'd love you if I was able to see you more.'

Aram's steady gaze was disconcerting. His next question was embarrassingly direct. 'Why?'

'Now that ain't easy to answer. But I'd be happier if you weren't living here.'

'I like it here. My father teaches me to make things and to look after the horse. He's strong, like you. There ain't nobody I love better, 'cept Ma.'

The women had started digging again, all except one who was hurrying across to the shed from where incessant hammering could be heard. Ben kept talking to the boy, fascinated by him and impressed by his intelligence. He listened to the confident little voice telling him how clever his Ma was at reading, and how she was teaching him his letters. A surge of emotion made Ben's heart feel as if it were expanding, and the reason for it was . . . pride. He was so proud of Aram.

A cloud extinguished the sun, and a chill wind whipped up some leaves and set them whirling. When the flurry died down again it left a pool of calm in which a curious silence overcame the man and the boy. The hammering had stopped in the shed. The distant women with bent heads and backs seemed to be conspiring together. And in the darkened space of time it took for the cloud to pass over, Jonathan Whitfield suddenly appeared.

317

'Put my son down,' he commanded, stepping out from behind the concealing hedge. There was menace in his tone.

Ben was unprepared. Aram wriggled to be free and he set him on his feet, allowing a few seconds' grace before the confrontation with Hannah's husband.

'Good day, Jonathan. It's been a long time since we met.'

'I ain't forgotten you. Why are you here?' There was no smile of welcome. 'Aram, get on back to the garden.'

The little boy ran off without a backward glance or another word to Ben, and his going was like learning that the sun would never come out again.

'Stay away from my son, d'yer hear,' Jonathan said. 'I don't want you near 'im ever again.'

'I hear you, but I don't understand. What's wrong with me speaking to Hannah's child?'

Jonathan's eyes glittered. 'She said if ever you showed up I was to tell you she wants nothing to do with you, and I'm saying our child's better off not knowing you. You ain't her family, so stay away.'

'I'll not believe she said any such thing until I hear it from her own lips. Where is she?'

'She ain't here.' The man was reacting as if he were being threatened. It didn't make sense.

'What are you afraid of, bor? I've never done any harm to you or Hannah. I was with you when we got the boy back in London, and I've done nothing to earn this reception. I came to offer help.'

'We don't need your help.' Jonathan's fists clenched. 'And if ever you try to lure my wife and child from here I won't be answerable for the consequences.'

Ben saw Luke coming back, his lob-sided walk more pronounced as he covered the uneven ground.

'Any sign of them?' Ben called.

'They've gone travelling with the Shaker woman,' Luke shouted back. 'Won't be here for days seemingly.'

'Get off this land, Rutherford. You're trespassing,' said Jonathan Whitfield. 'And if you ever come back there'll be trouble, I'm telling you. I'd kill Hannah and Aram both before I'd let you influence them.'

'That's dangerous talk.'

318

'Just don't ever come near my boy again.'

Any further discussion would likely have brought about a fight, and Ben wanted to leave before Luke was involved.

'There's no point in staying, bor,' he said to his brother-in-law when he was level with them. 'Seems we're not wanted.'

He swung on to his horse before Luke had time to argue, and jerked the reins so tightly the animal reared with a snort.

The weather turned to rain. Ben and Luke returned to Beaulieu the way they had come, and now the open heathland was a wild, desolate place where the forest ponies could find little shelter from the stinging rain, and the galloping riders had to trust their animals to avoid bogs since they could hardly lift their heads to see where they were going.

It was impossible to hold a conversation. Later, Ben decided, when they were sitting in front of a comfortable log fire and he was supping a tankard of ale to mellow his mood, he would talk to Luke about Hannah's husband and find out if he, too, thought the man was mad.

A week after Ben's visit a letter was delivered to the Shaker colony for Hannah. The rules forbade anyone having correspondence which was not first read by Mother Girling so the contents were known before they reached her. She was summoned to speak with Mother in a small shed made specially for her as a place of privacy where she could retire to pray. A bedstead took up practically all the space.

'Sister Hannah, I am greatly disturbed,' Mother said. The paper was held rigidly by the top and bottom as if it were a scroll. 'This letter has come for you and it contains matter which is intended to cause mischief. It's from the man who is married to your sister, which makes the sin worse, and I have prayed over whether to destroy it rather than risk it causing you to become unsettled.'

Hannah dared not let her feelings show. She knew about Ben's visit. Aram had said that Uncle Luke came with another uncle while she and Ma were touring towns as far away as Salisbury to gain more support for the Shaker mission. When she had questioned Jonathan she'd received a curt reply to the effect that Luke had brought Ben Rutherford spying and he'd packed them both off. She and Ma had both tried to discover the reason for the visit but Jonathan had been perverse and neither had managed to get any further information. Now Ben had written to her. Her legs threatened to give way and she wanted to snatch the letter, so hungry was she to see what was in it, but restraint was absolutely necessary. She was angry and resentful at Mother Girling's rule giving herself the right to open the letter first, but rebellion might mean it being denied her altogether.

'I'm sorry if it's made you angry, Mother,' Hannah said, as contrite as she could manage to be. 'I have no idea why he should want to get in touch with me unless it's with news of Emily. Is my sister all right?'

'It seems the Rutherfords have come into money. If there'd been an offer to help The Children of God with it I might have overlooked the sentiments expressed, but the purpose of the letter is to encourage you to forsake your calling, and that's downright wicked.'

'May I read for myself please, Mother?'

Mother Girling halved and quartered the missive into its original folds and replaced it in the envelope. For a dreadful moment Hannah thought she was then going to tear it to pieces.

'I think we should pray together, sister, so that you have strength to make the right reply. It might be as well if no one else is made aware of the letter. You may have a piece of paper to write back and, of course, I shall see it before it is posted. Mr Rutherford asks why I do nothing to end the suffering of my children. You will tell him that when I am fully accepted as Jesus in a woman's form God will appear in His glory to save all those who are true believers. Until then we rest in the confidence that we are abiding by His will and He will provide. Now, let us go down on our knees.'

Hannah's impatience grew as long exhortations were made to the Lord for her to be given divine guidance in the matter. There were no floorboards, and stones cut into her knees. When at last she held the letter she was desperate to run and find a secluded spot, but until she was out of sight of the shed she managed to walk with dignity. She thought of taking it to the privy in the hope that no one would disturb her while she read it, but it always smelt so awful, and even there she couldn't be sure that someone wouldn't barge in. With the precious envelope tucked in her bodice she crossed the field to the hen-house. Memories tugged at her heart as she bent low and crept inside the half-derelict structure to sit among the laying fowl. Their clucking and squarking reminded her vividly of the day of Luke's accident when she had first been aware of Ben's magnetism. As she drew out the paper and saw his bold handwriting it was as if he was there with her.

'My dear Hannah,' she read. 'I am deeply concerned for your welfare. Your husband has no right to keep you prisoner, which is how I see it since I can't believe you would stay in such a place of your own accord. The Shakers are blind, religious fanatics who should be asking Mrs Girling why she allows them to live in such poverty. If she were truly sent by God she would do something to make a better life for those that follow her.

'I came to see you but you weren't there.

'Things have been going well for me. I am going to buy a rope-yard about eight miles from where you are. Come to us when Emily and the children are settled. I'll buy a cottage for you and your son, and if your husband can be made to see sense I can find him work as a blacksmith.

'You are too sensible to be taken in by the Shaker woman. I beg you not to let your son be brought up any longer among such strange people. Leave, I implore you, with Ma and the boy before it is too late. I shall wait eagerly for your answer.

'Your devoted brother-in-law, Ben.'

A hen on a perch above her dropped excrement on her head. She combed her fingers through her hair and wiped the mess on her skirt. The unpleasantness of it typified her existence, but it also reminded her of the hen-house at Kean's Farm and how she had once been happy.

She read the letter twice more through a mist of tears. What had she been expecting? A love letter? Of course not. But she had anticipated something more than the harsh demand that she should give up her present life to please him. Prisoner of a sort she might be, but it was high-handed of him to be so critical of her husband.

It was plain that he was concerned for Aram as much as for herself, and as she read deeper into the letter she began to see things that added up. Once, when Luke had been staying nearby, he had casually observed that when Aram stared at him it was uncannily like being a boy again on the farm, with Ben using his eyes to gain advantage when he wanted things to go his way. If Luke had said the same to Ben it must have made him suspicious. Perhaps he had come to Hordle to see for himself. Well, likely he went home disappointed if he'd expected to see a child in his own image. But he'd been intrigued enough to pen a plea for her to remove Aram from an influence he feared.

He had no right to expect her to fall in with his wishes. Let him bring his wife and family to Hampshire if he had the money, but he wouldn't dictate what she, Hannah, must do – even though he was right in saying she was too sensible to be deceived by Mother Girling. She was living in the community of her own accord, because she was married to Jonathan and it was her duty to fall in with whatever he decided was right for them, and that was the way it would continue.

It had been Hannah's intention to maybe write two letters, one for Mother Girling's eyes, and one to be posted secretly to Ben. But now she had no need to deceive anybody. Later, when the children were asleep and the women were occupied, she composed her answer to Ben Rutherford.

'Dear Ben, I got your letter. I'm sorry you are wasting your time worrying about me. I am quite happy here with my husband and our son, and I resent the things you said about him. Please don't ever write to me again with suggestions that I am being kept against my will. Jonathan is a good husband . . .' Here she stopped writing and bit the end of the quill. Then she carried on, indenting the paper with the pressure. *'As for Aram, his father and I see to it that he has a fair education, which is more than can be said for many children, and he is being brought up to serve the Lord. I can see no reason why you should have any interest in my son's upbringing and I'll thank you not to criticise the life I've chosen for him.*

'I'm sure Emily wouldn't want me to join you.

'I will not comment on the things you said about Mother Girling, except to say that she knows of your opinion of her and wishes me to say that it is God she answers to, and He knows what is best for us.

'I'd rather you didn't come here again.

'Your sister-in-law, Hannah.'

It was not until Mother Girling had approved the letter the next morning and sealed it in an envelope that Hannah allowed herself to consider how she had effectively cut herself off from Ben forever. She had condemned herself to the Shaker life and destroyed the only

322

sure way of escape. Her stomach muscles contracted and her throat hurt as she held back from weeping. She could only be happy if she pushed all thoughts of Ben from her mind, and with an effort she had managed to do it over the years since their last meeting. But he had entered her life again without warning and her peace of mind was shattered. In spite of his intolerance, his new affluence which he probably thought gave him the right to dictate, his conceit and his cheek, she still yearned for him. Let it be inwardly said that if he'd not been married she would have been sorely tempted to leave her husband.

Chapter Thirty-Two

The next three years were not easy for Mary Ann Girling. Setbacks inevitably made it harder to keep the faithful from slipping, and there were no new converts to bring in much-needed money. She survived financially only through generous contributions from the curious, the irreverent and the sympathetic who still came every Sunday from miles around to watch the devout at worship. Vaggs Lane was regularly clogged from end to end with carriages and carts, making it impossible to pass through. Mary Ann accepted charity and endured the ridicule all in the name of the Lord.

Local officials tried to undermine her authority. In fairness they thought it the only way to improve conditions for the Shakers. A doctor was persuaded to issue a certificate saying that Mary Ann Girling was a lunatic and should be locked away, but when she was brought before the examining magistrates in Lymington they found her to be quite sane. The ordeal simply strengthened the faith of her flock, and her appearance in court was likened to Christ being brought before the Pharisees.

Unfortunately the doubts cast as to the sanity of Mary Ann brought the nephew of Miss Kitty Long down to the New Forest with two doctors to prove that his aunt was similarly afflicted. The poor lady was forcibly taken to the lunatic asylum at Laverstoke, and though Mary Ann successfully pleaded for her release it was only two more weeks before the doctors saw to it that Miss Long returned permanently to Laverstoke.

There was illness in the community, particularly in winter when the cold and lack of food was too much for even the hardiest constitutions. No one succumbed to any infections and faith in Mary Ann's promise of everlasting life increased. But in the spring of 1877 Mary Glaser was suddenly taken ill with pneumonia and died. She was buried in the churchyard at Hordle with only a macracarpa tree to mark the place, and for days afterwards The Children of God stood about in disbelief, stunned by the mortality of one of their number. It took a great deal of persuasion to bring them back to complete subjection. Mary Ann called a meeting in the chapel and preached forcefully, calling on her lambs not to be weak in a time of testing.

'Sister Mary has been taken from us because she didn't have sufficient faith,' she said. She had spent hours praying in solitude, and when she finally got up off her knees it seemed as if God was a fire inside her. 'I tell you, brothers and sisters, God's mercy is the greatest thing in Heaven or on earth, but if you are less than inspired by your faith then you will not be immortal. Sister Mary wouldn't have died if she'd lived as I do. I shall never die, and neither will you if you follow my example.'

The doubters were quelled and there was a period of renewed devotion, but by the end of another winter six more of the Shakers had been given final resting places beneath macracarpa trees in the churchyard, having fallen victim to consumption.

Smaller trials were an irritation to Mother Girling. She was hounded by critics, particularly in the church, and attempts were made to slander her. She was publicly accused of fraud and deceit, cruelty and licentiousness, immorality, indecency and hypocrisy, but she denied everything in long letters to the press. She knew God had given her the Holy Spirit to make utterances which could change the world, so why would the world not listen? The stigmata on her hands and feet were proof that she was chosen. Sometimes she walked about without shoes, and anyone expressing doubts would be shown the marks of the crucifixion. She tried to instil in her followers the wonder of living like Christ and labouring for each other, and she earnestly prayed for new souls to join them. None did.

Another spring had come and gone since Ben had written to Hannah and her reply had been sent. A year in which nothing was heard of the Rutherfords. So it was a complete surprise when Emily came visiting one day in early summer. Hannah was nursing a sick child and didn't see her arrive with her two fat little daughters. It was Beth who brought the news.

'Sister Hannah, your sister Emily's here. Announced herself as Mrs Rutherford and right posh she looks.' Beth had never been partial to Emily, so her tone was cynical.

Hannah was silent a moment. She'd known the day would come when she must face Emily but she had hoped for plenty of warning. Her heart thudded and she felt giddy as she stood up.

'Stay with Dick, will you please, Beth.' She rarely attached the prefix of 'sister' to anyone's name. Since discovering Emily's treachery she would have preferred not to use the term for her, either. 'The fever's at its height and I've been trying to keep him cool.'

She smoothed her skirt and patted her hair, not that it made any difference to the way she looked. Far better to keep her shoulders back and head high so that Emily could see straight away that she was not doing anyone a favour by calling.

It was not until some time after her return to the Shakers in London that Hannah had learnt the full extent of Emily's deceit. She didn't know which was the greater shock, learning that such deviousness lay beneath the beguiling mask her sister used to win approval, or that Ben had fallen for it so easily. She had betrayed her family with her lies. Well, now there was going to be a confrontation: things had to be said.

Hannah crossed the women's quarters where she knew Ma would be doing the weekly mending. She took a deep breath with each step, drawing the strength to look at Emily for the first time since she had become Ben's wife. There must also be a smile for the two children she had borne him. Primitive instinct urged her to approach with extended claws and scratch her sister with the ferocity of an enraged cat, but she recognised it as the product of jealousy and had to rise above it.

It was mid-afternoon and most of the women were gardening or making preserves, so Ma was working alone. Two plump children were standing behind her sniggering at the strange grandmother they had come to see, and Emily was seated on the edge of a chair as if afraid her clothes would be soiled if she made herself more comfortable. She was dressed in a flounced crinoline gown of peacock-blue satin. It might have been fashionable but it did nothing to flatter the wearer. Emily Rutherford was thinner than her Shaker relatives, and the colour drained her face of all liveliness, leaving dark shadows exposed beneath her eyes and under her cheekbones.

She got up and held out her hands to Hannah. 'I had to come,' she said. 'I was telling Ma how much I miss you.'

Hannah didn't respond to the overture. She kept her fingers laced together. 'Had to come?' she queried. 'You must be needing something from us. Or is it to flaunt your new wealth?'

'Enough, Hannah,' said Ma. But the reprimand was gentle. 'We must be glad that the Lord has prompted her to visit.'

'Why should we? She lied and schemed to leave us.'

'That's not fair,' cried Emily. The raised tone brought her children to her side and they accused Hannah wordlessly with their round grey eyes. 'I came to find out if there's anything I can do for you. Is this the only welcome I get?'

'You don't deserve anything better.'

Ma leaned forward. 'We're pleased to see you, Emily. And the girls. You don't know how I've longed to see my granddaughters.'

'We're *not* pleased to see you,' said Hannah. 'You lied to Ma, pretending you were going to look for me in London. How brave everyone thought you! And all the time you were going to Ben. You didn't tell *him* that I was wandering alone in London, did you? He didn't know until the day he came to get me out of prison, and by then you'd already got him to marry you.'

'How could I have gone to Ben? I didn't know where he was any more than you did.'

'Liar, Emily! You must think we're idiots if you expect us to believe that.'

'How could I have known?' Emily wailed. She stood up unsteadily. 'I shouldn't have come here.'

'Go easy, Hannah,' urged Ma. 'There ain't no sense raking over old grievances.'

But Hannah had been storing them up for a long time. 'I shall tell my sister just what I think of her,' she said, giving Emily a slight push so that she was back in the chair. It gave her the greatest satisfaction to be making her feelings known. 'You spoke to Ben at the Meeting Hall in Walworth. Don't deny it because there were witnesses. Harry Bourne saw you with him, yet you made out you didn't even know Ben was still in this country when I told you he had called on me. You knew exactly where to go when you left the Shakers, didn't you, Emily?'

'I didn't . . .'

'You didn't tell Ben about Aram – why? You made out I married

327

Jonathan because I loved him, and that's lying because you know how I was forced into it.'

'It made no difference,' shouted Emily. 'You were married and that was that. I've loved Ben all my life and what he didn't know didn't hurt anyone, especially him. Now I'll thank you not to say any more in front of my children.'

Raising her voice made her cough. The spasm was quite severe and Selena opened her mother's reticule to find her a handkerchief.

Ma got up and went to her. 'How long have you had that cough?' she asked anxiously. Clearly her maternal love was too strong for continued blame. 'Dear child, have you any medicine for it?'

'I keep getting colds,' Emily said. 'Ben wants me to see a doctor but it's summer now and I'm feeling much better.'

'Ben's good to you, then.'

'I don't see much of him. He's always at the ropeyard.' Emily leaned against her mother and her thin shoulders shook as she suddenly gave way to weeping. 'I know I behaved badly. I came to see if we could make a new start and see each other sometimes. I need you.'

Hannah stood by while Ma did the comforting. She had expressed her anger and now it had died down, leaving her strangely sorry for Emily. It sounded as if Ben wasn't the wonderful husband she had hoped for and it served her right if she wasn't truly happy with him.

'We've never stopped loving you and praying for you, sweet mawther,' Ma was saying. 'And we've missed you too. I'm so glad you've come. Reckon Hannah feels the same, don't you, girl.'

Hannah made no move towards reconciliation.

'I'm sorry if what I did upset you, Hannah,' said Emily, wiping her eyes delicately. 'But you've got to admit it made no difference to *your* life. I always knew how you felt about Ben, but you were married to Jonathan so you couldn't have had him anyway. I don't know what all the fuss has been about.'

It was difficult to argue any further, but a choked feeling in Hannah's throat made it hard to speak.

'Please be reasonable, Hannah. I'm sure you'd rather I had him than some trollope he might have picked up,' Emily went on. 'Please let's be friends again.'

Ma did the answering for her. 'We're Christians. Loving and forgiving is what life's all about so of course your sister wants us to be close again.' She drew her chair nearer to Emily's and patted her hand. 'There's so much news to catch up on.'

Another bout of coughing caused a temporary diversion and left Emily weakly dabbing at her eyes and nose. When it stopped Hannah wiped her own eyes. She said nothing, but went to her sister and put her arms round her, hugging the thin body in its shiny peacock-blue covering. Then she turned to the children.

'Come Selena, Patience. I'll take you out to meet your Cousin Aram and see the animals while your ma and your grandmother have a good gossip.'

Mother Girling suffered her next serious blow in August 1878, when the lease on the field in Vaggs Lane ran out. Quite unfairly she was asked to pay three pounds fifteen shillings rent before it was due. When she couldn't find the money she was advised to take her case to court, but it was against her principles. The only law she acknowledged was the one Jesus had taught, and she refused to be drawn into legal argument. The result of failing to speak in her own defence was a second eviction.

On Tuesday 20 August, the Shakers were once again turned out, and though it was not such harsh weather it was still an ordeal which caused almost as much hardship. Once more there was an encampment in Vaggs Lane. Everything they owned lined both sides of the narrow road for a hundred yards or more and shelters were again built with bedsteads and couches. Furniture was piled on top to support crude attempts at roofing with blankets. It was a wet month and rain soaked through everything.

That week Mary Ann received a summons to appear in court for causing obstruction of the highway. Rain soaked the cushions on which she knelt to pray unceasingly.

'Surely it's time for my children to be brought out of the wilderness,' she beseeched. 'I pray unto You, deliver them from this new tragedy, Lord.'

But the Lord was silent. And her children grumbled.

She prayed for herself, too, because she was guilty of complaining in her heart about God's treatment. She didn't know why He had called her to lead people into hardship and failed to give her hope.

She found herself looking back at her life with George Girling. He had been a good husband, but he hadn't understood her, nor the

329

reason why she'd had to leave him. She thought of the two living children of her body and wondered what her life would have been if she had dedicated herself to them instead of to God. She'd been born again through visions, with no choice other than to do God's will, but likely George was doing well now and she could have had a comfortable home in Ipswich. The thought disturbed her.

Ashamed of her weakness, Mary Ann prayed with renewed passion.

'I pray, dear Father, if You won't deliver us from all these trials grant me the words to help the disciples You have given me. Help me to protect them and provide for them.' She began with humility, assuring the Lord that she was dependent upon Him for all things and accepted His decisions. But bitter reproaches against the men who had deliberately planned the eviction began to colour her prayers. 'Reprobates! The Devil's at work in them. How can they see us turned out in the road and not feel shame!'

The next time all were gathered together she was prompted to tell them about Moses and the bronze snake.

'Remember, brothers and sisters, how God delivered The Children of Israel from the plague of snakes He'd sent to punish them for their sins. They'd grumbled because things weren't going right and God said they had to die. But He told them how they could be saved. He got Moses to make a bronze snake and hang it high on a pole outside the camp and He promised that those who'd been bitten wouldn't die if they looked up at it. Later it was His Son, our Lord Jesus, God hung on a pole outside Jerusalem so that all who looked up at Him could be saved.' Amidst the debris of what had so recently been their home she was inspired to give them the will to carry on. She spread her arms wide. 'We're all sinners and we've no right to expect God to spirit all these things back into the field and off the road. He doesn't work like that. We must repent. Repent, brothers and sisters. Repent!' Her voice rose so that the plea carried to ears beyond the perimeter of their meagre possessions and reached staring sightseers on the fringe. 'Look up at the cross, my dears, and be saved from death. Trust the Lord to look after you. Remember the greatest sacrifice God made because He loved us. He gave His Son. Remember and stop complaining. *We will be saved.*'

On Saturday she felt moved by the Holy Spirit to attend the court session. The pony-cart was made ready in which Jonathan Whitfield was to drive her into Lymington, and everyone clustered round to wish her well.

'Our prayers go with you, good Mother dear,' said Sister Lilianne. Lilianne was one of her most devoted followers, dependable and unchanging, an inspired witness on whom Mary Ann could rely when times were hard and others were faltering. They kissed each other.

'Bless you. Don't worry, the Lord never fails me.'

Brother Jonathan held the pony-cart steady while she got in and they drove off to the singing of a hymn she had written herself after the first eviction. They had been safely delivered on that occasion.

Mother was smartly dressed for the occasion in her black merino dress with a white frilled collar, a coloured scarf kept in place with a brooch and a tippet of ostrich feathers. Long curls hung down her back and on her head she wore a black straw hat trimmed with blue velvet. Her skin was as brown as a gypsy's from living out of doors. When she entered the courtroom she overheard a remark that she looked like the wife of a travelling showman, but she ignored it and walked to the table with her head held high. A chair was brought for her.

'Mrs Girling, you are here before the Bench to answer a complaint of obstruction under the Highways Act,' said the superintendent. 'Your goods are, I understand, lining the road in Vaggs Lane. Do you admit to the charge?'

Mary Ann's sharp features and pale blue eyes were disconcerting. She knew she could unnerve the man just by staring at him.

'I don't deny it. But you may be sure they are not there through any wish of mine. A great injustice has been done to my people and I am waiting for those who have done wrong to do right, if they will. If they don't it is highly likely the wrongdoers will suffer Divine punishment.'

'Do you understand, madam, that under the Vagrants Act no one in this country is allowed to lie about under hedges when there is a parish to go to?'

'I can't move my things until another place is found for me to put them.'

'Is it not true you have been offered a perfectly good refuge near to Southampton?'

'It came from a publican. I would rather die by the roadside than take chaste, respectable women to such a place.'

'You are without food, I believe.'

'We have supplies of bread, potatoes and beans which must last until we're given new ground to cultivate. The Lord always provides.'

The chairman, a thin, angular gentleman seated across the table next to the superintendent, had the courage to challenge her gaze. 'Why is it, madam, that you expect the Lord to give you everything when your menfolk stand around idle instead of taking available work on the farms around?'

'We're waiting for the millennium. It will come in our lifetime and we're preparing ourselves in prayer and perfect love to receive God in all His glory. Until then we work for each other and support each other in every way.'

She spoke with such conviction no one dared to query her faith. Worldly affairs, however, were another matter.

'But you won't enter into legal agreement.'

'No. We live according to the law of God and harm no one.'

'So you shouldn't expect consideration from a law you don't recognize.'

'All we ask is to be treated fairly and to rent another piece of land where we can be left in peace to serve God in our own way.'

There was consultation between the men of the Bench and it was decided that as Mary Ann Girling had been given such short notice to appear before them she should have a week's grace. Then, to her surprise and relief, the hearing was adjourned until the following Saturday.

'Though we hope it won't be necessary for you to come,' said the chairman, whose own daughter had been dangerously close to being converted by the woman's winning ways. Listening to her today had made him partially understand. There was something very seductive about her voice, and those eyes caused his thinking to be impaired. 'May your faith be rewarded, Mrs Girling.'

'Thank you. It always is, sir.'

On the way out Mary Ann was given several modest contributions from sympathizers which she accepted graciously.

'You don't give it to me, you give it to the Lord,' she said, dropping the money into her reticule. 'We do the Lord's work and that's where our comfort lies.' She left the court and climbed into the pony-cart, feeling strong and refreshed. 'It's going to be all right, brother,' she said to Jonathan. 'I'm certain of it. I felt the Holy Spirit settle on me while I was in there.'

'Praise be,' said Jonathan.

When they arrived back at Hordle it was to find that The Children of God had been offered the lease of two acres of land in Tiptoe, a hamlet only a quarter of a mile away from Vaggs Lane which still came under the parish of Hordle.

That night Mother Girling held a service of thanksgiving. 'Let there be joy!' she cried. 'Oh, glorious Lord, how great is Your mercy. We praise You forever.'

Not so many people were gathered as before the eviction, some having left ill and disillusioned after the soaking of themselves and their belongings, but those who continued in faith sang and gyrated once more to the music of Harry Bourne's squeezebox.

Emily had been twice to visit her mother, but Ben didn't go to the Shaker colony at all.

The letter from Hannah had made him so angry he had washed his hands of her. It had been a cold, clear signal that she didn't want his help and he chose not to be rebuffed again. All the same, there were days when he considered the success he was making of his business at West Borley and thought how much more rewarding it would have been if he'd had a son to inherit. Sometimes he deliberately tortured himself by picturing Aram Whitfield, who was now seven, and remembering how it had felt to hold him that day when Jonathan had made his preposterous threat. The threat didn't keep him away – it had been the ranting of a man deranged, a lunatic to whom Hannah remained loyal, in spite of entreaties to leave him. He couldn't understand her; he had given up trying. If he was ever tempted to go again to Hordle it would be to watch for the boy from a distance, but he refrained from making the short journey.

He heard about the second eviction of the Shakers via the newspaper which reported Mother Girling's appearance in court, and it was Emily who made him go.

'I know my mother can't be right in the head for wanting to be one of those weird people, but I'm really worried about her,' she said. 'Will you take me on Sunday? I can leave the children with Reverend Lawrence's wife for the day.'

He was reluctant to agree, but Emily had been very good about working with him since he had taken over the ropeyard and he owed her the favour of falling in with her wishes. So it was settled, then

Emily went down with one of her chesty colds and it was evident she was not fit to do anything except stay in bed.

'You must go without me, Ben,' she wheezed. She knew nothing of the exchange of letters between himself and Hannah after his visit three years ago. 'If only you could get Ma to come here. She'd aged so much last time I saw her and it really frightened me. Besides, it would be such a help if she was here to look after the children. I could do more for you then. You must make her understand how much we need her.'

That was the crux of the matter. Emily wanted help in the house and saw the advantage of using her mother as cheap labour. Ben smiled at her deviousness.

'All right, I'll go over there, but I don't reckon she'll be coming back with me, Mother Girling'll see to that. And what am I to say to Hannah?'

'Give her my love.'

So Ben went alone.

He wished Luke had been around to go with him. He'd suggested taking his adoptive brother into the business when he'd first bought out George Crummock, but Luke had no experience of working with hemp and no aptitude for learning. After a few months Luke declared that he had stayed in one place too long and was suffering from wanderlust. The call of the sea was strong. One morning he came downstairs with a canvas bag over his shoulder and left the house to go to Southampton. He was taken on by a captain sailing for Russia with a cargo of wool, and he would then be going on to China. Since then there'd been a couple of letters and it was plain Luke was happy to be back at sea.

Ben approached Hordle with his spirits as low as they could be, and was directed a quarter of a mile further on to a hamlet with the delightful name of Tiptoe. He had no trouble finding the place. All he had to do was follow a procession of vehicles trundling the same way. There were donkey carts, large brakes drawn by three or four horses, and conveyances from as far away as Bournemouth, Southampton and Salisbury. He was told the Shakers unwittingly provided regular entertainment on Sundays and the turn-out was nothing unusual. It was an extraordinary sight.

He was better prepared this time for the chaotic scene which met his eyes when he got there. The roughly made tents in the two-acre field had been drenched in the night, and their coverings of old clothes and blankets were now steaming in the August sun. It made Ben angry and he was impatient to have done with the unpleasant duty imposed upon him by his wife. He threaded his way through the carts and edged people aside, arrogant on the chestnut horse he had bought only six months since.

A meeting was in progress in the ramshackle wooden building which served as a chapel. In Ben's opinion it could have been put to better use as accommodation for the children and the elderly, but the Shakers had different priorities. He stayed at the edge of the crowd pressing to see what was going on, and was struck by the contrast between this place and the hall under the railway arches at Walworth. The further poverty of Mother Girling's people was reflected in their gaunt faces and thin bodies, yet they didn't look as if they were too undernourished. They still had plenty of energy.

The Girling woman stood on a platform at the rear of the building and she was dressed in white with a crown of flowers round her forehead. Her eyes, for once, were closed and she was reciting a psalm in a loud yet melodious voice which was compelling in its quality.

'Let them praise His name in the dance; let them sing praises unto Him with the timbrel and the harp. For the Lord taketh pleasure in His people.'

Dance she said, and dance they did. Ben was sickened by the sight of the ungraceful movements being performed in a space left for the purpose in the centre of the chapel. There was nothing indecent or impure, no hint of eroticism or seduction, yet the shaking of these people somehow seemed vulgar. One man, an uncouth labourer by the look of him, was stamping his feet so hard on the rotting timber floor it was a wonder it didn't collapse, and he extended his arms and whirled like a scarecrow in the wind. Quite by accident he struck a young girl a blow to the face with the back of his hand and she fell, but the music continued and nobody stopped dancing. The girl jumped up quickly and carried on, but Ben reckoned she would soon be sporting a black eye.

And there was Ma Jerram. He hadn't recognised her at first. Her hair had lost its bright colour, and on it she wore a round straw wide-awake hat. White bloomer trousers were partially covered with a petticoat-type garment reaching to just below her knees, and

335

as she took part in the bizarre, ritualistic swaying it was plain to see she was supple still. Her eyes, too, were closed, so she saw nothing.

Ben looked around, fearful of discovering Hannah similarly conditioned, but she wasn't among the dancers. She was standing to one side with another girl, and by keeping well back he was able to watch her unobserved, pressing his hand to his heart when it jerked fiercely. She was a woman now with no trace left of the carefree girl she had once been, and he remembered she would be twenty-four. Like all the women she was dressed in white. Virginal white. He didn't know how any man could be married to her and resist the temptation to take her to his bed, but that was the way these celibate beings lived, by all accounts. The men must be stronger than they looked; strong-minded to say the least.

Heat coursed through Ben as he took his first look at Hannah in seven years, and he hadn't bargained for this reaction. She was thin like the rest, and her eyes with the golden flecks were sad. Her full mouth was gentle in repose but it looked as if she had given up smiling. Hannah in her white dress with her golden hair cascading over her shoulders was like a forlorn angel. She was watching the proceedings, but he could tell her mind was elsewhere and he longed to know what thoughts were going on behind that clear brow. She was definitely not moved to ecstasy like some, but neither did she appear to be immune to the music. Her shoulders moved slightly in time to it.

There was no sign of Jonathan Whitfield or Aram, and Ben was glad. The man was anathema to him. The boy was an enigma. Having seen Hannah he didn't want to give time to anyone else and he forgot that it was Ma Jerram he had promised Emily he would seek out.

He moved round behind a group of women in homespun skirts and crocheted shawls until he could see that Aram was the other side of Hannah, pressed against her hip. The boy looked bored. He yawned. His hair was bleached by the sun to the colour of sand, and it had been trimmed to a thick wedge which touched the frayed collar of his shirt. Where the peak was on his forehead it fell forward in a tuft. His chin jutted slightly, and when he put his hand to his mouth to stifle another yawn Ben saw that he had long, capable fingers with broad nails. He gave a quick glance at his own and thought he saw a similarity.

336

Another few crab-like side steps between the people and he was close enough to touch Hannah. Her right hand was by her side, her fingers tapping out the rhythm of the hymn, and she was quite unaware of his presence until he clasped that hand firmly. She gasped. Her head shot round to see who had perpetrated the outrage. Her mouth fell open.

'Sssh,' he murmured.

She tried to loosen his grip but he couldn't let go. It was as if a cord was binding them which he couldn't, and wouldn't, break. The feel of her hand heightened all his senses. He was aware of the clean smell of her hair amidst the sweaty, unwashed bodies all around; the sound of his heart beating so loud it drowned the whining squeezebox; the taste of the dust in his mouth; the beloved sight of her; and to touch her was unimagined bliss. He felt like a man who had thirsted for years and was being given his fill of pure spring water to drink.

'What're you doing here?' she hissed.

He held her eyes captive. His mouth curved into a warm smile which lifted his lips higher one side than the other, and he wanted to fold her roughly in his arms. Instead he caught her chin with his free hand and held her face steady while he kissed her.

It was an outrageous thing to do. He couldn't have chosen a more public place to show her that she was as desirable as she had ever been, and he'd gained an unfair advantage in taking her by surprise. She moved her head, trying to escape, but he increased the pressure on her mouth and she shivered before relaxing into submission. He held her so close she could hear the beat of his heart, and her arms crept up round his neck as she kissed him back.

The music stopped. Dancing ceased and there was a horrified silence. The circle of dancers opened out further to reveal the couple in a close embrace, oblivious to everything around them, and a gasp was audible. Someone among the crowd of Sunday sightseers began to clap, and others immediately joined in. There were calls of 'Good luck t'yer!' a selection of cheers and jeers, and then good-natured laughter, until Mother Girling raised her voice to be heard above the commotion.

'Who is responsible for bringing the Devil into our midst?' cried the Shaker woman. Her eyes were flashing. 'Sister Hannah, leave this hall. You're bringing disgrace on us.'

Aram was pummelling Ben with balled fists. 'Leave my ma alone. Leave her alone!'

Hannah struggled to be free, but though Ben released her mouth he wouldn't loosen his hold of her.

'Bring the boy and come away with me, Hannah,' he urged, his lips close to her ear. 'He's mine, I know he is.'

'No!'

'Now, Hannah. Come with me now,' he begged. 'You've been here too long.'

Mother Girling was urging her own people not to bring down the wrath of God. Ben jumped on to the platform beside her.

'How can you be so simple as to believe this woman?' he cried in strident tones meant to be heard. 'She misleads you when she quotes from the Bible. She reads into it what she wants you to believe.'

'Close your ears to this blasphemer!' shouted the woman. 'He's been sent by the Devil to provoke us.'

Ben was undaunted. 'Have none of you read what Paul wrote to Timothy? Oh yes, I can quote the Bible too. St Paul said some shall depart from the faith and speak falsehoods. They'll forbid marriage, yet everything God created is good and not to be rejected. What state would the world be in if we accepted all Mrs Girling's nonsense as gospel teaching?'

'You, sir, are the one seeking to lead these good people astray, but my lambs know who is their shepherd. The world will never be in a better state until I am accepted as the one in whom God has placed His love. While I am refused, Christ is refused, because we are one. I won't be crucified, but I *shall* be glorified.'

'And where in the Old Testament do the prophets tell of your coming, like they told of Jesus? Nowhere, madam. Nowhere!'

Having made his point Ben dropped down again to join the crowd. A fight broke out. Those who had come for an evening's entertainment got more than they had bargained for, and within minutes the place was in an uproar. Fists were flying, and the normally passive Shakers were forced to defend themselves against the bullying of outsiders who had been given the chance to express their ridicule physically as well as verbally. Others supported the Shakers. The brawl spread to those who hadn't found room to get inside the shed and there had never been such a scene in Vaggs Lane.

338

At the centre of the trouble Ben tried to drag an astounded Hannah away, while Aram flailed them both and tears streamed down his young cheeks. The adrenalin flowed through Ben and he hadn't felt so exhilarated since he had helped to rescue Aram from the house in Seven Dials.

'I've a horse out in the lane.' His thumb and second finger met round her thin arm.

'You're hurting me.'

'Not half as much as you've hurt me. I want my son.'

He saw that the boy was going to be the only way he would get her to go with him, so he picked Aram up and swung him on to his shoulders. He was a heavy youngster and he didn't take kindly to being manhandled. He kicked and struggled, his feet pounding Ben's chest, but he was held tightly to stop him falling backwards into the crowd. Clouds of dust were obscuring everything, and Ben pulled Hannah behind him as he made for the square of light which had to be the door.

'Why are you doing this?' Hannah cried.

'Because I love you.' Oh, Lord, how he loved her. But there could have been no worse place to tell her so.

A path was made for them and seconds later they were out in the air with Aram riding high on Ben's shoulders and Hannah behind him. She was no longer pulling back. He could feel that she was going forward of her own volition, and his heart sang. She would soon be free.

They had just reached the gate and were within sight of the tethered chestnut stallion when a shot rang out. It scattered the crowd, terrified the horse and set up a movement of horse-drawn vehicles. Ben fell to the ground, trapping Aram by the legs beneath him, and Hannah sprawled across his body.

Jonathan Whitfield stood some way behind them with a smoking rifle in his hands.

Chapter Thirty-Three

The crowd dissolved. Hannah looked at Ben's chestnut horse and almost expected it to have the wings of Pegasus.

'It's all right, Aram,' she heard herself telling her son. 'Everything's going to be all right.'

And then Ben was shot.

'Dear God, what's happened?' Hannah scrambled frantically to Ben's side as soon as she realised he was hurt. 'Ben!' She pressed her hand hard against a wound in his shoulder to stop the blood pumping out. 'Oh Ben, don't die, for God's sake. Ben, I love you. Help him, someone!'

Reason told her that he hadn't been fatally hit. She looked round with wild eyes for the source of the outrage but people had closed in behind her, and in the midst of her fear for Ben she faced the awful thought that if the shot had been a fraction higher it would have struck Aram instead. Her son had pulled himself free and was bravely nursing a cut lip and bruised legs without giving way to babyish crying. Someone drew him back from the scene.

'Who did it?' she cried in anguish.

No one answered.

A local woman knelt down beside her with a strip of cloth she had torn from her petticoat, and she drew back Ben's jacket so that she could staunch the blood-flow better. A man took off his coat and made a pillow of it, and Hannah lifted Ben's head very gently to slip it underneath. As she did so he opened his eyes and gave a wry smile. She uttered a sob of relief.

'Can't say he didn't warn me,' he said.

'What're you talking about?' Relief was mixed with bewilderment.

'That husband of yours. Warned me he'd use a gun.' He moved and tried to get up. 'The bastard's dangerous.'

Hannah felt sick with shock. Jonathan had used a gun once before, and even now she couldn't bear to remember the terrible consequences.

'Help me up,' Ben demanded.

'You mustn't stand.'

'Help me up, I said, and take me to Jonathan Whitfield.'

Hannah was close to tears. 'You've got to see a doctor. Likely there's a bullet in your shoulder that's got to come out.'

'Likely there would have been, but it's only cut through the top. I'll have it seen to by my own physician.'

Ben took the blood-soaked cloth from the woman who still held it to his left shoulder and held it there himself while he got to his feet. He was standing unsteadily, supported by a neighbouring farmer, when Mother Girling appeared. She was a ludicrous figure in her white bloomers with the flowers still in her hair, but there was nothing funny about her expression. Her eyes blazed, and her hands were clasped together so tightly the knuckles gleamed like white bony knobs.

'Get this infidel off my land!' she commanded. 'He tried to turn our sacred chapel into a den of iniquity.'

Ben shook off the arm of the farmer and stood tall. 'Madam, this is your chance to work a miracle and prove you're who you say you are. I've not heard of you curing anyone or raising anyone from the dead. Heal me.'

'This is an age of evil and my powers can't be proved to unbelievers, but my hour will come,' said Mother Girling, her dignity restored. 'Now take yourself off before I have to give orders for you to be forcibly removed.'

'Be sure I'll be gone as soon as I've had words with the bastard who shot me.' Ben still held the cloth to his shoulder as he turned and searched the field for sign of his quarry. 'Jonathan Whitfield, you madman, come out and face me,' he yelled.

There was a hush following the challenge, as if the crowd held its breath. And then the blacksmith appeared, his hands empty and his deep-set eyes as dark as pitch beneath his brows. There were calls for him to be arrested, but no one attempted to lay hold of him. In his wake came Lilianne like a shadow.

'I ain't sorry,' Jonathan said. 'A man has a right to protect his wife. You sullied her in front of a congregation.'

'You're not fit to lick her boots,' said Ben. 'You force her to suffer poverty instead of working to make a home for her like any self-respecting man would do.'

'I give her my devotion and I work in all honesty for the salvation of her soul.'

'And neglect her earthly needs. What kind of devotion is that?'

Lilianne came forward. 'You deserved what you got, Ben Rutherford. I ain't never been so ashamed. To think I brought you up and treated you like one of me own, and this is the way you repay me. How could you speak to Mother like that?'

'Ma Jerram, how can I respect anyone dressed in bloomers,' said Ben. There was a general burst of unkind laughter but none of the principal assailants treated the remark as a joke. 'You may be taken in by this false prophet, but I'd swear your daughter isn't. If you love her, make her leave with me.'

'It's the last thing I'd do.'

'Stop it,' cried Hannah. 'I ain't an object to be fought over.'

The farmer who had helped Ben up stayed by his side. 'Press charges,' he urged. 'There are plenty of witnesses to testify you did nothing to justify being shot in the back.'

'No, I'll not bring in the law.' Ben raised his voice and addressed the Shakers. 'Do you call yourselves Christians? I've seen no sign of it. But I'll set an example by forgiving what's been done to me.' He turned to Jonathan Whitfield. 'Do you hear that, bor, I'm doing the Christian thing and forgiving you. In return I'm begging you to do right by Hannah and the boy. Take them away from here.'

'You should be asking the Lord to forgive your own sins first,' said Mother Girling. She lifted her hands high and in a loud voice appealed to everyone to move back. 'This ain't a side-show and I'll thank you all to go home and leave us in peace.'

Immediately, there was shouting about the right and wrong of the matter, and under cover of the confusion Ben left, but not before he had made one more appeal to Hannah.

'Come with me,' he implored her. 'I heard you say you love me.'

'I can't go to my sister's house with you married to her. Besides, I married Jonathan for better or worse.' The pain he was in showed in his face and he had an unnatural pallor. 'Oh Ben, get on home, and for goodness sake take care.' She tore the bottom off her skirt to replace the rag which was now too soaked to be of use. 'Here, take this. And see a doctor straight away about that wound so poison doesn't set in.'

'I can't leave you here.'

'And I can't come with you. Go!'

'Then make that husband of yours see sense. Tell him he might get a job working for Andrew Peterson.'

Ben shrugged his coat more comfortably over his wounded shoulder and strode away towards the chestnut horse. Hannah watched him climb into the saddle and take the reins in his right hand, but her eyes were too blurred with tears to watch him ride away.

There was no need for Hannah to speak to Jonathan about leaving. The initiative was taken out of her hands by Mother Girling the next morning. But before the dawn of a new day there were still traumas to be faced in the old one. Jonathan took himself off before Ben had got to the end of the lane, giving no one a chance to say or do anything. Mother Girling sought refuge in private prayer, and Lilianne followed Hannah to the pump across the field where they couldn't be overheard. There she reproached her daughter unmercifully, and quite unfairly.

'Don't you think Mother has enough worries without you adding to them?' Lilianne demanded. 'Have you no words of repentance for what happened?'

'No, Ma.'

'Ben Rutherford tried to undermine our faith in our dear Mother. And he showed the world he coveted you. You were no better, kissing him back and him being married to your sister.'

Hannah had to suppress the surge of anger which threatened her control. 'Which is worse, showing love or attempting to murder?' she asked. 'Have *you* no words of blame for my husband? No, you wouldn't have, would you. You've always coveted *him* and he can do nothing wrong.'

'That's a slanderous thing to say!'

'Look me in the eyes, Ma, and tell me you've never wished it was you married to Jonathan instead of me. No, I knew you couldn't do it. Well, precious good it would have done you in this place if you *had* been married to him. I don't even know what it's like to be a proper wife.'

'He loves you – and that's why your sin is greater than his,' Lilianne declared. 'Any man seeing his wife kissing another the way you did has every right to protest. Jonathan didn't mean to hit Ben, only to scare him.'

343

'He didn't mean to hit Shem either, but by what happened afterwards he might as well have done.' Hannah's temples throbbed. 'It's written "Thou shalt not kill", and that means it's just as wicked to think it.'

' "Thou shalt not steal",' quoted Lilianne. 'Haven't you tried to steal your sister's husband? "Thou shalt not commit adultery". How many of God's commandments have been broken?'

'I certainly haven't committed adultery,' said Hannah. 'Have you?'

The older woman's face flamed, but whether with temper or guilt it was impossible to judge and Hannah decided enough had been said. She took up a bucket of water and walked away before either of them could do any more verbal damage.

She spent a sleepless night beside Ma in the women's tent; Lilianne repelled her, as if she emitted some alien energy, and Hannah couldn't bear to touch against her.

The encounter with Ben was almost unbelievable. If it hadn't been for the bruise on her lip from the pressure of his mouth she could have convinced herself it had been a dream. All night she lay awake, and not a single detail of his visit escaped her scrutiny, from the moment his hand had touched hers until he rode off on the chestnut stallion, and every word he had spoken was indelible. To Hannah the most important thing he had said was that he loved her still. But what good did it do to know? They could never be together, and his coming today had caused so much trouble it would have been better if he had stayed away.

She loved him too. In reverie she stroked the back of her hand against her lips and opened them sensually as if she were teasing his mouth, but the fantasy produced an ache in her belly and in her chest, so great was her longing, and she had to bite on her index finger to stop herself crying out. She was afraid for him, and prayed he had gone straight to a physician when he got home. And then she wondered what he had said to Emily. She doubted her sister would hear the truth of how he had got a bullet wound in his shoulder, and guessed his ingenuity had been sorely tested to provide an explanation that would satisfy her. The ache grew worse as she tortured herself with thoughts of Emily's good fortune, and her only consolation was the knowledge that Emily had everything of Ben – except his love.

First thing in the morning Aram came to Hannah and said his father hadn't returned. Her immediate reaction was to rejoice – she didn't care what had become of him after what he'd done to Ben. However, deep down she feared for his safety, knowing he had a tendency of late to believe he was being guided by visions, and the first thing she did was to make sure he didn't have the gun with him.

'No, sister,' said Harry Bourne. 'That old rabbit gun still sits where I put it after 'e gave it to me.'

Brother Harry acted as if he felt awkward talking to her, and she found herself being peered at by other Shakers, as if they had been told not to associate with her.

Before breakfast she was summoned to the chapel where Mother Girling was waiting to speak to her alone. There was a wind blowing and the ramshackle timbers creaked.

'Hannah Whitfield, I can no longer call you sister,' Mother Girling said. She was wearing her black alpaca dress this morning and looked every inch a matriarch. 'I have prayed over your transgressions and I've been told I must ask you to leave our fold. You have earthly inclinations which cause you to sin and you'll never be able to live the pure and holy life God expects of those who love Him above all else.'

Hannah knew it would be pointless to enter into argument. Besides, the decision filled her with a certain elation.

'And am I to leave on my own? What of my husband?'

She felt the floorboards move. Mother Girling's piercing eyes altered focus to stare beyond her at someone who had come in the door.

'There's no need to answer, Mother,' said Jonathan, ambling forward with a heavy tread. His hair was unkempt, his clothes dirty, and the smell of sweat accompanying him was so pungent it stung the nostrils. 'I'm the one who's not fit to be among The Children of God, so I'm taking my wife and my son away. We'll not embarrass you again.'

'Jonathan!' Hannah laced her fingers tightly together and forced her feet to remain rooted. 'There's no need for you to come with me.'

He glowered at her. 'We'll go together. Likely I'd be better on me own than with an unfaithful wife, but I reckon as how I ain't got much choice.'

345

'No, Brother Jonathan, I don't reckon you have,' said Mother Girling. 'Since you saw fit to take vengeance into your own hands yesterday instead of leaving it to the Lord I reckon there's no place for you here either, though it'll grieve me to see you go.'

'We'll be gone before the day's out,' Jonathan promised.

Hannah's stomach muscles tensed and her hands became clammy. At last he was doing what she had pleaded with him to do for years, and she ought to have been pleased. But after yesterday's violence the prospect of setting out to make a new life with a husband capable of murder was frightening indeed.

Chapter Thirty-Four

On the day that they quit the Shaker settlement there was no precise thought in Jonathan's mind as to where he could take his family. They owned nothing and took nothing with them except the clothes they wore, yet from the first night they had a roof over their heads, thanks to Hannah's insistence that they walk through the lanes to Sway where Andrew Peterson lived.

'He's a good man, Jonathan,' she said. 'Mother has a high regard for him since he's accepted she's no hypnotist, and he gives work to people who need it.'

'I know that, but we're going further. Back to Suffolk maybe.' He strode ahead of them, brusque and unfriendly.

'And how will we get there with no money?'

'Walk. I can find jobs along the way to feed us.'

'That'll take forever.'

'I don't want to walk forever,' cried Aram.

'And nor you shall,' said his mother, taking his hand firmly. 'Not when there's chance of a place to work nearby.'

Jonathan didn't want to fall in with the suggestion, even though he saw the sense of it. He hadn't forgiven Hannah for being the cause of their expulsion from the community and every time he looked at her he saw again the shameful spectacle of her kissing Ben Rutherford. The wretch lived too close. If they were ever to live a normal life it would have to be far away from the danger of another such episode.

He could have left her, of course, but then she would have had every excuse to go to Rutherford, and Jonathan was not prepared to give her such an easy option. Nor could he cope with the thought of any hands touching her except his own. For all these years he had abided by Mother Girling's rules, but now he was free. He turned to wait for his wife and son who were several paces behind. The boy snatched his hand away from Hannah's and ran to him eagerly.

'I thought you didn't want us, Pa.'

Jonathan ruffled his hair. 'Of course I want you,' he said gruffly. He idolized the boy and his welfare was more important than anything else. 'All right, we'll see if Mr Peterson has a temporary job to tide us over till we get enough money to move on.'

'I knew you would.'

Aram's spirits lifted and he tramped along quite happily, his young legs trying to match his father's strides. How lithe he was. He was a child to attract attention with his thick, sun-bleached hair and bronzed skin. Daily he grew more like Hannah, and the pity of it was that he still showed no resemblance to Shem, unless it was in the way his hair fell in a quiff over his forehead. There was nothing about him either to suggest he had any connection with Ben Rutherford, though Jonathan tormented himself with suspicions. Even now, he studied the way the boy walked, praying he would never see a developing air of Rutherford arrogance. There was certainly none in the carefree hopping and skipping required to keep up.

Down a twisting hill and up another. They came at last to the place where a few grey buildings were grouped near a small square tower, and it could be seen that one was a laundry, another a dairy. Behind them was an elegant house which had recently been extended. Jonathan had been this way once when Mother Girling had been invited to visit but there'd not been so much development then.

They must have looked a sorry trio. A fellow wearing sand-covered corduroy trousers, a shirt with the sleeves rolled up and a green neckerchief, stopped to speak to them.

'Ain't I seen you on Sundays with them queer Girlingites?' he asked.

'We've just left there,' Jonathan said. 'We'd like to speak to Mr Peterson.'

'Would there be work for a blacksmith?' Hannah asked. 'My husband's very skilled.'

The man rubbed his stubbly chin. 'Reckon the master'll be interested. He's starting a new scheme shortly and he'll be wanting men as can handle iron, so I'm told. And yer in luck. He's at the house this week. Most of the time he's in London, 'cept for weekends.'

Jonathan put Aram on his shoulders to walk up the drive, and his pace made it necessary for Hannah to take small running steps to keep up with him.

'Oughtn't we to go to the back door?' she asked nervously.

'No. I've had enough of humility.'

Through an open window to the left of the front entrance he saw a large room in which a housemaid was singing as she flicked a duster over the sill. She saw them and smiled, and as soon as Jonathan rang the doorbell her feet could be heard clicking across the hall.

'We'd like to see Mr Peterson,' he said.

'What name shall I say, sir?'

'Jonathan Whitfield, blacksmith.'

'Just a minute, Mr Whitfield.'

The girl was very pretty and very young. She showed them into a small study where they had to wait half an hour or more. The room was sparsely furnished with a plain desk and two chairs, and there was no sign of money having been spent on luxuries, except for some Indian vases. From what Jonathan had heard the man was very generous to the local unemployed and preferred to use his money to pay a good living wage.

When the white-haired man came it was Hannah he looked at, and after an initial frown he brought her to mind.

'Ah, young lady, I remember you,' he said. His manner of speech was abrupt. 'You had the temerity to suggest the mesmerist I brought from the Isle of Wight once was a music-hall turn.'

'Yes, sir. I'm sorry if I offended you.'

'Not at all. If I recall you had a great deal of courage and I admired your faith in Mrs Girling. How is the lady? I hear she's been given tenancy of another field.'

'Yes, sir, but we've just left.'

Jonathan cleared his throat loudly. 'My name's Jonathan Whitfield and I decided it was time my wife and son and I had a life of our own, sir. I'm a blacksmith by trade and I'm looking for work.'

Afternoon sun slanted through a small window in the study and it touched on Andrew Peterson's mane of white hair, turning it to pale gold. He was a stately figure even though the blacksmith topped him by several inches, and when he turned his barrister's eye on this latest candidate for his generosity it felt to Jonathan as if he were back in the Army. Likely no falsehood would pass undetected here.

'Are you a good smith?' he asked.

'The best, sir. My father taught me.' Jonathan looked at the large vases. 'And I was with the cavalry in India.'

'India. We must talk about it some time.' Peterson's smile indicated it had been a wise reference. 'You're in luck, Mr Whitfield. The smith with me now is too old for the work I have in mind.' He went to the window and invited Jonathan to join him. In the distance a horse and cart had drawn up and men were shovelling sand from it, adding to a pile which was as high as the tallest of the labourers. 'Those men are bringing shingle from Milford beach. It's mixed with Portland cement and water to make concrete, and I intend to be using a lot of concrete in a building project I have in mind.'

'Indeed, sir. So why will you be needing a blacksmith?'

'You've seen the tower I've already built, my friend. Now I'm planning to have one erected three times the height across the lane there, and for that I shall need iron supports.'

Jonathan was intrigued. 'What purpose will it serve?'

'I'm interested in testing the strength of concrete as a building material. It's widely used in India, you know. And then I've about forty men working here who'll be out of a job if I don't start a new project. Since my brush with the mesmerist after investigating Mrs Girling I've become a great believer in the power of spiritualism, and that's where I turn for advice. Quite recently, through my medium, I've been given the plans for my tower directly from Sir Christopher Wren.'

'You mean the man who built St Paul's Cathedral?' This was ridiculous.

'I do indeed.'

'But he's been dead about two hundred years,' said Hannah.

'One hundred and fifty-six, to be precise. But his spirit is alive and has given me directions. The soul of a departed man will always communicate with a soul still in the body if it can find the right conditions, and that's what happened between myself and Sir Christopher Wren. His ideas will keep men in work for several years. If you're interested I'll take you on. What do you say?'

'I accept, sir.'

Andrew Peterson went into more details about the proposed tower, explaining the quite unorthodox methods he intended using. It all sounded absurd, but if the man was going to pay good wages it would be foolish not to give it a try. There would be a tied cottage

350

made available as Jonathan was more than a casual labourer, and it seemed there would be work for Hannah in the fields. The thought of making money again gave him confidence, and there in that small study he shed a feeling of inadequacy like an adder sloughing its skin.

'Tell me,' said Mr Peterson, 'are you a supporter of Mr Gladstone?'

'I am indeed,' said Jonathan, who knew very little about politics these days. At that moment he would have become the supporter of a Zulu chief if it was important to the job.

'Good. I'm a keen Radical myself. Always does to have men with the same sympathies around the place. You can start work tomorrow.'

It had all happened so fast, as if the Lord had guided them to this place. If they had been delivered from the influence of one eccentric only to be put in the hands of another, well at least Jonathan and his family were being provided with a few material comforts to make it easier. And they need only stay for a short time.

It was very hot in the blacksmith's shop and Jonathan's shirt was open to the waist in spite of it being only March. Beads of sweat glistened on the grey hair covering his broad chest, and the muscles of his arms had regained their former tautness since he had been daily wielding a hammer. Hannah stood by the doorway watching him for several seconds unobserved before going past on her way to the gate to look for Aram. He was a powerful man, a man one would have expected to be hungry for the intimate side of marriage, yet still, after seven months at Sway, he hadn't made her his wife.

Things were turning out better than she had expected. Her fears were unfounded and she was happier in many ways than she had been since leaving Seggenham. She had begun by making it clear that he wouldn't be welcome in her bed. After what had happened to Ben the very thought of Jonathan touching her had been loathsome and she had dreaded that first night alone with him. But he hadn't made any demands.

'Keep your chastity,' he had scoffed. 'When I want you I'll take you – whether you like it or not.'

He slept in the back bedroom every night with Aram while she occupied the one at the front, and not once had there been a suggestion of change. That was the way she wanted it, and yet it wasn't natural. She couldn't understand why her husband shunned her, unless it was because he was still angry at the way she had behaved that day with Ben, and womanlike she suffered a perverse resentment that he could resist her for so long. He had been jealous enough to fight over her.

She had written to Ben and Emily, telling them their new address and asking carefully after their health. She had to be diplomatic. In due course she received a letter back from Emily saying how pleased they were to hear of the Whitfields' move from Shaker clutches.

'I don't know how you could have endured the life for so long,' Emily had written. And then came censure. 'And I don't know how you could have left Mama there alone. It was cruel of you to leave without her.'

Hannah smiled at the extension to Ma's name. It told her quite clearly that her sister now considered herself to be more upper-class. But the reference to her neglect of their mother was quite uncalled-for. If Emily was so concerned, there was nothing to stop her making an effort to persuade Ma to leave Mother Girling, though no doubt she would be unsuccessful.

She read on: 'My poor Ben met with an accident on his way back from visiting Mama. He was riding by the marshes when he was struck in the shoulder by a stray shot from a poacher's gun. The man ran off, apparently, and Ben was in no fit state to chase after him so the wretch got clean away. Luckily the wound wasn't too deep, though I did have a terrible time worrying it would get infected. It could have been a lot worse. Ben is now fully recovered, but I am not well. My cough is very troublesome.

'My Selena gets prettier every day. She has grey eyes just like Ben's and her hair is dark like his. I'm afraid Patience is beginning to look a bit like you, though she too has Ben's grey eyes. His children certainly take after him in that respect.'

There was another page describing Emily's full social life. It seemed she entertained now that Ben had bought a bigger house away from the ropeyard, and her diary was always full of appointments to visit in return. Sadly her health was restricting her, but she hoped that by the spring she would be fit to resume her engagements.

Hannah had let Jonathan read the letter.

'You're very lucky Ben didn't press charges,' she told him. 'It was generous of him to say the shooting was an accident.'

'Maybe,' Jonathan grunted. 'And maybe he's lucky I didn't mean to kill him for molesting my wife.'

'He showed me affection. That's more than you ever do.'

She was stung into making the reply, but afterwards she regretted it. It sounded as if she was inviting his attention, and for several nights she felt apprehensive at bedtime in case he should act upon it. The reverse happened. Jonathan took to staying out until long after she had retired, and he became even more morose.

Soon after they arrived at Arnewood Towers Hannah began working in the dairy. Mrs Peterson took charge of domestic hiring and was pleased to have someone capable to see to the butter-making. In no time at all Hannah was showing two young girls the methods she'd learnt at Springly's Farm, and she was pleased to be using decent equipment again after the poor utensils which were all Mother Girling had been able to provide.

It wasn't until Christmas that Mrs Peterson discovered Hannah was also capable of teaching children to read and write. Quite by accident she came upon Aram Whitfield with a book in his hands, and to her amazement he was able to read from it quite fluently. He told the lady proudly that his mother had taught him his letters and that he could write as well. From then on the parlour of the Whitfields' cottage had become a schoolroom each weekday morning, and Hannah found herself with ten small pupils eager to learn.

On the March day when she was surreptitiously watching her husband at work the children had just finished their lessons, and she needed some air before going to the dairy. Jonathan was bringing a strip of metal out of the fire and it was red-hot, glowing like something from the depths of Hell, and it illuminated his face. She saw the planes and furrows exaggerated by the light, the heavy brows streaked with grey the same as his beard, and the set of his mouth as he concentrated. Now over fifty he was still a handsome man, and his return to tough manual labour had given him a look of great virility. In the past Hannah had been strangely fascinated, but now she felt only revulsion. He had destroyed any willingness on her part to consummate their marriage when he had nearly killed Ben, the man she loved so desperately. She hated him. There would never be a welcome for him in her bed. She moved away hastily before he saw her.

Work had begun on the new tower at the beginning of that year, 1879. Land had been cleared at the other side of Flexford Lane and the foundations had been laid. With still a little time to spare Hannah needed to take her mind off Jonathan so she wandered across to the site where men were busy erecting a set of frames made of wood over the eighteen-foot square base. There was plenty of dust and noise, shouting and hammering, and two men were pouring washed gravel into a box with long handles on a board platform. Hannah went over to them.

'What're you doing with that?' she asked.

'Measuring a cubic yard of gravel ready to mix with cement and water,' one told her. 'Want to have a go?'

'Not likely. I'll stick to making pastry.' She was used to being teased and she enjoyed it. 'What do you do with it when it's mixed, then?'

'Pour it into the frames and ram it down so it'll set hard.'

The frames were each about eighteen inches high. Hannah looked skywards and wondered how long it was going to take at that rate to build a tower three times higher than the one near the cottages. A lifetime, she reckoned; Jonathan would never be out of a job.

When Hannah got back there was a neat carriage standing in the yard, a woman and two children seated in it and a man holding the horse which was sweating from a fast drive. Her heart gave a lurch. Ben and Emily had come visiting. She ran over to them at once, pushing her tangled hair away from her face and wishing she had taken trouble with it this morning since it was obvious that Emily was fashionably dressed.

'How lovely to see you,' she cried. 'What a wonderful surprise.'

She looked first at Ben, adoring him instantly, and the months since they had met dissolved like sugar grains in hot water. Her face flamed with pleasure.

'We thought it time we checked on you,' Ben said. His black hair was long, touching the collar of his mulberry-coloured jacket at the back. 'Emily wanted to see you.'

His eyes were worried, and Hannah turned to her sister. She was shocked at what she saw. They hadn't met since the day of their terrible confrontation, and now she would hardly have known her. Emily was painfully thin and her skin was like parchment, the high

354

cheekbones so pronounced they made the hollows beneath them appear deeper than they were. She could have been at least ten years older than her twenty-six years. The two little girls beside her were prim and pretty and still decidedly overweight.

'We've been to see Mama first,' said Emily. She pushed aside the rug from her knees and held out her hand for Hannah to help her down. 'I want her to come and live with us but she refuses. I need her, Hannah. What can I do to persuade her to leave that dreadful Shaker woman?'

'Nothing,' said Hannah. 'Ma will be faithful to Mother Girling forever, I can tell you for certain.' The exertion of alighting from the vehicle brought on a fit of coughing and Emily held a handkerchief to her mouth. 'I'll just tell Jonathan and Aram you're here then we'll go to the cottage. It's too chilly to stand around.'

Jonathan grunted when told. 'It ain't me they've come to see.'

But Aram was as excited as a puppy. He skipped up to his two girl cousins, grubby from playing in the gravel heap, and they shrank back until he invited them to come and see the new work-horses Mr Peterson had just bought.

'Don't get dirty,' Emily said to them. 'Selena, keep an eye on Patience. And Patience, behave properly please.'

'Yes, Mama,' chorused the girls.

'Can we go to the stables, Ma?' Aram asked, belatedly.

All three children turned to look at her and Hannah was struck by the likeness between Aram and Patience. They were cousins, but they could have been brother and sister.

'Yes, you can go, as long as you ask first if it's all right for you to go near the horses.'

She was jubilant at the likeness. Maybe it didn't prove anything since neither child looked like Ben, but the stain of Shem Whitfield grew fainter every year.

Hannah took Emily and Ben indoors and stoked the fire. Her sister was pinched with cold and she made her sit in Jonathan's chair close to it.

'Your cough's no better, then?' she said anxiously.

'The doctor says all I need is some warmer weather and it'll clear up.' Emily hid her handkerchief away in her reticule. 'I'm better now I'm not near the hemp all the time. That seemed to make it worse.'

355

'You must come and see our new house,' said Ben. 'Emily now feels quite the lady, don't you, my dear?'

'Hannah, where is your water closet? I really must go,' said Emily.

As soon as she was out of earshot Ben turned urgently to Hannah. 'She's very ill, as you can see. I wanted Ma to come and look after her but she won't, so I'm asking you, Hannah. Emily needs someone with her . . . her family. I beg you, please come.'

'I can't. I've got a husband and child here, and I teach the children.'

'If you love your sister won't you try to help her?'

It didn't seem right that Emily should be the one in poor health when she had everything to make life easier for her. Hannah almost felt ashamed of her own robust constitution. Yet she had suffered so much hardship in the past few years it was a wonder she wasn't lying in an early grave. Since leaving the Shakers she had put on weight and she knew by the admiring glances she got from the men working on the tower that she was more desirable than she had ever been. Ben didn't touch her, but she didn't need any physical contact to be assured that his feelings for her hadn't changed. The scene in the Shakers' chapel was as vivid as if it had taken place yesterday, and she could feel the tension in him.

She met his gaze. 'Would it be wise for me to stay in your house?'

'I swear I would treat you as a sister.'

'Jonathan would never let me take Aram with me.'

'He's too possessive.'

'I know. But he has his reasons.'

They were looking into each other's eyes and the message contained in their depths had no bearing on the spoken words. Hannah found it hard to draw an even breath, and his breathing was equally ragged. She clasped her hands tightly together in front of her lest she should be too strongly tempted to reach out for him.

'Shall I speak to your husband?' Ben asked.

'No,' she said quickly. 'You know what his temper's like. I'll speak to him myself later, but don't let Emily hold out too much hope.'

She made tea for them. It nearly broke her heart to see Emily pick at a few crumbs of cake and then cough when they caught in her throat. There was no doubt that she had consumption, and even if

356

it responded well to warm summer days there was still the worry of what would happen next winter. Hannah tried to make easy conversation, and she made them laugh describing Mr Peterson's eccentric familiarity with Sir Christopher Wren.

'Whoever heard of building a concrete tower just as an experiment?' she said. 'And with plans passed on by someone who's been dead nigh on two hundred years!'

'Maybe it'll look like St Paul's Cathedral when it's finished,' laughed Ben.

'Then Mother Girling would have some opposition,' said Emily, clapping her almost transparent hands.

Ben's expression sobered. 'Don't go too near it once it gains height. It'll never stand the force of the wind. Once it's above the trees I reckon it'll collapse in the first big gale.'

Jonathan didn't join them. They sat for an hour drinking tea and talking over old times, and by then it was plain to see that Emily was very tired and needed to be getting home. Hannah walked with them across the yard, and saw her husband talking to Aram, Selena and Patience who were standing in a row and staring up at him with their big, grey eyes ...

Chapter Thirty-Five

Jonathan Whitfield stared into the furnace, his thoughts as hot and painful as the burning coals. It was two months now since the Rutherfords' visit and in that time he had wrestled continuously with his conscience, his faith, his suspicions and his fear. His conscience bothered him because he ought to have made peace with Ben Rutherford and apologized for the harm he had done him in the heat of jealousy, but he hadn't even been able to speak to the man. His faith was receding without the prompting and passion of Mother Girling to keep it alive. His suspicions were tied up with his fear, and it was these last two which plagued him most.

When he lay down at night he saw again three children standing before him with identical grey eyes. When he looked in the fire he saw them. Wherever he looked they were there, and one of them was Aram. The other two belonged to Rutherford, and the more he thought about it the more convinced he became that the same man had fathered all three. And it was all because of the letter from Emily Rutherford in which she had commented on the way her daughters took after their father about the eyes.

He had tried questioning Hannah but she always denied the possibility. She became angry when he doubted her word and he was left with new hope that Aram was his own flesh and blood. There'd been a witness to the raping, and Aram had arrived at exactly the time to agree with the date of his conception. Around then though, according to Lilianne, Ben Rutherford had escaped from Ipswich jail where he'd been imprisoned for horse-thieving, and she had hinted at things. He could never be absolutely sure.

The argument was tearing him apart. He knew it was ridiculous to let himself get into such a state, especially when he had no means of discovering if Hannah was telling the truth. He had to believe her. There was no other way.

And then, as he made shoes for the new work-horses, he conjured with a frightening means of proving once and for all whether or not Aram came from Whitfield stock.

There was one remnant of Mother Girling's teaching which remained firmly rooted in his soul but he'd been afraid to put its validity to the test. Oh yes, there was a sure way – an infallible way – to prove if Aram was his grandson, his son by spiritual adoption, but he would be dicing with his life. All he had to do was break the vow of celibacy yet again, and wait to see if the boy was taken from him in the same way that Shem and Clemmy had become forfeits.

He lifted the white-hot iron from the fire and took it to the anvil. It almost blinded him as he stared at it, and a pain started at the back of his neck, spreading up through his scalp and settling just above his eyes. His feelings for Aram were undergoing change. When he looked at him lately he saw the Devil with horns standing behind him pointing out signs of Hannah's deceit, and he wanted to destroy the fruit of it. And Aram's puzzlement at the fierce stare would result in him clasping the child so close to his heart he would cry out and struggle to be free. The fight within himself was so passionate he knew it had to be resolved soon one way or the other before he lost his sanity.

Jonathan brought the hammer down on the metal and started fashioning a shoe, the rhythm of the heavy tool taking over automatically to control a terrible urge to use ungovernable force. He loved Aram. He hated him. It was Aram who kept him from making love to his wife because he was terrified the act might once more bring God's vengeance down. Night after night he lay awake, his body aching for the release of physical union with Hannah, and he had to calm himself by consciously listening to Aram's steady breathing in the truckle bed by the wall.

But if Aram was Rutherford's child no harm would come to him.

A choice had to be made. He could no longer live with his wife and his fears together. If he went to Hannah's bed and Aram died as a result of it, then he would know for sure that he had been Shem's child. And he would have sacrificed him. The loss would be too great for any man to tolerate and he would have to take his own life. But he didn't know yet how he would feel if Aram didn't die, because then he would have proof that he had made a fool of himself over the cuckoo in his nest.

359

The decision was impossible to make, and when Jonathan at last put down the hammer he was weak from the strain and staggered backwards to lean against the wall.

'Pa, are you all right?'

Aram had come in unnoticed. He ran to his father, and Jonathan saw the anxiety in his young eyes, the love which a few minutes ago he had been prepared to risk losing in a cruel experiment. He straightened up.

'Yes, son, I'm all right. Reckon I let the metal get a mite too hot and it sapped me.'

It was a dark night and a strong wind was blowing, making the cottage creak and groan with eerie sounds. There was no moon to shed light through the small square window, but stars pinpointed the sky and gave just enough glow to lift the bedroom out of total blackness. Towards midnight Hannah drifted on the edge of sleep, becoming accustomed to the heavy gusts which kept thudding on the window-panes. It was new, completely different sounds which disturbed her. They were soft and stealthy. Her eyes flew open in alarm and she saw Jonathan standing beside the bed in his night-shirt.

He was looking down at her. She didn't know how long he had been there. Silhouetted in the starlight he appeared to be of giant proportions, the silver in his long hair glistening, and he was so quiet his presence had a menacing quality. Hannah went cold. She held her breath and pulled the blanket up under her chin, but he didn't go away.

'I've come to share our bed,' he said. The door was shut between the two bedrooms so that Aram wouldn't wake. 'I've decided it's time.'

He drew the covers off her and rolled her out of the familiar hollow she had made in the feather mattress. When he lay down beside her the springs of the bed complained loudly at his weight, and Hannah cowered as far from him as she could get without falling over the edge. How she had dreaded this moment.

He said nothing as he roughly removed her nightdress, tossing her like a pillow as he shook her out of it. The smell of him was unpleasant and she shuddered, her body going rigid at the first invasion of his fingers. He was coarse and gave no heed to the pain he caused when

360

he lowered his great weight on to her body. With one hand he squeezed her breast until she knew there would be black bruises in the morning. With the other he forced her legs apart. He was about to use her cruelly to satisfy an animal craving, and there was no difference between him and his son Shem. She cried out.

'What's the matter?' he asked. 'Isn't this what you want? I thought you were drooling to be a wife.'

'Not like this,' she wept. 'There's nothing nice about it.'

'And was there something nice about the way Ben Rutherford took you?'

'Stop it! Don't ever talk about me and Ben like that. You should've had more sense than to listen to whoever put such wicked thoughts in your head.'

To her great relief Jonathan rolled away and lay with his back towards her, his head burrowed into his arms. He said nothing more for a long time and Hannah dared not move. She was trembling so much her limbs ached, and she feared the next onslaught. At first she didn't realise that he was trembling, too. His shoulders were moving convulsively, as if he wept, and his legs were curled up into the foetal position. She watched for a few minutes, her own nerves becoming calmer. He was clearly distressed, and the weakness of this big man played on her emotions until she found herself kneading his back with sympathetic fingers.

'I'm sorry,' she said, and didn't know why she apologized.

'I can't do it, Hannah. Not because my body ain't willing.' It was apparent he was under great mental strain.

She said: 'I don't understand.'

'I wouldn't expect you to.'

'Try telling me.' But he was silent.

He left her a short time later, but Hannah had no sleep at all that night. For the time being she had been spared the hateful business of union with him, but Jonathan had made the first move and it wouldn't be long before he came again.

Two months after their visit to Hannah, the state of Emily's health was so serious that Ben Rutherford saddled his horse early and set off for Sway. Hannah had a generous heart and she wouldn't refuse again to come when she knew how bad things were. It wouldn't be for long.

361

He could see that his wife was dying, and his heart was heavy. The doctor visited her regularly, and Ben had known for a long time that she had consumption, though Emily carefully hid the evidence that she was coughing up blood. Her illness had now progressed to the point where she could no longer get out of bed, and Mrs Lawton, who came in daily, was severely overworked looking after the children as well as cooking and cleaning. This morning, when Ben had gone into her room and heard Emily calling feebly for her mother and sister, he knew that something had to be done.

Over the years he had learnt to forgive Emily's duplicity and had tried to rekindle the brotherly affection he'd had for her when they were young. He was sad that he was about to lose her. She had been a good wife and she had deserved a more attentive husband. Ben had given her most things she'd wanted since he had become wealthy enough to do so, but giving his time was different. Her company irritated him beyond endurance, and the only way to keep the peace between them had been to stay out of her way as much as possible.

Ben rode into Brockenhurst that spring morning with his family on his mind. The girls were being very good. They had grown used to being quiet so as not to disturb their mother and her illness was now something they accepted. But it would come hard when she was no longer with them and he didn't know how he was going to cope. Perhaps if they had something new to occupy them it would help. He remembered seeing a shop in Brockenhurst where hobby horses had been made for generations and he decided to stop long enough to buy one for each of his daughters.

The brightly painted wooden steeds on wheels with their fur manes and straight bodies were packed and strapped to his saddle-bag, and he was just about to remount when he saw several women hurrying towards the green. A waggon was parked there and a young man had unloaded his wares ready to tempt them to part with their money.

'Dear ladies, if ever you've wished you could cook a meal fit for the Queen, now's your chance to do it. These saucepans are the very same that's used at the palace, but you don't have to pay royal prices for 'em.'

The patter could be heard from quite a distance. Memories flooded Ben's mind of Amos Hanberry and the happy weeks they had spent together on the road. Their waggon hadn't been quite so elaborate but their selling techniques had been the same. Nostalgia made him delay a few minutes longer.

'Now you, my pretty young friend, I'll wager you've a magic touch in the kitchen and a husband who appreciates good food.' The fellow picked out the woman most likely to respond to flattery. 'Wouldn't you like to spend more time with him and less at the stove? Well, here's the answer. Buy my pots and pans and I'll guarantee you married bliss.'

Ben walked his horse over to the green and stood at the back of the gathering crowd. The young man looked familiar. He had a very long neck and a small head which nodded like a pecking hen as he emphasized the extraordinary value of his wares. His hair was oiled into place and he had an incongruously large black moustache. It was when Ben looked more closely at the waggon that recognition came with a jolt. The man's name was painted across the front: *Trust Michael Playfair, the fairest salesman in the country.* Other slogans decorated the sides and back of the vehicle Ben had last seen disappearing down the street in Bermondsey bearing the superior message that Christ had died for the ungodly.

He felt nauseous. The man was an imposter, a charlatan. He dropped the horse's reins, pushed the women aside and strode up to face the man who had conducted the ceremony at Bermondsey Methodist chapel and signed a document making Emily his wife.

'Good morning, Reverend,' he said, in a voice as loud as the pedlar's.

The wretch kept smiling, but a flush crept over his sallow skin. 'I'm honoured by the title, sir, but I'm not a gentleman of the cloth, as you can surely see.'

'Am I to take it then that you have never been an ordained Minister in the Methodist church?'

'Never. You're mistaking me for someone else, I think.'

'*I* think not.' Ben took hold of him by the collar and it hooked beneath his Adam's apple, making him splutter and choke. 'The last time I saw you was in Bermondsey in London, where you were masquerading as a man of God.'

'No, m'lud . . .'

Ben kept him prisoner and the surrounding women pressed closer, excited by the unexpected free show. Michael Playfair's legs twitched as he tried to break free, and Ben shook him like a terrier with a rat.

'You conducted a wedding. Don't deny it because your signature is on a document which no doubt is worthless.'

'It was someone else. I wouldn't know the first thing about weddings.'

'Perhaps you'll tell the truth to a constable. I'm taking you to Lymington right now.'

The pedlar changed his tune. He wriggled frantically. 'I was asked to do it. Your wife paid me . . . '

'My wife would never have done such a thing,' shouted Ben. 'You're making it worse by lying.'

'I swear she paid me! The lady was that desperate to get married . . . ' he looked up at his aggressor with a touch of daring ' . . . though goodness knows why, if it was to you.'

Ben let him go. He felt concussed, as if he had been hit over the head with a mallet, and his brain wouldn't function properly.

'Pack your wares and be off,' he muttered to Michael Playfair. 'I ain't telling the police right now, but if ever I see you round here again I'll have them on to you faster than a whippet can run a mile.'

The women were clapping their hands, though a few protested that the poor man had a right to peddle where he chose. Ben went back to his horse and mounted, pulling on the rein to turn in the Sway direction. He still had to go for Hannah.

Luckily he wasn't known in Brockenhurst. He had said too much in front of an audience and he hoped that word of the entertainment wouldn't spread as far as West Borley. If it did, everyone would know that his marriage to Emily was invalid. Above all the tale mustn't reach Emily's ears. Had she not been so ill he would have headed straight back to confront her with it, but he couldn't worry her with the news that they had been living in sin all these years. Nor could he let her know the extent of his anger at her cunning.

He rode through the lanes in a daze. It was his right leg bumping uncomfortably against the hobby horses which made him think of Selena and Patience, his *illegitimate* daughters. He went cold at the realisation. There was only one answer to the affair: he would have to ask a genuine Minister to come to the house quickly and make the marriage legal before Emily died – not so that she could die in peace, but for the sake of his children.

364

First, though, he had to fetch Hannah.

Jonathan had risen exceptionally early. He had lit the kitchen fire which was already blazing when she came downstairs, but he hadn't stayed for breakfast. In the still morning air she could hear the sound of his hammer across the way as it pounded relentlessly on a piece of iron which would be fit for nothing.

Much later she was about to go over to the smithy with bread and cheese for him when a horseman rode fast into the yard. Her heart almost stopped beating. Ben had come on his own to see her, but she saw at once that it wasn't a social visit.

'Emily's dying,' he said, without preamble. 'She's calling for you, Hannah, and I've promised you'll come back with me.'

Shock robbed her of an answer and she closed her eyes. She had tried to believe that all Emily needed was warm weather to improve her cough, but deep down she had feared the worst. Now it had come.

Ben came indoors, ducking his head to avoid hitting the lintel. 'That's not all,' he said. His face was drawn. 'I've just made a terrible discovery.'

She caught his hand, holding it in both hers to share his pain. 'Tell me about it.'

'I came through Brockenhurst. There was a travelling salesman on the green with a waggon and I recognized him.' Ben's voice was tight with emotion. 'He was the same Michael Playfair who supposedly married Emily and me in Bermondsey. *Then* he'd been posing as a Gospel preacher. Our marriage was illegal – the man had no authority to conduct a wedding and the licence isn't worth the paper it's written on.'

The revelation caused a flame to leap inside her but it had to be quenched. 'Oh, Ben.' Her eyes sought his with genuine sympathy. 'What will you do? Will you tell Emily?'

'How can I?'

She buried her face against his breast and heard the heavy beating of his heart. 'I'm so sorry.'

'As far as Emily's concerned I've no wish to remedy the situation, but for the sake of our girls I must take the Minister at West Borley into my confidence, and get him to marry us properly. And it must be today.' He put her aside. 'There's no time to lose, Hannah. Come with me and I'll tell you the rest of the story on the journey.'

'Wait for me here.' She crossed the yard and entered the forge. The heat was almost unbearable and Jonathan was still shovelling coal on the fire to get it white-hot. He looked up, but continued with what he was doing.

'Jonathan, I must go to Emily right away,' Hannah said, raising her voice to be heard above the roar of the flames. 'My sister's dying.'

'So that's what Rutherford's come for.' To her astonishment he didn't raise a single objection. When the fire was sufficiently banked he put the shovel aside and came towards her. His half-naked body glistened with sweat.

'I want you back straight after the funeral,' he said. 'And I warn you I'll know if Rutherford's laid a hand on you.'

She was so moved by his unexpected generosity that delayed tears sprang to her eyes. 'Thank you, Jonathan. I'm real grateful,' she told him. 'I'll take Aram with me out of your way.'

Aram appeared from behind a pile of bricks and would have run to her side, but Jonathan caught and held him. The boy was equally hot and stripped to the waist in imitation of his father, his lithe young body unnaturally pink from the heat.

'No,' Jonathan said. His great hand touched the rough blond head beside him but his gaze remained fixed on his wife. 'Aram stays here. That way I know you'll come back.'

An hour later Hannah was riding with Ben across the open forest towards Beaulieu, the Brockenhurst route being likely to produce another encounter with the despicable pedlar.

'I swear if I ever set eyes on him again I'll kill him,' Ben declared.

'Just be glad you can make an honest woman of Emily before it's too late,' said Hannah, to comfort him.

But it was not to be.

The Methodist Minister was found and urgently requested to accompany them to the Rutherford house. Ben trusted him with the awful tale of Michael Playfair and the Gospel car, and he agreed to hold the briefest of ceremonies to put right the wrong so wickedly done. Hannah and Mrs Lawton were to be witnesses. Thankfully the children were out visiting a neighbour who regularly invited them to play with her brood, so there was no fear of them discovering the truth.

With his prayer book in his hand the Minister followed Ben up

366

the stairs to Emily's bedroom. Hannah had rushed up there first to see her sister, but she had returned to the doorway.

'Emily's asleep,' Hannah said. 'She looks so peaceful it's a pity to wake her.'

The Minister went into the room. He stood over Emily for a moment in quiet thought, then lifted her limp hand, feeling for the pulse at her wrist. When there was none to be found he took the other hand and gently crossed her arms over her breast.

'I'm afraid, my dears, that Mrs Rutherford's sleep is everlasting.'

There was a moment of stunned silence, then Hannah turned to weep in Ben's arms. The Minister took the marker out of the page in his book where the wedding service began, and thumbed his way through to the section where there were prayers for the dead.

Chapter Thirty-Six

The sun shone on the day of Emily's funeral, but there were showers true to April's custom. Lilianne had arrived as soon as she could after the news of Emily's death reached her, but the journey was slow. Harry Bourne had brought her to West Borley in Mother Girling's pony-cart.

'I thought you weren't coming,' Hannah said. 'Ben reckoned Mother Girling wouldn't let you leave.'

'And likely that would have suited you,' was Lilianne's curt reply. There had been no communication between them since Hannah had left with Jonathan, and the meeting was difficult.

Consumption had claimed the lives of several Shakers and Lilianne had seen the way it progressed, but this hadn't prepared her for the shock of losing her oldest daughter to the dreaded disease. Now she was being buried in a strange churchyard where no other members of their family had a last resting place. Lilianne cried for her dear Emily. If only she could have persuaded her to become a devout follower of Mother Girling perhaps she wouldn't have died. The promise of everlasting life was the most wonderful, powerful part of her faith and her own good health was proof that a pure life led to riches beyond the imagination. She couldn't wait to get back to Mother and the community.

There were plenty of people at the funeral. Emily had been well-liked in the village and many came to pay their last respects. Others came to see the woman who was rumoured to be one of those peculiar Shakers who lived over in the Lymington direction; they stared at Lilianne as she stood at the graveside in the only dress and shawl she possessed. She was used to it. Every Sunday people came to stare at her when she danced, and she always pitied them for not recognizing Mother as the saviour of the world.

Ben Rutherford wore a black coat and his bare head was bent as he listened to the prayers at the interment. In spite of her dislike of him, Lilianne had to admit he had made Emily's life very comfortable. She couldn't help thinking, though, that her own money had played a major part in this. Without it, likely Ben would have been in prison still, or transported to some place on the other side of the world.

He was a handsome devil, and she could understand why both her daughters had been drawn to him. Yet he had always craved Hannah alone – the terrible incident in Tiptoe last summer had proved it. It was all due to Ben and his wickedness that Jonathan had been forced to take his wife and leave the Shaker community.

Earth was thrown on the coffin. The parson's voice droned. Hannah reached for her mother's hand in that emotional moment, and Lilianne held it loosely, unable to respond to this other daughter's need of her. She admitted to herself without any remorse that she wished it had been her in the coffin instead of Emily. The girl looked fit and strong, though her face was drawn and she had been exceptionally quiet all the time they'd been thrown together. If there was any conversation at all it was about Aram's cleverness, or her new life at Sway which only interested Lilianne in so much as it gave her news of Jonathan.

She missed him. There were times when she committed the sin of remembering how it had felt when he had made love to her, but it hurt to know that he was now free of his celibacy vow and could bed her daughter. She had half-expected to see Hannah several months pregnant when they met. The fact that she obviously wasn't had been a small consolation.

Emily's children stood at either side of their father, their sadness too deep for comprehension. Patience was crying fitfully and rubbing her eyes with an embroidered handkerchief, but Selena managed to contain her grief admirably and the only visible sign of it was the way her lower lip was held tightly between her teeth. Lilianne loved them. She watched them while their plump little hands were folded in prayer, and an unexpected nostalgia for the days at Kean's Farm assailed her. Supposing she'd still been living a normal life with a home of her own where the children could visit her – she would have spoilt them like any other typical grandmother. Aram too, most likely. But she had her own life to lead now and there was no room in it for selfish family ties.

Lilianne disentangled her fingers from Hannah's as soon as there was an opportunity, and walked with the family back to the Rutherford house where neighbours had prepared a tea.

'Ma, is it any good asking if you'd consider coming here to live and look after the children?' Ben asked her quietly. It was what she'd been expecting. 'I'd be mighty obliged. It would solve a big problem and the girls would have someone of their own to love them and care about them.'

They were standing near the window looking out on Emily's herb-garden. Lilianne took a bite from a small egg sandwich. 'You're right, it's no good asking,' she said. 'Much as I love the children, I can't leave Mother Girling. I don't want to. Your house-keeper's made a good job of looking after them while Emily was ill and I don't doubt she'll go on doing it.'

It was true. Annie Lawton, the woman Ben had been paying to run his house, had impressed Lilianne with her capability. She kept the children neat and tidy, and stood no nonsense. It was plain to see she was eager to be kept on.

'You're a hard woman, Ma Jerram.'

'And you're a man with a short memory. I couldn't live in the same house with you knowing how you betrayed Emily. I'll not be forgetting the way you behaved with Hannah not many months since.'

'Emily wanted you with her before, and she'd want you to be with the girls now,' Ben urged. 'You'd have no worries. A room of your own, Ma, with pretty things round you, plenty of food and a warm house all year. Now ain't that something worth having?'

Lilianne looked round the room at the porcelain and pictures, the chintz curtains and the nice furniture which was Emily's pride. After the years of hardship she had endured, for a moment it was tempting to succumb, but the Lord was always with her and she heard a voice warning her not to weaken.

'Treasures on earth, Ben Rutherford, ain't worth anything,' she said firmly. 'It's the treasures we store up for ourselves in Heaven that matter. I ask for nothing better than to serve my dear Mother for ever.'

The next day, Lilianne accepted a lift from a carrier who was going to Lymington, and from there she walked back to the Shaker encampment. She hadn't liked leaving the children, and she feared what would happen when Hannah and Ben were left alone in the house, but her allegiance was to Mother and she knew she must quit worrying about anything outside the bounds of her faith.

*

Hannah watched her mother depart, and grieved almost as much as she had for Emily. Ma was lost to her. Their few days together had been difficult. Like Ben, Hannah had tried to persuade Lilianne to make her home in West Borley, but she had met with the same response.

'Patience and Selena need you, Ma,' Hannah had said.

'The Lord needs me more,' had been Lilianne's reply. 'I'm dependent on Him to tell me what to do, and He hasn't said I must leave The Children of God to take care of Emily's family. They've got Mrs Lawton, but if Ben's that set on me being the one to bring them up then he'll have to let them come to Tiptoe. There's nothing I'd like better than to take them with me.'

'And have them brought up as Shakers! Never!'

'It's the only way I'd consider it.'

And so she had gone on the carrier's waggon, a thin, middle-aged woman who had now lost the boldness and good looks which had made her so attractive before Mother Girling had arrived in Seggenham. In the old days she would never have gone off and left Emily's two motherless little girls to be brought up by a virtual stranger. The change in her mother saddened Hannah almost more than the loss of her sister and she wanted to weep afresh.

She couldn't stay herself, either. She'd sent news to Jonathan of Emily's death and the date of the funeral, but he hadn't come. The work for Mr Peterson was too pressing, he had written, but he sent condolences, and gave instructions for her to be ready when he called to pick her up today.

She dreaded going back to him. If it hadn't been for Aram she might have dared to stay away, but her son was being held hostage just as much as when Mrs Humby had kept him. For Aram's sake she would always have to go back.

'Stay with me, Hannah,' Ben said.

He came in while she was packing a few things in a bag. She had thought he was at the ropeyard and hadn't been expecting him home until midday, when likely Jonathan would be arriving. Her heart missed a beat and caused a fluttering which made her head spin. In the last few days she had made sure she was never alone with him, but now there was no avoiding it as Selena and Patience had gone to a smallholding down the lane where some new kittens had arrived.

371

'I can't. I've got to go back. I've no choice,' she answered, keeping her eyes averted.

'You don't love your husband.' He was behind her and he put his hands round her waist, drawing her back against him. His lips touched her hair. Shivers coursed the length of her spine and she moved spontaneously, pressing closer so that his hands could move up to cup her breasts, but she was determined he mustn't see the light shining in her eyes.

'You're right,' he said. 'It's too soon after losing Emily anyway. But I can't bear the thought of you with him, and I want my son.'

She swung round at that and forced him to let go of her. 'Now let's have this out once and for all, Ben Rutherford.' She was deliberately angry. It was the only way she could cope with her feelings. 'It can never be proved that Aram is yours. I'm not saying he is, but I can't say he ain't, either. A few days after we were together in the barn, and before me month was up, Shem Whitfield raped me. I was going to be made to marry him and I thought it was for the best since you were supposed to be on your way to America. I didn't think I'd ever see you again.'

'I told you I'd send for you.'

'And what good was it to hang on to a promise like that with a baby on the way?'

He was contrite. 'I'm more sorry than I can say, Hannah. I ought to have taken you with me like you asked, but I was on the run. I couldn't risk any harm coming to you if we were together.'

'I would've risked anything, you know that.'

'I know it now.'

'Reckon I loved you from the minute Pa brought you home.' Her gold-flecked eyes could no longer conceal her love and she met his gaze fully aware that she was making their parting more difficult. Her lips curved into a gentle smile which invited the lightest of kisses.

'Likely the feeling was mutual, the way I took to the scrawny kid you were then. I sure as hell have loved you since you became a grown woman.' He touched her face, his fingers caressing her cheekbone and travelling down to the corner of her mouth and across it until her lips quivered ecstatically. They were ready and eager for the deeper kiss which followed.

'Aram's mine,' he said. 'I've not got the slightest doubt, and neither have you.'

372

She drew a long breath and held it a second, willing herself to think of her husband.

'Jonathan worships him.' She summoned up a picture in her mind of the man and the boy together at the forge in Sway. 'He became the son he lost when Shem took his own life, and he married me because it was so important for the baby to have the Whitfield name. I could never deprive him of Aram.'

Ben's face hardened. 'How can you even consider his feelings? The devil tried to kill me.'

'I'm married to him. Don't you see, he's been good to me in his way, and there's been so many tragedies in his life. He even lost Clemmy, and if I were to admit he's been doting on another man's child for the last seven years I reckon it would turn his mind. I can't do that to him, no matter how much you want me to, or how much I love you.'

The April sun shone through a budding apple tree outside the window and dappled the wall. There were signs of Emily everywhere and Hannah dragged herself away from Ben's reach, filled with guilt that she had allowed him to touch her before his wife was hardly cold in the grave. He didn't try to recapture the moment. Maybe he too was suddenly aware of the impropriety because he clattered some plates into place on the dresser and seemed to take pleasure in the noise.

'Emily loved nice things,' he said irrelevantly.

Hannah's heart ached. 'And I ain't used to them so I don't reckon I'd be happy here. I might break something.'

He swung round again, and now he was angry. 'You don't owe that bloody man anything. He took your youth and your child and put you into an intolerable situation.' His grey eyes glinted like steel. 'Hell, I'm afraid for you. Whitfield ain't safe if he can pick up a gun and use it without a second thought.'

'As long as I stay away from you I know everything'll be all right. I've got to go back with him, Ben. He's got Aram and he'll never let him go.'

'If that's what's bothering you I can soon ride over and collect the boy. He's got no right to blackmail you, and I ain't afraid to tell him so.'

'You won't do any such thing.' Hannah's voice rose. 'I won't have grown men fighting over my son like he was a prize to be won. Nor will I let him be torn apart by the people who love him. He believes *Jonathan* is his father and that's what he's going to go on thinking. There ain't no two ways about it, so let's not hurt Aram or ourselves. I don't want you coming near him, d'yer hear?'

'I'll bide my time,' Ben said. 'I'll have to be coming over to Sway soon anyway. Mr Peterson's put in an order for a quantity of rope. Seems he's going to be building that tower a strange way, but who am I to argue with business.'

He left the house just before Patience came in the back door with her pinafore undone and her boots covered in mud. She was brighter than she had been for days and she skipped through the kitchen.

'Aunt Hannah, I can have one of the kittens when it's older, Mrs Smith says so. You will make Papa say it's all right, won't you? Mama wouldn't let me have one.'

'I'm sure your Papa will let you, but you must make it right with Mrs Lawton as well. I shan't be here to ask them. I've got to go home soon.'

Patience's little face crumpled. 'I want you to stay.'

'I have to go and look after Aram.'

'But we need you more than he does. He's a *boy*.'

Hannah took the child on her knee and nursed her. 'Boys need looking after just as much as girls,' she said. 'More sometimes because they're not so clever at seeing to themselves.'

Through the window she saw the Petersons' carriage pull up at the gate and a knot of apprehension settled in her stomach at the sight of Jonathan alighting. He was alone. She'd thought he might bring Aram with him, but likely he'd considered it a risk. When he rang the bell she set Patience down but kept hold of her hand so as to gain moral support from the plump little figure in a grubby apron at her side.

'Come in, Jonathan,' she said.

'I'll wait here.' He was unsmiling. 'Are you ready?'

'Yes, I'm ready. I'll just make sure Mrs Lawton's around for the children.'

That night Jonathan came again to her bedroom. He was fully dressed and the candle he carried illuminated his gaunt features. His eyes were strained and dark.

374

Hannah clutched the sheet, dreading the invasion into her body which she knew could no longer be postponed. He fingered his braces and she waited for him to take off his trousers. Memories of the last time he had stripped to his shirt and forced the lower part of his body against hers made every muscle tense. She kept perfectly still, prepared for the rough removal of her nightgown, but moments passed and he made no move.

'You've no need to fear me, Hannah,' Jonathan said. His voice was low but it didn't hide his despair. 'I can't take you. I'd be breaking my vow.' He lowered himself on to the edge of the bed, and she sat up so that the candle was between their faces. The flame flickered with their breath.

'You're not beholden to Mother Girling any more,' she said. 'Her rules don't have to be obeyed here.' Her relief was so great she wanted to weep, and yet she was trying to find excuses for him.

'It ain't only Mother Girling. When Susan was dying I swore on the Bible I'd never take another woman since it was the only way to give her comfort.' His forehead creased into deep furrows. 'You're a good wife, Hannah. I couldn't ask for better. You keep me sane.'

'I know you don't love me. I don't love you either, but we're wedded and I'll be faithful to you.'

The candlestick tipped as he gripped it too firmly and hot wax dripped on the bedcover. 'If ever you left and took Aram away, the Devil would take me,' he declared. 'He's always at my shoulder just waiting, but *you* keep him at bay. Remember that, woman. My fate rests with you.' He got up and lumbered from the room, but his presence seemed to linger in the darkness.

Hannah reached up to unhook the plain wooden cross which hung above her bed, and held it to her heart.

Chapter Thirty-Seven

When Lilianne returned to the Shaker community in 1880 after the death of Emily her devotion to Mother Girling underwent a severe test. Precocious little letters came from Selena and Patience which worried her, and she was torn between her loyalty to her dear Mother, and her duty to be with her grand-daughters, giving instruction on the need for humility and obedience. The letters were read first by Mother Girling, of course, but she didn't offer to release Lilianne from her bondage; instead, she urged devout prayer.

'The Lord will look after the children. They have a good home and a loving father. They don't need you as much as God needs you, sister, and I beg you not to desert the fold. We'll pray together for you to be given the strength to do what is right.'

'I'm not sure what *is* right any more.'

Mother Girling reached out and touched her. 'Trust me. You gave up everything to follow me and I won't fail you. I am the present body of Christ, the only Christ.'

'How can I believe you, Mother?' Lilianne was appalled at herself, but having dared to speak out she found the courage to continue. 'Sometimes I marvel at the strength of your faith when nobody outside our family here recognizes you.'

'Even inside our family it's difficult for some to see God in my body,' Mother said.

They were sitting in the chapel, the only place where there was a stove. When Mary Ann had been working in the field her feet were painful. This evening she removed her boots so that warmth from the fire might ease the ache, and when she crossed her ankles the stigmata gleamed white, just as if a large nail had been driven through both her feet while one rested on top of the other. The largest mark was on the foot uppermost and was like the imprint of a jagged nail-head. It was embedded quite deep between the bones, drawn in by the weight of the body causing the head of the nail to sink into the flesh. Lilianne gazed at it. Her breath caught.

' "Not a bone of Him shall be broken," ' Mary Ann quoted, very quietly. 'You've seen my hands. Now look at my side.' She drew her blouse out of the top of her skirt and lifted it to expose her waist. A large oval scar, the size of a spear-blade, had the appearance of an old wound which had healed and left a white, sunken mark. 'I've had the stigmata from the day I gave myself to Christ. I became absorbed in Him and He in me.'

Lilianne fell down on her knees and touched Mary Ann's feet reverently. 'I'm convinced, Mother. Forgive me for ever doubting you.'

From that evening she ceased to worry unduly about Selena and Patience, but she prayed regularly that Ben Rutherford would see they were schooled in religious matters which would guide them through life, and asked for someone loving to be sent to them. Her own life was revitalized, her faith in Mother Girling restored, and she was happiest when she was giving comfort and support to those around her.

Towards the end of that year Beth Page came to Lilianne in terrible distress. She was expecting a child, though she had managed to keep the fact a secret and was then in the fifth month.

'It were an accident,' she said to Lilianne, when they were working on the allotment together one cold November day. The ground was hard and the young woman struck it forcefully with her spade as if trying to bring on a late miscarriage. 'He were desperately unhappy and I comforted him.'

Lilianne understood only too well. 'I know. It happens.'

'But what am I going to do now?' Beth had been a Shaker for twelve years and she was clearly frightened of a future on her own away from the only family she had known.

'First Mother must be told. We'll go together if you like. Then maybe I can think of something you can do.'

Beth had taken Hannah's place with the children and she had a wonderful way with them. Oh yes, Lilianne's prayers had been miraculously answered. Mother's sorrow at Beth's sin brought forth numerous prayers for her soul, but not enough compassion for her to be allowed to stay in the community. So a few days later Lilianne borrowed the pony-cart and took the girl to West Borley, where she exacted a promise from Ben. He was to give her a home, and in return she would take charge of Selena and Patience, leaving Mrs

Lawton free to run the house. Lilianne no longer had to worry about her grand-daughters. Their moral welfare was now in the most capable hands.

By 1883 the community had become much smaller. The Shakers continued to live in the two-acre field in Tiptoe. Mother Girling toured local towns and on occasions ventured to London, but she was not prompted by God to return to the city permanently. The reward for her tiring journeys was that she managed to collect enough money to keep her family together, and she continued to receive help from local tradesmen and sympathizers who had become dear friends. If there was not enough food to go round it was given to the children, and she still refused to allow the menfolk to work for a wage. They cultivated the land, putting every inch to good use, and if they hadn't eaten the day before they were careful never to give a sign of it.

Mary Ann Girling was frequently unwell. She suffered numerous headaches and loss of appetite, and she had grown thin. But her mind was keen, and her faith in God and herself shone brighter than ever. Her energy for preaching and dancing was undiminished and the power of her eyes was awesome in her gaunt face, but though she spoke with increased fervour at every meeting she failed to attract many new converts.

Lilianne worried about her more than anyone. Sometimes she tried to persuade her to make things easier for herself.

'At least move to a cottage, Mother dear,' Lilianne begged her. 'I'll live with you and cook for you, and the meetings can be held same as usual.'

'I'll not be tempted, sister,' said Mary Ann. 'My children would lose faith if I had privileges. My own welfare is unimportant. I've got God's work to do.'

During 1883 Mother Girling wrote a long message addressed to the Church and the World. It was printed in a four-page leaflet and called *The Close of the Dispensation*. In it she went to great lengths to explain her presence on earth. *'Great has been the mystery surrounding me,'* she wrote, *'yet it is holy, truthful, loving, divine.'* She said she was suffering on earth for love's sake. As soon as she was accepted as the Bride of Christ then He Himself would appear in His glory. *'The beginning of creation was a male: the end is a female – not to be crucified but to be glorified,'* she declared. She had overcome death and was immortal. It was signed: *'the God-father and God-mother, known by name as* JESUS FIRST AND LAST, *(Mary Ann Girling).'*

The leaflet caused uproar. Articles appeared in newspapers decrying the extraordinary woman for her blasphemy, and she was judged to be repulsive and irreverent. Accusers said she contradicted the plainest statements in the Bible and turned them to her own advantage. Preachers, laymen and journalists came to see for themselves the author of such a controversial leaflet. They were treated with utmost courtesy, and agreed that the Shakers led exemplary lives. They were happy people, and Mother Girling herself had a ladylike manner when she spoke in her compelling voice which still carried a Suffolk dialect. She had an answer for every direct question, yet no one was prepared to agree in public that she was the Saviour of the World.

One clerical gentleman politely pursued the matter of her immortality until her head ached.

'When I look into your face, Mrs Girling, you don't look any different or superior to ordinary women of your age,' the man said.

'I'm afraid you see me at a disadvantage, sir,' said Mary Ann. 'I'm very tired this afternoon.'

The gentleman, like all the others, would probably have dismissed her claims as coming from a tortured mind except for the one indisputable fact which none could explain away. The stigmata.

Andrew Peterson's tower was progressing favourably. It was soon as high as the cottages, and by Christmas 1879 it could just be seen from a distance rising like a campanile into the landscape. The walls were two feet thick and the first storey was complete, having two large porticos of thirteen feet by twenty and doorways in Gothic style moulded in concrete, one on the west side, the other on the east. The square shape was broken by the addition of a hexagonal extension on the north side which housed a spiral staircase, and the separately moulded steps were incorporated with the walls as the work advanced, inscribing a circle of nine feet, all according to Sir Christopher Wren's post-humous instructions.

The horses were Jonathan's responsibility as well as the smithy and he was sometimes called across to the site during the day. The work in progress fascinated him. Three rows of frames were used at a time, each row at a different stage of completion so that when the concrete in the bottom one had set hard the frames could be removed and placed on top ready for the new mixture to be rammed in. In this way three feet of the wall was drying and hardening while the next eighteen-inch section was being added to the height.

But what intrigued him most about the construction was the way the walls were being raised without the use of machinery. A derrick was now attached to the top of the framework and was being used to hoist the weighty concrete up in buckets. There was a pulley embedded in the ground with a rope carried over it to another pulley on the derrick. One end of the rope was tied to the bucket while the other end was attached to a horse which was required to walk away from the building. As it did so the bucket was then raised to the height of the derrick.

'It's the way things are done in India,' Andrew Peterson informed him one day. When he was at home he was frequently around to check on progress, and Jonathan was flattered that he chose to stop and talk to him about it. 'The wells there are deep so they use bullocks to haul up the water. I've always wanted to try the method on a larger scale and it's working so far.'

'How high do you intend the tower to be?' Jonathan asked.

'Over two hundred feet.'

It took a moment for him to comprehend the magnitude and he looked skywards, trying to picture how the structure would look when it was done.

'But you can't use horses to draw concrete up that high!'

'There'll be no difference to the weight,' shrugged Peterson. 'All we'll need is more rope, and the horses will have to walk further.'

On Sunday, 28 December there was a terrible disaster at Dundee where the Tay Bridge, which had been completed less than two years, was partly destroyed in severe gales. A northern mail train had been passing over it at the time and it had plunged into the river with the loss of about ninety lives. At a Board of Trade inquiry soon afterwards it was stated that the bridge had been badly designed, badly constructed and badly maintained. The tragic incident seemed far removed from the building going on at Sway, but it brought home to Mr Peterson the importance of ensuring his tower was able to stand against severe winds. So great was his concern that in March, a year after the foundations had been laid, he called a meeting of everyone involved in the work, accommodating them all in the drawing room of his house.

Jonathan looked around at the Indian rugs hanging on the walls and wondered why they were not on the floors. A collection of oriental pictures hung between them, some of gruesome subjects, and it was plain to see how strong was the Indian influence.

'The safety of all of you has been on my mind,' Peterson said, settling himself behind a large oak desk from where he could command attention. 'Building a tower is not a simple matter of erecting walls. A great many things have to be taken into consideration and one of them is to be absolutely sure there is no danger of gales bringing the structure down, as happened to the Tay Bridge. The outcome of such a catastrophe here doesn't bear thinking about.'

'You mean the whole lot might come down on the cottages?' someone asked in awe. Obviously the possibility hadn't occurred to him, nor to many of those sitting around. Jonathan was not such a simpleton. He'd been anxiously watching the height increase, trying to judge in which direction the tower would fall if the unthinkable came to pass.

'To prevent it ever happening I have been to Westminster to consult my friend Mr Rollo Massey, who is an eminent engineer,' Peterson went on. 'And I can put your minds at rest. We've done a great many calculations and I'm now quite satisfied the tower will be able to resist the highest wind pressure ever recorded, which is fifty-five pounds per square foot. Gentlemen, our tower will be standing for hundreds of years.'

The work went on all through 1880. Gothic-style windows were set in, wooden mouldings and sweeps being set in the frames at the right position and the concrete rammed against them to leave an imprint. For these the concrete was mixed with a dry red pigment which gave a pleasing effect and added interest. And for Jonathan there was no shortage of work as the horses toiled with their loads.

Rope was being bought in great quantity, the wear on it increasing as the pull became longer, and it was obvious that it would have to be replaced more frequently as the weeks went by. This meant good business for Ben Rutherford, from whom it was regularly ordered. Ben had come himself initially to discuss the contract but since then supplies had arrived by waggon and there was no need for him to visit often. Jonathan watched carefully on the days he came to see Mr Peterson, determined that he would have no opportunity to be alone with Hannah, and as far as he knew there'd been little contact.

But he'd not been able to keep Rutherford away from Aram. He'd seen them together sometimes heading for the tower, but though he'd agonised over the sight of Aram leaping and running beside the man who had gone up in his estimation since the shooting episode at Tiptoe he was sensible enough to know that forbidding them to meet would only cause trouble. Aram knew that the shooting had been an accident. At first he had asked questions and Hannah had dutifully refrained from apportioning any blame, but Ben Rutherford had assumed the role of a hero. It was fixed in the child's mind that his life had been saved by the uncle who'd been carrying him on his shoulders that night, and there was nothing Jonathan could do to remove the idea without incriminating himself.

Aram was growing tall and strong. Jonathan looked at him and felt a gnawing in his guts. At eight years old the boy wanted to learn how to shoe a horse, and Jonathan took him to the forge every day even though Hannah begged him not to for fear of any harm coming to him. He became capable of hammering straight and true. His father gave him a hammer, some nails and a few old horseshoes on which to practise, and he watched him attach them to a block of wood, his aim becoming straighter with every blow. It should have been a cause for pride, but it wasn't. It hurt to see he was showing more aptitude than Shem had ever done.

The months followed each other. Another summer and he still daren't risk Aram falling victim to the curse which awaited the Whitfield children. But though he hadn't taken Hannah the sin of taking Lilianne was still unforgiven and the danger remained. With great cunning Jonathan began to lure Aram towards more dangerous pastimes, inviting fate to strike.

'You're doing well, bor,' he said, when Aram rode a pony bareback for the first time. 'Reckon you'll soon be shoeing a pony if you can control one as well as that.'

'You mean it, Pa?' Aram cried. 'You really reckon I could? I know how. I watch you all the time.'

Jonathan's mind went back to the day when Shem had taken it into his own hands to shoe a colt, and the terrible scene that had followed. It made him think of Lilianne. He put his hand to his eyes to rub away the pictures of his weakness, and he was so ashamed he was forced to issue a warning.

'Don't ever touch an animal to put a shoe on it until I say the time's right,' he told the boy. 'It's dangerous. There's more to it than just hammering on a piece of hot metal.'

'I know that, Pa.'

'Don't do it just to show folk how clever you are. That's even more dangerous.'

'I won't, I promise.'

He ruffled the boy's hair, feeling the thickness, and he tried to convince himself that Shem's had been like it. It was becoming difficult to visualize Shem any more and he imagined likenesses, seeing what he wanted to see, but the only indisputable fact was that Aram increasingly resembled his mother. And no matter what he did he came to no harm. He didn't fall off the pony. He hardly ever so much as grazed his knees. His fingers were bruised when he first started using a hammer, but not any more, and he made himself useful in so many ways. His healthy young body was a sight to make a father's heart swell with satisfaction, yet as Jonathan watched him fill out there was a canker inside himself which grew also, and with morbid preoccupation he willed an accident to happen to Aram. Grief at the loss of him, knowing him to have been his own, would be easier to bear than the hatred building up as time went by without there being even the smallest sign to give hope that Shem had sired him.

'On the other hand, if there's small jobs you think you can do when I'm not here I'll not be cross at you trying,' he said, that same day. 'There's plenty of folk hereabouts who think what a clever lad I've got. They like to see how well you're learning.'

The subtle hint took root and Aram could always be found hard at work, doing things more suited to a grown man. And he began to show off, his promise forgotten as Jonathan had guessed it would be. When his father was not there he worked the bellows to control the fire, his young lungs expanding with the energy and his shoulders broadening. He told the coal merchant not to deliver fuel which clinkered easily, his boyish voice ordering the men about with authority. Jonathan was harsh with him. He began to expect more and more of him until Hannah complained at the way he was driving the boy.

'What's the matter with you, Jonathan?' she said. 'Aram's only ten. You can't expect him to take over the place!'

'He's old enough and big enough to earn his keep,' he answered gruffly. 'All the fancy reading you teach him ain't going to fit him for making a living.'

'He's got brains. Reckon he'll do better for himself than blacksmithing when he grows up.'

'What's wrong with blacksmithing?'

'Nothing.'

'Then don't try to fill my son's head with stuff that'll make him think he's better than he is.'

His feelings for Hannah were complicated. Sometimes he wanted her with a passion he hardly knew how to deny and all day the fire in his loins built up as he anticipated the union. But by nightfall the fears were on him and he had to refrain once more. He was as virile as he had always been and if he took his wife it was more than likely he would be creating new life. It had dawned on him that any new children he fathered would be under a certain shadow. Oh, the cruelty of it. It was then that he hated Hannah for no better reason than that she represented everything which was denied him. He hated God, too. God must know how impossible it was to be celibate, and it wasn't as if he would be doing anything wrong if he made love to his wife – a man had every right when he was legally married. Every right, except when he had sworn on the Bible never to touch a woman again.

A great deal of work was coming into the blacksmith's shop, for the tower floors needed iron supports fashioned to exactly the right measurement to fit with the ceilings, which were moulded in seven pieces of arched concrete. The ironwork was Jonathan's responsibility and he was always kept busy.

One autumn afternoon while he was in Lymington there came an urgent request for an extra rod of iron. Aram, then eleven years old, was alone in the forge, and the man sent with the order was short of patience when told the blacksmith was absent.

'Damn it – we aimed to get this section finished afore dark so as to have time to go down to the Three Bells. When will your father be back?'

'I can do it for you,' Aram said. 'The iron's made to size – all I'd have to do is shape it in the fire. I know how, I've helped Pa do it dozens of times.'

'You reckon? I'll be back in half an hour, then. Look sharp you get it right!'

The man had no authority. His priority was the ale he would be drinking later, and he hadn't been working on the tower for long enough to realise the importance of everything being perfectly to scale. The fire had not long been stoked and was glowing orange-red with a heat so fierce it hurt the eyes to look at it, but Aram was not afraid. He had been forbidden to go near the fire unless his father was with him, but he disobeyed, thrusting the piece of metal into the heat and holding it with the pincers instead of the tongs.

Jonathan heard the boy scream as he turned in at the yard and he left his horse without stopping to tether it. Hannah, too, came running from the cottage. They arrived together in time to see the workman frantically pulling Aram away from the fire. The weight of the iron had pulled him forward and he would have fallen into the furnace if the man hadn't returned within ten minutes instead of thirty, his conscience troubling him. The worst that happened was that Aram's hands had received a severe scorching.

'What the hell's going on?' Jonathan shouted.

'My son!' Hannah ran to the boy and tried to put her arms round him, but he shrugged her off. 'Come and let me put something on those burns.'

'I could have done it, Pa,' Aram said, his voice trembling, not with pain but with aggravation at the fuss. 'I know how. It was just I couldn't hold the iron steady.'

'Mad irresponsible lout! You know bloody well it's as much as *I* can do to hold those rods steady. And what were you going to do with it once you'd fired it?' Jonathan's anger was frightening. He ranted at the boy, then turned on the builder. 'And you! Would *you* have accepted a girder made by a boy of eleven? The lives of us all depend on the accuracy of those supports. Thank God I came back in time. Get out of my sight before I report you to the overseer.'

The man scuttled away, but Aram was undaunted. He faced his father with his hands by his sides, though the blood flowing into them must have caused him agony.

'It was only me that was in any danger, Pa. I know exactly how the supports have to be made. I know the measurements and the curvature and everything to the fraction of an inch, and I would have done it right.'

'Well, you won't get another chance to try. From tomorrow you'll be working on the tower carting cement. Likely they can do with a monkey to climb the scaffolding.'

Hannah immediately protested. 'Jonathan, you can't make him work on the tower. It's dangerous and I won't let him. He ain't old enough.'

'He'll do as I say. When he can obey orders I'll take him back to learn this trade properly.'

'You won't,' said Aram. 'I never wanted to be a blacksmith anyway. I'm going to be an engineer and I reckon there's more I can learn from the men on the tower than from you.'

'Aram! Don't speak to your father like that,' cried Hannah. But Aram ran off to put his hands in cold water in the horse trough.

Another second and maybe the boy would have toppled into the fire. Jonathan wrestled with his conscience, seeing the near-tragedy as a dire warning, and he was so confused he had to press the pulses at his temples to stop them throbbing.

Aram wasn't his. He knew it now with absolute certainty. But then he had never been his directly, and there was the slender hope that maybe the curse didn't extend to Shem's offspring. If he'd been raising Ben Rutherford's brat all these years there was no justice in Heaven or Hell.

Chapter Thirty-Eight

By the end of 1884 the tower stood like a giant finger pointing to the sky, serving no purpose and not even gracing the landscape since it had no beauty. But it was a structural triumph for Judge Andrew Peterson. He had proved that concrete was strong enough to build an edifice so tall it could be seen about forty miles away, and in a gale it remained as firm as a rock. He had also paid an above-average wage to the men he employed, and his answer to farmers who complained that he had unfairly raised the labourers' rate of pay was that he only took on men who would otherwise have had no work at all. His contribution to relieving poverty earned him congratulations from the Board of Guardians, as it was said he had reduced the Poor Rate by tenpence in the pound.

Hannah had thought the building would stop at the sixth floor, where a cornice broke the plainness of the concrete walls. Ninety-two feet was surely high enough for any building to be. She had expected to see it being roofed in the same way as the laundry tower behind the cottages, but work continued. Another hundred feet was added, a cornice again breaking the line between the tenth and eleventh floors, and at the point which was to finally be the summit.

'It's finished, then?' she said to Aram, on the day the octagonal extension containing the spiral staircase was completed. Her relief was so great she felt as if an enormous weight had been lifted from her.

'No, Ma,' said Aram. 'There's an observatory going on the top. I've seen the plans.'

Her heart sank. 'That means you'll still be working on the scaffolding.'

'It won't be so dangerous. It's going to be octagonal like the staircase and it ain't going to be so wide as the tower.'

'Mercy on us. Whatever does the man think he's creating?'

She worried incessantly for the safety of her son. He was thirteen now, and the hard work he did helping to mix concrete by hand, then hauling buckets of it over the pulley-wheel to the men at the top of the scaffolding, had kept him lithe and thin. He'd stopped growing for a while which was just as well because for a few years she'd been tired of him always needing new trousers. Soon, she could tell, he would be broadening out into manhood – and then he would be handsome enough to attract a host of girls. She dreaded the day she would lose him to one.

It wasn't easy to keep the peace between Aram and Jonathan. A great animosity had sprung up between her husband and her son over the past two years, Jonathan always expecting too much of the boy and having little patience with him. Verbally he was cruel. He taunted Aram unmercifully when he began working on the tower and found he was terrified of heights.

'So there's something you ain't clever at is there, bor? Something you can't brag about.'

'I'll get used to it,' Aram said.

'A scared workman ain't no use to anyone.'

'I ain't scared.'

'Tomorrow then you'll go to the top of the scaffolding when you're asked, instead of making excuses?'

Hannah saw the anxiety in Aram's face and couldn't stand it. 'Let the boy come to it in his own good time,' she urged. 'The men understand.'

'Leave it, Ma,' said Aram. 'I can go up to the top if I want to. It's just I'm needed more at the bottom.'

'Like hell you are,' scoffed Jonathan.

It was as if he had finally made up his mind that Aram was not from his stock and was punishing him. She caught him looking at the lad sometimes with a dark expression which furrowed his brow and tightened his mouth into a hard, bitter line, and she knew the doubts had developed roots which were curling and thickening round his gut like the ones filling a flowerpot when a plant needed repotting. They were taking up too much room and depriving him of the pure air, and even though his antagonism made her angry it saddened her to see him becoming a lesser man.

It took a year for Aram to pluck up enough courage to work on the scaffolding. He would walk up the spiral staircase to its limit and watch the men perched above him on the platform where the derrick was secured, but no one could persuade him to venture on to the structure until Mr Peterson spoke to him one day when he was with Hannah.

'I hear you want to be an engineer, Aram,' he said. He mostly supervised the work himself and took an interest in everyone he employed.

'That's right, sir.'

'I like ambition in a boy. I'll find you some books to read.' He was about to turn away when he had another thought. 'There's the College of Practical Engineers at Muswell Hill, in London. Opened a couple of years ago. Perhaps you should think about trying for a place.'

Excitement made Aram's eyes shine, and he clasped his hands together. 'Oh sir, I'd like that fine.'

Hannah broached the subject to Jonathan that same evening, and met with instant rebuff.

'College! The likes of us don't go to bloody colleges. It costs money, woman – a lot of money, and we ain't got it. So put such fancy ideas out of yer head.'

'We'll find a way. Maybe Ben would lend us it.'

She knew as soon as she had said it that she'd stirred a hornet's nest. Ben's name inflamed Jonathan at the best of times. To mention it in connection with Aram was just about the most foolish thing she could have done, and she put up her hands to ward off the blow which she was sure would result. His face turned almost purple, his shoulders rose, his fists clenched. But a shake of his grizzly head seemed to clear the threatened brainstorm.

'I'll pretend you never said that, woman.' His voice was dangerously quiet. 'I'll not have Rutherford providing so much as a brass farthing, so don't ever suggest it again.'

On the few occasions that Ben came to Sway Jonathan kept out of his way, but Hannah knew that he was aware of every move. She could feel his eyes everywhere. Hannah herself never made an opportunity to be alone with Ben, and they indulged in only the simplest conversation.

'How are you, Hannah?'

'I'm very well. And you?'

'Very well. And Aram?'

'He's doing fine.'

She wanted to tell him how proud he should be of the boy, but that would start fresh trouble. Sometimes he saw for himself. His eyes would meet Hannah's and the forbidden emotions were there, scarcely veiled, telling more than words that nothing had changed. They still loved each other.

Jonathan had never made any physical demands on her since the night of his confession, and Hannah counted herself lucky. But he was not easy to live with. Sometimes he was angry, at others he was moody and silent and there was a dullness about him, yet he worked harder than he had ever done. When there was no pressing need for ironwork he joined the men on the tower and did his share of labouring, and in the evenings he tilled the vegetable garden until the light faded. It seemed he couldn't rest.

Hannah herself was always busy, though these days she only supervised the running of the dairy, and had given up milking the cows in the byre. She scrubbed and cleaned the cottage until it shone, and in the afternoons she sat with the children of nearby families round her kitchen table to teach them letters. But what she enjoyed most was the work she now undertook for Andrew Peterson.

Mr Peterson was writing a book on his experiences of mesmerism, expressing his belief in an outside intelligence operating the nervous system of mediums and giving them the ability to communicate ideas in speech. His research had been hampered by the unsatisfactory method of employing public professional mediums so he had engaged a man whom he called a 'sensitive' to work only for himself – an uneducated labourer with a gift for being in touch with the spirits, and he wrote down in his own peculiar shorthand every communication which came through the sensitive. As over a thousand of these came flooding in, the papers recording them piled high, and it was then that he decided to take advantage of Hannah Whitfield's intelligence. He taught her to decipher his shorthand so that she could write the messages neatly, ready for inclusion in his book. There were drawings, too. It fascinated and mystified Hannah to see the man working in a trance on sketches he claimed had been given to him by famous painters long since dead, when at other times he was quite incapable of producing anything recognizable.

Andrew Peterson was not always an easy man to work with, but his irascibility was a small price to pay for the new dimension his work had given to Hannah's life, and when he had been quite unbearable he could always be relied upon to apologize.

'I'm sorry, Mrs Whitfield,' he would say. 'My sensitive informs me I've been told by both Plato and Lord Clive that I must control my temper otherwise it will warp my judgement. There'll be no hope for the progress of my soul, either.'

Sometimes Hannah saw Ma. A strange friendship had developed between Mother Girling and Andrew Peterson. They both had a passion for writing long letters for publication, and over the years they had learned to tolerate each other's views. The friendship brought the Shaker woman visiting occasionally, and Lilianne always took the opportunity to make the journey with her. Ma looked well, but she had aged a great deal and likely poor diet was affecting her bones because her spine was curving slightly, making her appear shorter than she had been in her youth.

Her visits were difficult. She would sit by the cottage fire and gaze into the glow for a long time without saying anything, and it was plain to see her mind was troubled.

'What's ailing you, Ma?' Hannah asked, when another year was partway through. 'I know we're not close but you can confide in me and I'll help if I can. Are you ill?'

'No, I ain't ill. It's our dear Mother.'

'She looks well enough to me. Certainly there's nothing wrong with her tongue. Poor Mr Peterson can't get a word in edgeways sometimes.'

'She drives herself hard, touring round and holding meetings. She gets so many headaches and she doesn't eat enough to feed a sparrow, yet she won't rest.'

'What are you afraid of?' Hannah took Lilianne's rough hands in hers. 'Mother's a strong woman, and when did she ever rest?'

'I know that. But so many have left us and I worry that no one's listening to her. We're down to fewer than fifty in the family now. What's going to become of the world, if no one hears?'

'Reckon it'll go on same as it's always done,' said Hannah. 'You ought to leave the Shakers, Ma.'

Lilianne snatched away her hands and tensed her body as if fighting temptation. 'You've taken to going to church these last years. Would *you* desert Jesus?'

'How can you ask me such a thing?'

'Because Mother is the Lamb's Bride and my heart's breaking at the way people turn their backs on her.'

Hannah wanted to weep for her mother's misplaced faith, but she longed to comfort her, too. Great sincerity filled the thin body with an inner strength, and there was so much goodness in her.

'It says in the Bible that Jesus sometimes forgot to eat. The disciples had to bring Him food. Perhaps Mother Girling just forgets.'

'I cook for her, the best we can afford, but she's got no appetite.'

'Then trust God to feed her if you believe she's immortal.'

The worried lines etched across Lilianne's brow smoothed out a little and she gave a trembling smile. 'Aye, girl, I reckon that's what I must do.'

When Ma and Mother Girling left that evening Hannah took a good look at the gaunt woman who had ruled her life for several years, and saw only the same matriarchal figure which these days was garbed in neat black. Her eyes were still as compelling and she had lost none of her charisma. If she was in poor health she hid it valiantly, and likely only those close to her were aware of it.

Chapter Thirty-Nine

The finished tower soared to two hundred and eighteen feet. The observatory on the summit was reached by climbing three hundred and thirty steps, passing thirteen storeys on the way which each contained a cold bare room. But nowhere was so cold as the basement, where two oblong tables made of cement stood side by side in the darkness. Jonathan took Hannah down there one day and they speculated on the reason for such a strange place.

'D'you reckon it's to be a mausoleum?' Hannah asked. 'D'you think Mr Peterson's built this great place as a sort of tomb for when he dies?'

'Could be a table for his ashes to stand on, and the other for his wife's,' said Jonathan. 'Likely we'll never know.'

She shivered. 'I'd rather have a good Christian burial.'

Only one job was left to complete the building work. The octagonal observatory which looked more Indian in design than English, was topped by a cupola, a domed roof which had to be faced with cement, and the only way it could be done was for a man to climb out through one of the Gothic-shaped windows to work from the outside. So dangerous was the project no one could be persuaded to undertake it until Andrew Peterson offered a princely bonus. The next day Aram came home with his head held high and his chin set firmly.

'I've said I'll do the cementing.' He looked at his father first, challenging him with his courage.

Hannah's face turned white, and she grasped her skirt to stop her hands shaking. 'You can't, Aram. I won't let you. Jonathan, tell him he mustn't do it.' Her voice was unsteady.

'Why should I?' said Jonathan. 'Seems he's the most suited. It needs someone small to get out there and climb on top.'

'No! Dear God, he can't work on the outside of that monstrosity.'

'I've already agreed,' Aram said.

'But you're afraid of heights,' his mother protested. 'Don't be a fool, boy. You could be killed.'

'Mr Peterson's paying fifty pounds to the man who'll do it. Likely that'll pay for my place at Engineering College, and that means everything. So you can't stop me.'

Hannah leaned back in her chair, her knuckles pressed against her lips as she took deep, gulping breaths. She was relying on Jonathan to make the boy see sense, but to her horror she saw a strange look of exultation sweeping over his face. He *wanted* Aram to face the danger.

For two days a high wind made it impossible to climb out on to the observatory roof. In that time Hannah did everything she could to try and make Aram change his mind. She pleaded with him, cajoled, tried emotional blackmail, but all to no avail. Aram had decided that the money was worth the risk, and he was deaf to persuasion.

'Maybe you could talk Mr Peterson into lending you the money to pay for college,' she suggested urgently. 'He's real interested in you.'

'If I can't pay for it myself I'll not be going,' said Aram.

In desperation Hannah took matters into her own hands and did the one thing Jonathan had expressly forbidden. She went to see Ben.

The weather was improving, the wind abating, and she knew there was not much time left in which to get help. As soon as the men had started work she saddled a horse and set out for West Borley. Gorse tore at her legs, and the forest ponies eyed her curiously as she sped along. Ben *had* to return with her. Aram's life was in danger: if he persisted in climbing out on to the cupola, there would be nothing to save him from falling if he slipped.

She went to the ropeyard but Ben wasn't there. He rarely worked in the yard now that his business had grown and she was told she would find him in his office close by the house. Her hair was damp. Her dress was wet at the hem, caught with twigs and bracken, and she looked so dishevelled that the elderly clerk sitting at a high desk got ready to usher her out of Ben's sanctuary, likely thinking she was a gypsy.

'State your business,' he said. 'This is a private office.'

'It's urgent I see Mr Rutherford. Tell him his sister-in-law's here. Hurry, please.'

The clerk was new and had never known Emily. He looked at Hannah with disapproval and lingered as if distrusting her claim to be related to the family. But Ben had heard her and he came through from the inner office, his height and breadth filling the doorway so that the light behind him was obscured.

'Hannah, my girl, what's the matter? What's happened? Are you all right?'

She ran to him, half-hysterical. 'It's Aram. You've got to stop him from getting himself killed. Oh Ben, I'm so afraid.'

'Daniel, go and ask Mrs Lawton to make some tea for Mrs Whitfield,' Ben said to the clerk, who lumbered away with his head hunched into his neck like a retreating turtle. Then he took Hannah into his arms and tried to soothe her. He cradled her head, his strong fingers working up through the golden tresses which had darkened to a glossy brown with the damp. 'Now calm down and tell me about Aram.'

'He's stubborn like you,' she cried, her face against his chest. 'I can't talk sense into him. He's volunteered to cement the cupola at the top of the tower because he wants the money to go to Engineering College. You must come and tell him it ain't that important. He's afraid of heights, you see.'

She could feel the tension in him. He was angry. 'Why didn't you tell me he wanted to go to college? You know I'd pay for him.'

'Jonathan forbade me to ask.' She looked up, her eyes full of despair, and fear of her husband was there for him to see. 'He doesn't know I've come today. He'll be terribly cross when he finds out.'

Ben didn't ask any more questions. He kissed her trembling mouth, then set her from him. 'I'll saddle my horse. While I'm doing it you go in the house and let Mrs Lawton look after you.'

Half an hour later she was riding back across the heath and through the lanes with Ben at her side, warmed by the tea and heartened by his presence. The relief at having involved him had brought the colour back to her cheeks, and though she didn't know what he would be able to do she was confident he could change the situation. She tried not to think what Jonathan would say.

The sun came out from behind a mountain of heavy cloud. Suddenly the day was beautiful and she threw back her head with the joy and luxury of being alone with Ben, her mouth curving into a smile, her breast rising as she took a deep breath of satisfaction.

'I love you,' she shouted recklessly, her voice carrying across the open space. She wanted the world to know.

He reached over, caught the reins of her horse and drew it to a standstill alongside his own. Both animals were sweating from the long gallop. Then he leaned towards her and their lips met, clinging and passionate, each hungry for the taste of love. Ben took the reins of both horses and held them tight with one hand, his other hand stealing behind her neck so that he could draw her face closer. The length of their thighs pressed together, and she took her foot out of the stirrup to stretch her toes in ecstasy.

'Leave Jonathan,' he urged. 'Leave him and come to me. I need you. We've wasted too long.'

She came back to her senses with a jolt and pulled away. Her stomach muscles tightened, and she pressed her free hand against it to quell a feeling of panic. 'I can't.'

'Aram's not a child any more. You stayed for him, but it seems he's man enough already to make his own decisions. Please think of yourself for a change.'

Tears filled her eyes. 'I can't, Ben. You must find yourself a wife and forget about me.'

'You know I can't do that.'

'Then you'll have to accept that we can never be together. I must stay with Jonathan.'

Ben jerked her head up roughly, and when he searched her face she saw the way frustration turned his grey eyes to steel.

'What a fool you are, woman. Don't you want to be happy?'

'Of course I do.'

'Then leave him. There's nothing to keep you tied to him.'

'There is.' She hesitated. It was not her place to talk of things which Jonathan had told her in confidence, and yet she had to make Ben understand that in many ways her husband's need of her was greater than his. She sucked on her lower lip. 'Perhaps it'll ease your mind if I tell you that I've never bedded with Jonathan. There've been times when I expected it, but he's afraid of the consequences if he breaks the vow he made to stay celibate.' Ben started to laugh. She was angry. 'It isn't funny! Reckon he's made me responsible for his soul, and as a Christian I'm morally as well as legally bound to him.'

'I admire your strength,' he said grudgingly.

'Jonathan was good to me when I was alone and pregnant,' she said.

His hand fell away and he let go of her horse. 'We're wasting time if I'm to talk sense into my son.'

With that he set off at a gallop, leaving her to follow as fast as she could, but before reaching Sway he thought better of his impatience and pulled up to wait for her so that they could travel the remaining distance together.

They had stopped for about fifteen minutes. Had they not done so they would have been there to put pressure on Aram and perhaps he wouldn't have gone up the tower. Likely it would have made a difference to all their lives. As it was, they arrived to see a group of about forty workmen gaping up at the summit where the boy was just emerging from one of the arched apertures of the observatory.

Hannah shook. She wanted to scream but was terrified of distracting Aram. The tiny figure of her son was like a magnet drawing her reluctant gaze.

He had a rope round his waist. He climbed out and started up the iron ladder to the highest cornice of the observatory. Hannah's heart thudded and she pressed her knuckles against her mouth. On top of the cupola he would have to lean over for the tools he needed. If he lost his footing the rope wouldn't be sufficient to save him. Great waves of fear swept through her as she lived the boy's feelings, his fear of heights and the traumatic knowledge that it would be fatal to look down. It was horrifying.

The sky to the east was a doom-laden black, made to look even darker by the sun which still shone brightly on the concrete and sharpened the stark lines of the structure. Clouds scudding fast immediately overhead gave the impression it was the tower that was moving.

Vivid pictures tumbled into Hannah's mind as she stared, transfixed with fear. She seemed to be seeing her brother Luke up on the barn roof. Scalding tears made her face burn with guilt and shame. Luke had fallen and broken his leg so badly it had changed his life, and as a direct consequence so had all their lives changed. Now Aram was fixing a roof, her son, the most-loved person in her life along with Ben. It came to her that in involving Ben she had put Aram's life in even greater danger because whenever he and Jonathan met there was terrible trouble. The shaking became uncontrollable.

397

'My God,' Ben breathed, his gaze homing in on the boy. 'And you say he doesn't like heights.'

'Do something!' she pleaded.

'Who the hell sanctioned it? That boy shouldn't be up there. I'm going after him.' He made straight for the door at the foot of the octagonal extension, where the stairs curled dizzily upwards. There was a shout from the watching men and Hannah saw Jonathan, his shaggy head higher than the rest. Within seconds he was in pursuit and he stopped Ben before he could vanish inside.

'Damn you, what are *you* doing here?' he demanded, trying to wrench the other man back.

'I'm going to bring my son down before he kills himself.'

'Aye, *your* son!' stormed Jonathan. 'Your bloody bastard! Well, if you're so sure of that, you can leave him up there because he won't come to no harm. If he was mine he'd be dead by now.'

'You're talking squit, bor,' shouted Ben, anger making him lapse into colourful Suffolk dialect which had almost disappeared from his speech since he had come south to live. 'He's Hannah's boy and that makes his safety doubly important to me. I'm going up there to make the fools realise they're exploiting him.'

'You ain't going anywhere.'

'Let him!' Hannah had run to join them and she was afraid of the madness she saw glittering in her husband's eyes. She seized his arm but he shook her off as easily as flicking a fly.

'Keep out of this.'

There was a scuffle as Jonathan tried to prevent Ben from going inside, and the other men immediately pressed forward to come to the assistance of the blacksmith, who was one of them. The rope-maker was from a different class: he was an outsider, and he was interfering. Sheer weight of numbers forced Ben back, though he struggled against them, and there was such a noise it almost drowned the piercing scream which came from the summit as Aram looked down and lost his footing. He tried to clutch hold of the top cornice, but panic robbed him of the necessary control and his young body plummeted like a stone.

A brief and terrible silence followed.

Hannah bent her head, gripping it between rigid fingers as she screamed. She had never experienced anything like the pain which tore at her heart before she fainted into the arms of one of the workmen.

The rope had been made at Ben's yard, and though it was not so stout as the ones which had been hauling buckets of concrete up to the derrick it was nevertheless of the best quality, and Aram was not too heavy. The length attached to him had been coiled inside the observatory and it spun out with speed as the weight took it like a dropped anchor. About thirty feet unwound before the limit was reached, the end being firmly secured to an iron hook in the wall. Aram's plunge was halted abruptly and he was left hanging against the side of the tower.

Jonathan was already on his way up the punishing spiral stairs, his boots clattering on the rough concrete, and he was shouting as he went. 'Aram! Aram, I'm coming!' His voice echoed up through the empty rooms.

Behind him came Ben, his youth making him more agile, and he caught up with the older man before they were halfway.

'For God's sake, bor, let me pass. I can be there quicker than you.'

But Jonathan wouldn't move aside and there was no room for Ben to get past him. Round and round. Up and up. The stairs were neverending. Jonathan was breathing torturously and his progress was slowing, which made Ben impatient as he pressed close behind him. Other men followed. At the eleventh floor they saw the boy through the unglazed window, his eyes closed as if the shock had rendered him unconscious. He was being hauled slowly back to the top, but the motion was making his inert body swing against the concrete and his limbs were grazed and bleeding.

'Quicker, man,' Ben urged Jonathan. He pushed him and the blacksmith stumbled but wouldn't give way, and Ben was left to curse and fret behind him, knowing that he could have reached the observatory by now if he'd been ahead.

The sun had gone and a squall of rain lashed at the tower, coming in through the apertures which gave light to the staircase at regular intervals. When they finally reached the last stair Jonathan clung to the extension of the central axis of the spiral which formed the door jamb, his breathing jerky, and at last Ben was able to push past. But as he stepped on to the narrow footway edging the observatory he was unsteady from the circular climb. Rain beating down almost blinded him and he shook his head to clear his vision so that he could go to the assistance of the man already leaning over the parapet to pull the rope.

When he looked down over the side of the tower his stomach churned. The people crowding at the bottom were like toys. And the rain had made the edge slippery so that the rope was sliding down again rather than holding, taking Aram back to the limit of its length.

'*Give it to me !*' bellowed Jonathan.

He lumbered forward, squeezing past to take hold of the rope in his calloused hands, and his strength was phenomenal. When there was enough play in it he wound the rope round his biceps and back over his wrist, flexing the enormous arm muscles to hold it in position while he continued to haul. Slowly, so as not to hurt the boy more than necessary, the rope came up the side, but drawing him over the edge of the cornice proved to be the most treacherous part as he was not able to help himself. Ben leaned out as far as he dared and guided him over the projection, but his head swam and he had to keep his eyes firmly fixed on his task since a glance down might have been fatal.

At last Aram was near enough for hands to grasp him.

'It's all right, my son,' called Jonathan. 'You're nearly safe. Yer Pa's got you.'

Ben's heart was pounding, and his relief when the boy was gently lifted over the edge and on to the precarious walkway was so great he could have almost shouted out loud. He chafed the boy's limbs to bring back the circulation while the other man untied the rope. Jonathan leaned back against the observatory wall, his face a purplish colour from the exertion, and the difficulty he had getting his breath made his chest rise and fall painfully. After a few seconds Aram opened his eyes.

'We've got to get him to a doctor,' said Ben.

'Ain't going to be easy down them stairs,' said the man who had been solely in charge.

'I'll carry him.'

But Jonathan had recovered sufficiently to protest. 'No one takes him but me.' He bent down and gathered the semi-conscious boy into his arms very carefully. His face was wet, and Ben knew it was not only from sweat. For all his strength the blacksmith was crying.

'Maybe you're my Shem's son and maybe you ain't, but it's not important any more. You're mine, bor, and I reckon I'd give me life for you.'

He edged through the narrow door and on to the staircase, having to hold the boy sideways in his arms and go down crab-fashion as he negotiated the steps. The men who had come up behind now had to turn-tail and go down ahead of him, and Ben followed, patient now and ready to take the burden if it became too much before they reached the bottom. Down past the thirteenth floor, the twelth, the eleventh. Progress became slower and the weight in Jonathan's arms became heavier, but he wouldn't relinquish it. Round and round and round. It had seemed bad enough climbing up, but the difficult descent was even worse, and Jonathan wouldn't pause. By the time they were at last at ground-level there were anxious people pressing forward to help as they staggered into the air.

Hannah had quickly recovered from her faint and she flew to her son's side as soon as the group emerged from the tower, her skirt lifted well clear of the ground and her hair sticking to her tear-stained face.

'Is he all right? Tell me he's all right.' She was breathless with fear. 'Give him to me.'

'He's too heavy,' said Jonathan.

The boy's arms and face were bleeding, but his trousers had saved his legs from being scratched against the concrete. Hannah walked alongside, touching her son with frightened fingers, and his eyes flicked open. Someone had arranged for a panel of wattle fencing to be brought to lay him on. Another had run to fetch blankets.

'My poor boy,' Hannah crooned. 'Thank God you're alive.'

'I'm fine. Stop fretting, Ma,' Aram said wearily. He was looking at his mother as if he was more worried for her than for himself. Then his gaze turned anxiously to his father. 'Sorry, Pa. I caused you trouble.'

Jonathan laid him on the makeshift stretcher and bent over, his eyes misted. 'It were my fault. I shouldn't have let you do it, but I'm real proud of you, son,' he said. 'You've got guts.'

He stood up and put his hands to his back to ease the muscles which had taken so much strain. Then without any warning at all he fell face downwards to the ground with a resounding thud beside the wattle panel.

'*Jonathan !*' Hannah shrieked his name and fell on her knees to help him. 'What's the matter with you? Oh God, what now?' She tried to turn him, but he was too heavy for her to move, and other hands were quickly there to give assistance. She looked up with new fear. 'What can I do? We must get him home at once.'

But it was too late for anyone to do anything. The strain on Jonathan Whitfield had been too great and he had suffered a massive heart attack. While everyone stood round in shocked silence Ben knelt down and lifted one of the brawny arms, feeling for a pulse-beat, but there was none. He drew Hannah gently to her feet.

'I'm afraid he's dead,' he told her.

Aram levered himself up and fell across the still body in a storm of weeping.

Hannah trembled uncontrollably, staring in disbelief. Then she turned to bury her face against Ben's sweat-stained shirt and his comforting arms closed around her as she started to sob.

The trauma of losing her husband, and almost her son, made Hannah ill for two days. Her head ached so badly it felt as if it rested on bricks instead of a pillow, and she couldn't bear the light. But she recovered enough to attend Jonathan's funeral.

She mourned him more than she would have credited. In exerting his strength to the very limit to save Aram, he had paid the highest possible price. She liked to think that, even if he could have known how it would end, he would still have put Aram's life before his own.

She had been Jonathan's wife for fourteen years, and losing him was like being robbed of something necessary to everyday living. She was stricken with remorse for her lack of love, but even while she grieved she gave thanks that it was him and not Ben who had been taken from her. A world without Ben in it was unthinkable. But she didn't encourage him to visit, and while she was ill she refused his insistent plea that she should be moved to his house in West Borley so that Beth Page could nurse her.

Ma came to the funeral, but she was no company. She spent too much time in prayer.

'Can't Grandmother stand up properly?' Aram asked. 'She's always on her knees.' He had almost forgotten his life with the Shakers.

Lilianne was devastated by Jonathan's death. She looked drawn and haggard. She was already overburdened with worry about the state of Mother Girling's health, and the loss of her son-in-law obviously affected her deeply; some would say too deeply. She hardly spoke, except to condemn Hannah.

'You shouldn't have let him put so much strain on his heart.'

'How was I to stop him? Jonathan was a very strong man, and you know he would have done anything for Aram.'

'Reckon the sacrifices he made were a tragic waste,' Ma said bitterly. 'I'll never believe Shem Whitfield fathered that boy.'

'That's a cruel thing to say,' cried Hannah.

'It's true, though. I'd eat my hat if it weren't. You've lived a lie all these years, Hannah, and I pray the Lord'll see fit to forgive you. I find it hard.'

They were alone in the kitchen and Hannah was desperately sorry for her mother who was always to be found in Jonathan's chair. She went and sat on the arm of it, drawing Lilianne's tired head against her shoulder.

'I know you loved my husband, Ma,' she said gently. 'If only Shem hadn't killed himself I reckon it would have been you Jonathan married, and you would have made him a much better wife than me. I'm right sorry things turned out the way they did.'

Lilianne didn't deny it. 'Likely it was God's will,' she said.

Sunlight stole through the open door. Men could be heard shouting and laughing as they cleared up the site now that the tower was finished. Life went on.

'In some ways you knew Jonathan better than me. Tell me about him, Ma. Tell me why he followed Mother Girling. I've never really understood.'

'He believed in Mother. You should all believe in her. She's the saviour of the world . . .'

'I want to hear about Jonathan.'

Ma fidgeted, pushed her grey hair back from her brow and twisted her fingers together. 'I can't talk about him.'

Hannah persisted. 'Why would he never make love to me?'

Now there was stillness. The fidgeting stopped. After a moment

Hannah saw tears sparkling on the thin cheeks, yet a subdued smile hovered at the corners of her mother's mouth.

'I heard tell he had a great weakness for women when he was young,' she said, as if to herself. 'There were tales he only married Susan for her money, but I believe he loved her in his way. He loved me too.' She stopped and pressed her lips together, likely afraid she had said too much. Then she went on. 'It was after Shem died he changed – all to do with swearing something on the Bible to Susan. He would have killed himself that night if Mother hadn't talked to him. She saved his life, Hannah. Do you wonder he followed her?'

They didn't hold such a close conversation again, but Hannah pondered long over what Ma had said. She remembered the night Jonathan had told her about swearing on the Bible. She'd thought he had never dared to break the vow he'd made, but it went deeper than that. Ma's manner, her tone of voice, spoke of a love fulfilled. It could be that he'd broken the vow right soon after Susan's death, and then seen Shem's suicide as punishment for his own sin. Why else would he have wanted to take his life?

She didn't let herself think about her mother's part in it. The time when poor little Clemmy had died Jonathan had nearly gone out of his mind. It was what came of living an unnatural existence, and the past was too painful to go probing too deep.

At Christmas Ben invited Hannah and Aram to West Borley and she happily accepted. It felt as if they were a warm, united family while she was there and she enjoyed every minute of the celebrations. The only person missing was Ma who had returned to Mother Girling and refused to leave her. Selena and Patience had become nice girls, less spoilt since Beth Page had taken charge of them, and there was the added pleasure of having Beth's small daughter toddling about the place. Aram fitted in well. He liked his cousins and they liked him. The fact that he could be their half-brother made Hannah watch with the keenest interest as friendship developed between them.

On Christmas Eve, when everyone was in bed, Ben and Hannah were at last alone. He had brought a small fir tree indoors for the young people to decorate, and firelight shone on the rosy apples twirling on red ribbons. There were parcels wrapped in pretty paper, bright baubles which glittered, and little tapers were still alight on the tips of the branches. The other candles had burnt low and the cosiness of the fireside gave a feeling of pure contentment as they sat side by side.

'I want to marry you, Hannah,' Ben said. The grey eyes resting on her were filled with love. 'There's nothing stopping us now.'

'Except that you were Emily's husband. The law forbids a widower to marry his late wife's sister.'

'I was never married to Emily. You know that.'

'Oh, Ben. To everyone's knowledge you were.' Hannah stroked his face, her finger trailing down his cheek with infinite tenderness. 'There'd be a terrible scandal in West Borley, and then Selena and Patience would suffer.'

'I've loved you since you were in pigtails, girl, and I'll not let you get away from me. We'll ride out the storm. And the girls are old enough to understand when I tell them what happened. They love you too, you know.'

'And I love them. Perhaps they would understand, but no one else would.'

'It doesn't matter about anyone else.'

'Yes it does. Your business would suffer.'

'I can survive that.'

But she wouldn't let him rush things. 'I love you too much to ruin everything you've worked for,' she said. 'And besides, it's too soon. I've only just lost Jonathan and I need a respectable time for mourning.'

'You're well rid of him.'

'How dare you speak ill of the dead.' She was angry. 'Jonathan was a good husband and father.'

So Ben apologized. 'I'm sorry. I hated his guts but I'm willing to acknowledge he brought my son up well.'

'I've told you before, it's just as likely Aram isn't yours.'

'Oh, Hannah! Admit it, you know he's our son.'

'No. He's mine, and though I'm sure in my heart you gave him to me I could never swear to it, so don't try and make me.'

He knew from experience that he would get nowhere with words, so he drew her to her feet and into his arms. She tried to turn her head away when he started kissing her, but he was forceful enough to keep her mouth imprisoned while he worked on arousing a response. It didn't take many seconds. She melted in his arms, her body soon moulding against his as he pressed her closer. His tongue explored her mouth. The tip of hers moved over the edge of his lips with sensual pleasure, and they clung together with mounting feverishness. But Hannah had not abandoned her resolve.

She pulled away. 'It's no good, Ben. Much as I love you I'm not going to marry you. It wouldn't be right.'

After Christmas she returned home, resisting all Ben's pleading.

With typical kindness Andrew Peterson allowed Hannah to remain in the tied cottage. Now that the tower was finished there was no urgent need to accommodate a new blacksmith. She continued to teach the local children, which made her feel that she was doing something to repay him, but Mr Peterson's generosity didn't stop at letting Hannah keep her home. His interest in Aram's ambition to become an engineer and his admiration for the boy's ability resulted in his insistence on lending the money for him to have a place at the Engineering College in London.

'I can't let you do it,' Hannah protested, when he came himself to the cottage to make the offer. 'When would we ever be able to pay you back?'

'Mrs Whitfield, in time Aram will be a successful man, and his honesty will ensure that he doesn't forget what he owes, either to me or to you. He's a remarkable boy and he'll make you proud of him, so you mustn't stand in the way of letting me invest in his future. He's going to be an asset to this country when he's fully trained.'

Hannah smiled at the compliments paid to her son. 'In that case then, I must accept, sir. And I thank you very much.'

At the start of the year Aram left for college, and his departure was the cause of further disagreement between Ben and herself.

'Why, Hannah? Why do you never let me do anything for the boy?' Ben's frustration made him shout. 'I would have given him the money, not lent it to him, then there'd have been nothing to pay back.'

'It's better for Aram this way. If he knows he's got to repay Mr Peterson he's going to try harder than if the chance was given to him on a plate. Sorry, Ben. I don't want him thinking you've any claim on him.'

406

Once again she wouldn't be moved, though her heart was close to breaking every time she shut him out. In body, heart and mind she longed to be an eternal part of Ben Rutherford's life, but by marrying Emily he had forfeited the chance of them being together.

Chapter Forty

In the summer Lilianne came to Sway in the hope that she could persuade her daughter to return to the Shakers now that she was alone.

'We need you, Hannah,' she said. 'Mother's very ill. She doesn't eat and she's got so thin a puff of wind could blow her over. I can't think what the good Lord's thinking about, letting her get so low. We're all worried about her.'

'Surely there's no need to worry,' said Hannah. 'Hasn't she told you she'll never die?'

'I keep telling myself to have faith. Maybe we're being tested yet again, but it seems cruel she should suffer so. She's in terrible pain, but she never complains.' Lilianne covered her eyes.

Hannah got up and gave her mother an unexpected hug. 'I'm real sorry. But what good could *I* do? I'm not one of her children any more.'

The hug was returned and they lingered over a rare embrace. Then Lilianne held her daughter by the shoulders and looked into her eyes. 'Come back to The Children of God and be saved, Hannah. It's not too late.'

'You know I can't do that. I was never a true believer in Mother Girling.'

'Don't you want God's love? It's the most wonderful thing to be working for.'

'Ma, don't you know yet that God's love is His greatest gift. No one can earn it, and I surely don't deserve it. I count my blessings daily and I try to thank Him by helping the children here to read and write.' Hannah drew away. 'I'm sorry, but good as she is I don't hold with Mother Girling's exalted claims about her relationship to God. I'd no option but to stay with her while Jonathan believed, but I'd be a hypocrite if I went back.'

For two days Lilianne went on trying to convert her, but it was no use. Hannah obstinately refused to accept Mother as the divinity she herself never doubted her to be. The truth was, Lilianne was lonely for her remaining daughter, the only one of her family left now that Luke was permanently away at sea.

On Sunday Lilianne set off alone on foot for the Shaker settlement. Anxiety lent her the energy to make haste, and she arrived in time for the evening meeting in the chapel.

How sad it was to see the small number of vehicles in the road outside. How heartbreaking that out of over a hundred and fifty followers only twenty were left to dance and sing with Mother as she led them in worship. Mother was preaching with every bit as much enthusiasm as in the past, and though her voice was not so strong there was no change in her manner. She wore her hat with the plume in it, and as she spoke it waved in the air.

'Give praise to the Lord, dear friends,' she urged. Her veined hands were raised in invitation. 'Praise Him at all times, and never cease to give thanks for His mercy. Let the words of the Bible show you the light of God's love and don't be afraid of its judgements. The time of the millennium is very near and all of you who have faith in me, the Bride of Christ, will be saved.'

There was no argument that evening. The people listened but none questioned. Perhaps they all believed and didn't need to challenge what she said; or maybe it was because she didn't have quite the same fire which in the beginning had brought converts eager to give up everything for her dear sake. The quietness of the proceedings was in great contrast to the pandemonium at her meetings ten years ago. Yet there was still a feeling of great joy when she urged them all to pray and sing, and it wasn't long before her charismatic enthusiasm had them all shaking rhythmically with ecstasy. Love for this tall, very thin woman was almost tangible.

By ten o'clock only The Children of God remained to get ready for their celibate retirement to bed.

'I'm glad you weren't long gone, Sister Lilianne,' Mother said, when the two were alone. The colour had drained from her face and she looked exceptionally tired. 'I feel more peaceful when you're here.'

The admission touched Lilianne deeply and she was thankful to be back even though she had failed in her mission to return Hannah to the fold.

Hannah, too, was lonely. With Aram away the cottage seemed

empty, and the only time laughter sounded through the rooms was when the village children came for their lessons.

Through the winter and early spring Ben had sometimes visited, but now that it was summer he no longer came. No messages were sent from him. No letters. It was as if he wanted to cut himself off from her completely, and for that she had only herself to blame. As the weeks went by she began to regret her stubborn refusal to marry him. Perhaps she ought to have let him do the worrying about his reputation and thought of her own happiness. If it hadn't been for his daughters she would have done so long ago.

Mr Peterson's work kept her busy as well as her teaching, and her days were fully occupied, but the yearning for Ben intensified and she was becoming desperate to know why he had deserted her. She reached a stage where she could think of nothing else, and knew something must be done about it. She would have to swallow her pride and tell him that she couldn't bear the separation. She would say that he was right after all, and if he was still willing to risk the consequences she would marry him. They would weather the scandal together.

On a warm day when the sky looked settled she borrowed a pony and trap and drove herself to West Borley. All the way there her heart was racing. Nervousness as well as the rough road made her draw in her breath sharply as she stumbled over the words she had rehearsed a hundred times. It was ridiculous to be nervous of Ben, but his silence over the past few weeks was so worrying.

As it was close on midday when she arrived she went straight to the house, thinking he would perhaps be home for lunch. The only people there were Mrs Lawton and the two girls.

'What a lovely surprise,' Patience cried when she saw her. 'Aunt Hannah, we've been longing to see you.'

Selena was more reserved. 'We've been hoping you would come,' she said. She bore an uncanny resemblance to Emily now that she was almost a young lady.

'Will you have a cup of tea, Mrs Whitfield?' asked Mrs Lawton. And when Hannah accepted gratefully she bustled away to the kitchen.

The house hadn't changed. It was still as Emily had left it, with pretty porcelain ornaments everywhere and an air of genteel refinement. Ben's presence couldn't be felt at all, and Hannah compared it with her cottage when Jonathan had been alive. There had always been his things lying around; his tobacco pouch and pipe, his thick socks hanging to dry in winter, and his coat on the back of a chair. It was good to have signs of a man about the house, yet there were none here.

'It's your father I've called to see,' Hannah said. 'Will he be back shortly?'

'He's away,' Selena told her. 'He's been gone for days.'

'He goes away a lot,' her sister added. 'We hardly see him. Selena says he's got a lady-friend. Her name's Mrs Marchment.'

Hannah felt as if all the air was pressed out of her lungs. There was a noise in her head and she felt giddy. 'Are you sure? Does she live near?'

'She lives in Dorset,' said the older girl. 'I know because he keeps having letters from her and she prints her name on the back of the envelope.'

'But you know nothing else?'

'Oh, no. He doesn't talk about her.'

It was almost too much for Hannah. She had to keep reminding herself through lunch that she had told Ben he must find someone else to marry. There had never been such a difficult meal. She had no appetite for food, yet for fear of offending Mrs Lawton she had to force some down. And as soon as possible afterwards she made an excuse to leave.

She cried herself to sleep that night, heartbroken at Ben's desertion. She felt as if she was drowning in self-pity and she had to talk to herself sharply in the morning when she saw her swollen eyes. All these years she had lived without Ben Rutherford. There was no need to feel so sorry for herself now that he had found someone else to love. 'What you've never had you never miss' had been one of Ma's favourite sayings.

But she'd had Ben once, for the briefest time.

The day dragged by. Andrew Peterson was so concerned about her he packed away his work earlier than usual and sent her home, thinking she was sickening for a cold. The next day was not much better. Hannah found herself trying to picture Mrs Marchment, who must be a widow if Ben had taken up with her. Was she pretty? What had attracted him to her? She tortured herself with questions to which she couldn't supply answers, and her head began to ache like it had done after Jonathan died.

411

She wondered how long it would be before Ben condescended to tell her about his new lady-love. No doubt he was embarrassed. Every time she saw two people riding up the lane in the days that followed she dreaded it might be him coming to introduce her.

When he finally came he was alone.

Hannah was waving goodbye to the children at the end of the morning's lesson and smiles lifted the worry from her face momentarily. It was hard to snuff them out when she saw him, so her welcome was brighter than she had intended it to be. He dismounted and strode towards her.

'You look lovely,' he said. And on a breath: 'How I've missed you.'

'Really!' The cheek of him riding in with flattery on his tongue to smooth his way. 'I wouldn't have thought so. It's so long since you've been.'

'I'm sorry. I didn't want to come until everything was settled.'

'You're getting married, then?'

'Yes, I am. How did you know?'

She was so distressed she wished she could tell him to leave without saying any more, but she loved him enough to want his happiness above everything.

'Tell me about her,' she said, trying to sound normal.

He lifted his eyebrows, and then laughed. 'Let me in first. I can't tell you about my future wife while I'm standing on the doorstep.'

They went inside where there were shadows to hide her misery. She fussed about stoking the fire and she put the kettle on the hob, keeping her head averted.

'What's her name?' she asked.

Ben captured her busy hands. 'Why are we talking at cross-purposes? You've always liked to joke but this one's lasted long enough.'

'It's all right, Ben, I know you've found someone to marry. You don't have to be afraid to tell me. Selena said she lives in Dorset.'

He looked at her in surprise, laughed again, and then drew her into a rough hug. His arms crushed her.

'You silly goose,' he cried. 'As if I would marry anyone but you.'

'But Selena said . . . '

'Selena is a nosy-parker. She looks at my letters and makes up what she thinks is in them.'

412

'But Ben . . . '

He silenced her with a kiss which lasted until she had to escape to draw breath. He gave her no peace. His mouth claimed hers hungrily again and again, and she surrendered without the least resistance. When at last he set her free she collapsed in a chair with her hair dishevelled and her skin sore from the roughness of his chin.

'Now, madam,' he said, grasping both arms of the chair and leaning over her. 'Would you like me to tell you about Mrs Marchment?'

'Yes, please,' she whispered.

'I've been doing business with Mrs Marchment these last few months. Her husband died and left her with a large ropeyard at Bridport in Dorset which she couldn't possibly run. I bought it off her. I've also bought the prettiest house you ever saw and I shall take you there as soon as we're married.'

She swallowed hard. 'We're going to live in Dorset?'

'You were afraid of a scandal if you married me here.'

'I wasn't . . . '

'You didn't want to ruin my reputation.'

'Oh, Ben!' Hannah began to laugh and couldn't stop. 'You're teasing me.'

'Reckon I am. Playing you at your own game, you might say.' He kissed the top of her head. 'So will you marry me now?'

'You know I will,' she said.

'Good. Because I've a licence in my pocket and arrangements are made for the morning after next at Lymington church. I hope that gives you enough time to get ready.'

She reached up to encircle his neck with arms aching to hold him. 'Tomorrow would have been all right,' she answered.

Ben and Hannah's wedding took place on a warm day towards the end of August. Ben arrived early in a large carriage with seats for at least six people. The reins of the two grey horses were in his hands, and four of the seats were taken.

She ran out as soon as they came. Her dress of cream silk, which had belonged to Mrs Peterson, fitted her slim figure to perfection after she had spent half the night taking in seams, and it rustled as she ran. A flower-trimmed bonnet covered her honey-gold hair. Ben caught her and swung her off her feet, dangerously upsetting the bonnet and making her squeal.

'You're a feast for my eyes, girl,' he cried.

Four of the seats in the carriage were taken. Selena and Patience were full of beaming smiles, and Ma even managed to look agreeable. The fourth occupant, praise be, was Aram whom she had thought to be in London.

'Aram, this is the happiest day of my life,' Hannah said to her son, after a warm hug. 'Please say you and the girls are happy too.'

She had his assurance. Selena and Patience echoed it.

After the ceremony the little wedding party stood by the church door to receive the good wishes of passers-by. Ben kissed his wife, and then his daughters. For Ma Jerram he reserved a special embrace which cancelled out their differences, temporarily at any rate.

Then he turned to the boy who was as tall as himself and put an arm across his shoulders.

'We're all family now, Aram,' he said. 'I want you to know that from this moment you're my son.'

'Suits me,' Aram responded.

Hannah's eyes misted with tears at seeing the two of them so close.

Chapter Forty-One

On 18 September 1886, three weeks after Hannah's marriage, Mary Ann Girling slipped quietly away in her sleep to whatever place God had prepared for her. Only hours before she had once more reassured her devoted children that she was feeling better. She had been in the world for fifty-nine years.

The sorrow and disbelief at her passing left her flock wandering about the field in Tiptoe in a daze. No one spoke for several hours. Lilianne Jerram knew that she had lost everything, and the glorious hopes she had fostered ever since the first meeting with her dearest Mother were broken into fragments, as if the mirror showing the brilliance of life everlasting had been shattered.

It was Harry Bourne who gathered the remnants of the Shaker woman's followers together and challenged their faith. He called them all, men, women and children, to the chapel where Mother lay in a coffin made of elm boards oiled to give it the appearance of oak.

'Our dear Mother wouldn't want us to mourn,' he said. 'This isn't the end for her, it's a new beginning and we must be filled with joy.'

'She promised us she would never die,' one man protested. 'How can we believe anything any more?'

'I've been on me knees begging the Lord for light to be shed on why she was taken, and now I know. Brothers and sisters, our Mother hasn't died. What she said was true. We only die in our sins here on earth, but we're born again to life in Christ Jesus, and if we trust in Him none of us'll die. She promised us.'

'Aye,' said Miriam Rawlings. 'I'm remembering she never once said she wouldn't go to the grave.'

'And don't ever forget she had the marks to prove she was the same Christ, and that being so I reckon as how she'll rise again on the third day. Don't lose faith, I tell you. We're all better people for believing what Mother taught us, and she'll be waiting to see we don't fall.'

Brother Harry's words were a great comfort to Lilianne and she began to sing very softly. One by one the rest joined in until the chapel was filled with the sound, and they swayed reverently to the beat.

The next morning there was a cold north-easterly wind blowing and the sky was dark. The gardener brought round Mother's pony-cart, and when her coffin had been gently placed in it Lilianne fetched a beautiful wreath of white dahlias and ferns the sisters had made to lie on top near the roughly engraved plate which read, MARY ANN GIRLING, *who fell asleep in Jesus*. Lilianne was wearing white like all the other women and children, and they carried posies of everlasting flowers. They set off in pairs behind the pony and trap, each brother accompanying one of the sisters, and at the head of the procession was William Girling, Mother's son who was the chief mourner, accompanied by Miriam Rawlings.

People came to cottage doors to see them pass. Black-clad on-lookers stood respectfully at the roadside. When they crossed a temporary railway bridge in Vaggs Lane they were acknowledged by about fifty navvies who stopped work to raise their caps, and further along the servants came running from their quarters in New Forest Lodge, from where the Shakers had been evicted years earlier, all anxious to see the curious funeral cortège. Other people joined the procession, and a number of vehicles fell in behind until there was a long, sombre line behind the coffin pall. Lilianne walked with Harry Bourne, relieved that he didn't speak. Her thoughts were too sorrowful for words. Three-quarters of an hour it took to walk to Hordle church where the men carried the coffin inside for the service. She didn't think she could bear it when 1 Corinthians XV was read, so deep was the meaning in connection with Mother's declaration that she was immortal. But it gave her fresh heart. Christ was raised to life. So would Mother be.

Mary Ann was laid to rest beside the path at the south-east corner of the church where eleven of her followers already lay under grass-covered mounds beneath the straggly macrocarpa trees. The sisters placed their posies of everlasting flowers on the grave, and The Children of God left as quietly and reverently as they had come.

That night they returned. In the darkness and the stillness over a hundred people congregated to the north of the church, and they formed a circle round the newly-occupied grave. The light from two lanterns held at the head and foot of it illuminated the pale flowers, and in the eerie glow it was possible to see the expressions of those nearest. The mouths of some moved in murmured prayers which were sometimes loud enough to invoke a quiet chorus of 'Amens' at their conclusion. Others raised their eyes to Heaven as if waiting for something miraculous to happen. A white owl flew out of the surrounding trees and gave a melancholy call as it went hunting, and children whimpered with tiredness. All night the crowd kept vigil, awaiting the dawn of the third day.

The first light produced a patchwork of grey amidst the heavy leaf-growth above them. The white of the women's dresses and the men's armbands seemed to stand out while everything else was lost in the gloom, and the yellow flickering of the lanterns made the vast array of flowers on the grave take on a separateness, as if they hovered above the dark, dark mound of freshly forked soil ready to float away. All eyes now focused on the grave.

'Ma, d'you reckon she'll come up through the ground?' a child asked, and was quietly admonished.

Silence fell for another few minutes, then the tiny voice piped up again. 'Shall we see her, Ma? The flowers'll be in the way.'

The wisdom of youth found a response in the old. After a quiet consultation the elders decided that maybe the child was right, and one by one the posies and bouquets were removed to another place, leaving the grave uncluttered and in utter darkness, until daylight at last came over the far wall and stretched out a finger of light to touch it timidly.

'Put the lanterns out, brothers,' said Harry Bourne. 'The time is very near.'

Lilianne stood next to him, her hands clasped tightly together, and she longed for some form of physical comfort to relieve the inward shaking which made her so cold. She wanted to touch Brother Harry just for reassurance, but that would be wrong. She wasn't afraid. At any moment their dear Mother would reappear and stand amongst them, fit and well like she had been that day in Seggenham when she had saved Luke's leg, and possibly his life. Through her mind went all the wonderful memories of Mother's goodness, and she didn't regret a day of her life since she had devoted it to her. The Lord had planned it this way, and soon He would reveal His purpose.

417

Brother Harry whispered: 'She is very near now, brethren.'

'Alleluia!' said Lilianne. 'Ain't it time we did some singing to make her feel welcome?'

She started to hum one of her favourite Easter hymns in a quavery voice, and as others took up the words she gained confidence. Soon the churchyard was ringing to the sound of joyful music, and curtains were drawn back in nearby houses as people awoke in surprise. The waiting crowd joined in.

Lilianne looked up at the sky which was now a pearly colour, and she prayed for the Lord to give some sign that their waiting was over. There were clouds overhead, but none of them was bright with the glory of God, and even the rising sun was hidden from view. She swallowed hard. Her heart was pounding and her legs and feet ached from the long vigil, but not for a moment did she doubt Mother's promise. At the end of the last hymn she was so near it seemed that everyone stopped breathing in expectation, and only the rattle of a passing milkcart briefly disturbed their concentration.

'Why hasn't she come, Ma?' asked the candid child.

By now the day had fully dawned. It was no different from any other. Labourers whistled on their way to the fields, dogs barked in the distance, smoke drifted through the trees as morning fires were lit, and somewhere a baby was crying. At last the twenty Shakers stopped singing and looked from one to the other in bewilderment as they stood around the undisturbed mound of earth. The rest of the crowd began to drift away in disillusionment.

'She hasn't come,' murmured Lilianne. Tears filled her eyes and overflowed on to her lined cheeks.

But when she turned to Brother Harry she saw that he was trembling, and his face was alight with some revelation seen only by himself.

'*I* saw her. She is Risen,' he declared. His eyes were brilliant. 'My faith made it possible to see, brethren. Halleluia.'

'I saw her too,' said Sister Miriam.

A third Shaker echoed their assertions, but no more came forward.

Lilianne fell to the ground in despair beside the flagging dahlias she had picked and arranged in a wreath with such loving care the day before. She had seen nothing.

'Don't weep, sister,' Harry Bourne said. 'Our dear Mother's in Heaven at last. She was too good for this world, we all knew that.'

418

Lilianne lifted her head. 'Why was my faith not strong enough to see her? I loved her as much as any of you.'

'Three of us saw her, my dear. Perhaps it was not meant for her to be revealed to a greater number. Who knows the way God works? He may think that's all the proof that's needed.'

He tried to console her, tried to give explanations, but she took a handful of earth from the mound and knew that if she cared to dig deep enough she would come to the oiled elm coffin with Mary Ann Girling's body still lying inside it undisturbed. That was not to say her spirit hadn't flown to new realms, the same as everyone else's did who put their trust in God. But there would be no visible sign.

The other Shakers were leaving and urged her to accompany them, but she stayed by the grave, watching still. She felt lost and frightened. Abandoned. For so many years her life had been given to Mother and in spite of the hardships she had been happy. She buried her face in her hands and wept, even though she knew Mother would disapprove of such defeatism.

Supposing there had been no truth in anything she had preached. Doubt was like a knife stabbing at Lilianne's vulnerability. She began to recall passages of scripture in which it was foretold that the Second Coming would be heralded by earthquakes and fire, and the Heavens would disappear. God would never repeat the suffering of His dear Son. The world had been given the chance just once to turn away from evil by following Him, and not enough people had listened. Perhaps He had given Mary Ann Girling a special mission to spread the Word, else why would she have carried the stigmata? But likely she had overstepped the mark in claiming to be Lord Jesus returned as a woman. It was all beyond Lilianne's understanding.

After a short time she became calmer and she started to pray for guidance since she couldn't see anything in her life ahead except a void which had to be filled. And when she opened her eyes at last she was not alone in the churchyard. A man was at the gate. Lilianne blinked to clear the haze created by pressure on her eyelids. He came nearer, shouldering a heavy seaman's bag, and she was afraid he was a figment of her imagination. Surely it was Luke.

'I'm here, Ma,' he cried, hurrying towards her with his lob-sided gait. 'It's going to be all right.'

He drew his mother into his arms and cradled her there as if she were a child in need of protection. He smoothed the grey hair away from her brow and gently gathered it in his hands to stop the wind blowing it in her eyes again.

'Mother's gone,' Lilianne wept. 'Where am I to look for God now?'

'Same place as always,' Luke said. 'Inside yourself. He comes to *you*, Ma. If you've got faith you don't have to look.' He kissed her temple, and caressed the tear-stained cheeks. 'I've come to take you home.'

'My home's in Tiptoe, son. I don't want to go anywhere else. Ben and Hannah wanted me to go to their fancy house in Dorset, but that ain't for me.'

'We're going back to Suffolk,' said Luke. 'I'm tired of the sea and it's time I settled.'

Lilianne brightened. 'To Seggenham? We're going back to Seggenham?' She brushed the dirt off her white dress, becoming warmer as a slight tingle of excitement increased her pulse-rate. A vision of the marshes and the never-ending sky came into her mind where she ought to have been seeing Mother Girling received in Heaven. She drew a long breath and let it out slowly.

'Not Seggenham. Nor too near Ipswich just in case they still have a record of me being a horse-thief,' he said. 'There's plenty of other places. I've money enough to take up farming again.'

There was a choking feeling in Lilianne's throat. Too much was happening all at once and she couldn't cope with it. Guilt surfaced because she was overjoyed just hearing the name of her home village, and she was sorely tempted to leave the remnants of the Shaker family. She thought of the rich farmland she had tilled with Matt at the start of their marriage, the satisfaction of seeing crops grow where before there had been none. It had been grand being a farmer's wife.

'I need you, Ma,' Luke said earnestly. 'Say you'll come with me.'

Even as she was on the point of agreeing she knew that she couldn't desert the brothers and sisters with whom she had shared both ecstasy and adversity for so many years. Not straight away. Their closeness to each other made it impossible.

'You'll have to go on without me, son,' she said. 'Maybe I'll come later if there's no one here to keep us together.' She rested her cheek against Luke's chest and he put an arm round her. 'Reckon I'd like it back in Suffolk. Right now though I have to stay close to Mother's grave.'

'She ain't in there, Ma.'

'I know that, but I need time to get used to being without her.'

Luke tried plenty more persuading but she wouldn't be moved. Finally he hoisted the bag back on his shoulders. 'All right, I'll be on my way. But I'll let you know where I am when I'm settled in case you change your mind.'

'Yes, boy, you do that,' said Lilianne.

Alone in the churchyard again she sank down on her knees beside the grave to give thanks to the Lord for Luke's return. And she had to come to terms with the lack of faith which had prevented her from seeing the ascension of Mother Girling. She had loved her so devotedly. Yet if she admitted the truth she had always known deep in her heart that she was not the Second Coming of the Messiah. She had never been seen by angels. Mary Ann Girling had been just one more false prophet, no matter what she had believed about herself.

If it hadn't been for Jonathan likely she would never have become a Shaker, Lilianne mused. She had loved that man until the day he'd died, and loved his memory still. When it came to the Day of Judgement she would have to account for her sins, and that was surely one of them. But she didn't feel she'd sinned against Hannah. Seeing her daughter and Ben Rutherford so happy together had made her realise that she ought to have understood their need of each other all those years ago.

They had been good years, in spite of the hardship. There were no regrets that she had followed Mother to the end. She had taught people the two greatest Commandments; to love God above all, and to live for each other. That alone must have made everything worthwhile. In Lilianne the influence of Mother Girling would never diminish.

Brother Harry returned with the pony-cart in which he had brought a small macrocarpa tree to plant at the head of Mother's grave.

'We were worried about you, sister,' he said. 'When you didn't come back this morning we were afraid you might have left us. A few have done so already.'

'Reckon I'll stay for a little while,' she answered. 'A month or two, maybe. Then I might go back to Suffolk to where I first heard Mother preaching.'

'I saw your son Luke down the lane. I thought perhaps he'd persuaded you to go with him.'

She knotted her shawl across her chest and gathered up her skirt with more confidence. Then she touched Harry Bourne on the arm in a gesture of affection.

'Brother, I've been in despair these last few days, but my life has been in the hands of Jesus long enough for me to know I ought never to have worried about anything. Luke needs me. I reckon if anything was Divine Providence it was his turning up right now.'

'We need you too.'

'I know. But Luke is my son and he's come back to me.'

'You *are* going with him then?'

She kissed Brother Harry on both cheeks. 'In a month or two, like I said.'

She helped him to plant the tree and shovel the earth into place. When it was done he handed her up into Mother Girling's pony-cart and they set off for Tiptoe. She didn't look back at the churchyard. The leaden sky was clearing ahead and the sun was coming out.